OPERATION FOOLS MATE 24

M.L Baldwin is a former Tank Commander who joined the Second Royal Tank Regiment in 1996 and served with them on operations in Northern Ireland, Kosovo, Iraq and Afghanistan over a 19 year career. He was awarded a Mentioned in Dispatches (MiD) during his last tour of Afghanistan. After leaving the forces he decided to try his hand at becoming an author, which is where you join him now in his journey. Inspired by the likes of Clive Cussler and Tom Clancy, his debut novel Operation Fools Mate 24 is book one of an exciting series of books which he hopes people will enjoy reading as much as he has enjoyed writing them. Using his own first hand experiences of life on the front line of combat operations, he hopes to bring a level of realism and excitement that will both shock and excite his readers. The modern battlefield is full of technology, but ultimately, it's the human element and a certain degree of luck that play its part the most. His expertise in his field have garnered widespread acclaim and featured interviews on BBC Radio, whilst his articles in leading publications such as The European, NationalWorld, MSN, the Daily Star (UK), The London Economic and others, have helped solidify his reputation as a sought-after authority in the field. Keep watching for more exciting titles. In his own words, "I'm not finished yet, I'm only just getting started."

Also by M.L Baldwin

THE OPERATION FOOLS MATE SERIES

OPERATION FOOLS MATE

24

By M.L Baldwin

www.mlbaldwin.co.uk

Contents

Bad men need nothing more to compass their ends, than good men should look on and do nothing.

John Stuart Mill

Dedicated to all the brave men and women of this great country who in their lifetime have ever had to put on a uniform and put the needs of the country before their own selves.

For all the sacrifice, the hard work, the blood, sweat, and tears,

Thank you.

May you all find peace and happiness in whatever life you choose to settle into.

Prologue

11th April 2025

He wiped sweat away from his eyes for the tenth time in as many minutes as he tried to prise the remaining two screws out of the computer's server rack, which had stubbornly refused to budge. Cursing, he reached down to his tool roll, selecting a screwdriver with a smaller, finer head.

"Everything okay? You going to be much longer?" the voice behind him sounded. He stopped to look over at the young Royal Air Force Military Policeman, his escort who had been with him since he arrived. Smiling he replied, "Just a few stubborn screws, that's all. Looks like the rack has been twisted in the past, it's making it harder for me to remove the drive. I should have it out shortly."

He watched, as trying not to look bored, the MP went back to looking at his phone, his fingers dancing over the screen, the sign behind him stating, *Mobiles not to be used in this area.*

He leaned back into the confines of the rack, adjusting his sweaty palm on the grip, wiping his face again. After a few heaves and grunts, his hand slipped on the screwdriver; and it fell clattering to the floor amid a torrent of curses as he pulled himself back out of the rack.

The MP looked up again, glaring at the engineer as he held the broken screw aloft and stated,

"I'm going to need to go and get another set of screws from my van. It's out in the car park. I won't be long."

The MP shook his head irritably. "You can't just go out and walk back in mate, you'll have to go through security again." Looking at his watch, the MP shook his head in frustration. "I need to be out of here by 5pm, can't you just use the old screws?"

He shook his head sadly. "Afraid not, two of them are broken." Then he looked down at the drive the MP was holding and continued. "And if that drive slides out, you could have a system crash, the whole network could go down."

He stood up, wiping sweaty hands on his trousers, waiting for the MP to think it through. Trying his best to look unconcerned, he looked up around the huge room, thinking it was no wonder they called this room 'the cathedral'. Measuring thirty metres wide, seventy metres in length and the height of three storeys, the immaculate white windowless room contained only one automatic sliding glass door with vast banks of computer racks, the hard drives softly humming away and the lights blinking rhythmically. The whole room was temperature controlled, and even with all the systems working, the air conditioning pumps helped to keep everything at a modest twelve degrees.

The MP looked frustratingly at his phone screen at the last message. He'd been chatting to Tasha all month after meeting her online, and now finally after all that leg work, she'd arranged to meet him tonight, in the hotel, but he had to be away from there soon or he'd be late. And those pics... she was stunning. And some of those messages... He felt a stirring in his groin as he thought lustily about the night ahead, angrily interrupted as the engineer cleared his throat. He looked up at the man, then looked at his watch. It was already 16:20, the engineer was supposed to have been finished by now. He'd already watched the man these past few hours, updating the computer drives and slowly, almost lethargically, going about his business, and now this? Why hadn't he brought all his gear in with him? And the traffic being what it was on a Friday afternoon, he knew he had to leave soon. His mood darkened as he thought of what awaited him, what he could lose thanks to this man's laziness. Suddenly he had a thought. The security for the building was tight, but not for him. He could be out and back in within minutes, his clearance and passes allowing him to bypass all of it. Besides, the engineer had security clearance himself, it wasn't like he was any old Tom, Dick or Harry off the street. He quickly formulated the plan in his head.

"Where's your van parked?"

"Contractor's bay, it's the yellow van with the..."

"Yeah, I know what it looks like," he shot back irritably, holding his hand out for the keys.

3

The engineer delayed, his face uncomprehending as the MP shot out, "Yeah, give us your keys and I'll go and get these bloody screws. It'll only take me five minutes. If you go back out, we'll be here all bloody night going through security again. You don't want that, do you?"

The engineer nodded in understanding, handing over the keys and smiling as he replied, "Open the side door, you'll see the yellow-and-black case. If you open the case the screws will be at the top in a clear bag."

The MP nodded as he was told, committing to memory what was being said, before placing the hard drive on the floor and walking towards the door, turning quickly to add, "Don't touch or do anything until I get back."

The engineer smiled, waving his hand in acknowledgement, leaning back against the wall looking unconcerned as the MP left the room.

As soon as the door closed behind the MP, the engineer collapsed slowly to the floor, his knees almost buckling as he breathed out with relief. The sweating – he cursed himself – it had nearly given him away. He was trying his best to look normal, but lying wasn't natural to him, and he needed this to work, he *had* to make this work. He watched the door like a hawk, counting down the seconds in his head, making sure the MP wouldn't come back in. After a count of thirty, he knew he wouldn't be coming back just yet, so he quickly jumped up, running over to where the hard drive had been placed on the floor. Picking it up, he took a photo of the security tag on the back, before removing it to allow access to the drive. Darting over to his laptop, he flipped it over, undoing the screws on the back and quickly removing the outer shell, pulling out an almost identical black hard drive to the one in his hand. His laptop didn't work, and he hadn't used it all afternoon. Had the MP been looking more closely he would have seen that, but thankfully he'd spent most of his time looking at his phone. Instead, he'd used his laptop to sneak in the copied hard drive as it had been passed through the security scanner, with the hard drive sat where it was, the operator looking at the X-ray machine had assumed it belonged to the laptop. The original hard drive had been checked for viruses earlier in the day, which was why the MP hadn't let it out of his sight and only now, with him gone, did he have the chance to swap them over.

He picked up his phone, quickly accessing the photo of the security tag, and pressed both the volume button and the on/off button. Usually, a screenshot would have been taken – but this was no ordinary phone. He remained watching the door, expecting any moment to see someone coming through it, as a few seconds later a fresh new security tag emerged from the hidden printer in the phone. His heart was racing as he quickly checked and double-checked the position against the photo, before applying the security tag and looking over his work. Satisfied, he dashed back over to place the new hard drive exactly where the old one had been left, careful to wipe away any trace of his sweaty fingerprints. Then with a renewed sense of urgency he placed the stolen hard drive back into the laptop casing. There was always a possibility they could check the equipment when he left, and he couldn't take that chance.

He swallowed nervously, as finally he hurried up to the rack, removing the original unbroken screws, and hiding them in his pocket before resuming his position over by the wall where he waited.

He was sure he'd be discovered. He looked around, trying desperately to calm his breathing down. His chest was heaving with the effort and his clothes felt clammy and cold against his skin, the sweat running down his back in rivulets. He ran his hands through his hair as he took a moment to try and compose himself, quickly checking the floor and the area around him, looking for anything that could give him away. Finally, satisfied with what he had done, he slowed his breathing and closed his eyes. It would be all right, everything was going to be all right. The hardest part was over.

He looked up as the MP strode back into the room, the automatic door opening softly as he whistled to himself. His eyes scanned the room, looking to the floor, then the hard-drive rack, then finally back at him. *Has he seen something?* the engineer thought.

His stress and anxiety turned to relief when the MP smiled as he walked up to him, his anger and frustration now gone as he triumphantly produced the clear plastic bag and the van keys, handing them over.

"Now let's get this done, shall we? I'm sure we've both got better places to be than here."

Twenty minutes later and the engineer was finally walking out of the last set of security doors, waving and smiling to the civilian security team who watched him leaving, unconcerned.

He walked up to the van, casually unlocking and opening the side door, placing the case inside, before closing the door and climbing into the driver's side, the laptop and its hidden cargo now on the passenger seat beside him. It was only once the driver's door was closed and he felt totally segregated from the outside world did he breathe out a sigh of relief, the nerves and stress of the past few hours finally being released. He started to cry, the tears flowing freely down his face as the realisation of what he had just done dawned on him. He wasn't a bad man, why had they picked him? He looked about nervously, there was still a chance someone could see him. He reached over to the glove box and pulled out his personal phone and a box of tissues. Wiping his nose and eyes he looked into the rear-view mirror, chastising himself for his weakness. "Come on, Pat. Nearly done, stick with it, you're nearly free of all this."

After a few moments of composure, he felt ready for what came next. He fired up the phone, checking around him, scanning the near-empty car park to check he wasn't being watched as the screen blinked to life. He keyed in the messages, selecting the only number stored there and simply wrote, *Done*.

After a few moments the phone vibrated, as he read the response.

15-16 Drayton Industrial Park, Southampton. SO11 5TP. 20 minutes.

"Oh, I'll be there in twenty minutes you bastards," he said angrily as he looked over at the laptop.

He started the van, looking up once more at the building, a quick thought entering his head. It wasn't too late to stop this. He could run back in, tell them what he'd done, tell them how he'd been blackmailed, the pictures and videos he'd been looking at weren't his, he'd blundered onto the websites accidentally. Yes, that could work. It seemed reasonable. He was about to switch the engine off. But then... *No.* He shook his head. Who was he kidding? It hadn't just been the pictures or the videos. He knew that it had been his weakness that had led them to his door, and now they had him. If he didn't meet them in twenty minutes and hand over the drive that he'd taken, they'd release everything – his family, his friends, his wife, his kids, everyone he knew and loved would see him for what he was. He was about to cry again, when angrily he shouted to himself, turning the sadness to rage.

"Stop feeling sorry for yourself. This stops today, it stops now!"

He put the van into gear and reversed out of the space, quickly looking up one more time at the sign on the front of the building.

National Air Traffic Services – Helping to keep the skies above the United Kingdom safe.

Ignoring the sinking feeling in his gut, he drove out of the car park and onto the main road.

Fifteen minutes later and he was at the location – ramshackle warehouses with a rusty chain-link fence running around the perimeter. He planned for this to be simple: he'd hand over the hard drive to whatever piece of shit was blackmailing him, and they'd hand over the evidence they had against him. He'd had thoughts about reporting what had happened to the police, but only after he'd got his hands on the evidence. He *had* to get that back first.

He looked around him, trying to see if anyone was about. The place looked deserted. Over at the far side he saw some cars in various states of disrepair. All were on bricks, with wheels missing, some had doors and bonnets stripped off. Clearly the place was used as some kind of salvage yard.

He saw the roll-up door to the warehouse nearest him begin to rise, the protesting squeals of the runners, long deprived of oil, sounding loudly, as someone from within opened it, keeping out of the daylight. It stopped, and a lone figure, a tall man wearing blue oil-stained coveralls, stepped out into the light, smiling at him, waving him in.

He looked over to the glove box, pulling out the large hammer that sat there, his insurance policy. If they tried anything silly, he'd come out swinging. Whatever happened today, this was finished, one way or another.

He drove the van inside, watching as the light began to disappear behind him as the roll-up door was pulled back down.. He switched on the van's headlights, illuminating a man in a suit, standing in the middle of the concrete floor, shielding his face from the glare. He remained seated in the van, checking his surroundings – the warehouse was empty, except for the two people in it and the floor was strewn with rubbish and old machinery, a relic of a business folded long ago. He waited as the man in the coveralls finished closing the door and walked to the centre, to stand by the man in the suit. Satisfied there was no one else in there, he stepped out of the van holding the hammer and laptop.

"You both stay over there," he warned.

Both men remained standing. He could see in the lights the one with the suit was smiling, beckoning him closer, inviting him to join them. Keeping the van's lights on, he walked towards them, his body casting a shadow as he moved in front of the van, the light giving him some sense of security. As long as he could see, he felt safe. He continued a short distance, stopping five metres from them.

"Well?" his voice echoed out across the empty space.

The smaller man in the suit spoke, the Slavic accent apparent in his voice.

"Mr Brinkman, you've done very well, thank you for your work today."

Work? he angrily thought to himself, *that wasn't work, it was bloody blackmail.*

Trying to keep his voice calm, he replied, "Well, if you want to call it work, then that's fine by me, just so long as I get paid for doing it. Now, onto my payment – where's the evidence? I want it all: every scrap of paper, every megabyte of data you have on me."

The man spoke again, his tone almost apologetic. "Mr Brinkman, first hand us the laptop, and then we'll give you the files."

The man in the coveralls began to move towards him.

Quickly he knelt on the floor, putting the laptop down in front of him and cocking his arm holding the hammer back, ready to strike.

"Stop!" he yelled, causing the man to freeze immediately, looking over to his colleague in the suit for direction. They shared a few words in a language he couldn't understand as he looked back to the man in the suit – he was clearly the one in charge.

Almost apologetically the suit began, "Mr Brinkman, what are you doing?"

"I'll fucking smash this thing up – you'll lose it all, the hard drive – the data, whatever is on it that you so desperately want. Now stay where you are!"

The man in the suit smiled wickedly, quickly exchanging more words with the boiler-suited figure. His heart began to beat faster as the man walked slowly, menacingly, towards him.

"I'll do it!" he threatened as the figure advanced closer, almost daring him to strike.

"*I'm warning you!*" he shouted. The figure kept advancing.

He yelled angrily as the fear quickly turned to desperate rage overwhelmed him, bringing the hammer down repeatedly, over and over, smashing the laptop, the case buckling and denting, before breaking open. The black hard drive now spilled out onto the concrete. His hands scrabbled for it as he pulled it closer and struck it over and over again, pieces breaking off and flying in all directions. He kept expecting at any moment to feel the hands of the advancing man on him, trying to stop him, Panting heavily, almost exhausted, he looked up. Instead the man was laughing at him. *What the fuck is going on?* he thought. Confused, he looked down again at the pieces of broken circuitry and electronics. Didn't they care?

Suddenly the van's headlights flicked off – a third person had snuck in behind him – plunging them all into darkness. He panicked, the fear rising as he yelled, lashing out with the hammer at the darkness where the man had last stood. His feet crunched on the broken laptop, causing him to stumble as he felt two pairs of vice-like hands wrap around him tightly, pinning his arms and legs as he writhed on the floor. He tried to move, but their grip was just too strong. He became aware of someone close to him, reaching down and removing one of his shoes, then suddenly a sharp pain in between his toes. They'd injected him with something. Almost immediately he felt weightless; his arms and legs were light, as if he was almost floating. He looked on, confused as the warehouse lights came on.

There were three of them in there, two men were kneeling, pinning him to the floor, both wearing coveralls. The third man, the one in the suit, was stood over him, replacing a needle into a small black case. He looked over, his voice soothing and sympathetic as he replied, "Nearly done, Mr Brinkman. Just rest now, won't be much longer."

He tried to speak, to say something, but nothing came out. He tried to turn his head, to look about, but couldn't. Suddenly it dawned on him, he was paralysed. His heart began to beat faster, he could feel it almost exploding from his chest as the fear of being a prisoner in his own body took hold. What were they going to do to him? He could still move his eyes, and they darted about manically, looking up from the floor at the man in the suit, trying to make sense of it all.

The man in the suit watched him amusedly, like a cat toying with an injured bird as he saw the confusion on his face.

"Ah, you're wondering why we let you destroy this?" he said, as he bent down to pick up one of the broken pieces of hard drive, holding it close for him to see.

"Mr Brinkman, it was never about you retrieving the hard drive, that's just what we wanted you to think."

The suit bent closer, his gaze boring into him, full of malice, waiting for his eyes to finally indicate he understood. The engineer's eyes went wide with shock as finally it dawned on him what he had just done. It hadn't been about getting the original hard drive out; it had been about getting their copied hard drive in. What had been on it? What had he just done?

He wanted to shout, tell them all to fuck off, to scream at them to go to hell; to cry, hell, even to bite them, but he couldn't. All he could do was watch helplessly as they carried him mutely over to his van, opening the door, carefully placing him into the driver's seat. One of them gently replaced his shoe, even taking the time to make sure it was laced up correctly, as they all worked around him. He sat there, staring straight ahead, a prisoner in his own body, as another laptop, similar to his was placed on the passenger seat. Gloved fingers carefully opened it and reached over, taking his fingers and pressing them firmly onto all the keys. Then it was booted up, the display illuminating off the windscreen, allowing him to see what was being done. He watched as their hands worked the keyboard, opening up the word processing document, displaying the note. His eyes began to well up. He couldn't read it all, but he could make out the last few lines, his eyes reading them over and over.

I'm sorry, please forgive me. Love Babs.

There was only one person in the world to ever call him Babs. His wife. He knew then, they'd written a suicide note for her to see. He was about to be murdered.

He tried to think, tried to reason, how could he get out of this? How long would the paralysis last? Perhaps it would wear off, perhaps someone had seen them go into the warehouse? He kept hoping and praying as he watched a pair of hands reach over to start the van's engine, kept thinking there was a chance, as the doors were closed. Even as the driver's side window was lowered slightly and the exhaust hose was placed inside, he still thought deep down somewhere that he could survive. It was only when the van's cabin began to fill with smoke, and his breathing became laboured that he knew, he finally knew. He was going to die, and the whole world would now know his secret. He just hoped his family could forgive him.

***

The police found his van and body three weeks later, after it had been phoned in by workmen coming to prepare the warehouse for demolition. He'd already been reported as missing by his family, but the van's GPS tracker had been disabled some time ago, making it impossible for the police to locate him or the van; it was only when they traced his last day alive that they'd seen the CCTV of him in the NATS carpark looking visibly upset in his van. The last person to see him alive, the RAF Military Policeman, had confirmed he'd seemed upset and anxious, appearing distant and careless. The MP had decided to keep his rendezvous and messages about Tasha a secret. The police wouldn't need to know any of that, especially as he'd had the embarrassment of being turned down anyway. After promising to meet him, he'd driven all that way to find the hotel room empty and no sign of her. The police added the MP's report to the evidence that supported the conclusion of a man under immense stress, whose secret was about to be exposed. They found the laptop, with his fingerprints on it and his suicide note to his family, signed off with *Babs*. His grief-stricken wife had confirmed it was his, only she ever called him Babs. The message had to have been written for her and therefore, the police ruled the note was genuine. On the laptop various indecent images were found along with videos of children, and the investigation was quickly wound down. After all, who would really care about one more dead paedophile? Some of the investigating officers believed it to be a blessing in disguise, and quietly welcomed the coroner's findings. There were other more urgent cases requiring resources and funding, so the verdict was officially filed, *death by suicide*.

The days turned to weeks, the weeks turned to months, and over time people began to forget all about the paedophile called Patrick Brinkman, little realising what he had done. His actions had set in motion a chain of events that one day would see a country in ruins and its population fighting for its very survival.

1

Sunrise

Mike's eyes opened slowly, adjusting to the darkness of the room. He knew it was daylight outside as he saw the thin sliver of light projecting from below the curtains. He sat up on the side of the bed, running his fingers through his brown hair. He looked over to the smart home assistant. "Turn on the bedroom lights please." The robotic chime kicked in as the lights in the bedroom blazed on. His eyes squinted against the brightness, waiting for them to adjust before standing up and walking to the bathroom. He paused at the bathroom door, looking back at the empty bed and the space where Kate would have usually been. His wife of six years and counting had only been gone a few days but already he was wishing she was home. He'd only spoken to her last night, it had been 10pm in the evening here, but in Chicago Mike knew it was 4pm and the conference that Kate was taking part in would have been finished for the day. She worked as a sign language interpreter, assisting businesses and media companies in translating spoken words to sign for TV and film. One of her latest ideas had been to try to incorporate British Sign Language, or BSL as it was called in the UK, and its American counterpart, ASL, into one language, understood on both sides of the Atlantic. It was this idea which had seen her invited to a media meeting conference in Chicago, a week-long event. Mike smiled to himself as he thought of the time Kate had tried to teach him a few signs when they first got together, but after seeing his attempts, they both agreed one signer was enough for the family. Besides, the last thing he wanted to do was to attempt a conversation with someone only to be asking them where to buy dog food, or how much a haircut cost. Some things were best left alone.

Mike remembered her excitement at being asked to attend the conference as she packed her bags, but also her apprehension at the nine-hour flight – she had a fear of flying that just couldn't seem to be conquered. "Don't worry, darling," he'd reassured her. "It's the safest form of travel, you know that." She'd smiled at him with her usual *yeah, I know* face. It had been a quiet car ride to Heathrow on the morning that he dropped her off at the airport.

He knew her work was important to her, but damn, it felt strange to now be the one left behind, Mr Homemaker, especially after so long in the army, being the one used to serving overseas. Mike went into the bathroom, brushed his teeth, turned on the shower and whilst waiting for it to warm up, glanced at himself in the mirror. *Not too bad for forty-eight*, he thought. Thankfully he hadn't started his time as a civilian by letting his fitness go. It was one of the perks of having a gym in their basement at home. *Mind you*, he thought to himself, *that's always hard when one of your wife's hobbies happens to be baking*. And Kate did make a mean bakewell tart! Usually, fitness was the first thing to go when soldiers left a life in the military. He had been to enough regimental reunions to see just what being out of the military could do to you. But one thing he didn't miss was the parade ground. The only part of army life he'd tried to actively shy away from was the parades, and if he was honest, he was never really known for his parade-side manner, choosing instead to volunteer for the guard room if ever a high-profile parade came up.

He looked down to the bruises on his upper arms – they were at least starting to fade now. A little present from his instructors Ewen and Ariel. To help keep himself in shape Mike had also joined a local gym three years ago that specialised in teaching the Israeli martial art of Krav Maga. It was a combination of martial arts that took the best of Aikido, Judo, and Karate, combining it with boxing and street fighting to make a very effective way for someone to defend themselves. Mike remembered the look from Kate when he'd mentioned he'd joined, with Kate saying to him with concern, "Aren't you a little old to be throwing yourself around a gym mat?" Secretly he wondered that too, but Mike had always worked on the mantra, 'better to have and not need then need and not have'. And since then, he had spent three years learning all manner of self-defence techniques.

It hadn't been easy; the bruises were testament to that, and he remembered for the first year his instructor Ewen seemed to spend more time patiently talking the moves through than they had spent actually using them. Finally, after year two, Ewen had felt Mike was ready and before long, the two were sparring at what Mike considered to be a reasonable speed. Then to add another level, Ewen began to introduce his partner Ariel into the mix, with Mike having to learn to deal with two attackers. One of the techniques Ewen always instructed him to use was to turn one attacker into the other's path, causing them to trip or tangle with each other. Now three years in, Ewen had started to teach Mike the faster take-downs, moving on to disarming multiple opponents with knives and guns. Mike enjoyed the sessions and enjoyed the chats with Ewen and Ariel, as he found out over time that they had both been members of the Israeli Defence Forces. It was there that they had met, fallen in love and decided to leave for the UK to make a fresh start before opening the gym together which was where Mike met them.

Mike was brought back to the present with the mirror in front of him steaming up as the shower began to heat up the room. He stepped in, thankful for the piping hot water and he began to hum one of his favourite tunes as he washed himself, happy with the way life was going.

He'd been out of the army now for eleven years, having served eighteen years in the 24th Royal Tank Regiment. He'd served overseas and seen active combat in Kosovo, Iraq and Afghanistan, before eventually taking voluntary redundancy. He'd met his wife and had decided for once in his life to put someone else first instead of his career. Besides, he knew he wasn't getting any younger and he didn't want to end up as some forty-something singleton looking for love.

When he'd met Kate, she was already living in Poole, an area of Dorset he knew well, thanks to the Royal Armoured Corp (RAC) having its two main training areas located there. First, there was Bovington, home to the oldest tank regiment in the world and where the RAC began its driver training for tank crews. After doing basic army training the newly qualified recruits would come to Bovington to learn how to drive the tank, how to fix it and what it could and couldn't do. Then situated about five miles away from Bovington was Lulworth on the south coast. This had been established in 1914 as a secret tank range where the first tanks from World War I could train and practise their shooting before being shipped to France for the fight. Now it had evolved into the RAC's school of gunnery where all gunners, operators and tank commanders would learn their craft before being able to work as a crew. Between these two places Mike had spent many months and had happy memories of being there, so when Kate asked him to move in with her, the answer had been very easy for him.

Using the money from his redundancy, and from Kate's savings, they had started up and ran a successful online business which made a handsome profit for them after five years, after which time they had sold it on. They reinvested the profit so that each year they had a very healthy return, meaning they would never have to work again unless they chose to. This gave them the freedom to travel and see the world, living in a sort of semi-retirement. However, being semi-retired could only last so long, and soon Kate was thinking of something else to do, as was Mike, which is where her job teaching British Sign Language came in. She'd already been working as an interpreter when they'd met, so for her it was simply a case of picking up the phone and getting her old job back. For Mike, though, the decision had been harder, as the only thing he really knew how to do involved the military, and he wasn't too sure how he felt about going back into that line of work.

It had been a chance encounter with one of his old bosses, Peter Rawlinson, that had opened a new door for him. Peter had set up a company called Aurora after leaving the military, the company being in the process of developing the design and integration of battlefield drones to work with armoured vehicles. Over a few drinks Peter could see Mike had some fresh and exciting ideas, and it wasn't long before Peter was offering Mike a place within the company as a consultant. Mike had helped develop and design a number of the platforms, all highly secret and classified, with only a small select few, knowing exactly what they could do. But the platforms needed approval from the Ministry of Defence; a slow, laborious process of testing that could take years with plenty of red tape to cut through. Until that happened, the projects were dead in the water, and with no new work, and Mike's consultancy role now on hold, he was back to having time to spare. For now, the most exciting thing going on in his life today would be to see if their cat Daisy had left him anything in her litter box.

He finished showering, changed into jeans, T-shirt and blue jumper and made his way downstairs to start the morning ritual of checking the cat tray (nothing there, Daisy was slacking), cup of tea, breakfast and a catch-up on the news. He made himself a cup of tea, got some cereal and sat down to watch the TV, turning over to one of the news channels. It was top of the hour, so the latest headlines began to play and straight off the bat it was over to what was happening in one of the former regions of Russia. Last year, a new region of Russia called Tumat had decided to follow in the footsteps of Estonia and Latvia and break away from the motherland. The area was in the north-eastern edge of Russia, close to the Arctic Circle on the coast of the East Siberian Sea and from what Mike had seen on the map was far larger than the United Kingdom. The area had not been happy with the ongoing war in Ukraine, now dragging into its third year and what had started out as riots had eventually led to an all-out coup resulting in the region's military overthrowing the old Russian regime, installing a new government. This had all happened last year and since then the west had been posturing as to how to treat this new breakaway republic. Mike smirked to himself as he remembered a joke from one of the late-night comedians who had remarked that "If this new republic is set to be called Tumat would that mean its citizens are to be called Tumatos?" It was a poor joke, but it meant people would not forget the name of the region.

For the past year everyone had wondered what the Russian President would do, would he roll in the army and crush the uprising? Would he try to assassinate the new leader elect? Many an analyst had hazarded a guess, but all had been proven wrong. Russia had done nothing. They had lodged complaints within the United Nations about the coup and expressed concern about the level of violence conducted during the takeover, but that had been it. Since then, the people of Tumat had been left to their own devices – within a year they'd established a government, elected a new President and even had a new flag made. *Not bad efficiency*, thought Mike, *perhaps our own government could learn from theirs*.

The camera was showing parliament square, where thousands of people stood waving the new flag, all happy, cheering, some even crying. Clearly, emotions were running high. A young reporter who Mike had seen before, was shouting over the crowd, attempting to report on the unfolding events.

"As you can see here there are emotional and excited scenes as the people of Tumat prepare to celebrate their first year of independence. Tomorrow will mark the first year since this country shook off the shackles of the Russian President. A President who has taken his country to war, with the disastrous invasion of Ukraine, a war that even now is still ongoing. A President who has increasingly shown hostility toward the west. But now perhaps this is the

sign of things to come as the new Republic of Tumat waits to celebrate its first birthday. Along with this fresh new country comes a fresh-faced new leader, the charismatic and energetic President Iylanovitch, former TV star and critic of the Russian President. His rise to power being largely thanks to the way he handled the road to independence for Tumat. Always an advocate for peace, some say it was his leadership that prevented the revolution from turning into a blood bath, as forces loyal to the people led the takeover of the parliament building, allowing a new reformed government to take charge. It was only eight months ago the United Nations recognised this new country, and it can only be a matter of time before the talk turns to future agreements with the possibility of NATO membership being discussed. But for now, I think President Iylanovitch will just enjoy his country's moment as he and the people of Tumat prepare to celebrate their anniversary tomorrow."

Mike lowered the volume of the TV so it faded into the background and took a sip of tea. As he did so he was startled as a ginger mass of fur began her assault from the left.

"Daisy!" he exclaimed happily, as the cat jumped up onto the breakfast bar. She began purring loudly and nudging into his hand holding the teacup. Mike had to be careful not to spill any. Daisy had clearly not been happy that Mike's attention was on the telly. As if to prove a point she rolled onto her back and playfully nudged his cereal bowl.

Mike began to rub Daisy under her chin as her big brown eyes looked back at him. *Butter wouldn't melt*, thought Mike.

"Okay, girl, okay, guessing someone wants a fuss, but you know you shouldn't be up here. Kate would kill me if she found out."

As if in response Daisy meowed, then shuffled closer, her paw touching Mike's arm.

Mike continued to stroke her chin for a minute before finally relenting. He stood up and went over to the cupboard, pulling out one of the sachets of cat food.

"Right, let's see what flavour you get today," said Mike, looking at the sachet.

"Looks like it's chicken and liver. I hope you realise how lucky you are, lots of cats have to hunt for their food," Mike joked.

He looked down as Daisy sat at his feet, staring at him with her soft beguiling eyes.

Mike smiled and filled the cat bowl with the disgusting-looking meal. *Definitely not one for humans*, he thought, as he placed it down, stroking Daisy as she tucked in – clearly she was not thinking the same.

As Daisy ate her breakfast, Mike went back to his, resuming his seat at the breakfast bar and continuing to eat his cereal. The TV was now showing a harsh-looking young man standing in front of the large crowd talking. Mike left the volume low; he'd heard it all before. No doubt the President was keen to make an impression, they always were. And besides, whatever he had to say, it wouldn't stop him eating his breakfast.

He took another sip of his tea, watching as the screen changed to the familiar footage of Ukraine, the war that still continued after all this time. Mike raised the volume to hear what was being said, as he knew two of his old squadrons were deployed to both Poland and Latvia, countering any further Russian aggression in the area. Thankfully, so far, they hadn't been needed – the Ukrainians had been doing all they could to stop the Russians. But the war had grown into an endless tug of war as the western weapons had an impact on pushing back the Russians, only for the Ukrainians to run out of spares and supplies. Then the Russians would use their endless supply of manpower to push the Ukrainians back to where they started, back and forth like a pendulum.

As the war stood, the momentum had swung away from the Russians and Ukraine was advancing on all fronts. It was this new offensive the news was reporting on. The scene cut back to the news studio and to one of the many ex-forces analysts, some retired Captain or Major who would give an almost military-style daily briefing, showing the gains and losses so far of both sides on a large map of the region in the background. It was almost like he was reading out the weather as he droned on about casualties here, equipment losses there. From what Mike could gather from listening, the war had not been going too well for Russia – Ukraine had been receiving new supplies of western weaponry and its forces had been training in Germany and the UK, safe from any Russian attacks. The Russians, however, seemed to be having either supply problems or manpower issues as the Ukrainian troops had encountered an increasingly weakened Russian army.

Mike remembered that since the end of 2023 Russia had gone 'dark' – a term referring to zero information going in and more importantly none coming out as all the western or pro-western journalists were kicked out of Russia, being replaced by more pro-Russian journalists preaching the Russian President's line about 'the special military operation'. Since then, the news coming out of Russia had been sketchy at best and had resorted more to school yard gossip than factual news. Everyone had heard about Russia's 'ultra-hypersonic missiles', faster than anything the west had, its 'Poseidon torpedoes' that could send radioactive tsunamis crashing against an enemy's coast, next generation hovercraft with the lift capability to carry four tanks each, and lately he'd been hearing about a so-called 'mass conscription' with reportedly fifteen per cent of all fighting age males within Russia being called into service.

But where were they? Perhaps Russia was planning yet another offensive over the winter? Mike downed the cup of tea in one gulp and continued watching as the news now cut from the ex-military briefing to another scene. A reporter was speaking live from the Ukrainian front line, with a column of what looked like Marder German vehicles flying huge Ukrainian flags in the background. From the way the reporter was getting animated and the excitement in her voice, Mike could tell she was close to the action, and as if to emphasise the point, every now and then the cameraman would pan frantically around the area, with a few shaky shots, proudly showing off the latest blackened destroyed hulks of what was once the pride of the Russian army. Mike wondered to himself where it would stop. Would the Russians let the Ukrainians cross over into Russian Federation territory? Would they have the resources to pull that off? He knew from previous news reports the the allies were closely controlling the logistics of what Ukraine could use, so maybe in effect it was NATO that had the say on how far it would go. Mike certainly didn't think they'd want the Russians to be backed into that much of a corner.

After he finished breakfast, he switched off the TV, picking up his phone from the kitchen worktop and checking his messages for any further potential changes to his day. That morning, he'd already planned to go down to the marina to check on the boat before coming back home, then spend an hour or two in the gym before going to meet his lifelong friend Chris in Bovington, who was currently working for the Armoured Trials Development Unit (or ATDU for short). Mike thought back through the years to how he and Chris had first met. Chris had joined the same army regiment as Mike in 1998, two years after him, and both had hit it off from the start. They had joined the boxing team and had become opponents, each representing their respective squadron in the inter-squadron boxing tournament. It was during the match that Mike had learnt the hard way that Chris had a mean right hook. That's not to say he didn't get a couple of punches on him too; Mike had been chuffed when he felt his right fist connect with Chris's nose, causing him to stagger backward. But it had been Chris who had gone on to win the bout – he stood a foot taller than Mike and had a longer reach. And every time Mike had thrown a punch, he was hitting fresh air as Chris had pivoted around him, his arm cocked, ready to spring one back in response.

The match had gone the distance, with both men unable to knock out the other and Mike remembered being very thankful, on legs like jelly, as the bell had rung for the last time. His gloves had begun to feel like they were full of lead and his face ached, one eye swollen as the match ended. Chris, on the other hand, had looked fresh and composed, albeit sporting a newly broken nose, and was springing around the ring looking like he could go another round. Chris had won the match on points, no surprise there, but the one thing Mike would always remember is that once the bell sounded, Chris came right over to congratulate him. After the tournament the boxing team had been allowed into the Sergeants' Mess bar for a drink to celebrate the wins. It was there Mike had sat, his face bandaged, to lick his wounds and numb the pain of both the injuries and the defeat with something alcoholic. Chris had come over to join him with two bottles in hand. He'd offered Mike one, which he'd gratefully accepted. It was at this point that Chris had told Mike he'd boxed before and had remained undefeated, usually knocking out his opponents. The fact Mike had not only lasted the three rounds but also broken Chris's nose was something for him to be proud of.

It had been a strange way to form a friendship, but one that was formed on respect and, after their unorthodox introduction, what followed was a friendship that had spanned seven operational tours, including two in Iraq and Afghanistan. Both men had been through some great and equally horrific times, but they would always have each other's back and had both advanced up the rank structure roughly at the same time. Even after Mike had left in 2014, they had kept in touch, meeting at least twice a year. And when they did meet, it had always been like they had never been apart. When Mike took redundancy, Chris had been a Sergeant Major, but was now a Captain, having been in the ATDU these past two years and working on all manner of new and wonderful things for the army, or at least that's how Mike understood it.

He'd always imagined the ATDU to have some kind of new flying tank or stealth tank ready to combat the latest threat and the thought of finally getting to go in and see it for himself gave him a childish shot of excitement. *Finally, I can see behind the curtain,* he thought.

Mike had received a call from Chris the previous week asking for him to come visit the ATDU building today at 2pm. When they'd met in the past it had always been in Mike's neck of the woods in one of the many cafés or bars that Poole had to offer. Mike had wondered at first how a civilian like himself would be allowed into a military building, but Chris had already seen to his security clearance. When Mike had questioned why he wanted the meeting there, Chris had just replied with, "There's something I want you to take a look at and we can chat about it on the day. Trust me, it'll be worthwhile."

Mike had thought it would be nice to be on familiar ground again with people in the military. He really missed the banter they all had together, the sort of chat enjoyed by people who live and work closely like that. *Bonds and friendships forged in fire*, if he remembered correctly, the bumper sticker he once read.

Mike remembered when he'd served in the regiment, he knew the names of over three hundred people. He still remembered the day he left, shaking hands with nearly all of them, all the well-wishers saying, "keep in touch," and "good luck, mate." But, as with all things, life gets in the way – family ties, location, work, personal circumstances, take your pick. Now the only people he knew from the army he could count on one hand. And of these he only met two regularly. One was Chris, and the other Peter Rawlinson, former brigadier and Mike's old Commanding Officer.

Come on, Mike, stop daydreaming, he thought, as he snapped out of his trip down memory lane.

He checked the phone and the last message from Chris had read, *Yep, all good, see you here for 2pm.*

He put the phone into his pocket and tidied away the cup and dishes before walking into the hall. He took the house keys out of the front door as Daisy sidled up to him and began rubbing her body and head against his leg, as if wishing him goodbye. He smiled and reached down, giving her a stroke before saying, "Okay, little lady, I'll be back shortly." As if in disgust at Mike leaving her alone, she walked away gracefully, tail in the air, showing the part of a cat that owners usually saw the most, her backside. Mike chuckled to himself as he put his shoes and coat on and checked he had his wallet and phone, then left the house. The garage door clicked to life, the motor humming softly as it raised up and over to reveal the third love of Mike and Kate's life. Mike allowed himself a small smile as he looked at the car parked before him. In their garage sat a 2021 Porsche Turbo S in crayon grey, the sunlight glinting off the bodywork. The headlights and shape of the front of the car always gave the impression of a smile, causing the car to look happy but almost docile. But in the back of the car sat anything but docile, an engine capable of launching the car up to sixty mph in less than two seconds and onto speeds of two hundred mph. Both Mike and Kate had a passion for cars, and after the success of their earlier business venture they had both decided why not, they were only here once. The car had cost a hefty sum but had more than made up for it with the numerous driving tours they had enjoyed. Now, however, it was simply a trip to the marina. Mike opened the door and got in, sinking into the driver's seat, the smell of leather filling the air. *What is it about the scent of leather that fires up the senses*, he wondered, as he turned the key, the engine revving to life before settling into a rhythm, like a cat waiting to be released from its cage. He put the car into gear, rolled out of the garage, making sure the door had closed behind him and made his way to the marina.

With the light traffic the drive to the marina only took ten minutes, even though the school holidays were in full swing. Mike knew that in about an hour the traffic would increase as holidaymakers poured in from all over the UK to make the most of the beaches that Poole and Bournemouth were famous for. He parked the car and walked down to the marina, the sun already beating down. The sky was clear, except for a flock of seagulls aimlessly floating on the thermals overhead. It was clearly going to be one of those glorious summer days.

He stepped onto one of the floating pontoons and walked to the finger pontoon where their boat *Valkyrie* was moored. This was the fourth love of their lives. Mike had passed two people he knew on the pontoon, giving them the usual "Morning" before arriving at his berth. There she was, a forty-two-foot motorboat, built by one of the many great British boatyards, but she was looking a little sorry for herself as she was currently halfway through her four-month renovation. Mike could have paid one of the many marine engineers in the area to do the work, but he enjoyed getting his hands dirty, the work keeping him physically and more importantly mentally active.

The boat had been Kate's idea to give Mike something to focus on; not long after he'd left the forces, he had been known at times to become Mr Miserable, moping around the house bored, thinking of things to do. Kate had suggested they get a boat, to give them an escape onto the water and to also get Mike up and out of the house. So, in 2018 they'd bought their first boat. Now, five years later, and they had already moved on to boat number three.

He unzipped the back cover, carefully stepping off the pontoon and onto the swim deck, then ducking under the canopy, Mike stepped into the cockpit area. Normally he would have brought along his toolbox with a whole array of jobs on his to do-list, which no matter how much he seemed to work on the boat, would always get longer, never shorter. He remembered someone once saying, "that 'boat' is an acronym for Bring Out Another Thousand." He smiled to himself as he thought of all the lovely places they'd be visiting once the work was completed and all the fun times ahead of them. Then Mike was brought back to reality looking at the mass of wiring protruding from behind the helm, realising that there were still many more hours of work needed before that dream came true. Mike spent the next thirty minutes checking over the boat, running up both engines, checking nothing was leaking and that the engine temperatures were running normally. Then he gave the interior of the boat a quick wipe down, before switching everything off and checking the battery charger was still on and connected.

Happy with his checks, he made sure everything was locked up, but before step-ping back onto the pontoon, he checked the canopy was zipped up tight as the wind could tear the canopy apart if he left any fasteners or zips loose, and then he tested if the dock side ropes were secure. Once happy that *Valkyrie* was secure, he turned and started back along the pontoon toward the marina offices. Mike wanted to check in with the marina staff that everything was still all good and there were no outstanding invoices.

As he walked away from the berth, he had a quick glance back at the boat, the summer sun shining off the water, before continuing down the pontoon toward the marina office, thinking how lucky he and Kate were to be in the fortunate position to own one. They'd had friends and family down on the boat last summer and it was a great way to see the south coast. He'd certainly be making the most of her when she was ready again. Mike walked into the office to see the marina staff, Gerald, Julie and Dave all behind the main desk looking at the wall-mounted TV on the far side of the office. Curious, he looked up to see what had grabbed their attention. It looked like the news was showing Southampton Harbour, he remembered it as one of the ports they had visited on *Valkyrie* before they had started the renovations. The camera was setup on the dockside, overlooking the harbour channel. Whoever the camera operator was, they were doing a shitty job as the camera kept erratically panning left and right, before finally focusing on what appeared to be a large container ship no more than two hundred metres away. Mike recognised it as one of the types that was regularly seen loading and unloading in Southampton Docks. She looked large, about four hundred metres long with a light-blue hull and a large white logo in the centre and some white superstructure that towered over the rest of the ship about a quarter of the way along the hull. The ship was fully loaded with containers and was at least the height of a twenty-storey building. There were two black-and-white pilot boats and a police boat floating next to it. Something about the way the ship was positioned looked wrong though, as Mike could see it was lying across the harbour channel, blocking it. It reminded Mike of the container ship that that had got itself stuck back in 2021 in the Suez Canal. That had taken weeks to clear, so who knew how long this would take to get moved. Mike tried to focus on what was being said on the TV but Gerald, who was obviously excited by the drama unfolding, wanted to be the first to tell him.

"Look at that, Mike! It got itself stuck about fifteen minutes ago. Look at the size of it! How are they going to fix that? Someone's going to get fired over this, my bet is the captain was drunk. It was just like that car transporter that tipped over in 2018."

Mike glanced at Gerald as Julie interrupted his rant. "Gerry, we don't know that, we don't even know what happened, it just veered off course, maybe they had a rudder failure."

"Julie, do you mind turning it up a bit just to listen, I think the reporter is going to give an update," Mike said.

The volume increased as the news reporter, who was just off camera, continued.

"*Live from Southampton Harbour, where again, for those of you just joining us, at about 10:30 today the container ship* MV Trojan *has run aground in the area of Southampton Harbour. We don't yet know what has caused this to happen. Is it mechanical failure? Or is it crew error? But as you can see this is a large vessel, and you have to begin to wonder, how on earth are they going move this? At the moment, as we understand it, the port authorities are working with the coast guard and tugs are being moved into position, but these vessels fully loaded can weigh as much as one hundred and twenty thousand tonnes. That is a lot of weight to just push aside, and we don't even know yet how badly this ship has run aground. Later on, we will be talking to a former captain from the Maritime Transportation Board to explain what possible causes there are and just how the port authorities can begin the recovery process."*

"Look at that!" Dave yelled excitedly. "The boat looks like it's sinking!"

"What?" replied Julie. "Why? It hasn't struck the bottom, it can't be!"

They all continued to watch the live feed and could see in the short space of time since they began watching that the ship had indeed begun to settle stern first. The water around the ship began to foam and bubble, which Mike could see was an indicator that air was escaping from the hull.

But what would cause that? Mike thought to himself. The huge white logo on the side of the ship was a good reference point that it was sinking, as the water could be seen creeping up the hull.

Suddenly the crowds that had gathered on the shoreline began pointing, excited heads bobbing back and forth, deep in discussion. As all of this was happening the news reporter finally caught on and said, "Bob, focus on the back of the ship, it looks like it's sinking!"

Slowly, gracefully, the ship began to settle stern first onto the seabed. Mike wasn't too sure about the water depth, but he knew it wasn't deep enough for the ship to just disappear. The angle of the ship increased and some of the containers on the stern of the vessel began to slide off into the water, one nearly hitting the police boat that had gone too close. Some of the containers simply sunk out of sight, whilst others began to bob away from the vessel, looking like some strange form of lifeboats. Everyone in the office watched transfixed, no-one saying a word as the scene played out in front of them. Even the reporter was silent as the hull of the container ship seemed to level out as she sunk down on a more even keel. It couldn't have taken more than three minutes before the MV Trojan sat upright and proud on the seabed, most of her hull underwater but a mountain of containers and her superstructure still towering above the water. One thing was for sure, thought Mike, this salvage job just got a whole lot worse.

"*My God,*" the reporter finally said. "*Umm... I'm not quite sure what the port authorities are going to do now, but let's just hope and pray that the crew were able to get off the vessel to safety...*"

The volume of the TV suddenly muted, as Dave had the remote in his hand. "Guys, wow, that's something you don't see every day. That ship sunk far too fast, didn't it?"

"I've never seen a ship sink that perfectly and quickly before" Julie replied. "Any chance it had the hull ripped open on the seabed?"

"As far as I'm aware it's all mud and sand on the seabed," answered Mike, "not quite sure what would cause that except explosives."

"Well, whatever it was, if anyone had ordered anything online don't count on next-day delivery!"

They all turned to face Gerry.

"What do you mean?" Mike asked.

"Well, Southampton Docks are now officially out of business, closed for the summer holidays." Gerry beamed, clearly enjoying the moment. "How are any boats going to get in or out of the docks now? All those containers sat in the dock waiting to be loaded and unloaded. Anyone waiting on a delivery will be waiting a looong time."

"Gerry, sometimes I think you get a little too excited at this sort of thing. I bet you used to poke dead animals as a kid." Clearly Dave had heard enough of Gerry's ranting.

Mike stood there thinking about something that had seemed familiar about all of this as the three of them carried on discussing what they had just seen. It only lasted a second before he shook his head, clearing the thought. *Couldn't be.* He smiled to himself. *You're a civvy now, stop imagining things.*

He looked at the others as they chatted. It was Julie who broke the conversation, looking at Mike before asking, "Sorry Mike, ignore these two, what was it you wanted to talk about?"

He explained to them that he had just come in to see if there were any outstanding invoices that needed paying, and that he'd checked on the boat, and she was all securely tied up. He didn't need to tell them the latter part but after what he had just seen on the telly, he was being extra cautious.

Thankfully and surprisingly, there were no bills to pay, so after having another quick glance at the TV and saying his goodbyes, Mike left them watching the news and made his way out of the office and back to the car. Now he had somewhere else to be.

2

And So It Begins

When the attack came, it was fast – the knifeman's right arm exploded out, knife poised for the killing strike toward Mike's chest. Upon instinct, Mike's body flexed backward and he pivoted to his right, increasing the distance of the knife to his body whilst at the same time bringing his arms closer to the attacker. Mike's right hand arched behind the knife, his palm outstretched as it slammed into the knifeman's inner elbow, whilst simultaneously he cupped his left hand and brought his left arm up and around to grab the outer wrist of the knifeman's now outstretched arm. This one, fluid movement caused the knifeman's arm to fold in at the elbow, bringing the knife away from Mike and toward the assailant's exposed body. Using his left hand, Mike bent the assailant's exposed wrist into a devastating lock, practised countless of times, rendering the arm useless. Mike knew the pain would be severe as the knifeman yelped and he dropped the knife to the floor. Mike kicked the knife backward as his opponent tried to counter with a devastating roundhouse punch aimed to his head. Mike had already predicted the move and on instinct his right arm released his hold on the elbow and blocked the punch, batting it away and deflecting some of the energy. The punch still connected, but with nowhere near as much force as intended. To keep on the offensive Mike stepped forward, launching a devastating headbutt. Using his legs to spring up, he felt his head connect with the knife man's lower jaw, before his opponent's legs turned to jelly. Clearly the head butt had caused some damage.

Mike could hear the second assailant coming at him from behind, and with one swift motion, with his assailant's arm still locked and useless, he side stepped, forcing the knifeman into the path of the second attacker. Two became one as they were tangled, falling to the floor, cursing. Mike stepped back to reassess the threats, quickly using the time to glance around, checking for further danger. He could see the first man was struggling to get up and Mike was contemplating running away when he saw the second opponent already on his knees and quickly rising, the distinct shape of a pistol being drawn from his waistband.

Realising time was against him, Mike launched himself at the gunman, his right leg sweeping out into a devastating kick that was aimed toward the gunman's chest. To his horror the gunman, as if sensing the move, brought his elbow up to block and Mike grimaced as his leg connected with it, the force of the kick being deflected. The pistol was out of the waistband now, the gunman almost on his feet, trying to bring the pistol to bear onto Mike. Purely on instinct, Mike shoulder-charged the gunman. One hand locked around the gunman's free hand, preventing any further attacks whilst the second took hold of the pistol body, tilting it upward and outward, causing the trigger guard of the pistol to trap the gunman's finger, preventing him from firing the pistol. Mike pushed himself against the gunman, increasing the pistol's angle, giving the gunman two options – one: keep hold of the pistol and break his trigger finger, or two: release the pistol and continue the fight. The gunman chose option two; he released the pistol and wrapped his arm over Mike's arm, which was still holding the gun, trapping it. Mike now had a dilemma as both men had each other's right arms trapped with their left, with no clear way to strike. Straining, he could hear the knifeman behind him struggling to get up and knew it was only a matter of seconds before the knifeman recovered and plunged the knife that lay on the floor into his back. The gunman, as if sensing his dilemma, looked Mike straight in the eyes, his face a mask of rage, his teeth clenched in effort and snarled, "And what now, Kolboynik?"

Thinking clearly, Mike rolled backward, allowing his full body weight onto the gunman's arms, pivoting and bringing his knees up into his opponent's chest. He heard his opponent groan as the air was smashed from his lungs, winding him as the gunman was levered up and over Mike, the move causing him to release his hold on Mike's arm holding the gun. The gunman rolled over in a heap and looking up he saw Mike, pistol in hand in a perfect firing position. The pistol was aimed squarely at his chest.

"STOP!"

Everyone froze. Mike lowered the pistol, his chest heaving as the adrenaline coursed through his body, before stepping forward to the gunman, extending his hand in an offer to help him up. The gunman's face broke into a smile, showing nothing of the earlier anger or aggression as he pulled himself up standing next to Mike, patting him on the shoulder in appreciation.

Meanwhile, the knifeman had got to his feet, walking to the discarded knife and picking it up from the floor, before approaching the fourth person in the room, the one who had shouted the command.

"Damn, Mike, that was a good move," the gunman exclaimed. "Good thinking on your feet."

"Thanks, Ariel, only thing I could think of," he replied before raising an eyebrow and asking, "Kolboynik?"

Ariel smiled back, replying, "Yiddish for 'smart arse', a know-it-all. I just fancied getting into character. Besides, three more seconds and Ewen would have had you."

The knifeman walked toward them, rubbing his arm. "Actually, I'd have had you in two. Damn silly of you, Mike to get in that situation to begin with. Remember what we taught you – don't concentrate too much on a pistol. You could have quite easily finished Ariel with a punch to the neck, he would have gone down choking, then you could have had the pistol anyway." Mike nodded, happy to be receiving the instruction.

"Thanks, Ewen, I'll remember that next time."

"See that you do, or there may not be a next time," Ewen replied, placing a hand on his shoulder to emphasise the point. It wasn't that Ewen was being harsh, he was being pragmatic. They didn't teach manners and etiquette there; it was hand-to-hand combat.

Ewen walked over to Ariel, handing him the plastic knife, a prop with a plastic blade that would withdraw into its handle if ever there was an attempt to use it. It was made specifically for teaching hand-to-hand combat and would ensure no one would get hurt. The pistol that Mike had in his hand looked and felt real as it was a deactivated weapon. Both Ewen and Ariel liked to teach with a weapon that was as realistic as possible, so that students could get used to the feel and weight of the real thing. The pistol had a top slide which could be pulled back to simulate it being cocked, but more importantly some of the grab holds that Ewen and Ariel taught involved pushing against the top slide, which even if only pushed back a millimetre would stop the pistol from firing, something that could mean the difference between life and death.

Ewen looked to the fourth man in the room before saying, "Okay, Gregory, you saw how Mike improvised against multiple attackers and weapons, let's see you go through the same. In the middle of the mat please." His arm shot out, pointing to where he wanted his student to stand. As Gregory walked there, Ewen turned to Mike. "You've been at it now for an hour, do you fancy heading home or do you want to watch Gregory?"

Mike walked over to the side of the gym and picked up his watch, lying on top of his belongings and checked the time. He still had a few hours to kill. "Ewen, if you don't mind, I'll head off and hit the gym at home to stretch some of these muscles."

Ewen smiled and nodded his head in approval, he understood more than anyone the importance of fitness, especially at his age of fifty-nine; he didn't look a day over forty and had a body that was hard and lean from all the years in the IDF.

Mike picked up his things, his face wet with sweat and waved goodbye to Ariel as he made his way out of the door. Ariel waved back and smiled, before his face settled into the cold unreadable mask of the attacker, preparing to launch again, this time at Gregory, knife in hand. Mike smiled; it was proving to be a very good day.

Twenty minutes later and he was back home on the treadmill, doing one of his three times a week gym sessions. No way was he going to let civvy street give him a belly, he thought, as he passed the five-kilometre mark. He had his earbuds in, music was pumping, and he was in the zone. He always started off at a slow and steady five kph for the first kilometre, just to get his blood pumping before cranking the speed up to a steady seven kph. After only five minutes he was covered in a new sheen of sweat, his breathing heavy but constant. He was just reaching the six-kilometre mark when suddenly his phone, connected through his earbuds, began to ring. He glanced at the screen, recognising it was an American number. *Kate wants to chat*, he thought. He quickly tapped his left earbud, halting the music and answering the call, breathing heavily as the treadmill began to wind down.

"Huh-hey, babes-huh-you... huh-okay?" Mike asked, breathing heavily.

"Hey, darling, I caught you at a bad time. What are you doing there?" she asked, clearly hinting mischievously.

"Not what you're thinking, funny girl. Actually, I'm in the gym!" He laughed, his breathing slowly beginning to return to normal. He looked at his phone for the time. It was 11:20.

"Anyway, what's up? It must be, what, 5am there?" he asked. Kate replied, "Actually it's 05:20 and it's all good here, I'm actually calling because I just wanted to hear your voice."

"Forgive me if I'm wrong, but you're at a conference for sign language, it should be your hands doing the talking and no voices allowed."

"Mike! I swear your jokes get worse the older you get. What happened to the funny man I married? Is this what I've got to look forward to as we get older?" He could hear the humour in her voice. That's what he loved about Kate, she also had the gift of banter, and he knew there was never any offence given or taken.

"Nope, you've also got the bonus of the beer belly, moobs, failed eyesight, grey hair and lack of mobility. But one thing that won't ever change is my great taste in women! Hence, I married you. You're a lucky girl, you know!" he added jokingly.

Kate laughed before replying, "I love your modesty, that's why I married you!"

"And there I was thinking you married me for my large—"

"Mike!" she interrupted. "How do you know I don't have you on speakerphone? Anyone could be listening."

Mike chuckled before continuing, "*Personality*, I was going to say personality."

"You were not. I knew exactly what you were saying. Besides, it's like I always tell you, you always have a knack for doing more with less..."

"You cheeky..." he started, and then they both burst into fits of laughter.

After it had died down, they began chatting about how the conference was going so far and how she had settled in. Kate mentioned how Chicago was lovely and that they should both pencil in a visit for the future. Mike then began to tell her about his day so far, leaving out what he had seen on the news in Southampton. He chatted about their boat, saying it was all fine and that Daisy was good. Mike let Kate know her parents, Roy and Martha, were both well and that he had been keeping an eye on them which was especially important as Martha was seventy-six and Roy eighty-two. Mike and Kate had moved them close a few years ago to a bungalow only three streets away. Since then, they had always made a point to pop in, not to intrude but merely to ensure they were happy and didn't need or want for anything.

Suddenly out of the blue Mike asked, "Babes, what's up? You haven't rung me this early to chat about Daisy or the boat or ask me about my morning?"

She took a deep breath before saying, "You remember you used to tell me all about how you would have to do those big briefings in the army?"

"That's right, I'd have to chat to sometimes hundreds of people in a room, why'd you ask about that?"

"Look, if I'm being honest, I'm a bit nervous about this morning. I've got to go up on the stage and do a speech on the merits of ASL and BSL being integrated. It's not the subject matter that worries me, it's being in front of all those people. You know what I'm like in crowded rooms, I hate being up there with everyone looking at me. So, I guess I'm kind of asking you how did you do it...? I mean, how did you get the confidence to do it?"

Mike took a moment before replying, "If I'm being honest, you're always nervous about doing something like that, even the most experienced people have nerves – it's how you control them that counts. Remember watching the documentary on that pop star who would throw up before every concert, regardless of how many times he did one?"

"Oh great, so all I need to do is chuck up all over the front row, and as they wipe away the puke, I'm all smiles!"

He laughed before continuing, "No, silly, what I mean is that the nerves are normal, it's natural to feel nervous. First, breathe slowly, talk slowly, don't rush. The audience are not there to judge or criticise you, they're there to listen to what you have to say. They want to hear what you have to say. Secondly, when you're talking, don't stare at the audience, instead pick a spot just above their heads, and when you start to talk pan your head slowly left and right. You'll not see the audience anymore as your eyes will blur them out and focus instead on the space above them. They will think you're looking at them and the fact you're turning your head will look like you're chatting to them all, it's what the experts call 'controlling the room'."

"The experts, being you?" she asked doubtfully.

"I'm serious, darling, it works and has been proven to work. Contrary to popular belief I don't blag my way through everything, just most things."

She chuckled and Mike could hear her tone relax. His words had had the soothing effect she needed.

"Okay, anything else?" asked Kate.

"Yes, remember, babes, you know the subject, you don't need to read a speech or read it from an autocue, you've spoken to me many times about this. How many times have you made me listen to your speech? Imagine you're chatting to me in that room. Hell, even imagine I'm at the back of the room listening to you."

"Mike you *never* listen to me!" Kate replied jokingly.

Mike laughed as Kate continued. "Look, seriously, I'm really missing you. It's only a few days I know, and I know when we first met, we managed seven months apart, but this really sucks. Promise me if I ever agree to go away again, you'll come with me?"

"Look, darling, if I was there, I'd probably be a distraction to you. I know how important this is to you, you've spent years putting it together with your team. So yeah, next time I'll be right beside you and happy to distract, because I think right now a distraction is just what you need..."

There was silence on the end of the line. At first, Mike thought he'd said something to upset her. It wouldn't have been the first time he'd blundered into something. "Kate, you still there, babes?" he asked tentatively. He looked at the phone screen, the call was still connected, but for some reason Kate wasn't responding. They had always suffered from a poor phone network in their area, so he assumed it was playing up again. *She'll call back*, he thought as he hung up the phone and waited. After five minutes of waiting Mike looked back at his screen. He had a full signal bar and was confused as to why the call was cut. Finally, he decided that she'd been happy with his advice and had finally managed to get some sleep. He knew Kate had a big day that morning and he didn't want to disturb her further. He checked the time, it was 11:45. He knew he still had time to finish his workout before seeing Chris, so without any more thought he restarted the music, cranked up the treadmill and continued the run to nowhere, with the dance tunes getting him back in the zone.

After a shower, change of clothes and some lunch he felt like a young man again, his body refreshed and vibrant as the endorphins kicked in. The time was 13:20, plenty of time for him to get in the car for the drive to see Chris. He checked that Daisy had food – he didn't know how long he'd be with Chris, especially as he had no idea what the meeting was about, so he didn't want Daisy to go too long without a meal. She followed him to the door again, conducting the same ritual as this morning, purring, nudging into his leg, happy to see him off. This time, however, instead of walking away she stayed by the door as he gave her one last stroke before leaving the house, then made his way to the car. Little did he know that this would be the last time he would see his home for a very long time....

3

New Beginnings

The drive from Poole to Bovington took Mike ten minutes longer than usual, with extra traffic building up as families ventured out for the day. The British summer had kicked up a gear as Mike saw the temperature on the vehicle's dashboard display showing twenty-nine degrees. He drove with windows and sunroof open, preferring fresh air to the artificial cold of the air conditioning. During the journey the radio played the news, dominated by events unfolding in Southampton Docks. Business leaders were already beginning to warn of supply chain problems; Southampton was a major artery for trade into the UK and this would no doubt affect things. Various maritime experts were discussing options to salvage the ship with one expert saying it could take months to remove. The other curious aspect of the incident being reported was that the crew were missing. The bridge structure was still above the waterline and the coastguard had sent teams aboard to find them. No one had been found. Experts were saying perhaps the crew had abandoned ship in some panicked state before the ship ran aground. *"But where was the lifeboat?"* they'd asked. *"And why no distress call?"* It was a very intriguing situation and Mike listened intently during his journey.

Before long he was there, and he slowed to make the junction that would take him to his destination. He switched off the radio as he approached the main gate, ready to speak to the sentry.

He pulled up to the main gate for ATDU with the barrier down, blocking the road, expecting to see an armed guard. To his right side, level with the car's window sat a small camera with microphone and speaker. A sentry box stood to the far side of the road, empty and forlorn; in days past there would have been a guard there to check his credentials, however, these days everything was done digitally. A voice sounded through the speaker, courteous but firm. *"Good afternoon, sir, may I ask what your business here is today?"* Mike leant out of the open window and replied, "Afternoon, my name's Mike Faulkes and I've got a meeting with Captain Chris Richards here at the ATDU at 2pm."

There was no acknowledgement, no instructions, just an audible click as the microphone disconnected and the barrier began to rise. Mike smiled to himself as he drove through the gates toward the car park.

He'd always driven past the Armoured Trials Development Unit. It seemed quite funny to him that with all his years of being in the army he'd never once set foot in here, and now here he was, a civilian, and just like that he was in.

He pulled into the car park situated across from the large blue steel building that served as both the hangar for the vehicles hidden within and the administration building. The car park had space for twenty-five cars, but Mike counted only six there, including his own; parking wouldn't be a problem at least. He parked up in a space away from the other cars, switched off the engine and had a glance around.

The ATDU complex was located just outside Bovington Camp, opposite the through road leading in and out of Bovington village. It was a small garrison village of about four thousand people who were either families of serving soldiers or had settled there after serving in the forces. Typical of one of the many small Dorset villages, it had its own school, hairdresser, local convenience store, pub and takeaways, all designed to make the families and soldiers feel at home. The ATDU complex was separated from the main camp, having its own perimeter fence and gate that ran around the grounds. With its own access to the driver training area day or night, the vehicles could enter the training area to conduct tests and trials required of them without waking up the camp and without too many people in the village seeing what was going on. Although the village was made up of forces personnel, that didn't mean people wouldn't talk and the military way of thinking was better to not show anyone to begin with, then there wouldn't be any rumours to end with.

The main building sat in the centre of the complex hidden by trees dotted throughout the area. It was almost as if nature was trying to hide the building, Mike thought, as he looked at it.

He exited the car, closing the door, checking it was locked before making his way through the tree-lined pathway toward what he guessed would be the main doors into the complex.

Before he could get to the doors, they were flung open, and Chris came bounding out, all smiles. He was dressed in military uniform wearing MTP (Multi-Terrain Pattern) combat trousers and shirt with his beret tucked into his pocket.

"Mike! Great to see you, mate. I'm glad you made it down here." As always, Mike could see he'd still been hitting the gym, keeping himself in shape as every time he met him, he seemed to be even bigger than the last time; not in a 'all you can eat buffet-type way' but more of a 'smashing it out in the gym way'.

"Chris," he replied with an expression of mock concern on his face, "I thought you'd said you were spending more time in the gym?"

Chris froze for a second, not quite sure what to say, his mouth open wide, before laughing and grabbing Mike in a big bear hug and lifting him off the ground. Mike grimaced as the older bruises on his arms began to ache, Ewen and Ariel's gift was still giving. "That's what I love about you...you *small* people always have a big sense of humour!" They both laughed as he released Mike, putting him back on the ground.

At five feet nine inches, Chris was only an inch taller than Mike, something that he always liked to bring up whenever Mike cracked a joke about him. Chris was medium build, but muscular, thanks to the early years of boxing and then in the later years skiing for the army and more recently hitting the gym. He had short black hair, a smooth face that was always smiling and piercing blue eyes that seemed to melt even the most ice cold of receptions. He was professional, honest and held himself to a set of high standards, sometimes too high, Mike thought, as he was his own worst enemy. Many a time Mike had seen him beat himself up over a mistake that anyone else would just shrug off, but that's what made Chris one of the army's brightest and best – it was no surprise he'd managed to make the rank of Captain, which for someone who had started through the ranks as a Trooper was one hell of an achievement.

Chris saw Mike rubbing his shoulders and asked, "Don't tell me you're still doing that bloody Crab Maja stuff?"

Mike looked at him with raised eyebrows, replying, "It's called Krav Maga, and yes, I'm still doing it. It's actually good for the mind and the body. You should try it."

"Getting thrown around a gym by two former IDF soldiers who just so happen to be lovers doesn't sound like it's good for *your* body. Besides, did you ever think you could end up being the meat in their sandwich?" asked Chris mischievously.

Mike looked at him with mock seriousness, replying, "I don't think I'm Ewen or Ariel's type. You are though – I've already shown them a picture of you. They both commented on how butch you looked; I'll be sure to pass on your comments. Maybe next time they're passing here they can pop in to help fulfil that fantasy of yours. You've clearly thought about it."

Chris stared at Mike, not too sure what to say, until Mike couldn't keep the serious face any longer, his face cracking into a grin. Seeing this, Chris laughed.

"You bastard, Mike, you had me going then!"

Mike knew that despite Chris's joke, Chris was as tolerant and understanding as any person you could meet, especially as Chris's brother was gay and living in Brighton on the south coast.

Mike looked down at Chris's chest, his fingers pointing to the rank slide on his uniform. Instead of showing the usual three pips for a Captain they showed the large crown denoting Chris was now a Major.

"And what's this all about? I thought you were a Captain? You've been promoted again?"

"Umm... yeah, I'll explain all that later. In the meantime, how've you been keeping? How's Kate?"

Both men chatted, catching up on the last three months with Mike explaining that Kate was away at a conference. Mike briefly mentioned the boat's progress and that overall life was good, as Chris listened, giving the occasional nod. But Mike could see he was now distracted, looking over his shoulder toward the car park.

"And when were you going to mention that?" he exclaimed, Mike turning to see what he was pointing at.

"Ah the car, I thought you'd seen it before?"

"Mate, if I'd seen it before I would have asked for a drive! You'll be taking me out for a spin later?" Mike got the feeling Chris's hint was more of a statement than a request.

Mike chuckled, he'd forgotten what a complete petrolhead Chris was; Chris had a multitude of cars over the years that would have rivalled any collector. He remembered joking with Chris when the fuel light came on in one of his cars, he would simply trade the car in and get another. But truth was, Chris had an abandoned farm in the local area that he'd bought some years ago with plenty of space to store the cars, so he never had to sell any. Instead, he opted to keep them safely away from the elements. Mike also knew Chris worked on the cars himself, choosing to strip them down and rebuild them. From memory, the last time they'd met he had a Chesil Speedster 356 Replica, which in June on the Dorset roads was a joy to drive. Mike looked, but couldn't see it in the car park so was hoping he hadn't traded it in.

"You still got the 356 Replica? I was hoping to get a drive in that myself," Mike asked hopefully.

"Still got it, mate, but she's sat in bits back at the farm – I need to strip and rebuild the engine, but the one thing I need and I never seem to get is the time to do it. You know how it is."

Mike nodded before asking, "I'll show you round the car if you like?" turning to walk toward it.

Chris glanced at his watch before replying, "Not yet, mate. Remember what I said about time, afraid that applies to today. There's loads I want to show you and talk about. Come inside. I'll show you round."

"Am I still allowed in there?" Mike asked, pointing toward the building. "Remember, mate, I'm a civvy, and last time I checked that was out of bounds to people like me."

Chris reached into his pocket, pulling out a plastic credit-card-sized ID. He handed it to Mike. "It's all good, your security clearance came through, hence the guy on the gate let you in. This is yours for the day, this will get you in and out of the camp. So long as you don't get your phone out and start taking pictures it'll all be okay."

Chris stepped back. "Come on, let me show you around then we can chat some more," he said, leading the way toward the now open doors. They walked through and into the main hall which was a large open room, light spilling in from the huge windows on the side of the building. A stairway led up to the left with two doors leading off along the wall on the right side. At the far wall was another door, made more solidly than the others. This, Mike guessed, led to the vehicle hangar. Chris walked to the middle of the room, with Mike following, before stopping and then he pointed up the stairway. "Upstairs, mate – it's just our offices, nothing special up there, but we'll go get a brew there later."

"Okay, mate," Mike replied, looking around as Chris continued.

"So, the far door leads to the hangar, I'm guessing you knew that already, I'll give you a tour there in a second. The first door on the right leads to the toilets. If you need them, they're unisex, mate, so don't freak out if you see women in there. We've got a few working with us, some are from the Engineers and some are from the REME (Royal Electrical and Mechanical Engineers)

The REME had a whole task of jobs to do. It was the British army's version of the RAC, Kwik Fit, and a car dealership all rolled into one. Any vehicle operated by the army would have a fleet of REME fitters ready to work, day and night, rain, snow or shine, indoors and outdoors to fix and maintain any vehicle that the army was working with. They used to joke with Mike that "You play with it, you break it, *we fix it.*" But as any of the fitters would tell him, the satisfaction they would get from fixing a vehicle that was damaged, bogged in or broken, and getting it back on the road again would more than make up for the work involved. They were always integral to any troop, squadron or regiment and all would have their own 'fitter section' consisting of mechanics, electricians, gun fitters and vehicle recovery specialists. What they didn't know about vehicles, well, it wasn't worth knowing. It made sense for the ATDU to have its own fitter section on-site.

Chris began walking toward the second door. "And in here is our briefing room-cum-brew room-cum-'I've had a bad bloody day and want to tear the arms off someone room'. Surprise, surprise there's a lot of shouting that goes on in here." Chris chuckled to himself as he said that last part.

They walked through the door into a large rectangular room with a concrete floor.

Along one side was a fitted kitchen unit that ran the length of half the room. It had a sink, cooker, microwave, full-size fridge, a large kettle and what Mike would call a 'brew area' - basically, the essentials to make tea and coffee. There was a collection of mugs next to the kettle and each one had the owner's name written on it. Above the kettle attached to one of the cupboards was a laminated piece of paper which Mike recognised as the brew list. When he had first joined the army, and was attached to a troop, as the newest member he was expected to make the drinks for everyone. So, with twelve people in each troop that was always lots of drinks for him to remember.

To save constantly having to ask what they wanted, he instead made a 'brew list' with everyone's preferred drink on it. Then when he was told "Oi! Put the fucking kettle on," off he would go, coming back with twelve cups of something that everyone could moan about. He smirked as he saw the nicknames for drinks choices: there was 'NATO' which meant tea, white with two sugars, then there was 'Julie Andrews' which meant 'white none', a reference to *The Sound of Music* and there was 'Whoopi Goldberg' which meant 'black none,' a reference to *Sister Act*. It was the little things that made you smile, he thought to himself.

Mike's eyes scanned further into the room as he saw on the far side a large wall-mounted sixty-two-inch flat-screen TV which was state of the art. However, it also had what looked like a 1990's TV cabinet sat underneath. In the cabinet he saw a DVD player, games console and about one hundred DVDs all loosely stacked. Everything you'd need if you had to work the weekend here and needed a break, he thought. In the centre of the room were a collection of sofas, clearly from a catalogue during the 1980s. All the sofas were showing high mileage, the material looking worn in places and sunken cushions which had seen years of use. Clearly this room was where the crews had spent most of their time relaxing when not working on the vehicles. The other side of the room had some tables and chairs, all pulled together in little groups, where Mike guessed people sat reading or researching or just talking to each other. It reminded him of one of his troop rest rooms back in Germany when they were based there, and he smiled as feelings of nostalgia returned that he thought had long gone.

Chris saw Mike looking at the kitchen and as if reading his thoughts said, "Big kitchen I know, but it saves us wasting the time to keep going up to the cookhouse on camp."

Mike looked around the room again and realised that there was no one there, in fact, he hadn't seen anyone since he'd arrived. He looked at Chris quizzically, asking, "How many people do you have working for you at the moment?"

Chris paused before answering. "Usually about fifty, but with most of the camp closed for summer leave, most people are away. Now we're down to just fifteen, including me, but that's only because I've got to keep a team here to keep the testing going every day on the tanks. They're all over at the squadron offices in camp getting their paperwork and passports checked for a trip we've got coming up next month.

They'll be back in an hour. Anyway, come on, I'll show you the tanks – that's what I want you to look at."

Of course, Mike quickly thought to himself, *it's summer leave time.* Contrary to popular belief the army didn't always work seven days a week, fifty-two weeks a year; soldiers and their families needed time off like everyone else. If there was no requirement to work during the Easter, summer and Christmas periods, the camps would be almost empty as the soldiers would be stood down for two- to three-week periods. Sometimes this could be longer if the unit had recently been away on a deployment. But it wasn't a simple case of, 'last person turn off the light and close the door'. The camps had to be protected and maintained. So, a small volunteer force of soldiers would stay behind to do their 'guard duties'. This small force would hold the fort so to speak, providing protection to the camp and manning the gates, effectively keeping the lights on until the remainder of the unit, now fresh-faced and relaxed, came back off leave. This was why Mike realised the camp was looking deserted and the car park was empty when he had arrived.

Still unsure as to why Chris had invited him over, Mike followed him out of the rest room and down the hall toward the end door. The door had a keypad on it and Mike respectfully looked away as Chris keyed in a six-digit number. The keypad lit up green followed by an audible hiss as the door unlocked. Chris opened the door then ushered Mike through.

Mike's eyes blinked as they adjusted to the slightly darker interior of the hangar as the large, long LED lights hanging from the ceiling flicked on as one. "Motion Sensors," said Chris, "all part of turning the army green, reducing its energy usage. They flick off every ten minutes, so it saves leaving any lights on. The noise you heard was the dehumidifier system. It keeps the tanks moisture free, a bit like what you've got on your boat."

"Oh, so you do listen to what I say?" Mike said jovially as he stood to the side of the doorway.

Chris looked back with raised eyebrows and smiled.

Mike's eyes were drawn to the huge profile of the rear of the Challenger 2 (Chally2) sat hulking in front of him. They were stood at the back of the tank, its one hundred and twenty millimetre gun protruding over the rear decks. The turret was to the rear of the vehicle, the gun stowed in its clamp, something the crew would do in peacetime if the turret didn't need to be moved around. The sleek lines and sharp sloped edges made it look menacing even without the usual green-and-black disruptive-patterned paint job. The door they had entered was to the rear of the building from where he could look down the hangar's whole length to the far wall. He saw the back end of what he counted to be ten Challenger 2 tanks, all parked with their guns over the back decks or 'gun rear' as the crews called it. At the far end of the hanger, he also saw a Challenger Armoured Repair and Recovery Vehicle, CRARRV for short.

The CRARRV was the REME's version of the tank. Effectively built upon a Chally 2 hull, it had a huge dozer blade on the front and a crane system on the back. It allowed the fitter section to keep up with the tanks and go where the tanks went. If a tank became stuck or needed repairing, that's where the CRARRV would be in its element. The crane was used to help lift out generators, gear-boxes and engines alike, and the dozer blade was ideal for digging trenches or helping dig the tanks in. Overall, it was a brilliant bit of kit and Mike had lost count of the times he had seen it used to help tanks and their crews out of trouble.

Mike looked around the hangar trying to size it up: roughly one hundred metres long and fifteen metres wide with a concrete floor, designed to take the weight of the large vehicles. The roof had large metal rafters with smaller skylights set into it, designed to let the light through. On the right side of the long wall were eight hangar doors – they were electric roller ones allowing vehicles easy access to the building. Huge extractor fans sat in the roof, designed to suck out any poisonous fumes that would accumulate when the huge diesel engines of the tanks were running.

On the back wall of the hangar were a series of cages; large metal lockers with mesh grilles and a lockable door, which were designed to store the vast array of equipment to go with an armoured vehicle. A tank was a high maintenance piece of kit so the crews needed a vast array of tools, similar to the tools of a car (albeit much more heavy duty) to keep it on the road. As well as tools, each tank would also come with equipment to maintain the weapon systems, and also the cam and concealment kit. This consisted of huge camouflage nets and poles to hide the tank from view when not in use. There would also be crew equipment, food, water, helmets and headgear. The headgear was necessary for crews to be able to talk to each other over an intercom system as, without it, there would be no way to hear anything over the sound of the deafening engine. All this kit was usually kept off the tank for safe-keeping.

Mike looked further down the hangar toward the CRARRV and his eyes were drawn to the tank furthest away. It was the same type of tank as the others, a Chally 2, but this particular tank Mike had seen before at one of the open days that the tank museum ran. It was called 'Megatron' from what he remembered. It was what the army had called Theatre Entry Specific – TES for short. Megatron was painted in the usual military olive-green-and-black camouflage pattern but had what looked like a more modern digital urban digital camouflage pattern on the forward face of the turret. The biggest difference, though, between Megatron and the other Chally 2's in the hangar was this tank had the extra armour packs on the sides of the hull and turret, with frontal armour that increased protection but also increased the size and weight of the tank.

From memory, Mike recalled the road weight of Megatron was closer to seventy-six tonnes, which was twelve tonnes heavier than the others. It was this slight size difference that had drawn his eye to it. He knew from previous history the other onboard upgrades consisted of a driver's front-and rear-facing camera, which could also show a thermal picture, which made night driving a breeze. The turret usually had a machine gun mounted on the loader/operator side which was mainly there for anti-air defence, but in the modern age was next to useless as the operator had to be heads up (have his head and body outside of the turret, exposing himself to incoming fire.) Instead, in its place was the Remote Weapons Station (RWS) which was a large mounting system for an L7 General Purpose Machine Gun. The mount had a large box on the left for holding ammunition and large sensor head on the right about the size of a small suitcase that housed the sighting system. Like the driver's sights it was thermal and could see very well at night. The whole unit could swing through three hundred and sixty degrees independently of the turret and was remotely operated from within, via a TV screen and controller, not unlike a video game. When Mike had deployed to Iraq in 2007 the squadron's tanks had all been TES upgraded so he knew first-hand what the tank could do, and that the RWS offered a huge degree of protection for the operators from any gunfire.

Chris began to walk toward the side of the closest tank with Mike following behind, listening in as Chris began to explain.

"The first nine tanks you see are prototypes, ones we're testing. At first, you'll not notice anything unusual about them. However, as you get to the running gear…"

Chris stopped by the side of the tank and pointed to the tracks. Mike looked down to what he was pointing at. He could see some small changes to the running gear from when he'd last worked on one.

"Chris, I was never a D&M (Driving and Maintenance) man like you remember; gunnery was more my bag. Mind explaining what I'm supposed to be looking at?" Mike asked amusedly.

Chris smiled, replying, "Sorry, mate, force of habit. What we have here is a new type of track, road wheel, and suspension unit. The track has titanium-backed track pads with a new kind of rubber material that's in development which can withstand over one thousand degrees of heat. It's something the eggheads have called SVB – don't ask me what it stands for, it's written somewhere upstairs in my office."

"Okay," Mike replied, trying to make it look like he knew what they were talking about.

Chris continued. "The bushes in the track links are made from the same SVB material, as are the roadwheels. The Hydrogas suspension units have been upgraded so the track is now low maintenance. Remember those lovely days of changing the track pads every five hundred miles?"

"How could I forget those!" Mike exclaimed. Every tank soldier would fondly re-member the art of what was called 'track bashing'. The track on a tank was more fragile than people would believe and required lots of maintenance to keep it all running smoothly. Each track consisted of around seventy-six links, and each link weighed forty-five kilos and had two track pads on it. That was one hundred and fifty-two track pads per track. The track pads were fitted to dampen the shock of the sixty-four tonnes of tank riding over it and to reduce vibrations from hitting the running gear. Every five hundred to one thousand miles the track pads would wear out and need replacing. Each worn track pad would have to be hammered out with a sledgehammer and removal tool, the new pad then hammered in the opposite side. Trying to replace a whole track's worth of pads was a bitch of a job when the crew and tank were back in camp, but usually they were out on the ground, often in boggy terrain and covered in mud. It certainly wasn't a job for the faint-hearted and Mike had lost count of the number of grazed knuckles he'd received from missing the pad and hitting the track with the sledgehammer. Not a job he wanted to return to, he thought as Chris continued.

"Well, now the track and pads have much more longevity, we've had these on here for six months and counting, racking up an average of two thousand five hundred miles so far and we've not yet had to change any road wheels or pads."

"Low maintenance then?" Mike smirked.

"Very, they're also running a new type of engine, still multi-fuel like the old one, able to run off most diesel and petrol types, although they do need to be manually switched over at the engine."

"How much horsepower are you getting out of the engine?"

"At the moment they're putting out two thousand three hundred horsepower, almost eight hundred HP more than the original engine!"

"Wow, that's impressive! Who makes the engines? What speed are you getting out of the tanks?"

Chris looked at Mike and replied in a more hushed tone, probably out of habit. "The manufacturer is keeping quiet, not even we know who it is as there's no identifying marks on the engines. Our fitters are going ballistic trying to find a label or identification plate. I'm guessing whoever they are, they want to keep quiet about working with the military. As for speed, with the new track and engine, they'll do fifty miles per hour on the road."

Mike raised his eyebrows in surprise. Genuinely impressed, he replied, "Wow, that's quick, but why are we whispering?"

Chris paused for a second before replying, still whispering, "I thought it would add to the drama," before laughing and returning to a more normal pitch. "Sorry, mate, again – force of habit!"

He continued. "We've got all the hull and engine parts being tested here and we've also got a team over at Lulworth testing the new turret. It's got the one hundred and twenty millimetre smoothbore barrel which will allow us to get the newer two-piece ammunition from the Americans."

"Of course," replied Mike, remembering back to his gunnery lesson days; the ammunition on the Chally 2 was what the British army would call 'three-piece ammo' in that it has three pieces that all work together to fire the gun. It was deemed a safer choice than the two-piece ammunition. If the tank took a hit, carrying three-piece ammunition, it would be less likely to set off the tank's own internal ammunition, thereby giving the British tanks a better survivability rate. The problem, though, with three-piece ammunition was that the UK was the only country to use it and that meant logistically it could only supply itself. Another problem was the factory making the ammo in the UK had been shut down some years before.

Mike added, "If I remember correctly, most of the ammo for the Iraq invasion had come from a South African factory. Logistically not very ideal."

"Exactly that," replied Chris. "With Ukraine now taking most of our war stock of ammunition and no way to replenish it, all our tanks that have the older one hundred and twenty millimetre rifled guns are on borrowed time. Hence the need to get the Challenger 3 out to the troops."

Chris walked round to the front of the tank and gestured for Mike to climb up. As he was about to, Chris stopped him suddenly, stating with mock concern, "Shit, sorry, mate, I forgot – with your old knees, do you want me to go get the steps for you?" Mike looked at him as he smirked. Ever the joker.

Using one of the tank's towing bollards as a step and with a combination of left leg and left arm he pulled himself fluidly up onto the right-hand mud guard of the tank, all from muscle memory. He guessed that was something you just don't forget how to do, like riding a bike. He walked along the side of the tank, keeping his arms holding onto the turret as he remembered one of his old instructors yelling, *"YOU WILL ALWAYS MAINTAIN THREE POINTS OF CONTACT WHEN ON THIS TANK!"* Walking along the part of the tank they used to call the 'catwalk' led them to the back of the tank above the main engine. Chris climbed up first and Mike followed. The area above the engine consisted of giant steel louvres and decking that would hinge up, allowing the crew access to the engine compartments when required. It was this area called the 'back decks' that they were now stood on. When it was cold, the crews would think nothing of sleeping on the back decks as it was normally the warmest and usually the safest place to be, as it was off the ground away from the bugs and creepy crawlies that always wanted to get to know them better. Standing there now on the tank with his old friend again brought back good memories.

Chris carefully made his way up and onto the forward edge of the turret toward the operator's side. Both hatches into the turret were open, and he gestured Mike into the commander's hatch.

With a grace he thought he'd forgotten, Mike walked up to the hatch, sitting on the cupola edge and lowering his legs through the opening, before finally placing his hands on the cupola edges. Then using his arms, he lowered himself down into the tank's interior and onto the commander's seat below.

Mike settled into the seat, immediately at home in all so familiar surroundings. He looked around the interior of the turret seeing everything as he'd remembered – even the smell seemed familiar; the smell of the vinyl on the ripped commander's seat, the smell of gun and hydraulic oils coming from the huge breech of the main gun that dominated the operator's side, the smell of the rubber coming from the brow pad on the commander's primary sight. It would never have made a scented candle, but if it did, he'd buy one. Mike saw the lighting inside the turret was currently set to white with the interior lit up brightly. However, these lights were dimmable and at the flick of a switch could turn to red, which would bathe the turret in a demonic glow and was usually reserved for when the crew didn't want the light escaping out of the turret at night. With no outside windows and only the hatches, there was little in the way of natural light to enter the turret. For this reason, when the Chally 2 had been designed, the manufacturers had painted everything white, which not only gave the interior a light look, but also a clean, functional one as well.

If the lights were on, then that meant the power had been left on – *Did Chris plan for us to come into the turret all along?* Mike wondered.

He sat there for a few seconds, alone in his thoughts as he heard Chris huff and puff his way down into the operator's hatch; first, two boots appeared, then legs, until his slender frame eased its way into the hatch and down onto the operator's seat.

He waited for Chris to settle in before saying, "You okay there, mate? Made a bit of a meal getting yourself in didn't you? You want me to go and get you some cod liver oil? Don't want you hurting yourself, looks like too much time in the office and not enough time in here."

"I'll be honest, mate, it's been a while since I've been in *this* side of the turret, now that your fat arse is sat in *my* seat!"

Mike smirked as he looked around, his head instinctively ducking under the commander's control handle as he looked into the gunner's station. The gunner in the Chally 2 sat lower than the commander, both sharing the one hatch. The gunner would get in first, climb down to his station and then the commander would get in behind him. There was a backrest to the rear of the gunner's seat that would fold up to give the gunner some degree of comfort and stop the commander from kicking them in the back accidentally. Once the backrest was up, the gunner was cocooned in position with all manner of electronics, computers and sighting systems around them. For the uninitiated it could be quite a claustrophobic place to be, and took some getting used to. It wasn't uncommon for gunners to suffer motion sickness in their first few outings.

Mike noticed from looking around the turret that the equipment that usually would have been stowed in the cages was already fitted. Every station had the head-gear installed and plugged in. The radios were fitted, the gunner's tools were in their tool bag under the gun and even the onboard water tanks were full.

Seeing what he was looking at, Chris replied, "The cages you saw earlier were empty, all the gear for all the tanks is onboard. Part of the testing process is that the tanks must be at combat weight, otherwise why bother testing the tracks?"

"Even the water tanks being full?" Mike asked.

"Yep, even got the turret bins full of cam and concealment kit, these tanks are all combat heavy. We've got an armoury at the back of the building where the L94's and L7's are kept." (Mike quickly reminded himself that the L94 was the coax chain gun and the L7 was the General Purpose Machine Gun or GPMG that sat on the loader's side). Chris continued. "Every time they go out, they even take weapons with them as well. In fact, the only thing we are missing is the add-on armour. I'd asked to get it fitted, especially as Megatron already has it but was told no. I'll keep trying though."

"I've always said you can be trying," replied Mike playfully.

Ignoring the comment Chris said, "So what do you think then, mate? Blast from the past?"

"It's strange isn't it. There are some things I don't miss about the army and some things I do. This is one of those things I *do* miss."

"You think you'd still remember how to fire it up?"

"Is that a bonus question?" Mike asked, raising his eyebrows as he looked around the turret, his mind casting back to the start-up checklist.

He was quite surprised at the amount of information he'd retained. He was fully expecting to have forgotten most of it, but it was as if once the tap was opened it flowed out of him. After a few moments of looking around he nodded confidently.

"Yeah I think if I had to, I could start up the old girl."

Chris said nothing, closing his eyes and rubbing the end of his nose with his thumb and fore finger. Mike had seen it before, it was a sure sign that Chris was deep in thought. Something was on his mind.

Rather than sit in silence any longer Mike asked, "Right, come on mate, what's going on? You haven't brought me onboard just to sit and talk through start-up procedures. What's on your mind?"

"You know you're always telling me when we meet up that you're happy and life's great. But I also know that in civvy street you're bored."

Mike opened his mouth to reply, but Chris raised a hand quickly, cutting him off and said, "Look, I don't mean with married life or with Kate, that's not what I mean. I know you're more than happy in that department – I've seen your wife and I've seen your car. You're 'living the dream' as we used to call it."

Mike raised his eyebrows, looking at him curiously.

"Look, since you got out of the forces, what have you done, what have you really done?" Chris asked.

Mike was about to reply, when he realised Chris still didn't know about any of the work he'd done with Aurora and Peter Rawlinson – he'd never told him. Should he mention it now? No, he thought, he'd signed the non-disclosure agreements, he could still be called back to work for them. He'd keep that part of his life private and confidential; his friend would understand, he knew how it all worked. Mike began to reply, raising his left hand and using his fingers to count down the items on the list as if to emphasise a point.

"We've established a business, we sold the business at a handsome profit, we've got a steady income coming in from some investments, we've got a boat, we've got a bloody *great* boat. We've got a great house, we've got a fantastic car, and like you say we're living the dream."

"Okay, smart-arse!" Chris said jokingly before continuing. "That's all good, that's what you've both done, but the question still stands, *what have you done* since getting out?"

Mike sat there thinking for a second. What was Chris up to? What was he getting at? Where was he going with this?

Chris let him sit there in silence for a second before finally relenting and giving Mike his opinion.

"Mike, when you were still in, you had a wealth of experience, we all knew that you were never going to be cut out for a desk job. You were always better out on the ground, leading, – that's where you were at your best. Suddenly you're out in civvy street not knowing what to do. Granted you've kept yourself busy, but you're not employed anywhere, you're not working for anyone, you're still drifting, a nomad. Meanwhile all that experience, all that knowledge of working on armour is just lodged in your head going nowhere. It's being wasted. Do you remember that night in Iraq at the police station? Of course you do. Me, you, and the six other guys of our troop sat on the roof of the police station in Al-Dayr. You're the guy in charge, we've got no comms, almost out of ammo, a whole town out for blood. And you held it together and thought of a way to get us out of there, a *bloody* good way to get us out of there."

"Mate, that was twenty years ago, a *long* time ago, and I don't intend on being in that situation ever again."

"Okay," Chris continued, "then let's bring it more up to date: "Afghan 2010, the sniper that caused us so much trouble. It was your idea on the ground that helped us to get to him. A perfect example of creative thinking – you know they still teach that to the officers at Sandhurst, right?"

Embarrassed with the flattery, Mike held up a hand to stop Chris. "Look, that wasn't my idea, I'd read about similar stories in World War II in Italy and as for teaching officers, does that happen? It must be like herding cats."

That last comment made Chris smile as unperturbed he continued. "Okay smar-tarse, what about Afghan in 2013? Did you read about that in a book?"

A look of mock horror came to Mike's face as he thought about the events that Chris was alluding to.

"No, I did not! And I hope they're not teaching *that* at Sandhurst! I can't imagine any other scenario in the world where that would have been acceptable."

Chris could see Mike was taking it all within his stride, humour included, but he was also trying to get Mike to be serious. He knew from working with Mike that joking aside, behind those eyes of his was a very intelligent and sharp mind, full of great ideas that was now just treading water. It was that Mike, the serious Mike of old that Chris was trying to get to the fore.

"Look, mate, all I'm trying to say is you can be very creative when others are out of ideas. You've got a whole wealth of combat experience, you work well under pressure, you're great at leading a team, you're more than experienced on working on armoured vehicles, and you clearly still know how the Chally 2 works. Kate's realised that she needs something to get on with, hence she's gone back to her old job. It doesn't mean that she's not happy, but people need to feel valued, feel like they've still got something to contribute. I've seen it with you this past year, you need something going on in your life, you're not good sitting back and watching from the sidelines. And besides – and this really is serious – your jokes are becoming crap."

Mike sat looking at Chris as he digested what he'd just said. He knew Chris meant well, but he really had no idea about the work he had been involved in with Aurora. However, seeing the enthusiasm in his friend's eyes, he didn't want to burst his bubble. He took a deep breath before asking, "All right, so apart from the cheap psychiatrist session, what is it you're asking of me?"

Chris smiled. Finally, serious Mike had arrived, he thought.

"What I'm asking you is... would you like a job?"

Chris proceeded to outline what he had in mind. First, though, he brought Mike up to speed on what Mike had already guessed at from seeing the news. He'd been promoted to the OC (Officer Commanding) of the ATDU after his counterpart had been demoted and sent away. The old OC had been caught sleeping with a journalist and had been giving her more than he should have in bed. The army hated a scandal, so to keep it quiet he had been quickly removed from the post and Chris, being the second in command, was promoted quickly to fill the gap. This had happened four months ago, and Chris had been told not to get too comfy in the job as a replacement would be found shortly.

However, four months later there was still no replacement. The army was facing serious manpower and equipment shortages thanks to the various years of cutbacks, resupply of Ukraine and overstretched personnel. He talked about the constant deployments overseas, Estonia, Poland, Latvia – not to mention the strikes in 2023 that had crippled the country. Soldiers were tired of having to do their own jobs and then being expected to do the jobs of others, especially as those they replaced stood on picket lines complaining about too little money, whilst still earning more than the soldiers did. Also, the constant drain on resources – replacing equipment and ammo to Ukraine – had taken it's toll on the UK defence programme. Money was tight and the recently elected new government, had only promised to pull even further on the purse strings.

'Welfare not Warfare' was the term Chris used.

This meant training and development budgets were being slashed and people were being expected to work more with less. The team from the ATDU were being cut down as replacements were becoming hard to find. Normally the regiments would nominate individuals to come to the ATDU for a period of two years, but as regiments were losing soldiers and also being asked to do more themselves, they were loathe to send anyone. Chris said some of the applications of the more recent postings were not worth the ink on the paper. It was for this reason Chris now found himself in charge of the ATDU. "One applicant for one of the drivers had been in the unit less than two months and had discipline issues and the other had been deemed unfit by his regiment as he had a bad back. How is he supposed to work on the tank with a bad back?"

The ATDU was in danger of being either cut back to a shadow of itself or being removed completely from the army as it was being deemed almost irrelevant in this modern age. Even now, after Ukraine showing what the tank could do, civil servants, analysts and members of the newly elected government were deciding that tanks were obsolete, irrelevant and replaceable.

Already the Chally 3 upgrade programme was being questioned, with the proto-type tanks Chris currently had in Bovington and Lulworth possibly being the only ones made. Of the five original Challenger 3 tanks made in 2024, and lauded on the news, all of them were away in the Middle East taking part in an advertising drive with the MoD, desperately trying to generate more orders. Until that happened, or something serious happened in the meantime, tanks as Mike knew them were in danger of becoming an endangered species.

What the ATDU needed now were fresh voices, fresh ideas and more importantly a way to survive the next round of cuts.

The ATDU were flirting with the idea of creating a civilian-led department con-sisting of ex-soldiers, all of whom had experience working with armour. The benefit would be that they wouldn't be expected to leave after two years, would have real world combat experience on the vehicles and would be allowed to think freely and develop better and more cost-effective ways to work the vehicles.

After explaining all this Chris then said, "That's where you come in. I'd like you to put together a team of people and lead this from the front, what you used to do best."

"But I'd be a civilian, though, not back in the military?" asked Mike sceptically.

"Yes, mate, you'd be one hundred per cent civilian. It wouldn't be a nine-to-five post though – the hours would be dependent on the job, but you'd be back on armour, working with people you were used to working with and getting a decent wage, I bet."

Mike sat there looking around the turret, his mind running through all the options. What would Kate say? Could he make it work? Balancing the work he did between Aurora and the ATDU? Then it hit him, the two were the perfect fit. He could help get Aurora *into* the ATDU and help bolster the Chally 3 programme. It could work, it *would* work – he'd make it work."

Mike paused before replying, carefully thinking through which words to use. He was desperate to say yes but knew there were two people in every relationship. Even though he guessed at Kate's answer he needed to know for sure. "Look, mate, it's a great offer, and I'm tempted, but it's a big decision and I'm going to need to speak to Kate about it first. Please don't think I'm ungrateful for the offer – you're right in some ways – I do sometimes feel like I'm treading water, but there's two of us in this and I'd better square it away with her as well."

"I understand, mate, totally. Please think on it." Chris then lifted his arms to the hatch-opening, raising himself slightly before smiling and saying, "Fancy a brew? I don't know about you, but my arse is going numb sat on this bloody seat."

A broad grin spread across Mike's face as he replied, "With an arse as big as yours you'd think it would be sufficiently padded, mate. And yes, I'd love a brew. You better have proper tea though, none of that decaff crap."

Chris continued out of the loader's hatch before replying with a mock northern accent and a wink, "Yorkshire tea, lad, Yorkshire tea!"

4

The Penny Drops

Five minutes later and they were both relaxing in Chris's office, kettle boiled with two cups of tea, chatting through how the new role would work if Mike were to accept it.

They'd only just taken a sip of their drinks, when they heard the main doors downstairs being flung open and the advancing thick-set stomp of military-style boots on the hallway floor. The steps got louder as the person came up the stairs, clearly in a hurry.

"Major Richards! Sir, you there?"

Chris looked to Mike before pulling his black beret out of his pocket and placing it on his head, adjusting it so the cap badge was above his left eye.

"In here," he replied. Mike turned to see what was happening, cup in hand as a sweaty figure wearing military combats arrived at the doorway. The soldier immediately stood to attention, throwing up a razor-sharp salute, his eyes darting between the two men. He was young, perhaps eighteen years old, and Mike could tell from the way he looked nervously about him that he was expecting to be shouted at for disturbing them. Mike could see from his beret colour and cap badge that he belonged to the King's Company Royal Hussars or (KCRH). His name tape read 'Smith'. From the awkward way he stood, Mike could see he was a recruit, probably from one of the driver or gunner courses that had been running before everyone left for summer. He was breathing heavily, trying to keep still as sweat ran down his face. Mike thought to himself, *I wouldn't want to be him on a hot day like today, especially as there are better things to be doing.*

Chris returned the salute before replying, "Well, what is it, Trooper? You going to stand there all day sweating and become my new door?"

"No, sir. It's the CO, sir, he's asked to see you immediately, sir."

"Why didn't he call me? Why send a runner?"

"I don't know, sir. I was in the guard room when someone came in and told me to run down here and get the message to you."

Chris picked up the phone on his desk and began to dial a number. Whilst he was doing this Mike began to question the new arrival.

"Why didn't you just take the duty Land Rover? It's about two miles from the front gate to here, did you run all that way?"

The young Trooper stayed ramrod still, but his eyes flicked over to Mike, replying, "I was told to run here, sir, so thought that's what I had to do. I did it in ten minutes though." The last part was said with a small amount of pride.

"Well, that is fast... but also bloody stupid," interjected Chris. "Next time, use the duty vehicle, that's what it's there for. You're supposed to be an Armoured Corp soldier, we think on our feet, not bloody run on them. What if the guardroom needs you again? It'll take you another fifteen minutes going *uphill* to get back."

The soldier stiffened at the quick retort, his eyes staring straight ahead, probably now wishing he had brought the Land Rover. No doubt he'd heard far worse when going through training.

"I'm sorry, sir, I... it won't happen again," he stammered.

Chris replaced the phone's handset back in the cradle with a confused look on his face. Mike looked at him, expecting him to say something, but instead he stood up and reached into his pocket, pulling out a mobile phone. Mike recognised it as one of the earlier models from five years ago, so he knew it would be an army-issue job. Chris activated the screen and looked at the display before dialling in what Mike assumed to be the CO's landline. As he did this, he could see the young soldier was still stood to attention, his uniform soaked with sweat which was now dripping over the floor.

"Okay, lad," he replied, easing his tone down, "stand easy. Go down the stairs, toilet's first door on the right, go get yourself a drink of water, catch your breath and then make your way back to the guard room. No need to run, just get yourself there, okay?"

"Yes, sir. Thank you, sir."

Before he turned to go, the Trooper threw up another salute, which caused Chris an issue as he still had his mobile phone in his right hand. Awkwardly he threw his hand up in some kind of salute, dismissing the soldier. Once the Trooper had left, he looked over at Mike, remarking curiously, "Something's wrong, both the land line *and* the mobile phones are playing up. I can't get through, yet my phone's showing full signal bars. Can you try your phone?"

Putting his cup down, Mike stood up, pulling his phone out, and saw that he, too, had a full signal. He dialled his home number from memory, expecting it to connect to his landline. Instead, he got silence; no engaged tone, no ringtone, nothing.

"Sorry, mate, looks like mine's dead as well..."

Mike stopped mid-sentence as he thought back to something that had been troubling him that morning. He recalled a meeting he had had with an old friend.

Chris, still staring at him, said, "Penny for your thoughts?"

Mike looked up at him, replying, "Do you remember Brigadier Peter Rawlinson? Used to be our old Commanding Officer back in 2003?"

Chris looked up, thinking before replying, "Ah yes, Lord Farquaad! You still meet up with him, don't you?"

Mike grimaced at Chris's use of that old nickname. Their old CO had been small in size, but large in stature, which had led to the younger lads choosing a nickname of the character from the film Shrek. In the film, however, the small character had delusions of grandeur, but those who had actually got the opportunity to work with Peter Rawlinson found him anything but, hence the nickname had quickly been dropped. Chris had never got to work with Peter which was probably why he only remembered him by the nickname.

"I do. We've become good friends over the years. Anyway, Peter told me something that... Oh, forget it. I don't know, maybe I'm just being paranoid..." Mike trailed off.

"Oh, it's Peter now is it!" joked Chris. "You have been making friends in high places."

"Says *Major* pain-in-the-arse," Mike retorted jokingly.

Chris was about to speak when suddenly, looking at his watch he realised the time. He stood up, shaking any silly thoughts from his head and replied, "Come on, we need to go see the CO, and we can take your lovely new car for a spin. I'm driving though."

The drive from the ATDU complex to the camp's main gate took less than two minutes, as they passed the hapless Trooper Smith still walking up the hill. Both men smirked, not out of spite, but because they had both been that guy – young, impressionable, naïve and following orders to the letter. One memorable occasion sprung to Mike's mind when he'd been given a shovel which he was told needed to be returned to the QM's (Quarter Master) department, but before he went there, he was to also hand in a letter to the Squadron Sergeant Major (SSM). Being a young Trooper, Mike hadn't questioned the order and carried it out. He'd arrived at the SSM's office and stood to attention, before he had handed him the note, only for the Sergeant Major to open it up and read it out aloud. "Dear Sergeant Major, I feel I am due a promotion, please give me a promotion now. Lots of love, Trooper Faulkes. P.S. If you don't promote me, I'm going to bash you over the head with this here shovel!"

Ah, the fun times, he thought to himself, even if it had cost him five extra guard duties. They pulled up to the camp's front gate.

This time there was a sentry box that was manned, but this was by two civilian guards that were employed by the military. One sat in a grey booth with a window, controlling the two gates; the other, who stood outside, walked toward the car, scrutinising the two occupants – and their car.

Clearly also a petrolhead, thought Mike.

He approached the driver's open window, looking across to the passenger side at Mike before looking at the driver, recognising Chris immediately.

"Afternoon, Major Richards."

"Afternoon, Ted. He's with me," he replied, nodding his head in Mike's direction. "We're here to see the CO, I've heard he's looking for me."

Ted nodded, glancing at Mike then back to Chris. "Righty-ho, sir. Do you need a car pass?"

"Yes please. Also, have you been experiencing any problems with your phone lines?"

Ted reached into his pocket to pull out a crumpled-looking car pass, before reaching through the window and putting it onto the dashboard, then replied, "Yes, sir, we've been having problems all day with our bloody systems. They keep coming back on though, but I think they've been off for the past hour or so now."

"Okay, and thanks for that," replied Chris, nodding toward the car pass.

"No problem," replied Ted, before adding with a smile, "Nice car!"

They pulled away from the gate and made their way to the main car park; there were more cars parked here than at the ATDU. Some of the cars looked like they hadn't been moved in months. Mike guessed these were owned by soldiers living on the camp who were posted away for long periods, the cars left there for safe keeping.

As they got out of the car and locked up, Mike looked at Chris. "What was all that about back there with the car pass? I should have gone to the guard room and booked the car in. Why'd he have that pass ready in his pocket?"

"Because nowadays, mate, thanks to advances in technology, we don't have to. While we were sat there chatting, your plates were being ANPR-checked by the camera. Underneath, the car was being scanned by a sniffer camera that senses any form of explosive residue and finally our faces were being photographed and scanned onto a computer database system by a hidden camera in the booth. If we were wanted for anything other than a parking ticket, they would have known. The guy sat in the booth is for show, all the real work goes on in the guardroom behind the main desk. That's where we are being watched and scrutinised. The car pass is merely for visitors, to make them think that it's all old school. That's why I got you security cleared last week – if I hadn't, you wouldn't have made it in."

"So, there has been some money spent in some areas then?"

"Yes, there has, but unfortunately not in all the right areas," Chris replied, scrunching his face up to show his disdain.

They walked across the car park along the main path that ran the length of the whole camp. From what Mike could remember there would be a large five-storey building off to his right which served as the accommodation for soldiers who were based here on courses. The building also had the cookhouse on the ground floor so soldiers wouldn't have to walk elsewhere for a meal. In front of these buildings were the smaller accommodation blocks for both Officers and Senior Non-Commissioned Officers (SNCO's). Again, this building had its own cookhouse, keeping everything practical and organised.

In front of them was the CIS Signals School, a one-storey building devoted to nothing except the radio systems on the tank, where the crew would learn how the radios worked, how to make them secure, how to fix them, how to get the best out of them and how the effects of the terrain and atmosphere could help or hinder in getting a transmission out. Also, it was here that crews learnt about the different type of code that could be used if the radios were ever compromised by, for example, the enemy listening in.

Beyond the Signals wing, down the hill would take them to the vast tank hangars that ran the width of the camp which would house all of the Driver Training Tanks or DTT's. These tanks were strange-looking beasts, with the hull of a Chally 2 but with the turret removed, instead replaced with a large glass viewing and seating area. The recruit drivers would take it in turns to drive the tank, putting into practice what they had learnt in the classroom, whilst the other recruits sat in the viewing platform with an instructor, riding along and observing them from above. The instructor had a console in his position where he could manually input faults to ensure the driver was indeed checking his instruments correctly, and then test them, expecting them to be able to find the fault and fix it.

As well as the DTT's, there would be all manner of armoured vehicles, both tracked and wheeled that would be hidden from view, all waiting to be tested on the driver training area.

To the left of the tank hangars were the administration buildings where all the kit and equipment used on the DTT's was stored, repaired and tested. Also, there were REME sections based there, workshops, maintenance shops, gun fitters, welders' sheds and all manner of other things – everything needed to make Bovington work like the well-oiled military sausage factory it was.

Off to their left was their destination, a white two-storey building, drab looking and pretty nondescript, housing all of the headquarters' element of the camp. Usually out of bounds to soldiers, it was where the Senior Officers and Warrant Officers would work. If you ever got called here as a junior soldier, it usually meant you were in trouble or were about to get what was lovingly referred to as 'voluntold' for a rubbish job.

Both men walked through the double doors, Mike's trip down memory lane coming to an end, as they made their way upstairs to the first floor. Chris led Mike through another pair of double doors off to his right and into a long corridor with several offices branching off to the left. All the office doors were closed, expect the far one, which they walked through. Mike found himself standing in a large open office with a desk and a window along one wall, and a closed door, which he knew would lead into the CO's office. To the left of the room sat a flat-screen TV, next to a water dispenser and two plastic polypropylene chairs.

Behind the desk a middle-aged woman wearing glasses was sat busily typing away, and beside her a desktop fan ran on full power trying to cool the room down. She stopped typing, glancing up as they entered the room and said, "Ah, Major Richards, the Colonel is expecting to see you." Chris acknowledged with a quick, "Thank you, Rachel."

Chris motioned for Mike to sit over in one of the chairs. "Hopefully won't be too long, mate. When we're finished here, we can go for a drive to a pub I know down the road. Of course, *I'm* still driving though," he said with a wink and a smile.

Mike walked over to the drinks dispenser and poured himself a water using one of the white plastic cups before taking a seat. Chris walked over to the Colonel's office door, quickly checked his beret was on straight and his shirt was tucked in before knocking. *Ever the professional*, Mike mused.

"Come!"

Chris opened the door and stepped inside, closing the door behind him. As he did so, Mike could hear the voices inside increase in volume as if on a control, before fading, and becoming a murmur. Clearly it wasn't just the CO in there.

The CO's secretary had decided Mike didn't warrant any further investigation as she continued to type away, the rhythmic clicks of the keyboard and the hum of the fan now the only noises he heard. Mike sat there wondering, *Why would the CO be interested in meeting me? What had Chris said to him?*

He gazed around the room, thankful the fan was on. He hadn't realised how hot the room was at first, but a river of sweat had begun to form on his back as he sat there in what was known throughout the world as the most uncomfortable chair ever made. He glanced around the room, his eyes settling on the TV which was on but had been muted. It was still showing that morning's sinking ship at the port.

Suddenly the CO's door opened and two men in uniform walked out. Mike saw from their badges and rank that they were both from the Signals corps, one was a Sergeant, the other a Corporal. Both men looked sheepishly at each other before walking out of the office. Mike was left wondering what had caused such a look when they were closely followed by the CO. He followed them out of his office and into the corridor, his voice echoing down the hall.

"I want these phones back online by 18:00 tonight, gentlemen, I don't care about your excuses, get it done!"

The CO, clearly angry, walked back into the office, his eyes darting over to Mike as he passed. He slammed the door, causing his secretary to jump slightly at the noise. Something had him troubled, thought Mike, clearly the military phone system was having the same issues as the civilian lines were. What on earth could be causing that?

Mike's thoughts were interrupted as the secretary finally spoke.

"Terrible, isn't it?"

He looked away from the door toward her.

"Excuse me?"

"I said it's terrible, isn't it, all that pollution spilling into the sea, all those containers full of God knows what just being emptied into the water, just so some terrorist can make a point."

"Oh," he replied, suddenly understanding, and he looked back at the news being played on the TV. "You're talking about the ship that sunk this morning. Sorry, yes it's bad."

"And the one this afternoon."

A confused look came over his face as he looked over at her. She hadn't stopped typing and continued the rhythmic tap on the keys as Mike replied, "The one this afternoon? You mean *this morning* at Southampton Docks?"

As if to prove a point she stopped typing, raised her glasses and looked at Mike like a school mistress educating a child.

"No, I mean the one in *Portsmouth* Docks. The one in Southampton Docks was this morning. *Two* ships, *two* docks. Where have you been hiding?"

Sighing, she put her glasses back on her nose and continued to type.

He looked back at the TV, paying more attention this time as he began to read the text scrolling along the bottom.

MV Titan *sinks in Portsmouth Harbour... Crew were nowhere to be found on the bridge prompting speculation the ship was abandoned before being sunk... Witnesses reported seeing loud explosions and fountains of water before ship sunk... Police now believe both incidents are linked and are appealing for witnesses...*

Mike stood up and walked closer to the TV, almost as if being closer to the screen would somehow give him more clarity. Something wasn't right here. His mind thought back to earlier in the day, the calls being cut out, the military phones not working, both port attacks. He tried to think back through the years, to a conversation he had with Peter Rawlinson. *Could this be happening?* he asked himself. He quickly ran through all the possible options. *It could be a coincidence,* he thought, *but then both ships at the same time? Both ports and the phones and internet all down? Damn! What was it Peter had spoken to me about?* He desperately tried to remember their conversation from all those years ago. He began to think about the exact specifics of what Peter had told him. It had a name... *What had Peter called it? Follys Mate? No... Fools Mate. Yes, that was it, Operation Fools Mate, yes.*

He pulled out his phone and looked at the screen – it still showed as having a full signal – four full bars and 5G. Once again, he tried to call his home number – nothing. He tried the internet, tried accessing his emails, but still nothing. He tried to search online for 'phones not working'. Again, the same result, nothing, he didn't even get the '404 web page not found'.

Suddenly the TV flicked off, the news feed dying before being replaced with a test transmission page showing white lines and different coloured bars, causing the receptionist to stop typing and look up. She tutted to herself and spent a few moments looking for the TV remote on the desk, removing her glasses as she began to search through the other channels, all of them showed the same blank page. "Oh, come on, bloody thing!" she remarked to herself. Eventually she admitted defeat, turning the TV off and dropping the remote back on the desk, shrugging to Mike apologetically before continuing to type away.

He looked at the blank TV screen, his eyes narrowing in thought, before deciding his next move. It was extremely risky and he thought quickly about what he would say if the call went through. *I'll simply say I've mistakenly dialled it in,* he thought to himself. With a little bit of hesitation, he slowly dialled 999.

Mike could hear the line click, then static on the line, followed by a buzzing noise, then nothing. Total silence.

He hung up and tried again, and again, until after the fourth attempt he knew that something extremely serious was taking place for the whole of the emergency network to be down. He had to confirm it though. It could still be his network or his phone playing up. He remembered exactly now what Peter had said to him, almost word for word, and he knew there was one final way to check. Another conversation that he's had with another of his ex-military friends was now springing to mind.

The receptionist had stopped typing again and looked up at him. "Is everything okay?"

He tried to remember her name, was it Rachel or Rebecca?

"Umm, Rachel, isn't it?"

She smiled. Clearly, he was on the money.

"Rachel, I've forgotten something from my car, I just need to run outside to get it. If Major Richards comes out, can you give him my apologies and tell him I'll be no more than ten minutes?"

"Sure thing, I'll ask him to wait here. Hope you find whatever it is you're looking for."

Mike hurried out of the office and out of the building, running down the camp toward the main gate, cursing as he remembered suddenly that he'd left his ID card back in the ATDU offices. As he passed the two gate guards, he quickly stopped by the one he remembered as Ted.

"Ted! You remember me, I was just with Major Richards a few minutes ago, we came into camp and he was driving a Porsche 911."

Ted looked at him curiously before replying, "Of course I remember you, sir. You in a hurry to be somewhere?"

Mike pointed to the red phone box that was just outside the camp gates. "I need to urgently make a call using that, but I don't have my ID with me. If I go off camp, will you let me back in?"

Ted looked at his colleague in the booth, who gave an almost imperceptible nod. Then he looked back to Mike. "I'm only on for another twenty minutes, so you'd best be quick."

Mike started to jog again, turning his head as he went. "Thanks, Ted!"

Mike crossed the main road, watching for traffic as he made his way along the path to the phone box that was now no more than five metres away. Across from the phone box and slightly uphill was a post office with a small car park. As he slowed to approach, his attention was drawn to a silver four-by-four parked in the car park with two men in it who were watching him. There was nothing unusual in seeing the four-by-four, it was a standard Land Rover Freelander, most farmers in the area had those, but Mike noted both men were of military appearance – but they were also paying a significant amount of interest into what he was doing. Something about them set off his senses, senses that he always had in the past relied on when serving overseas. *Come on, Mike, you're near an army camp. Of course there's going to be military, get a grip of yourself,* he thought. Ignoring his nagging doubts, he continued toward the phone box.

Mike opened the door to the phone box, a faded red thing that had seen better days, the same musty smells emanating from within that all the UK phone boxes seemed to have. The heat from inside was stifling and he kept the door open with his foot, allowing the small breeze in to try to cool it down.

He controlled his breathing, slowing it down, as he picked up the handset; the metal flex cable needing to be unwound as it had coiled in on itself. The handset felt surprisingly cold and clammy, a welcome distraction in the heat of the summer.

He pressed the receiver and waited. A tone. He heard a dial tone. Music to his ears, he thought. He pulled out his wallet and his phone from his pocket. The payphone looked to be the more modern type, requiring a credit card instead of coins. He pulled out his card and tapped it against the smartcard reader, watching as the digital display showed he had just put £5 into the phone. Satisfied that he had enough to make a call, he picked up his mobile and looked through his contact list. After finding the number he needed, he dialled it. The number was ringing. "Come on. Pick up... pick up!" he kept repeating to himself, his impatience beginning to show. The phone rang twelve times. He began to think it might all just be a wasted effort and was about to hang up when he heard the line open at the other end.

"Hello?"

"Elizabeth! I'm sorry to bother you, but is Peter there?"

"Mike? How are you? How's Kate?"

Mike tried to keep his impatience in check as he was forced through the usual pleasantries. Eventually deciding he'd waited long enough, he urged,

"Elizabeth, I'm sorry to sound rude, but I really need to speak to Peter, it's extremely urgent."

"Oh," he heard her exclaim, a little taken aback by his abruptness. "Okay, Mike, well if it's *that* important, I'll go get him now."

He waited another two minutes, checking the amount of credit remaining on the phone, as suddenly Peter's voice could be heard approaching the handset. Suddenly his voice boomed through loud and clear.

"Hello? Mike, you there?"

Mike closed his eyes then began what was perhaps one of the most important phone calls of his life.

After only five minutes he was finished, hanging up the phone, and he was about to leave when he thought about another call, equally as important.

He checked he still had credit for the call, picked the phone back up and dialled another number. As the phone rang, he looked out of the phone box, toward the four-by-four and the two men that had piqued his interest earlier. He noticed that the man in the passenger side had a mobile phone and strangely seemed to be talking to someone. The driver was staring directly at Mike and clearly, he was the focus of their attention. *How has he got a working phone?* Mike thought, *and why are they interested in this phone box?* His mind snapped back into place as the phone was answered on the sixth ring.

"Hello?"

"Martha, it's Mike, how are you both? You both okay?"

Kate's mum sounded both relieved and surprised at the call. "Mike, is that you? How are you doing? We weren't expecting a call from you just yet."

"Who is it?" he heard in the background. It was Kate's Dad, Roy.

"It's Mike, he's just calling to say hi," Mike heard her reply. Her voice had become muffled as she pulled the handset away to answer him.

She came back on. "Mike, what's going on? Have you seen the news, all the stuff about the boats sinking?"

"Yeah, I've seen it. Look, I don't have a lot of time, but I'm at a work meeting and I might be here sometime, so can you both do me a massive favour?"

As Mike was talking, he noticed the driver of the four-by-four getting out, leaving the passenger in the vehicle and walking toward the phone box. Mike saw he was stocky, about five feet eight inches, wore khaki cargo pants, desert boots and an unusually large jacket given that it was approaching nearly thirty degrees in the sun.

"Certainly, what is it?" replied Martha.

"Can you go round to ours, use the spare key we gave you and feed Daisy for me?"

"Of course," Martha replied happily, "any excuse to see the little lady." Mike knew that meant Daisy would be spoilt, with lots of fuss and probably too much food.

"Okay, but please don't overfeed her, Kate will kill me if you do."

Mike instinctively closed the door to the phone box as the driver now stood outside seemingly waiting to use the phone. Mike was aware of the heat inside the box, but valued privacy more. No one liked having their conversation heard. Besides, there was something odd about him, and Mike didn't want his back to him in an open doorway as he chatted.

Martha chuckled before replying, "Don't worry, we won't. Have you spoken to Kate yet? Has she called you?"

"I spoke to her this morning, but the lines were terrible, you know what it's like. She's fine, though, so there's nothing to worry about. In fact, by about now she should be finishing her speech, so once the phone lines are back on I'll give her a call tonight."

"The phone lines? What's wrong with the phone lines?" Martha asked curiously. "You sound fine on the phone now?"

Lowering his voice, he replied, "Long story short, Martha, but I'm calling from a phone box to your landline. If you try your mobile phone now it won't work, there seems to be a UK-wide problem on anything to do with the internet or mobile phones. So, remember, if you need to call anyone from now on, use your landline for the time being."

"Okay," Martha replied hesitantly.

Knowing Martha knew little about technology he knew she wouldn't understand too much, so he tried to keep it simple.

"Listen, Martha," he continued, "there's another thing I need you to remember, okay? And that is..."

Mike was interrupted mid-sentence by two loud thuds on the door to the phone box. He turned to see a rather angry face staring back at him. The driver clearly wanted Mike to hurry up so he could use the phone. *Bloody typical*, thought Mike, *he's seen me using the phone and now he wants to use it!*

Martha had also heard the thuds that had interrupted their conversation, her voice showing a trace of concern as she asked, "Mike, are you okay? What's that noise?"

Still staring at the driver, Mike replied, "It's all okay, Martha, just some idiot who doesn't have any manners trying to hurry me out of the phone box."

Although the driver stared back, he showed no reaction at all to the taunt. Eventually he looked away, allowing Mike to continue with his conversation.

"Okay, Martha, like I was saying, I need you to remember something and it's going to sound strange—"

"Mike," she interrupted, "can't it wait until you're back later? You know what I'm like at remembering things—"

"No, it can't wait," he replied, urgently cutting in, "I need you to remember our house and what it has in the garage. You remember all the food supplies that we keep in there?"

Mike's mind's eye quickly thought about the garage shelves back home stocked full of tinned provisions and long-life foods. Ever since the days of the Covid pandemic back in 2020, Mike had always encouraged Kate to keep it stocked. "If ever there is another emergency," he'd said, "then the food supplies won't last long." Mike remembered that at the time Kate had joked with him about opening a corner shop and selling it all on, but she also knew the seriousness of what he said had warranted keeping the garage stocked.

"Mike, love, if we need any shopping, we get our online deliveries. Don't you go worrying about us."

Mike closed his eyes for a second, trying to think of the best way to word what he was trying to say.

"Martha, that's not what I mean. What I'm trying to say is, just remember it's all there to be used. If anything happens over the next few days and I'm stuck down here, use our spare key, and you and Roy go to stay at ours."

There was a silence on the phone. At first, Mike thought Martha had hung up, then after a few moments she replied with concern in her voice, "Mike, what's going on? What aren't you telling me? Why would you say that? Is it to do with those ships again?"

"Martha, listen to me, I promise I'll tell you all about it when we see each other again, but until then I just need you to be aware, that's all."

Again, Mike was interrupted by another two loud thuds on the phone-box door. The driver was clearly impatient and wanting in. Perhaps he had family to call as well, thought Mike. But it was no excuse for his rudeness and Mike was getting angry, not helped by the fact that the heat in the box had risen and sweat was now pouring off him. The phone receiver had become hot and clammy against his ear and it reminded Mike of the long-distance calls to loved ones he'd had when on operations. He turned angrily again to face down the driver, but this time the driver had kept his back to him.

Mike looked down at his watch, conscious of the time, before adding, "Look, I've got to go. Pass on my love to Roy and if you do manage to speak to Kate, tell her I love her."

"Oh, okay, Mike. You take care and don't worry, I'll remember what you said. We'll see you when we see you."

Mike could hear Roy in the background shouting, "Bye, Mike."

"Lots of love, bye."

Mike replaced the handset slowly, trying to calm himself as he thought about the person waiting outside. Usually not one to go looking for trouble, he now calmed his mind, replacing the angry thoughts in his head for quieter ones, before finally deciding he was composed enough to leave the phone box. There was still much to do, and he still needed to chat to Chris about what he now knew. He opened the phone-box door, immediately feeling the relief as a slight breeze hit him, cooling the sweat on his skin. The irate driver was stood off to the side, barely acknowledging him as he waited for Mike to leave.

Mike turned to him, unable to resist saying something, remarking in a loud voice, "Hey, fella, don't know where you're from, but around here we have something called manners. And when someone's on the phone it's not polite to keep banging on the door."

The driver looked up at him blankly, trying to get past Mike, but Mike had kept himself in the doorway, effectively blocking it, determined to at least give the guy a piece of his mind. The guy just looked back at him, clearly not registering what Mike had said. Mike was about to leave it and walk away when he had another thought.

"Mind me asking, but why are you so desperate to use a phone box when your mate has one of the few working phones I've seen?" As if to prove a point Mike signalled to the four-by-four with the passenger inside, who now looked like he was sitting up straighter, watching the events.

The driver looked to see where Mike was pointing before looking back at Mike, his eyes glaring through him.

What is this guy's problem? thought Mike. *Why the attitude and why no reaction? Why the jacket?*

"Look, mate, I'm talking to you," Mike said, his voice more assertive, but he deliberately kept his hands by his sides. He didn't want to provoke the guy. "Don't you speak English?"

Upon saying that last comment, he could see the guy flinch, almost as if he understood what Mike had asked. At the same time, he looked back toward the four-by-four to his friend in the car. Mike guessed he was looking for some kind of instruction or acknowledgement and was even more baffled when the guy, clearly having had enough of the standoff, went from merely standing to an attack.

Mike had practised this countless times before in Ewen's gym and he remembered everyone had a tell, a sign that an attack was about to happen and if you knew what to look for, then you could prepare yourself for most things.

The speed of the attack still caught Mike off guard, as he found himself being grabbed by the collar of his shirt as the driver tried to manhandle him out of the box. Mike allowed himself to be grabbed, his own hands grabbing the attacker's wrists, twisting in a fluid motion, breaking the hold of the attacker and allowing himself to step out of the confines of the box into a larger expanse. Looking confused, the attacker's eyes followed Mike as he hurried backward away from the box and onto an open grass area. Mike needed room for what was about to happen next. The confused look was quickly replaced by anger as the driver now advanced toward Mike. Mike didn't have time to think as his attacker tried to knee him in the groin, a very typical telegraphed move that Mike easily countered and blocked by raising his own foot and kicking the attacker in the shin. He pushed the driver away to give himself space and time before finally getting a chance to try to talk.

"Woah. Look, mate. Stop, STOP!"

The driver wasn't listening. Clearly in some sort of rage, he began to advance on Mike, his arms outstretched in some kind of wrestling manoeuvre, his eyes focused, staring at him. Mike was trying to think of ways he could disengage, to try to calm the man down, but he wasn't listening. Ewen's words of wisdom echoed in his head from one of his many training bouts – *Sometimes you may not be able to understand or reason with your opponent. He may not understand you. But he will understand your fists and your feet. So, win that argument first. And then, when you have beaten him, maybe then, he will start to see things your way.*

5

Cobwebs

Mike crouched into his first position, the semi-judo-style stance that he had first learnt all those years ago and got ready to fight. He tried to keep his mind clear, his peripheral vision focused on threats that could come from anywhere around him. Seeing his stance the driver smiled, almost relishing the fight that was about to take place. This was one strange guy, Mike thought to himself.

The driver threw a roundhouse left punch, slow, wide and clumsy, but with a lot of weight behind it. Mike easily stepped back slightly, allowing the fist to pass harmlessly by, before launching his own savage left that hammered into the driver's nose, causing his head to snap back. The driver recovered instantly, throwing a fast right fist, direct and short, designed to hit, but Mike blocked and parried the punch with his own right fist hammering into the same spot as before on the driver's nose.

Mike heard a crunch and was sure he had broken his nose. Blood began to run freely down the driver's face and drip onto his jacket as his smile vanished, replaced by a look of surprise followed by anger. He clumsily lunged at Mike, his arms grabbing thin air as Mike side stepped and followed through with a kick to his chest, which usually would have winded any opponent, but Mike felt something was wrong, as his foot connected with something hard beneath the jacket. This guy had body armour on.

Mike tried not to look surprised as his opponent turned to face him, the smile now a bloody grimace as the driver beat his hands to his own chest, his face a mask of rage. Mike heard the thuds as they hit something hard, the driver confirming what Mike had just found out – he was indeed wearing body armour. The driver approached Mike again, this time keeping his hands up boxing style and he looked more professional as he bobbed and weaved. Mike guessed quickly that his opponent had underestimated him, thinking it would be an easy fight, but now seeing Mike could handle himself, was becoming more of a challenge. The driver got close, too close, Mike thought, as he slipped on the grass after he attempted to parry a kick the driver had aimed at his side. Seeing him slip, Mike's opponent saw an opportunity and rushed forward, throwing a combination of lefts and rights toward Mike's head. Mike could do nothing but try to block the punches that came in quick succession as he tried to get away. He raised his elbows to the sides of his head, trying to lessen the damage, the punches smashing against his arms, Mike feeling the force of the impact and grimacing as the older injuries from Ewen's gym screamed out in agony.

Without seeing it, Mike felt the kick to his chest, the breath exploding from his lungs as his opponent sought to get him on his knees. Mike did just that, falling forward, feeling the blows connecting to his head as he momentary lost his balance and went down on one knee. This brought him lower to his opponent, but in a move that meant Mike would not win 'Gentleman of the Year', he gave an uppercut into the groin area, hearing his opponent yell in a deep guttural pain that even Mike winced at. The blows stopped and Mike was able to buy himself the time and space he needed to stand up, shaking his head, trying to clear his grogginess. He looked around, hoping to see someone coming to his aid, trying to think of ways to stop the fight. This was becoming crazy, he thought, all this over a fucking phone call. His opponent was lying on the ground muttering through clenched teeth in a language Mike didn't understand.

Mike heard shouts from across the road. He looked up to see the gate guard Ted, trotting over the road, clearly coming to investigate what was going on. *Thank fuck,* thought Mike, *finally some help to calm this crazy bugger down.*

His opponent, who was still on the ground looked up, still in pain, but the pain seemed to clear quickly as he realised he would soon be facing two opponents. Mike was still thinking about how to explain all this to the police when suddenly things took a dramatic turn. The driver unzipped his jacket and Mike could see it wasn't body armour he was wearing – it was an assault vest. Mike instantly recognised the weapon magazine's strapped to it. He saw the driver begin to fumble for a pistol tucked into his waist and knew things had just gone up a gear. Whoever this guy was, he was here to kill.

Ignoring Ted's shouts, Mike lunged forward, any thoughts of de-escalation now gone. He shoulder-charged the gunman, forcing him back down to the ground, Mike's right knee coming up to do whatever further damage it could to his groin area. Mike's hands went for the driver's as the gunman tried to free the pistol from his waistband. Thankfully the pistol had a large sight on it and was now snagged in the gunman's trousers and in his desperation to free the pistol, he'd taken his eyes off Mike, choosing instead to look down, handing Mike the initiative. Mike's hands closed around the gunman's as the weapon came free. He tried to lock the slide back like Ewen had taught him, but his sweaty hands slipped on the pistol's cold metal exterior, and instead his hand locked the gunman's and the pistol was held up to the sky.

In desperation, the gunman began to squeeze the trigger, the pistol firing a succession of rounds into the air that caught Mike by surprise as he was reminded how loud a weapon could be. The gunman's face was so close Mike could smell his bad breath and sweat as both men fought for an advantage. The gunman was manic, looking at Mike with wide eyes, shouting, as he released his left hand from the pistol and tried to gouge out Mike's right eye with his thumb. Mike quickly grabbed his thumb, twisting it back into a pressure point and exerting a huge amount of pressure. Normally when he had practised this, the opponent would tap out and give up, but this time, in a real-world scenario, his opponent didn't simply give up, instead he yelled in pain but continued to fight. Mike knew it would take more as he exerted extra force, feeling the thumb finally dislocate with a hollow pop. The gunman stopped yelling and merely grunted as he pulled his hand back, the natural reaction being to defend the injury.

Mike, taking advantage of the fact he was on top, now took the opportunity to move his own free arm up and under the gunman's, effectively getting him into an arm lock, but being careful to keep his head away from the pistol. Unable to move, the gunman now found himself being rolled over onto his front as Mike used his own body weight and leverage on his opponent's arm to roll the gunman over, whose arm was now being bent at a distorted angle. Mike's arms and legs were beginning to scream in protest, and he knew his strength wouldn't last forever. However, despite the pain and the noise, a strange calm had settled over Mike, all those years of practice in the gym finally being rewarded. All he had to do now was disable the gunman until help arrived.

Once Mike had the gunman in the position he needed, lying on his front, he wrapped his legs around the gunman's neck and began to put him into a choke hold. As if sensing the balance was shifting, the gunman tried to free himself. Finding an unknown reserve of strength, the gunman released his grip on the pistol and Mike felt it fall harmlessly to the ground by his head. Then he began to attack Mike's arms and legs using his one free hand, his dislocated thumb flapping uselessly as his fingers tried to scratch and claw. He felt the man's nails tearing into his arms and legs, blood beginning to flow, but he could do nothing to stop the attack as his own arms and legs were being used to slowly choke his opponent; Mike was using all his own strength just to hang on in there. Mike had a plan though, and the plan was working and soon it would all be over, or at least that's what he thought.

Suddenly Mike heard automatic gunfire and screams coming from the road. He felt his opponent was almost out, but not wanting to be caught in the open he quickly released the gunman and kicked him away, the prostate semi-conscious body rolling forward with a groan. Mike crabbed backward from the danger as his hands located the gunman's pistol on the ground. Without stopping, he picked up the pistol before moving further backward, keeping himself low as he headed into a small depression in the ground in front of the post office. Cautiously, he raised his head to see what was going on.

In the middle of the road, parked at a forty-five degree angle and blocking both lanes, sat the four-by-four he'd seen earlier. The engine was running, the driver's door was open and the passenger he'd seen before was now in a perfect firing position, pouring fire into the guard hut. He was holding what looked like a machine pistol with a folding stock and was firing short three-round bursts. *I'd forgotten all about the passenger*, Mike thought angrily to himself, realising he was lucky to have only had to fight one of the gunmen. He guessed quickly that upon seeing his colleague about to get captured, and the threat that the gate guard posed, the second gunman had jumped into the driver's side then driven down to the main gate. Mike couldn't see Ted anymore, who he'd last seen on his way across the road to help, and he could only hope that Ted had managed to find cover somewhere. He watched as the gunman reached down into his assault vest, pulling loose a small object before throwing it into the direction of the guardroom.

Mike watched horrified as he expected the object to explode – it was a grenade. Counting down the seconds, Mike realised after the count of four that thankfully it wasn't a fragmentation grenade but was instead a smoke grenade; the second gunman clearly wanting to keep the guard force pinned down, unable to see. The second gunman resumed firing and Mike quickly realised it was now a gunfight, and looked down at the pistol he had in his hands. It looked to be an MP-443 Grach, a Russian copy of the SIG Sauer P226 that Mike had used in Afghanistan. Most semi-automatic pistols worked the same way – so long as you could operate one you could operate them all. With that in mind, Mike pressed the magazine release, ejecting it, and counting the rounds he could see inside. Three rounds, he counted, so that meant he had four rounds in total. He knew there would be one in the chamber, but even so he pulled the slide back a fraction to 'check chamber' to see if he could see the glint of brass in there. Sure enough, there it was – so he *did* have four rounds, not enough to start a war, he thought, but at least he could defend himself. He slotted the magazine back into the pistol, ensuring it was seated correctly before looking back over the depression. He heard a noise behind him and looked back, the pistol pointing to the new threat. In the doorway stood two young teenage boys, phones in hand, happily taking video footage of what was going on. Mike tried to get their attention without alerting the gunman in the road.

"*Psst! Oi*," he was whispering, gesticulating wildly with his hands, waving them around desperately.

They both looked at him with a vacant expression, as if he were stupid, as Mike hissed, "Get down! Get yourself into cover, get away from the glass doors."

They ignored him and continued filming, looking at Mike as if he were talking another language before turning their heads back to the carnage going on below them. Mike heard the firing stop. Hoping it was finished, he peered out over the depression again. What he saw made him take a sharp intake of breath.

The second gunman was walking calmly up the path toward his position, reloading his machine pistol and throwing the used magazine into his jacket. What worried Mike even more was that the gunman no longer considered the guards a threat. Were they dead? The first gunman was now coming to and had rolled and crawled his way down toward his colleague. Mike watched as the second gunman reached down to help the first to his feet, muttering something into his ear. Whatever it was, it pissed off the first gunman who pushed his colleague away, beginning to fumble in his jacket. Mike saw to his horror the first gunman had also been concealing a machine pistol on an underarm sling. He saw it had its butt folded, allowing the gunman to hide it in plain view beneath the jacket, and now, eager for payback he brought it out to play. The last thing Mike saw before he ducked down into cover was the same bloody grinning face carefully taking aim toward him, as he opened fire.

The teenagers behind Mike screamed as the bullets began to head in their direction, any thoughts of filming lost as the glass windows around them shattered into thousands of pieces. The grass around Mike exploded in a flurry of turf as angry metal hornets whizzed mere inches past Mike's head. *Christ*! he thought, *incoming fire was never this loud, was it?* It had been a long time since Mike had been shot at and the feelings he'd felt back then had not diminished. Upon instinct he released the pistol and tried using his hands to dig a little deeper, trying to coax at least another centimetre or two, which could literally be the difference between life and death. He had no idea how long he was lying there, no idea how many bullets had come his way, but he knew that if they wanted to, the two gunmen could keep him pinned there, one keeping up the fire whilst the other flanked around to finish the job. He reached back to the pistol, careful to keep his head low as he scanned his left and right side.

The boys behind him had scurried through the broken remains of the post office. Mike could see trails of blood and hoped they hadn't taken any rounds and that it was only from cutting themselves on the glass. One advantage, Mike thought to himself, was that the position he was taking cover in was uphill to the gunmen, meaning as they tried to shoot him the rounds were passing overhead higher than they normally would. Had the positions been reversed, and they were shooting downhill the bullets could have easily found their way into Mike's small shelter of cover. After what felt like minutes but was probably just seconds, he could hear new gunfire coming from his front, different in pitch. He recognised it as the distinct noise of an SA80 assault rifle being fired on single shot, as the user was selective in their fire. He began to hope that finally help was on its way.

He looked cautiously over the edge, ready to dive back into cover as he scanned his front, trying to locate the gunman. He saw both were now running back toward the four-by-four, one putting down covering fire, whilst the other advanced a short distance, before they would repeat and do the same. He could see the slight sluggish movements in one, so knew which one he'd fought, and as if to answer the question, the very same man looked back up toward Mike, trying to see if he was out of cover. Mike thought for a few tense moments he'd give another burst in his direction, but his partner, clearly losing patience, almost pushed him into the four-by-four's passenger side, as both gave one final burst of fire toward the camp before speeding off into the direction of Wool village.

Mike stood up, running toward the road, pistol in hand, tempted to fire at the speeding vehicle, but quickly shook the thought from his head, knowing that to do so would open him up to all sorts of potential legal charges. Although he'd had a right to defend himself, if he fired at them as they drove away that would be seen in the eyes of the law as intent, and he really didn't want to spend the next few years in jail. He stopped just short of the road, the pistol hanging down by his side as he watched the vehicle disappear into the distance. *What the hell just happened?* he thought, his breathing heavy as his body now began protesting at the past five minutes of abuse.

Thinking quickly, he turned to the road where he'd last seen Ted, his eyes focusing on a lone figure lying prostrate, a crimson river already beginning to form beneath it. "Ted!" he yelled as he sprinted toward the body.

Ted was lying on his side, one arm outstretched, the other tucked under his body, his eyes open and lifeless, looking back at the camp gate, his mouth slightly agape. Mike carefully knelt beside the body, his hand touching his shoulder gently, respectfully. He'd seen enough gunshot wounds in his time to know the bullets Ted had taken were fatal, even if you didn't count the two crimson-red dots above Ted's left eye. Mike knew this man had died whilst trying to come to his aid and he felt sorrow which quickly turned to anger as he looked down to see four-bullet holes to Ted's upper body. Whoever the gunmen were, this had been senseless overkill and Mike began to wish he'd taken those shots at the fleeing vehicle.

His senses were coming back to normal as he heard shouts and activity all around him. People still in shock began to emerge from doorways and to appear at windows, the fear and surprise etched on their faces. This was something no one had been expecting. Looking up toward the main gate, he saw the booth that housed the guards was now a smoking ruin. Ironically, it had been made of wood and plastic, providing no cover from the automatic fire. He saw the body of the second guard lying half out of the open doorway; he'd tried to crawl for cover, again unarmed and an easy target.

The smoke rising from around the guard room began to dissipate as shouted orders could be heard from inside the building. Two soldiers dressed in full combat gear, carrying helmets and SA80 assault rifles began to assume fire positions overlooking the road as the Quick Reaction Force (QRF) began to deploy from the camp, taking control of the situation. Not wanting to be shot by an overzealous guard, Mike had already unloaded the pistol and put it on the ground beside him, making sure to remove the magazine and cocking the working parts to the rear, before raising his hands and putting them behind his head, his eyes still locked on the sight of Ted's body. A young Trooper moved toward Mike, his weapon raised, keeping Mike in his sights. Mike didn't flinch or move, knowing that to do so could invite his own death. As the Trooper moved closer, Mike could see he was young, but his eyes remained focused on the target, on Mike, his finger lightly resting against the trigger guard of his weapon.

Mike looked down at the ground trying to look as compliant as possible as the Trooper stopped just short of him weapon still aimed, shouting, "Who are you? Identify yourself!"

Mike calmly replied in a slow steady voice, "Friendly, I'm a friendly, I'm with the base, I'm visiting Major Richards. There's a pistol that is unloaded down by my right side, that's the only weapon I have, I took it from one of the gunmen. It's been unloaded and is safe to handle."

The Trooper paused, looking down at the pistol and then at the damage to Mike's face, his weapon remaining steady as he thought over his next move. "Okay, I want you to remain where you are, you are not to move or make any sudden movements. Do you understand?"

Mike nodded his head slowly.

Without taking his eyes off Mike, the Trooper shouted back, "Corporal!"

Mike remained kneeling, his hands on his head as the QRF began to set up a cordon around the main gate. Soldiers came racing from all over the camp, eager to be of any assistance. Some were ordered to send messages, whilst others were used to help keep the scene as secure as they could. Whilst all this was going on around him Mike began to think, his mind trying to log every detail of the gunmen while it was still fresh in his memory; their description, the weapons they'd used and the vehicle they'd just driven away in. After no more than a minute, a Corporal came running over, Mike guessed him to be the QRF commander. He was slightly overweight and red-faced, looking almost comical in his body armour, his helmet lying askew on his head. He glanced at the body beside Mike, reaching down with a finger to check for a pulse. As he did so Mike stated, "He's dead."

The QRF commander snapped his head to look at Mike, snarling, "I'll be the fucking judge of that. Who the *fuck* are you?"

Before Mike could reply, the Trooper responded, "Corporal, he says he's visiting a friend in the camp, a Major Richards, and that he's got caught up in this somehow. He's taken a pistol off one of the gunmen and it's unloaded at his feet."

The Corporal looked down at the pistol, then at the bruising that was beginning to show on Mike's face, thanks to the earlier fight.

"I've got two witnesses who saw you shooting that pistol at us, and then when *your* friends drove off, you ran after them. Got left behind, did you?"

Mike grimaced as he heard the words, 'your friends'. Clearly someone had got their wires crossed. This wasn't a good time to be on the wrong side, he thought.

"Look," he replied, "on the base is Major Richards, he knows who I am – go get him and he will vouch for me. I'm not a part of this, Corporal. You've got the wrong man."

The Corporal brought his face closer to Mike's, to emphasise what he wanted to say. "I've got people dead in there," pointing towards the guard room, "and from where I'm standing, I've got the *right* fucking man!"

"You're looking for two gunmen, in a silver—" Mike tried to reply, the sound cutting off as the Corporal slapped him with the back of his hand. Mike's head whipped to the side, tasting fresh blood in his mouth as he slowly turned his head back to look directly at the soldier who'd struck him. Inside, his anger began to build again, but he kept himself in check, as looking past the overweight Corporal, he saw the Trooper still had a weapon aimed at him, leaving Mike in no doubt that if he offered any resistance, the weapon would be used.

Mike felt his hands being pulled off his head as the Corporal placed them in plastic cuffs and tied them behind his back. Once this had been done, he saw the Trooper with the weapon aimed at him visibly relaxing, the barrel lowering slightly. Clearly, they were relieved Mike had been detained. The last thing Mike saw was the smiling face of the Corporal as he placed a set of blacked-out goggles over Mike's eyes to prevent him from seeing where he was being taken. With little care, he was forced up onto his feet, the pain of kneeling on already sore and tired muscles causing Mike to grunt with effort.

Resigning himself to his fate, he kept his head down and his mouth shut as they led him away. For now, he was going to have to play them at their own game.

6

The Saviour

Rawlinson Family Farm – 15:20

Peter gently brushed the grey horse stood before him, enjoying the relaxing rhythm and the soft warmth of his favourite animal.

"Now, now, Ajax. Good boy, easy does it."

He chatted constantly to the horse as he worked the brush down its body, moving slowly so as not to startle the animal. As he groomed, he ran a practiced eye over it for scrapes and bumps, as ever on the lookout for anything out of the ordinary that required attention. Stepping back to admire his handiwork he offered Ajax some carrots, the horse's large velvety nose seeking them out gently. Next on the agenda was some food, ready made up and hidden in the feed bin.

Ajax whickered with excitement as he heard the familiar squeak of the feed-bin lid being opened, and within seconds had his nose buried deep into the bucket, ravenous, as if never being fed before.

"Okay, boy, easy does it," Peter said with a laugh, enjoying the sights and sounds of the contented horse and the peace and tranquillity that the barn offered. Nearby stood a figure dressed in grubby jeans and a faded polo shirt, an eye patch over his left eye, waiting patiently with a rope in his hands.

Peter looked up to the man and said, "Make sure after he's fed, he gets his new bedding put into his stall, will you, Patch?"

The lone figure nodded, replying, "Of course, boss. I'll also check his hooves and top up the water."

Peter smiled. "Thanks, Patch," turning to walk back to his house from the stables, the sun beating down on him, basking the paddocks and fields in a flash of colour that almost looked like it had been airbrushed. As he walked away, he looked back at the stable block that housed his eight horses, seven of which he'd owned since they were foals and were bred and nurtured for his love of polo. It was a game he'd been introduced to back in his army days which he now enjoyed as a family hobby. His son and daughter had grown up loving the sport and as a family they'd become one of the south-west's most competitive family teams. Peter smiled with pride as he thought of last year's championships; they hadn't won, but came damn close to doing so. He still remembered the speech he'd tried to give his son afterward who had taken the defeat to heart. "Remember, Morgan, champions are not born champions, they *earn* it. We'll get better and we will win." *Oh God*, he thought, it all sounded tacky now, perhaps he should have said something else.

He smiled as he walked toward his house. It had once been a working dairy farm, and when he and his wife Elizabeth had bought it in 2014 it had needed more than just a little tender loving care to get it up to spec. But with extended family behind them, they'd managed it and succeeded in transforming a ramshackle old farm into a beautiful Georgian-style house with thirty acres of land. Granted, it had stretched the budget, and Elizabeth had her doubts, but when they had all turned up for the first viewing and saw the beautiful lines of the house and just how much land the property had come with, it was love at first sight.

Peter had bought the old farm to provide security and stability to his family after a very long and turbulent army career. A career that had seen him serve all over Europe, into Canada and parts of the Middle East and he'd served in the invasion of Iraq in 2003 as the Commanding Officer of what was then known as the 24th Tank Regiment. He'd been known to have a quick, calm, decisive mind and was always able to get the best out of the people he worked with. It was because of these traits that he'd advanced up the career ladder of the army quickly, becoming a Brigadier and finding himself posted out to the Middle East in 2010 on a two-year deployment. The army had needed someone in the Middle East to help the British defence industry promote its UK products and more importantly to see what the competition had been up to. There had been many new defence companies springing up in the area and the UK government had wanted to see for itself what new and exciting technologies were on the market.

Due to the length of time he'd be away, he had been allowed to bring his family along and promised Elizabeth and his two children the mystery and romance of somewhere as magical as the Middle East. "Think of all the exciting new things we shall get to see as a family and the new experiences," he'd told them. He remembered the excitement on his children's faces as they boarded the plane – they'd seen and heard the stories of Lawrence of Arabia and now they were going to enjoy for themselves the exotic places they'd only seen in the movies.

The first twelve months had flown by in a fantastic rush of fine expensive dining, cocktail parties, charity events and excursions. His family had settled in amongst the large group of expats living there and the constant sunshine had been a blessing compared to the rainy weather of the UK. His children had found a new love for the great outdoors, thanks to the consistent, stable weather and were always out with their new friends. Peter had found there was no end to the constant requests for him to attend functions, no doubt related to the fact his new job was all about creating relationships and promoting team GB. He picked up quickly on how cutthroat the world of civilian defence business could be and how to diplomatically navigate the waters, finding the right balance between courting relationships with potential future clients, whilst at the same time trying not to associate with anything that could be seen as politically or morally insensitive. Despite all the parties and social gatherings, he was still a serving Brigadier and still representing his country at the highest levels.

Elizabeth had loved it. For the first time in as many years she'd been able to see Peter on a regular basis, with no fast deployments away, no phone calls at an ungodly hour and for once it seemed Peter and his family were getting a look at what a normal nine-to-five life was like. However, as with all good things, life had a habit of throwing an unknown quantity into the mix, something to test people when they least expected. It was in the beginning of Peter's second year. In late 2011 he'd been on his way to a meeting with another defence contractor, whose company had been experimenting with drones, and had an exciting new concept, a drone that could 'loiter' on the battlefield at high altitudes for weeks, with the ability to self-charge its electrical motors using only the power of the sun and the wind. Peter had been looking forward to the meeting and had scheduled it toward the end of the afternoon, expecting to finish the day taking the family out for a sunset cruise on a rental boat.

The meeting had required just him and his driver, Corporal John Sampson and they'd both driven there expecting nothing more than cold drinks and some welcome company. However it wasn't to be. The Brigadier had been targeted for a kidnap attempt by one of the most serious terrorist organisations in the area, with a plan to at best ransom and kill him, or worse, just kill him. It had only been thanks to the quick reactions and bravery of the Brigadier's driver that they'd escaped with their lives, although not without injury, as Peter had sustained a gunshot wound to his leg and John had lost his left eye as they'd fought to evade the ambush.

After the failed attempt, the Brigadier and his family were immediately flown back to the UK, their fantasy life in tatters. Peter had been told to take some time off and heal from his injuries, but Peter being Peter, this hadn't lasted long. In no time at all he was made Commander of the 143 Wessex Brigade, which saw him oversee the formation and running of a brigade that existed on paper only, its mission to assist with any form of government or civil emergency that required troops. Initially he'd been told it would require little or no effort on his part, being one of the few postings that were known as a 'jolly' suggesting an easy posting to relax in, and that he should concentrate his time and effort on a hobby.

When he had dusted off the 1950s style folder in front of him, he was shocked to see the plans were outdated and designed for the Cold War, relying on units that no longer existed. They needed an overhaul, modernisation, to be made fit for purpose – and what better person to do it than an injured convalescing Brigadier with a sharp mind with nothing to do. So, he spent the time sat in his office, his leg in plaster, formulating and planning scenarios where the 143 Wessex Brigade could be used. His area of influence and control extended from the North Dorset and Somerset borders all the way down the south-west of the UK into Cornwall. This meant the garrisons of Tidworth, Bovington and Lulworth could all fall under his command in certain scenarios. He realised that he had almost forty thousand reserve soldiers in these areas, split into small detachments based in and around all the local towns and villages within the area. He began to contact these smaller units, introducing himself, making them aware of their new identity and that they were all to play a part of a larger unit. Then, he informed them of the roles they would effectively play if the worst were to ever happen.

After planning the likely scenarios in which the 143 Wessex Brigade could be used, Peter then began testing the units, organising exercises involving the reservists being deployed to fictitious mass casualty events, such as air crashes or biological agent attacks. Peter had at first expected the reserve units to complain, not wanting their soldiers to be messed about, but instead the opposite happened. The reservists, expecting nothing more than their annual two-week camp, relished the opportunity to show their potential. At the end of the day, they'd all volunteered to do something worthwhile and sitting in their camps practising drill and cleaning weapons was not the excitement most of its volunteers had joined up for.

Using his previous experience, Peter began to liaise with the civil services, the fire brigade, the police, the ambulance services and even the councils, to see what sort of planning they had put in place and if it could be used in conjunction with his own. Soon all the civil departments in the south-west were beginning to update and refresh their own outdated plans, realising that if the military were doing this, then so should they. Slowly the MoD became aware that this new unit that up to that point had existed only on paper, was slowly being born and forged into something real, something that could be used should a crisis arise. And that's exactly why, when the floods hit the UK in 2013 it was the 143 Wessex Brigade that was mobilised first, being the only effective unit in the area that had planned for and trained for the scenario. Also, in 2016 after the Salisbury poisonings it had been the 143 Wessex Brigade that had been deployed to provide the bulk of the personnel required to help cordon off the area and search for any possible areas of contamination. All of this had been possible thanks to the planning and forethought of one man, Brigadier Peter Rawlinson.

Peter had relished and enjoyed his time as the 143 Wessex Brigade's commander and the job had meant he'd built up a host of contacts within the military and civil government that he wouldn't have met had it not been for the job. However, he was also conscious that his family were beginning to grow up and move on without him and he realised that his time in the military was going to have to come to an end at some point. So, in 2014 he decided, for the good of his family, that he would semi-re-tire. And this was how they had come to own an ex-dairy farm with stables situated in the sleepy Dorset village of Godly-Morton. He had called it semi-retirement, as he was only fifty-one years old at the time and he and Elizabeth both knew they were not going to settle down to a quiet life and gardening just yet. But what would he do now? he had thought to himself. He had received endless job offers from friends who had established their own companies, but he didn't want to be working for anyone other than himself. It didn't sit well with him having to work for someone else and as Elizabeth had always told him, "You are your own man, Peter, and no one can put a fence around you. I think you should start up your own company and be your own boss."

So, with his wife's blessing that's exactly what he did. He found a small local company near to their home that specialised in commercial drones but was on the verge of bankruptcy. He bought the company, became its CEO and using his military contacts, began to design, research and test military-capable drones. His time in the Middle East had taught him how the defence industry worked and more importantly how the business model operated, and with his military background it made sense to work within the defence sector. In 2015 Aurora Defence Systems was created and had originally started with a team of just four including Peter. Now it boasted a workforce of nearly fifty people, most of whom were ex forces, as Peter preferred to hire people who had left the navy, RAF and army, whose skill sets were too important to waste within the civilian sectors.

When they had first started the company, the drones were the size of a football, but now, with the capability to carry weapons, they had grown to the size of a small light aircraft. They also had a large research team that had begun to work on some new and exciting prototypes for the military, but these were highly secretive and, frustratingly, Aurora could not advertise or promote these to any new customers. The MoD were dragging their feet on the budget requirements, as well as the approval, and even though they'd successfully tested the platforms, and given the MoD more than what they had asked for, they still dithered and delayed. Peter had been angry at having to put the project on hold but knew when it came to the MoD procurement teams there were two speeds: slow and backwards.

As well as his workforce, Peter had also employed on a more personal level his old driver, Corporal John Sampson, or 'Patch' as he now preferred to be called thanks to the menacing patch over his left eye. Patch had left the army in 2014 and fallen on hard times – it seemed no one had any urge to hire an ex-soldier with one eye – and he had ended up resorting to sleeping rough, spending nearly two hard years on the streets of Bristol before he was found and taken in by Peter. Peter had promised him nothing but hard work and a roof over his head with a good wage. To Peter, it was a way to repay Patch for saving his life; to Patch it was the chance he needed to settle down and start to live a normal life again.

Patch had met two other homeless veterans during his time on the streets – Tony and Alan – and upon hearing their plight, Peter quickly went back up to Bristol and found them, bringing them back with the same promise of work and wages. Peter had given them two simple rules to follow to keep the peace. The first was no talking about the past – he didn't care what they had done in the past so long as it stayed there. All he could promise them was a future and he hoped that would be enough. The second rule was absolutely no drugs. Again, he didn't care if they *had* taken drugs so long as the habit had been left on the street. He was not going to have drugs in his house with his family around them. All three had sworn to follow the rules and for the past nine years had worked hard, becoming close friends with each other and the family, always joking that they were now 'part of the furniture'.

He walked toward their home, the sun still beating down on him, his eyes squinting as he saw his wife Elizabeth standing by the back door looking out. Was she looking for him? he thought, as he saw her look in his direction before waving manically. Whatever she wanted it must have been serious as she left the house and jogged down the path toward him. He was hoping it wasn't bad news – only recently they'd had to get one of their horses checked by the vet, with them taking some bloods. Perhaps they had rung with results?

She was shouting to him as he got closer. "Peter, it's Mike on the landline, he says it's urgent!"

A look of confusion appeared on Peter's face as his hand instinctively reached down to his pocket. He reached inside and pulled out his mobile phone. Seeing it was on and he had a signal, he raised it up to show Elizabeth before asking, "Why didn't he call my mobile?"

Elizabeth shrugged her shoulders with her typical *I don't know* look.

Peter had by this stage reached her, and seeing the flour on her hands, knew she had been baking.

"Ooh, what's for tea then, darling?" he asked, smiling expectantly.

"Peter, it's not for you, I'm baking for the cancer charity," she replied archly, adding, "If you're lucky I might save you some."

His look said it all as they both hurried up to the back door and into the kitchen across the flagstone floor.

"It's in your office," said Elizabeth, as she went back to the kitchen worktop, a mixture of eggs, flour and bowls all scattered about.

"Thank you, darling, and I'll expect at least *one* cake." He grinned as he already knew Elizabeth would have made him two.

He walked across the large hall and through a large oak-beam door, into a spacious office, with a window and desk at one end. The telephone was on his desk, he wiped his hands on his trousers before picking it up.

"Hello? Mike, you there?"

"Peter, have you seen the news today?"

Peter stiffened as Mike skipped the pleasantries and went straight to business, something clearly bothering him.

"Not yet, I've been a bit busy in the stables and why the landline, you've got my mobile number?"

"Peter, I need you to turn on the telly in your office, check if it's still working, I need you to do this *now!*" He could hear the forced tone in Mike's voice on the other end. He'd never heard Mike like this, so it had to be serious.

"Okay, Mike, give me a second."

Cradling the phone in his hand, he reached over to the TV remote on the desk, hitting the button and waiting a few seconds as the screen flicked to life, showing the latest reality show about buying homes in the countryside.

"Okay, the TV's on and working, mind telling me what this is about?"

"Thank God," he heard Mike mutter, as he then shot back, "Can you put the news on, find one of those twenty-four-hour channels?"

Peter flicked over to the news channel. Immediately the scenes that Mike had seen earlier came to life. The news channel was showing the scene at Portsmouth with the MV *Titan* sunk up to its hull, police boats and tugs still aimlessly floating near the ship.

"Okay, Mike, I've got the news on now, looks like a ship in Portsmouth has an issue. What am I looking at exactly?"

"I think that Operation Fools Mate is in play."

Peter froze for a second as he let Mike's words sink in. Looking around the room as if to check no one was within earshot he replied slowly, "Say that again."

"I said, I think Operation Fools Mate is in play."

Peter pulled out the office chair and sat down, slightly shocked – that was a name he thought he'd never hear again. Clearing his thoughts, he quickly replied, "Come on, Mike, think clearly. Listen to what you're saying. Why on earth would you think that? What are you basing this on? I'm only seeing a ship that has sunk, an accident, nothing more."

"No accident," Mike interjected. "It was done deliberately, and earlier this morning a second container ship was sunk in Southampton Docks, again, done deliberately. Since 2pm all of the UK's mobile phone networks and internet have gone down, including the emergency network, and the army are reporting all their VoIP comms and intranet systems are no longer working. Also, less than ten minutes ago we started to lose the TV stations, thankfully it hasn't got to you yet."

"Wait, did you say the emergency network?"

"I did, try calling 999 now, you won't get through."

"Hang on, Mike."

Knowing Mike would be telling the truth, but wanting to be certain, he pulled his mobile phone out and tried to dial 999 – it was the same response as Mike had earlier; a click, a hiss and then cut off.

He rubbed his chin thoughtfully as he remembered the details of Operation Fools Mate. Then he asked, "Okay, if this *is* in play, then how is it you are calling me, if all the phone systems are down?"

"I'm in a good old-fashioned red phone box outside Bovington camp. As soon as I saw the emergency networks were down, I remembered all about the PSTN networks."

"I'm sorry, Mike, you've got me there. PTSN what?"

"You remember one of our guys called Tiny, he left in 2009 and ended up working for a telecoms company?"

"I don't remember him, no, but go on anyway," he replied, eager to know where Mike was going with this.

"I've seen him since at a few regimental reunions. Anyway, during one of our conversations he mentioned the older phone networks called PSTN or Public Switched Telephone Networks, were due to be replaced by 2020."

Peter interjected, "Yes, I'm aware of that, Mike, that's why I future-proofed Fools Mate, I took this into account, which is why the plan *could* take down the phone systems. I knew they were to be replaced. That still doesn't explain how we're talking now."

"But the phone companies underestimated the costs, and with Covid shutting the world down, the upgrades were all delayed."

"Really? So, when did they upgrade the networks then?"

"They haven't. It was supposed to have all been completed back in 2023, but it's been delayed again. So, the old phone boxes that were to have been replaced in your report years ago are still around, with good old-fashioned copper wires. All the new systems are digital, so can be brought down by cyber-attacks, but the older systems still go via the old telephone exchange in Milton Keynes. Unless you physically cut the wire you can't cut the line, hence they're still working. But I can't call mobile phones, it only works landline to landline."

Of course, Peter thought, he hadn't considered the older systems, expecting them to have been replaced long ago. If someone were to use the plan today, then Mike was right, they'd overlook the phone boxes.

He was shaken from his thoughts as Mike urgently asked,

"I need to know your thoughts though, could this be happening? Could this *really* be happening? Am I over thinking this?"

Peter thought it over quickly, his mind racing as he thought aloud.

"Well, as you know, to work properly the plan requires an unknown player, someone blameless to muddy the waters..." He thought back to something he had seen in the news earlier that week. Suddenly, as if a light switched on, it all fell into place. *Of course,* he thought, now it all made sense.

"Peter, what is it?"

"I think I know who the player will be, our mystery friend."

"Who?" asked Mike.

"Tumat. The new republic distancing themselves from Russia. It fits the profile perfectly. Only last week the new president had given a speech, acknowledging mistakes of the past, forging new alliances and making a stronger country free from tyranny. It had all been very ambiguous, very vague."

There was silence on the line as both men thought over this new piece of information.

Peter closed his eyes, rubbing his chin as he tried to control his thoughts and think through his next move. He was hoping Mike was wrong, but he knew Mike, he knew he wasn't the sort of person to jump to conclusions and was certainly not the sort to ring the panic alarm unless it was necessary. His mind began to focus clearly as he thought back to what Mike had just said. "Hang on, did you just say you're at Bovington?"

"Yes, I'm outside the main gate. I'm here visiting Chris Richards. He's a Major now and in charge of the ATDU."

Peter looked out of the window to the stables. He could see Patch walking Ajax back to his paddock. Slowly, deliberately, Peter began to think through the options, of what was happening and more importantly, of what could be done.

"Peter, you still there?"

Pulled back from his thoughts Peter quickly replied, "I'm here Mike, just thinking, give me a second."

"Okay."

"Mike, just remind me, how long ago did the phones go off?"

"Er, at about midday, I don't know when the internet went down, probably not long after that."

After about thirty seconds of thinking, Peter finally said, "Okay, Mike, you're at Bovington, I need you to stay there, get an audience with the CO, use Chris if you have to, tell him all you know about Fools Mate. I know it won't be easy, he'll probably call you crazy but you have to try to get the camp alert state raised. If what we think is happening, is happening, then we don't have the luxury of time."

Peter could hear the doubt in Mike's voice as he replied, "That's going to be a pretty tall order. I know I like to talk, but there's no way they'll believe me, hell even I'm struggling to believe it."

"Look, I'll come down myself to tell them, I just need to do something first and get the ball rolling, see if I can get something in play. In the meantime, you need to be aware there's only two people in the world who know of Fools Mate, and we're talking to each other. You need to warn them, and you need to do it now. I don't care how you do it, but that camp needs to raise their alert levels. You know the stakes now; you know what we're playing for."

"Peter, I'll do what I can. In the meantime, how long before you're down here?"

Peter thought quickly before replying. "No more than two, maybe three hours. I'll get there though."

"Well, I guess there's not much else to say then but good luck."

"You too, Mike. You too."

With that, he heard the line go dead. As soon as he replaced the receiver it was as if the pressure in the room had been released. "FUCK!" he shouted to no-one.

Hearing his outburst Elizabeth came in from the kitchen. This time her apron bore the fruits of her labours. "Darling, you okay? Was Mike all right?" she asked, concern etched over her face.

He was about to reply when the images on the TV suddenly flicked off, the footage now replaced by the same test transmission Mike had just reported. He reached for the remote, changing channels, seeing the same test picture being broadcast on them all. His mouth open in shock, he ignored his wife, stepping over to the office window and opening it, leaning out and shouting, "Patch, I need you, Alan and Tony in the office immediately!" His shouting made Elizabeth flinch and seeing her startled he took her flour-covered hands into his and said, "Darling, I need you to stop what you're doing, go upstairs and pack us both an overnight bag. It doesn't mean we're going anywhere, I just need you to have a bag ready in case we have to leave."

A look of confusion spread across Elizabeth's face as she digested what he'd just said. "Peter, I... I don't understand. Pack a bag? Leave? I'm baking cakes. Tonight we're going to the Daltons for dinner. What are you on about? Leave?"

Peter pulled her to him and kissed her forehead. "I love you, darling, I always will, but for now I need you to trust me. I know about the dinner party, I know about the cakes, but something is happening, something big, and if I'm right, and I hope to God I'm not, but, if I'm right then we need to be ready to move quickly."

"Peter, please tell me what's going on. What did Mike want? And what's got you so spooked? I know you, and this is the first time I've seen you like this."

She was interrupted as Patch appeared in the doorway followed by Alan and Tony. All three men were breathing heavily. Patch was quick to say, "Sorry, boss, we came as quickly as we could. What's up?"

Still holding Elizabeth in his arms he looked up, his warm loving demeanour replaced with a face more intense, focused, and his eyes sparkling with a fire within.

"Patch, I need you to get the car ready to go, we've got a bit of a journey ahead of us and we want to be leaving in the next thirty minutes. Once the car's ready, go pack yourself an overnight bag, whatever happens you'll be coming with me. Alan, Tony, I need you to secure the stables, get all the horses in, all the paddocks closed then report back here as soon as you're finished please."

The three men looked at each other, seeing the fire and energy radiating off Peter made them all instantly alert. Patch was the first to reply, "Right, boss, we'll get on it now," before all three men hurriedly left the room.

Elizabeth looked up at Peter. Her eyes shone fiercely as a flash of anger crossed her face. "Peter, I am not the *fucking* damsel in distress, don't you dare charge off and leave me here without an explanation. Those years have long past. I'm not an army wife now. I want to know what's going on. Whatever it is, *we* can handle it. This is our home, and I don't expect us to simply run away. What is it, what's got you so spooked?"

Peter smiled as he saw the drive and passion in Elizabeth. He'd been an idiot to try to shield her from what he knew. To think he could just click his fingers and his wife would dutifully skip to his tune. What was he thinking? She was tough, resilient and she had been his rock, keeping a loving family with two wonderful children going while he was off, charging all over the world getting the glory in his tank. She was the one who should have been given the medals. Well, she was right, those days were over, now it was Team Rawlinson all the way. He closed his eyes for a second, opened them again, gave her a kiss on the lips, and then began to quickly tell her all he knew about Operation Fools Mate.

The Rawlinson farm had become a hive of activity as everyone seemed to have a job to do and there was a real buzz in the air. Elizabeth seemed to calm somewhat after Peter had spoken to her. He was right to tell her, he thought, as he watched her cross the hall quickly, tidying up the kitchen and getting everything put away. He'd gone back into the office, pushing aside one of the paintings and from memory keying in the combination to the hidden safe. He sifted through the papers, pulling out an A4-sized folder and a small leather-backed phone book, before sitting at the desk and dialling one of the numbers. It answered on the third ring and he immediately recognised the voice.

"Hello?"

"James, it's Peter Rawlinson, are you able to talk?"

"Ah, Peter, of course I can talk, how's that lovely wife of yours? You still living the dream in Dorset?"

"James, I'm so sorry to be a bore, but we're time critical on something going on here. Have you seen the news about what's going on in Southampton and Portsmouth?"

"Ah, yes, the sinkings. I think they're being put down to eco-terrorism or something. Why do you ask?"

"I think it's bigger than that. A lot bigger. And I need to speak to you about it, but not over the phone."

"Well, it can't be that important, Peter, otherwise someone would have called *me* about it. I'll tell you what, why don't you call my office and have Margaret pencil in a meeting for tomorrow, say sometime in the afternoon? We can discuss it then."

"James, tomorrow may be too late. I need to speak to you now."

There was a pause on the end of the phone as James absorbed what he had been told.

"Peter if it's *that* important, why don't you call Sir Charles at five? I'm sure he'd like to know before me if you have any gossip of that nature."

He recognised the slang that James had used to describe MI5. Clearly the person he was talking to did not want to be disturbed any longer.

"James, have you tried to call anyone using your mobile? In fact, have you received *any* calls from anyone today?"

"What kind of bloody stupid question is that?" the voice on the end of the phone responded. "Of course no one's called me. I'm on leave, and it would have to be a world war starting off somewhere for someone to disturb me."

"James, what if I told you that could be closer to the truth than you realise?"

"Peter, what the hell has got into you? I know it's summer and it's hot, maybe the heat has affected your thinking." James scolded.

He tried to keep his voice cool and calm, knowing he was clinging to a thin thread that was getting thinner by the second.

"James, I can prove how serious this is. It's simple. All I need you to do is try to call someone using your phone. I guarantee you won't get through. Then use your phone to call the emergency services, 999. Again, I guarantee you won't be able to. Finally, try using your bat phone, I promise you that won't work either. I think that someone is deliberately disrupting our communications and I know why, and more importantly it's not the end of what's happening, it's just the beginning. But I really need that meeting with you."

"If what you're saying is true, how are we able to speak now? You're calling me right this second," James's voice sounded suspicious.

"Simple, we're calling on an old landline, an old PSTN dial-up," he replied, remembering what Mike had just told him. "I know what an old fossil you are – like me, you keep a landline in your office just in case your mobile plays up, and I know it's not been upgraded yet, you're always forever moaning about it."

James guffawed at the use of the word 'fossil'. There was a pause before he continued. "All right, Peter, I'll play along for now. What's your number there?"

He recited from memory his land line number and James jotted it down.

"Okay, Peter, I'll try the numbers like you say, but I'm warning you, if this is your version of a joke, if you're playing some kind of stupid game, then I'll forget we're friends..."

James hung up abruptly. Peter knew he'd just gambled years of friendship with him, especially when he had mentioned the term 'bat phone'. That had been a codeword reserved for the most serious of cases, a term for an emergency so powerful that the message needed to go straight to the top. He looked down at the folder on his desk, becoming aware of someone standing in the doorway; he looked up to see Elizabeth staring back. Breaking the silence she said, "I've packed our bags just in case, one for you, one for me, and the guys are getting the farm locked down." She walked over to him, placing her hands on his shoulders, slowly rubbing them to help him bear the weight of what he knew. "Was that James on the phone?" she asked.

He looked back at her smiling and replied, "Yes, I need to meet him. I'm waiting for him to call back shortly."

"I couldn't help but hear *bat phone*?" she quizzed.

Still smiling he replied, "Don't worry, it's not for the caped crusader, although right now I'd accept any help we could get. It's the codeword for James to chat to the PM."

"The PM? You mean *the* Prime Minister?" she asked, shocked. "Why would James be able to talk to him?"

"Honestly, Elizabeth, sometimes you don't listen to a word I say, do you? Don't you remember? Eight months ago, being invited to a party at James's house?"

"Yes, but you can't expect me to remember every party we get invited to. I thought it was to celebrate another one of his divorces, or engagements. I never can remember with him."

Peter looked at his wife with mock disapproval before she continued, "Anyway, what was it about the party, why so important? Did he marry the Prime Minister's daughter?

"No," he replied, smirking, "it was to celebrate his promotion to the highest military rank in the UK. James is the CDS, the Chief of the Defence Staff."

Elizabeth looked on as Patch appeared in the doorway.

"Boss, the car's outside ready to go. Alan and Tony are just waiting outside.

Peter looked up, nodding his thanks.

He stood up, looking at Elizabeth. "Darling, would you mind waiting here in case the phone rings? I'm expecting a very urgent call."

Elizabeth sat down in the chair looking back at him. "Go on then, go rally the troops," she said, smiling and waving him off.

He nodded his thanks and walked out, following Patch into the farm's courtyard. The other two were leaning against the side of the blue Range Rover, waiting for him. They both stood up as he approached.

"Paddocks are all secure, boss, horses all locked away, everything's secure."

Peter looked at Alan and nodded his thanks.

All three men looked at Peter questioningly before Patch asked, "Okay, boss, I've known you for a long time, I've not seen you rattled or startled before, but that phone call you had earlier – something's up. What is it? What do you need?"

For the next five minutes Peter told them what he'd told Elizabeth, about the threat that was coming for all of them, and what he'd found out from Mike. After he'd finished no one spoke, all of them digesting in surprise and shock what they'd been told. Patch shook his head slowly as Alan looked at the ground, deep in thought.

Finally they all looked back up at him as he took another deep breath and continued. "I've never asked too much about your pasts, I've never needed to. I know you've all served in the military at some time or another. And I've always told you all to look to the future, forget the past, make new lives for yourselves and become new men. And for these past years you've done just that."

All three nodded silently before he continued.

"But what I need to know now are two things: firstly, do you have any families? Anyone counting on you back home? If something like this happened, something that could threaten our country, would you rather be here defending my home? Or would you need to go to protect someone else? Would there be a loved one you'd want to defend? I need to know because shortly I'm going to have to go away, and I don't know when I'll be back. This is far bigger than me or my family. But I need to know this place will be looked after – more importantly, I need to know Elizabeth will be protected and looked after. I need people I can trust. I trust all three of you, but I need to know that your heart and head are up to the task. If there's somewhere else you need to go, a distraction that will pull you away from here, then tell me now. I'll be happy to let you go."

The three men looked at each other. A brief silence before Tony spoke first. "I can't vouch for the other two, but there's no one missing me. This has been my home since you pulled me off the streets."

Peter nodded in acknowledgement before looking to Alan. "Alan? What about you? Anyone at home you care about?"

Alan looked at the ground, his feet shuffling uncomfortably before looking back up. "The only person I cared about died a long time ago. Since then, *this* has been my home." He waved his hand around the courtyard to emphasise the point. "If you're saying there's a threat to your home, then it's a threat to my home too."

Peter put his hand on his shoulder in thanks before looking at Patch. "John." He used Patch's first name to emphasise the warmth he felt for him. "I've already asked so much of you, you've saved my life before, and for that I'm eternally grateful. It cost you more than just your eye, I know, and now here I am asking for more. I'll understand if you don't want to be a part of this."

Patch looked away toward the house then back at Peter. "Boss, since getting out of the army all I ever had were people looking down on me. Walking on by and judging me as I sat on those cold wet streets. People would stare down at me as if they were better than me. They didn't know me, didn't know what I'd done, what I had seen or been through, didn't know what I *could* do. Society forgot me, and it forgot *us*," he said, nodding his head to the other two before continuing, "but you didn't. You found us, you helped us, you gave us a home, you gave us respect, dignity and the chance to stand back up and be someone again." His voice was slow and emotional as he spoke.

Peter wasn't an emotional man, but something Patch was saying was tugging at his heart.

He looked away, wiping his eyes as Patch continued, "You ask us if we have anywhere else to go, a home to go back to or family to see? Well, as the others have said, we *are* home, this is *our* home, too, and you and Elizabeth and your kids are *our* family."

"Okay, Patch, okay," Peter said softly. He hadn't expected such an emotional response from the three men. He'd clearly underestimated how much the farm and his family had meant to them all.

A few seconds' silence descended as all four men digested what had just been said. Suddenly Tony looked back at Peter and asked, "Boss, the second thing? You said there were two things you wanted to know. What was the second?"

Peter looked at them all smiling back at him, as suddenly, wanting to change the mood, he asked, "And now I want to know about your past, your *military* past. Just how badass were you all?"

Alan looked up with a glint in his eyes. "I was a Corporal with 4 Para, served seven years, did three tours, two in Afghan, one in Sierra Leone."

"Okay," Peter answered, looking over to Tony who replied, "Eight years in the Durham Light Infantry, did two tours of Afghan, left a Lance Corporal."

Alan looked at Tony, shocked, and asked, "Eight years and only a lance jack?"

Tony shook his head slowly, thinking of the past. "Yeah, I got bust down the ranks twice for drinking and fighting. Stupid thing to do, I know that now..."

"No one's perfect," Peter cut in, not wishing Tony to think too negatively of the past. He then turned to Patch. "I know your history, but do you want to tell it to these two?"

Patch looked at them both and smiled. "Corporal, nine years in the 24th Tank Regiment. Did one tour of Kosovo, two tours of Iraq, and two tours of Afghanistan."

"Oh Christ!" exclaimed Alan, breaking the mood, "I forgot you were a bloody tankie! That's like having someone in a wheelchair on the battlefield."

"Says the man that used to jump out of perfectly good airplanes!" replied Patch, smirking.

All four began to smile, the mood lightening as Peter continued, "So, seeing as I can't get rid of you silly sods, let's see if I can make the most of you. Tony, Alan, I want you both to go to the shotgun cabinet, you know the code. I want you to take a shotgun each, a belt of cartridges, at least twenty per man. From this moment on, until I say otherwise, it's operational tour rules – no one moves around here without a weapon close to hand. You're to treat anyone coming onto the property as strangers, no one is to come onto the farm without either myself or Elizabeth's say-so. Questions?"

Alan quickly cut in. "What about the police?"

"You're on private property, with the landowner's permission within fifty feet of the boundary. You'll be fine. Just don't point the weapons at them. Anyone else and you're cleared to use *minimum* force. The shotguns are for show only, unless you come under fire."

Now it was Tony's turn to cut in. "Under fire? You really think this could come to that?"

"I hope not, but we've got to prepare for the worst and hope for the best. Your job is to protect Elizabeth. If the farm comes under attack and you can't defend it, then leave it. It's not worth dying for. Get Elizabeth out of here and leave the farm. Oh, and if possible try to break open the stable doors and let the horses loose. I don't want them stuck inside starving if you leave."

Patch quickly cut in now. "What about your son and daughter? Where will they be staying?"

"It's okay, Morgan is away backpacking in Brazil for the next three weeks and Phillipa is in Liverpool at uni, they'll be safely out of the way for the time being."

All three nodded in understanding at what was being asked of them. Alan and Tony went into the house to get the shotguns. Patch went inside to load the bags into the boot of the four-by-four. Peter was walking back inside into his office when he heard the phone ringing on his desk. He arrived just as Elizabeth picked up the phone. "Hello, James, it's Elizabeth. Yes, yes, urgently, I'll go get him. Okay. Bye, James."

She stood up as he entered the room, pointing to the phone handset on the desk and mouthing, "James."

He walked past her giving her a peck on the cheek, "Thank you, darling," he said, picking up the handset.

"James, I take it then that we're still friends?"

The Chief of the Defence Staff was gruff and excitable.

"If you have an answer for what's going on right now, I'll have your bloody children. There are no communications currently existing between any departments. I can't get through to anyone and all the country's emergency lines are down. I can't even raise anyone on the 'bat phone'. So, Peter, over to you. I'm listening now. What's causing this, you mentioned this was just the beginning?"

Peter thought to himself, *Thank you, now we are getting somewhere*, as he replied,

"I'm sorry but I can't tell you over the phone. I've got my car and driver ready. If you give me the clearance to visit, I can be with you in an hour."

"Sod that," came the reply, "an hour's too long, I need you here within the next twenty minutes to brief me."

"James, I can't get there in twenty minutes. Even with a police escort it will take me forty."

"Well," the CDS replied, "looks like now I get to surprise you. There's an RAF Merlin already en route to your farm, should be there in the next ten minutes. Be ready to brief me in twenty. See you then."

And just like that the line went dead...

7

Out Of The Frying Pan

Mike had no way of knowing how long he had been there. He guessed it had been no more than an hour, but it could have been longer – his mind was playing tricks on him as the adrenaline rush of earlier began to fade away. Damn, he was thirsty, he thought, as he imagined a cold glass of something, the ice chinking and the condensation running down the glass. His arms and legs had begun to ache as the bruises and scrapes from the fight began to make themselves felt, and the left side of his face was bruised – he could already feel it swelling. He still tasted a little blood in his mouth from where the Corporal had back-handed him, but compared with his earlier fight it was nothing. The sweat on his clothes had cooled and dried, making his skin itch, but with his hands still plasti-cuffed behind him he was powerless to do anything about it.

He had been placed into one of the holding cells in the guardroom – a cold concrete room with a drab, faded yellow interior, complete with a buzzing fluorescent light that occasionally would blink off and on. He was in the centre of the room on a plastic chair with his hands tied behind his back and his ankles plasti-cuffed to the chair's legs. The plastic restraints were tight and Mike winced as they began biting into his skin. To ignore the pain, he tried to focus on what had unfolded as he looked straight ahead at the grey steel door with a small hatch in it. He had remembered being in this very room when he was younger, only then he had been a guard commander on duty and had brought a camp cot in here to get some sleep. There were no windows, and he had no idea if it was day or night outside as frustratingly, he wasn't able to look at his watch. His hands had gone numb, so trying to coax some feeling into them he began flexing his fingers, hoping the blood loss would somehow be minimised. He knew, though, that when the cuffs did come off and the blood flowed again he would suffer some very painful pins and needles in his hands and feet.

He could still remember as they'd brought him here, the sounds of the chaos and carnage going on as people screamed in pain, and shouting as they tried to make sense of what had happened. What would have been worse for them was that he already knew the phone lines were down, so when people had rung 999 expecting a calm, assured operator, they would have only had static and a cold dial tone. He knew that at the very least the camp would be expecting ambulances and a police presence to take charge, but how would the emergency services know about the attack? He hoped that whoever was in charge had been able to get the casualties the care they needed, and he thought back to the two young kids by the post office. Were they okay?, he wondered. Once this little hiccup had been resolved he'd ask about them.

As time went on the shouted orders became normal spoken words again and the sense of panic and shock in people's voices was being replaced with a degree of calm and measured thinking. Mike guessed that whatever was going on out there, someone was taking charge. That didn't mean he was any more relaxed though – he still had to try to get an audience with the CO and sitting here tied to this chair he wasn't going to achieve that. Where was Chris? he kept thinking. Surely by now Chris was wondering where the hell he was. He looked at the door and was almost willing Chris to come bursting through, all smiles, with a cold glass of water in hand.

Surprisingly he heard someone at the door, the heavy bolt being thrown back with a slam and the door opening with a creak, the hinges screaming for some WD-40. However, his hopes were dashed as it wasn't Chris. Instead, filling the doorway was Corporal Webber, the QRF commander from earlier. Mike had managed to look at his name tape as he had the blackened goggles removed after they frog marched him in, head pushed down. Corporal Webber had given Mike a few slaps to the back of the head outside the gate on the way in. Mike had noted that once he had been plasti-cuffed and blindfolded the slaps on the back of his head had increased, so clearly this guy was a very brave man, making the most of a detained subject. He remembered the Corporal chuckling as Mike had been led purposely into a wall head first, smacking his nose in the process, with blood freely running down his front. The Corporal's voice masked his malice as he sneered, "Oops. Sorry about that, mate, didn't see that there." It was this man who was now stood before Mike as he sat there staring back at the fleshy jowls of the Corporal's face which scowled, trying to intimidate him. Mike kept staring as he said, "I need to speak to Major Richards NOW!"

Corporal Webber just smiled then turned to someone Mike couldn't see and said, "Yeah, I apprehended him myself. He put up a bit of a fight, but I soon had him under control."

Whoever he was talking to was laughing, clearly buying the bullshit this guy was selling. Mike could hear the crunch of broken glass and the sounds of furniture being moved – it seemed that whoever was in the guardroom was trying to clean up or sort through the chaos that was in there. He watched as the chubby Corporal moved off to the side of the door and two people entered the room, each carrying a plastic poly propylene chair. Mike could see both were with the Royal Military Police thanks to their red berets and badges of rank. One was a Corporal the other a Lance Corporal.

They planted their chairs in front of Mike. The older of the two, the Corporal, had decided to put his backward, his legs astride the chair, his hands lazily lopping over the back. *Ah*, thought Mike, *he's going to be bad cop.*

"Guys, I need to speak to Major Richards immediately, I have information concerning the attack on the camp and possible future attacks. Can someone please get him, or at least inform him I'm being held here." Mike remained as calm and controlled as he could, trying to appeal to some measure of sense with these two men.

No one said anything. They both looked at him like he was made of stone. Eventually the RMP Corporal said in a broad London accent, "I'm thirsty. You thirsty?" He looked to his partner who said nothing. "Of course you are, it's bloody hot in here." He then turned to Corporal Webber at the door and said, "Excuse me, mate, can you get us two lovely cold glasses of water for me and my illustrious friend here." Mike watched as the overweight NCO wobbled his way from the door. Still nothing was said as all three men sat there staring at each other. About thirty seconds later the Corporal re-appeared carrying the water, eyes still glaring at Mike as he passed each soldier a glass. After they had taken the glasses he turned and left the room, no doubt to brag to some more mates about his conduct that afternoon. Meanwhile the two military policemen made a big show of slowly drinking from their glasses before putting them on the floor beside them. Eventually, after smacking his lips together with a big "Ahhh," the older of the two began to speak. "So we already know now that you speak English, and we've got a number of questions for you that we'd like you to answer. And depending on how fast you answer and how truthful you are, depends on how quickly you can get out of the room."

Mike leant forward slightly, feeling the plasti-cuffs biting into him. The little display of power he had just witnessed had angered him. He should be trying to explain the past hours' events, but something about this didn't seem right. They weren't recording the interview, there was no legal representation and why only a Corporal interviewing him? Why not a senior rank? Mike resigned himself to the fact these clowns were not there on official police business but were merely there to have some fun with him. Mike noted that both the RMPs had their name tapes removed, so all he could see was the rank on their slides.

"Aren't you going to at least introduce yourself? Doesn't a detainee – which I'm guessing I am now by that little display – get the opportunity to know who he's talking to?"

The Corporal leant forward as if to mirror Mike's movements and replied, "Why do you want to know who we are? You want to take us out on a date? All you need to know is that *we* are the people interviewing *you*."

"Okay," Mike replied, his tone icy, "I'm going to call you... Bad Cop, as clearly that's who you're trying to be, and your mate there, the lowly NCO, I'm going to call him... Shit Cop. Yes, Bad Cop and Shit Cop." Mike sat back, showing both men he was relaxed, although mentally he was far from it.

Both men looked at Mike, the senior of the two smirking. "That's not very nice now, is it, especially as all we want to do is be friends in here. How's the cuffs by the way? Hopefully not too tight?" His tone was far from sympathetic.

Mike sat stone quiet not saying a word. Bad Cop continued speaking slowly as if talking to a child. "I'm not sure if you're aware but one of us here is beginning to stink, and I think might be wanting a nice cold shower, a change of clothes and a lovely cold glass of something wet. Perhaps a water or maybe a beer."

Mike leant toward Bad Cop and said, "And you can make that happen, can you?"

Bad Cop leant backward, throwing his arms up in the air theatrically. "Of course! You tell us what we want to know, and we can all be friends. We like friends here. All we want to do is get along nicely. Don't we?" He looked sideways at Shit Cop. They really wouldn't be getting their own TV show with this performance. Mike noticed that Shit Cop said nothing, just stared back, clipboard in hand, pen poised to write. They were really trying to hammer home the intimidation.

"Okay," said Mike, "so ask away." It had to be better than just sitting here saying nothing, he thought, and besides, he had nothing to hide, he wasn't the enemy. Hopefully talking to these two clowns might help free up the problem. God, he thought, he really could do with a drink though.

The look of surprise on Bad Cop's face almost made Mike laugh as he was taken back by the answer. Clearly, they were expecting him to say nothing.

"Okay," he said, nodding his head. "So firstly, what's your name?"

"Mike Faulkes."

Mike saw that Shit Cop began to scribble intently.

"And where are you from, Mike?"

"Poole."

"And your friends earlier on, are they from Poole?"

"No, I only had one friend here today I was visiting, and he works in the ATDU."

Upon hearing this, Bad Cop raised an eyebrow. "ATDU? Does he now? And what does he do, this friend of yours in the ATDU?"

"He's the squadron commander. His name is *Major* Richards and he's the reason I'm here."

Again, the look of mock surprise on Bad Cop as he replied, "Of course he is, of course he is, he's the squadron commander of the ATDU." He turned to Shit Cop again, slapping his arm and forcing him to make a mistake as he hurriedly jotted down what was being said. Then he continued sarcastically, "Why didn't *we* think of that. This guy's innocent! It just so happens he comes here carrying Russian weapons and his mates are also heavily armed. Was that personal protection by any chance?" He raised a quizzical eyebrow.

For the next twenty minutes the questions kept coming at Mike thick and fast:

"What was your mission here?"

"Why did you attack the camp?"

"Why did your team leave you behind?"

"What have you done to the phone systems?"

"Why can't we call the emergency services?"

"Where would your team have gone after the attack?"

"Why were you at the phone box?"

To each question Mike kept repeating the same answer in as calm a voice as he could. "Just get Major Richards." The temperature in the room was climbing and Mike was finding it difficult to keep his cool, his anger slowly brewing away, aware that time was precious, and these idiots were wasting it. *Where the hell is Chris*, he kept thinking, surely he'd be looking for him by now.

Mike realised the conversation was always going to go back to the gunmen. Clearly these guys didn't believe him. He was about to say something when Bad Cop decided it was time to earn his Oscar. Suddenly bursting up from the chair, he flung it sideways, hitting the wall, his face red and angry. He got right into Mike's face.

"Right! Stop fucking us about. We know you were part of the team that hit us today, we've got witnesses that saw you firing on our men, and we've got witnesses who saw you running after the car. You were holding a weapon when we captured you, you resisted arrest and you're still talking this bullshit story. We've got three people – *three good people* – dead outside, and two others injured. Do yourself a *fucking* favour and tell me what your mission is. Who are you after? Where did your friends go? TALK TO ME!" he yelled, flecks of spittle hitting Mike.

Mike sat looking up, staring impassively back – inside he was raging, wanting nothing more than to shout at these two. But he knew these guys – no matter how amateur – had the upper hand. Losing his temper and shouting was going to get him nowhere. He closed his eyes, trying to bring some clarity to his thoughts, then opened them again. Thankfully Bad Cop had recovered his chair and sat back down. Speaking slowly and calmly Mike replied, "Okay, so have you seen how badly bruised my face is, do you think I tripped up on a kerb on the way here?"

This time it was Shit Cop who spoke. "We know how you got those injuries. Corporal Webber has already told us. Outside the main gate you put up a fight, he had to detain you and that's how you were injured."

"What?" exploded Mike, as finally he lost his cool, almost jumping out of the seat. The plasti-cuffs on his ankles bit into him and he fell back down. A reminder that he was powerless. He tried to control his anger as Bad Cop sat there smirking.

"You're not going *anywhere*, mate." His tone was menacing. They had control in the room, and they knew it.

Mike calmed his thinking, controlling his voice as he continued.

"I sustained these injuries fighting the same gunman as you, that's how I managed to get his pistol from him. If, like you say, I was one of them, then why no body armour, no assault rig, no extra magazines? All I had on me was one pistol with four rounds."

This time it was Bad Cop who answered, his hands cutting through the air. "Who knows? Maybe it was just a case of shit planning, maybe you forgot to get it out of the car, maybe your mates didn't like you and took your gear, maybe you're not as good as you think?" He finished the point with a raised eyebrow.

Mike continued unperturbed, "Look, I wasn't running to get into the vehicle, I was running to take a shot at the vehicle, but seeing as it was fleeing and no further danger, I held my fire. I was *not* apprehended or arrested, I ran to the front gate to check on Ted, the gate guard who died trying to save my life. He saw me struggling with the gunman and ran to help. It was this action that got him shot in the road – why would he have been out there otherwise, running toward a gunman whilst unarmed?"

Upon hearing this, Mike saw them both look at each other as if both thinking the same thing. Then it was Shit Cop who answered. "How do you know the name of the deceased? Was he your target all along?"

"Oh, for fuck,s sake!" Mike raged, losing his temper. He'd thought he might have been getting somewhere. His throat was dry and beginning to ache, he really wanted a drink. Fighting back the urge he continued. "Right, we can clarify this. Firstly, let's get the CCTV up, check it all out – you'll see I'm telling the truth and it will verify my story."

Bad Cop leant forward, hands resting on the chair. "Ah, but you see that's where we run into a little problem. You see, someone has hacked into our system, all the cameras right now are conveniently offline. Which means everything you've said cannot be proven. It's just your word, and that I'm afraid isn't worth much at all right now. I don't think you're understanding exactly how this works."

Mike could sense the condescending tone. He sat back before replying slowly, "Oh, but I know exactly how *this* works. You see, I was in the British army for eighteen years in the 24th Tank Regiment. Would you believe this is not my first time in this room? No more than fifteen years ago, I was actually sat in this very guardroom as guard commander and I used to sleep in this very room on a camp cot on the floor, just there, where your chairs are sitting." Upon hearing this, Mike noted both men seemed to sit up a little straighter as he continued, his voice calm now and matter of fact. "I've had my fair share of detainees and I know that you're supposed to offer them food, water, and a blanket when you first arrest them. I also know that they are not to be interrogated or talked to without a legal representative in the room." As if to illustrate the point Mike looked around the room, as if searching for such a person. Continuing, "I also know all forms of torture and intimidation techniques including stress positions are forbidden both by the Geneva Convention and by the European Court of Human rights. That means your little stunt with the water earlier could see you both arrested. Also, these plasti-cuffs – which I might add I've had on now for over an hour – are too tight and again illegal as they should have been removed the second you put me into this room."

Mike had noted that Shit Cop's face had a look of someone who was starting to realise they were out of their depth. But Bad Cop sat there looking unconcerned. *Damn*, thought Mike, he really was playing it cool.

Mike was about to continue when the Corporal smiled and replied with a flourish, "All right, so you know the rules, fair enough. The cuffs are staying on, though, because you're dangerous, and for my own safety and that of my colleague as I still deem you a threat."

"So I'm a threat," replied Mike, playing the Corporal at his own game. "Then why am I being interrogated by a mere Corporal and *Lance* Corporal? I know from previous experience that as soon as you pass out of training you're given your Lance Corporal rank. For all I know your colleague there could have joined yesterday. Not exactly the experience you'd need for this then, is it?"

Both sat there silent as Mike, now feeling invigorated, continued, his tone acidic and dry. "There's supposed to be a duty officer, at the very least it should be some young impressionable upstart wanting to make a name for his or herself. Why aren't they here? Instead, I get Bad Cop and Shit Cop – some brand-new lance jack, still wet behind the ears, and an underperforming Corporal who's probably showing off in front of his young impressionable partner. Now both of you are clearly after your own comedy show with this performance. But I'm afraid your only audience is me and I've got to be honest, guys, your material's starting to wear thin and is in need of a rethink."

"Actually, there's *two* in the audience."

All three looked up to the doorway to the stranger now stood there.

He was tall, over six foot, Mike guessed, and was wearing the uniform of an RMP Sergeant. He was lean, tanned and clearly didn't spend his time sat behind a desk. His hands were resting on his gun belt as if he was auditioning for a cowboy movie.

Oh no, Mike thought, *first Bad Cop, now Shit Cop and now here's the bloody Sheriff.* He wondered if all this was part of the act and waited with bated breath to see what would happen next.

Upon seeing the man in the doorway, both Shit Cop's and Bad Cop's' faces dropped. Suddenly Bad Cop stood up, trying to hide the surprised tone in his voice. "Sarge, erm, how long were you standing there for?"

The Sergeant didn't answer straight away. Instead, he looked past Bad Cop and nodded toward Mike before answering, "I've been stood there long enough. So, what's going on in here then?"

"We're just trying to clarify a few details; this man was one of the attackers from earlier. He's been brought in for questioning by us to try to clarify the facts before the police get here."

The Sergeant's hand reached out to Shit Cop, who stood up and handed him the clip board. He said nothing as he stood there reading the notes that Shit Cop had written down. Mike watched, wondering what the Sergeant was playing at. What angle was he trying to spin now? The look of surprise on the other two seemed genuine enough, so perhaps they really hadn't expected the Sergeant to come in and disturb them, thought Mike.

As he read the details on the clipboard, Shit Cop asked, "Sarge, do you know if there's any details yet on the police, has anyone managed to get in contact with them?"

The Sergeant merely looked up at him, then looked over to Mike. The subtle message was clear. *No talking in front of this man.*

As he continued reading, without looking up, the Sergeant asked, "Corporal, how long ago was this man detained?"

"We've had him here now for nearly two hours."

"And in that time have his restraints been removed at all? Has he been offered the use of the bathroom? Have you offered him *any* drink or food?"

The Corporal's eyes darted nervously about as he saw the Sergeant was now looking to the empty glasses by the chairs.

"Er, not yet, Sarge, he's been deemed a serious threat by the QRF commander. It was upon his recommendation that the restraints be kept on."

Upon hearing this the Sergeant looked directly at the Corporal, talking as if he was a teacher educating a student. "That's why you post an armed guard at the open door. If he tries anything, then the *guard* is there to stop him."

The Sergeant looked closely at Mike, asking, "How did this man get the cuts and bruises to his face?"

"When he was captured, he was resisting arrest, he put up a fight with the QRF commander who apprehended him."

"And since he's been in here, has he shown any signs of violence?"

There was a pause. The Corporal didn't know how to answer. Mike saw him look to his colleague for support before the Sergeant asked again, this time more forcefully.

"*Well?* Did he or did he not show any sign of violence towards you?"

"Er, well, no, Sarge. He just sat there and chatted to us. But his answers have been quite sarcastic – clearly, he thinks he's funny."

The Sergeant merely nodded in response as he resumed reading the report. After another minute, the Sergeant had seen enough. He looked at them both.

"Okay, why don't you two come with me and we'll have a little chat and then I'll be back shortly." He turned to Mike. "We won't be long I promise, and then we can clear all this up."

All three left the room and the door closed behind them, leaving Mike alone with his thoughts. After only two minutes the door opened again and this time the Lance Corporal RMP walked into the room. He walked behind Mike and without saying a word Mike felt the ties on his feet being cut. He looked to the doorway where the RMP Corporal was standing, hand on his pistol holster. The threat was clear to see.

The Lance Corporal pulled Mike to his feet and walked him out of the room and to the cell next door. His feet felt like they were going to explode as the blood rushed to circulate. After so long with the restraints on, the pins and needles began to take hold and the all too familiar feeling of dead legs began to appear. Mike was curious as to what was going on, clearly something had changed. Was this all part of the act? He really was confused, and a sense of dread began to creep up his spine. What if no one believed him? What if he was about to get carted away to a prison? He quickly wondered if he shouldn't try to escape. His feet were untied so at least he could run. Perhaps he could get himself out the door and through the guardroom. If he could get outside to speak to someone maybe this would all be sorted out.

He quickly realised, though, that his feet and legs were in no condition to run and as if to prove the point he stumbled as he walked, the Lance Corporal being forced to help him up. He also knew he wouldn't get far; he didn't know how many people were behind him in the guardroom and the last thing he needed was to give Corporal Webber an excuse to shoot him. He knew his only hope now was either that Peter would soon get to the camp to be able to clarify what had happened, or somehow Chris would find him. Now, he thought, both options were looking pretty slim.

Mike was walked into a neighbouring cell, an exact replica of where he had just been. Same paint job, same sickening fluorescent light that buzzed above his head, but this time there was a desk in the middle of the room with three chairs, two on one side one on the other. Mike was placed into the single chair that was facing the doorway. The plasti-cuffs on his hands were cut and his fingers suffered the same fate as his feet as at last the blood flowed back into them. He brought his hands forward from behind his back and looked at the cuts and welts as he began massaging his wrists. In the corridor outside the doorway stood the RMP Corporal 'Bad Cop' who had been questioning him earlier. He wasn't sure what had been said but he stood there now solid as a statue, staring straight at Mike, watching his every move through the open door.

Mike was beginning to get some feeling back into his feet and hands, as he continued his slow rhythmic flexing of his toes and fingers. After a minute he looked down at his watch. The time was 17:30. It had been nearly two hours since the attack on camp now. Surely Peter would be arriving anytime soon. As he wondered about his friend, the RMP Sergeant entered the room carrying a briefcase, followed quickly by the Lance Corporal from earlier. Mike noted that both had their berets on and the gun belts they normally carried were now missing. Both said nothing as they sat down, and Mike noticed this time everything seemed more organised and formal. The Sergeant opened the briefcase, pulling out a dictaphone, a folder, some pens, a bottle of water and a white piece of rag. He offered the water and rag to Mike who nodded in thanks as he quickly broke open the bottle. Careful to sip and not gulp the water, he sat there happily drinking, the water helping to clear the gravel he felt in his throat. Using the rag and some water he began to wipe away the blood from his face and began to feel slightly more normal again. Eventually the Sergeant, having finished arranging the items on the desk, sat the briefcase on the floor. Mike didn't want to get his hopes up but perhaps the Sergeant was going to be one of the good guys. It was the Sergeant who broke the silence.

"Right, Mike – you don't mind me calling you Mike, do you?" Mike replied with a quick nod as he continued drinking.

"Right then, Mike, I'm Sergeant Mahony. Firstly, I want to apologise for your treatment earlier, it was unacceptable and not how we should have done things. I was late getting here but now that I *am* here things will be done correctly and by the book. Hopefully between us we can clear up what happened earlier and if after everything's been said and done you want to lodge a complaint then I'll be more than happy to help you get that filed. Okay?"

Wow, Mike thought, *this is a change of direction. Perhaps now we can get somewhere.*

He nodded his head, "Look, I get things are up in the air at the moment and you guys are having to make the best of it. I know no phones are working and comms are down, but can I *please* get a message out to—"

Mahony interrupted with a friendly but forceful tone. "Mike, I know you want us to talk to this Major Richards, and we will, but first I've got to get the facts. So just help me now and I promise I'll get the message to him myself."

Mike knew he'd have to play ball; things had changed, and this guy was the key. If he just kept stamping his feet and demanding things, the shutters would close quickly on the shop and it would be back to Shit Cop and Bad Cop.

"Okay, ask away," Mike replied as casually as he could.

"Right, before we start – introductions. Myself you already know, my scriber here, who I believe you lovingly referred to as Shit Cop, is actually called Lance Corporal Reynolds."

Mike looked at the young Lance Corporal as he merely nodded at him. Sergeant Mahony then continued. "Moving on to Bad Cop, that's Corporal Stevens back there in the corridor. He will be acting as guard today should you try anything silly. I must remind you he is armed and will not hesitate to use lethal force should he feel your behaviour threatening." Mike looked up to Corporal Stevens as his name was mentioned. He stood there like stone, his eyes watching Mike like a hawk.

"I appreciate you don't have any legal representation at present, but with things being as they are, we can't get through to anyone, so if you're happy to continue we can carry on this interview, but I'll be recording it for legal reasons so everything you say can be played back if necessary. Again, on those two points are you happy to proceed? I appreciate it's not how things are usually done but I'm sure you want your side of the story heard and don't want to be detained any longer than necessary. Do you agree?"

"Look, I just want to clear up this bloody mess and be on my way, so let's just get on with it." Mike's tone was icy as he thought to himself, *Keep it calm, Mike, keep it calm, you need this guy on side.*

Sergeant Mahony pressed record, then placed the dictaphone in the centre of the table as he began the interview. He asked Mike to explain what had happened, and Mike brought him up to speed on everything from meeting Chris that afternoon to the events up to his detention. He left out the part about the Corporal being overzealous on his arrest because he didn't want to come across as bitter; besides, he'd deal with that another time.

All the while Mike was talking, even though the conversation was being recorded, Lance Corporal Reynolds was again back to scribbling in his notes, recording all of Mike's answers. Sergeant Mahony, meanwhile, was leaning back in the chair listening intently to what was being said, occasionally nodding in agreement or looking over to what his junior partner was writing down.

After he'd finished, Mike sat back in his chair watching the reactions of Sergeant Mahony. Did he believe him? he wondered to himself.

Taking a deep breath, Sergeant Mahony leant forward, his elbows resting on the table as he clasped his hands together, his chin resting on them. He was deep in thought looking at Mike, his eyes studying his face and his hands. Suddenly, as if making his mind up, he looked up to the doorway, shouting, "Corporal Webber!"

As if on cue the QRF commander appeared in the doorway. "Yes, Sarge!"

Sergeant Mahony stood up and walked toward the Corporal, pointing at Mike as he talked. "Corporal Webber, we've got a little bit of an issue here. I know you've already explained to us and my apologies for asking again, but in your own words, would you mind just repeating what you told us about when you came out of the gate and saw this man?"

Corporal Webber looked toward Mike, defiance in his eyes. "The suspect was caught outside the gate trying to rifle through the pockets of the victim. He had his back to us, and didn't see us coming. Between both myself and Trooper Murphy we captured him. He had tried to pull a pistol on us, which is how he ended up with his injuries, and the pistol has since been seized as evidence."

Corporal Webber seemed to stand a little taller after his statement, almost as if relaying it again had given him a confidence boost. He looked back towards the RMP Sergeant who was nodding his head in thought.

"And when you apprehended him, who made the pistol safe? When it was handed in to us the working parts were to the rear and the magazine unloaded. Did you do that?"

The Corporal looked up for a moment in thought before saying, "That was me Sarge, I unloaded it and left it outside the gate for the forensic team."

"And were you wearing gloves at the time?" Sergeant Mahony asked, his head cocked inquisitively.

"Er, no I wasn't, Sarge, I forgot to put them on. Sorry about that."

"Okay," again, the nodding head, "and when you say he got his injuries as you apprehended him, how exactly did they occur?"

"Sarge?" The look of confidence was quickly replaced by one of confusion, as the Corporal looked back at him.

"How *did* you apprehend him? I want to know exactly what happened when you approached him. You've already said he had his back to you. Did he turn to face you? Did you pin him to the ground? Help me to visualise it. Paint a picture for me." Sergeant Mahony's tone was quiet but his eyes bore into the Corporal as if he was trying to read his thoughts.

"Er, it happened really fast, Sarge, I don't remember much. One minute we were on the ground, fighting, and the next I had him secured."

Mike could see the Corporal had begun to sweat. Secretly he was enjoying the show. Clearly, Mahony was going somewhere with this and Mike was intrigued to see where.

"Okay, so you've got him on the ground, what kind of hold did you use? Was it an arm bar? Leg lock? Choke hold? What? You see, we're all taught arrest and restraint in our training, it's our job and it's hard to do. So how did *you* do it? You're not exactly looking match fit, are you?" Sergeant Mahony looked down to the Corporal's expanding waistline, as if to emphasise what he meant.

Corporal Webber's eyes darted between Mike and the Sergeant. *What is he thinking now?* Mike wondered. Mike had decided that despite the lies from the Corporal he would remain quiet. He wanted to see this play out further.

As if a sudden inspiration came to him, the Corporal blurted out, "The pistol! I'd taken the pistol from him and had it pointed at him. That's why he stopped fighting!" The look of triumph had returned to him.

"Ah." Sergeant Mahony replied as if all was clear. "The pistol – so now you've got the pistol in your hands, pointing it at our man here, and he, realising the pistol is pointing at him, stopped fighting and you've then detained him, am I correct?"

"Yes," he replied, nodding furiously as Sergeant Mahony continued, "So can I ask then why did you not use your own weapon? Why engage a man in hand-to-hand combat, who you can see is about to pull a weapon on you, especially when you already have your own weapon, an SA80 assault rifle? You could have simply stood back, issued a challenge and detained him. Why the need to get in close?"

Mike saw the confusion and nerves behind the man's eyes replaced by a flash of anger as he replied, "I'll say it again. It happened fast. Why didn't I grab my own weapon? I don't know – maybe I thought I'd be a hero for the day. What does it matter? I arrested him, and we got him back in here. Why are we making such a big deal of it? We've got one of the bastards and that's all that matters!"

"All right, Corporal, all right, calm down. I'm just trying to establish the facts, like you've already said we've got one of the bastards." His tone was soothing as Corporal Webber's face flashed red with anger.

"Didn't you say there was a Trooper with you? Another person who will confirm what you've said?" Again, Sergeant Mahony's tone was low and quiet, almost disarming, Mike thought.

"Trooper Murphy? Yes, he helped me bring this fucker in. He's already confirmed what I've said," the Corporal answered, still with a slight edge to his voice.

Sergeant Mahony turned to Lance Corporal Reynolds who was still recording the notes.

"Corporal Reynolds, I want you to go and find Trooper Murphy please, and bring him in here."

The young NCO put down his pen and paper and stood up as Corporal Webber quickly responded, "But Trooper Murphy is on the gate, Sarge, he won't be off for another two hours."

Without looking at him, Sergeant Mahony said, "If he's on the gate then get some-one to relieve him and bring him back in here. We're going to clarify a few things."

Mike looked on, watching in fascination as the mood in the room had turned. Could it be Mahony was beginning to believe him now?

As the Lance Corporal disappeared out of the room, Mike saw Corporal Webber's Adam's apple bob up and down as he swallowed nervously. All three men in the room said nothing as they waited for the new arrival. Mike took the time to again try to move his fingers and toes, the silence deafening.

Suddenly both men entered the room. Mike noted the young Trooper from earlier was sweating more than usual and his chest heaved as he looked around the room. He was still wearing his body armour, but his helmet and weapon had been left behind. Mike guessed it was sitting just outside on the floor. Trooper Murphy's eyes were darting all over and Mike knew he'd been lying to the RMPs and was clearly nervous of the truth getting out. Trooper Murphy went over and stood next to Corporal Webber as Lance Corporal Reynolds resumed his seat, pen poised ready for round three.

"So, Trooper... Murphy!" Sergeant Mahony began. "We're having a little bit of difficulty with establishing the facts. Corporal Webber says you were one of the first on the scene and that you were with him during the arrest of our... suspect."

As the Sergeant talked, Mike saw Trooper Murphy's eyes were darting between himself and Sergeant Mahony. Mike had guessed Corporal Webber had already briefed him of the story and that he was going to go along with it.

"However, before I ask you for your version of events, I just want to ask one simple question. Were you wearing gloves at the time of the incident?"

The Trooper, sensing a trap, looked first to Corporal Webber before replying, "No, Sergeant, they're back in my room."

"Why did you leave your gloves there? Why weren't you wearing them?"

The Trooper's face creased in confusion at the question and then he replied, "It's the summer, Sarge. It's hot as hell today – why would I need to wear gloves?"

The Sergeant nodded in understanding then stood by the table looking down to Mike as he continued.

"Okay, this is a question for *both* of you then. Perhaps you can help me understand. If you look at this man, you'll see grass and mud stains on his jeans and T-shirt. Do you both see?"

Both men's heads turned to follow the gaze of the Sergeant whilst Mike sat wondering where this was all going.

"Perhaps he doesn't have a washing machine?" The cockiness in Corporal Webber's voice broke through as he smirked. The look was quickly gone as Sergeant Mahony's head whipped round, unimpressed. He stared at the Corporal as he continued, his tone icy, "It's not this man's laundry habits I'm questioning... It's the integrity and honesty of both of *you* that I'm going to question."

"What?" the Corporal exploded. "You cannot be serious. Are you telling me that you're doubting our word, two serving soldiers over this piece of shit!"

Sergeant Mahony now stood imposingly over both men as he looked down, glaring at them as he replied, "*Piece of shit?* Interesting that you use those choice of words. Earlier you called him a bastard. Corporal Webber, if I didn't know better, I'd say you were judge, jury and executioner. He's already guilty in your eyes and you haven't even looked at the facts."

"What facts?" the Corporal spat out. "Seeing as you seem to know it all why don't you explain them to us?"

Sergeant Mahony, as if to defuse the situation, relaxed slightly, walking over to the other side of the room, leaning against it as he continued in a more relaxed manner.

"Firstly, this man has grass and mud stains all over his clothes from where he has been involved in a fight, clearly on a grassy area. The area where you apprehended him is concrete; a road. Why don't you both have grass and mud stains on your uniforms?" To emphasise the point Sergeant Mahony pointed at them both before continuing, "Also, his head, face, arms and legs are cut and bruised as if he's been in a bar fight. I don't know who he's fought with, but he wouldn't have knuckles looking like that if he hadn't got in a few hits himself. Whoever he hit would be marked up, showing an injury. But again, look at you two – fresh-faced as clean linen. There's not a scratch or bruise on you. If you had both been wearing gloves then I could understand the fact that your own knuckles were clean, but you weren't, like you've both already clarified – so how did this man get his injuries if both of you are stood there unmarked? Whoever he *was* fighting, it wasn't *you*. If, like you say, he resisted arrest, then I doubt you'd be looking like that. I've detained enough people in my time to know you *always* come away with something, especially when they're fighting you."

"But what about the pistol, he was going to shoot us?" Corporal Webber blurted out.

"Ah, the pistol, yes, I'm glad you mentioned that," replied Sergeant Mahony. "Yes, the pistol that you yourself picked up and used. Yes, the one that you handled without wearing any gloves. That's currently being processed and has been taken away for fingerprints. Naturally, seeing as you handled it, Corporal, and it was you who safely unloaded it, it will have your prints and DNA all over it. That should easily prove that part of the story. No doubt, though, I'm expecting it *not* to have your prints on it. I doubt you ever even went near it."

The Corporal said nothing, his face going red as his anger started to rise.

The Sergeant now stood in front of Corporal Webber, examining his face intently, his eyes scrutineering every detail of the red face sweating in front of him. He said in a menacing tone,

"When you arrested him, as you say you did, he had four rounds in the pistol, no extra magazines, no body armour, no assault vest, no assault rifle, no radio. Where do you think all that equipment had gone to? Seems strange to plan an attack with just one magazine on the pistol then simply come along with no gear, don't you think? Did your man here eat it perhaps on the way to the guardroom? Our witness reports stated that they saw the gunmen heavily armed and heard the suspects speaking in another language, possibly Russian. The pistol that we have, the one you supposedly handled is called an MP-443 Grach. It's a *Russian* pistol."

"Exactly!" shouted Corporal Webber, "a Russian pistol! Where the fuck did he get *that* from? Did he just buy that off Ebay, did he?"

The tension in the room had risen again as suddenly everyone was aware how hot it had become. The Sergeant and the Corporal continued to glare at each other until Sergeant Mahony smiled and stepped back. "Of course, I'm getting ahead of myself," he said almost apologetically, placing his hands on his hips. "How about instead of us going round and round in circles we just have a look at some footage?" He turned and went back to his suitcase on the desk and retrieved two mobile phones.

"Footage? What footage?" This time it was Trooper Murphy who quickly cut in. Corporal Webber was still glaring at Sergeant Mahony.

Still smiling, Sergeant Mahony placed two mobile phones on the desk. One had a cracked screen and looked damaged, the other looked to be in better condition.

"These were taken not long ago by two bystanders who were filming the attack. They reliably informed me that it also captures the moment when this man was detained by yourself Corporal Webber.

"Wait!" It was Trooper Murphy who interrupted.

He saw Trooper Murphy take a deep breath and was about to speak when the Sergeant interrupted quickly. "Trooper Murphy, before I forget, I must remind you that at present, your statement has not been signed by yourself. Therefore, it's not legally binding yet. If your recollection of events has changed since we last spoke, then now's the time to tell us. However, if I now watch this footage and *confirm* your statement to be false, then I'm afraid we can do nothing to help you."

The Trooper looked again at Mike, then at the Corporal. Mike could imagine the turmoil going on in his head as he was torn between telling the truth and not dropping his fellow soldier in it.

Finally, he took a deep breath, looked at Mike and it all came pouring out. "I'm so sorry, sir, it wasn't my idea. After you were gone, after Webber had taken you away, I was left outside guarding the gate. He came back after thirty minutes telling me what he'd told the others, what he'd already told the military police."

All eyes now turned to Corporal Webber whose face was red with rage. He suddenly launched himself at Mike, trying to get his arms around him, but even though Mike was sitting and appeared relaxed, he had been expecting it. He'd been watching the NCO's demeanour change and knew the fight or flight reflex would kick in. Some people would curl up and wish nothing more than to slink away. But the way the NCO had been glaring at him, Mike knew the fight option was on. Had Mike still been manacled to the chair then it would have been a nice cheap and easy attack, but Mike wasn't manacled, and his bonds had been cut. With speed that startled all those around him, he launched himself backward and sideways as the chair slid

121

across the room. Remembering one of his early lessons in Krav Maga, he ducked under the outstretched arms of Webber, watching as his mask of rage turned to surprise as his opponent swiftly sidestepped and his momentum carried him on and over the table, knocking over the dictaphone and briefcase. Mike was now behind his opponent and quickly dropped one arm under his neck and the other over his head, getting him into a full nelson, ensuring that Webber's arms were locked uselessly at a forty-five-degree angle, unable to do anything except flail aimlessly.

"Get off me you fuck. LET ME GO!" the helpless Corporal shouted through clenched teeth as Mike began to exert more force on the hold, forcing the Corporal's head into his neck, choking him.

Lance Corporal Reynolds had jumped up and taken a step back as the assault began. Meanwhile, Sergeant Mahony, as if also expecting the attack, merely stood watching on, amused, almost as though the whole scene playing in front of him was a show. Corporal Stevens, who was outside, pulled his pistol and was about to walk in when the Sergeant's arm shot across his chest in warning.

"Stand down, Corporal Stevens, it's all okay, I was expecting this to happen. No need for that."

With a look of bewilderment, the Corporal holstered his pistol and went back to standing guard.

Mike was now stood in the middle of the room with the Corporal in the submission hold, not sure what to do next. He'd expected the soldiers in the room to at least rush him, but instead, everyone stayed where they were, watching. Even the young Trooper Murphy was watching in fascination. Finally, it was Sergeant Mahony who broke the tension.

"Mike," he said, his voice soft and reassuring, "Mike, let the lad go, you've proved the point I was trying to make."

"That was self-defence, he was coming to attack me," Mike began to explain. "That's the only reason I did what I did."

The Sergeant's face seemed to soften. "I know, Mike, I saw the camera footage, I know what really happened. Just let him go now, okay?"

Mike could already feel the Corporal's legs going weak, so quickly released him, making sure he fell forward against the table, so as not to collapse in a heap on the floor. With a splutter and cough Corporal Webber began to suck in lungfuls of air as Mike moved back toward the far wall.

Still angry and red-faced, Webber pointed an accusing finger at Mike, tears welling in his eyes as he shouted out between breaths, "Did you see that? That was assault. He tried to *kill* me. I'm pressing charges, I want him arrested!"

No one in the room moved as the angry Corporal again spat out, "Didn't you *fucking hear me*? I want him arrested! You're a bloody policeman, arrest him!"

Sergeant Mahony looked disgusted as he watched Webber rage on in front of him. Eventually deciding he'd heard enough he said, "Corporal Stevens, Lance Corporal Reynolds, I want you to escort this *soldier* next door to the cell that Mr Faulkes has just recently come from. I'll be speaking to him shortly. For now, I want him placed under arrest for wasting police time and interfering with a police investigation."

The two Corporals stood on either side of Webber as he was walked out of the room continuing to shout and rage at Mike. "He's the one who's done this, he should be arrested. It's HIS FAULT!"

Mike heard the raging man's voice become muffled as the door to the cell was closed. He stared up at the Sergeant with a look of admiration on his face.

"I'll be honest, I didn't expect that. I was expecting you to be like the other two."

The Sergeant held up a hand to stop Mike as he quickly turned to face the Trooper. "Now, Trooper Murphy, I've not finished with you yet. I'm very disappointed in the way you conducted yourself. I appreciate you're a junior rank but even when things get tough you're expected to make the right decision. I'll chat to your Troop Sergeant later, but in the meantime get yourself back out on guard and I don't want you talking to anyone about what happened in here. Do you understand me?"

The Trooper, sweat running down his face, slammed his feet to attention, body ramrod straight as he replied, "Yes, Sergeant, I'm sorry, Sergeant. I didn't mean for it to get out of hand."

"Right, off you fuck then." Sergeant Mahony's thumb jerked toward the door as the soldier charged out of the room, picking his rifle and helmet up as he went. Only then did the Sergeant turn back to Mike.

He walked up to him and offered his hand to shake. Mike burst into a smile and gladly accepted as both men shook hands. "Mr Faulkes, I'm so sorry about all of that..."

"Please call me Mike," he quickly interjected.

"Okay Mike. Well, like I said, my apologies about all that, I just didn't want him in the room with us. Well, you're free to go. Major Richards is at the med centre."

"The Med Centre? Why there? Is he okay?" Mike asked, confused.

"It's where we've sent our casualties from the attack. So far, no one's picking up the calls on the emergency lines, so we've taken all the wounded and dead to the med centre. Major Richards had been told that there were three dead from the attack at the front gate. I think he thought you were one of them. That's where I was when I bumped into him and that's how I was able to get the phone footage. We both watched you take on that gunman and then get arrested. He told me to come to the guard room and get you out, hence, I turned up when I did."

"Hang on," replied Mike, finally understanding. "Are you saying you knew I was innocent right from the get-go? And that all that bullshit of an interrogation was just for show?"

The Sergeant put his hands up in mock defence. "Hang on now, first and foremost I'm military police and I had two soldiers accusing you of something that I couldn't just overlook. You might be friends with Major Richards, but I don't know you from Adam. I had to see for myself, and like you say, the evidence just didn't stack up. Besides, after seeing and hearing how you disarmed a Russian agent I knew you'd be able to handle yourself."

"So, my knight in shining armour turned up on an old three-legged nag with a broken sword and forgotten shield?" Mike stated with a smirk. "This bloody army never changes!"

Both men smiled, happy for the tension to finally be over.

"Right, I need to be going, I've got to find Major Richards. Thanks again for getting me off the hook." With a quick nod and a smile he turned and left the room.

8

Foot in the Door

Mike walked back outside, passing three soldiers inside the guardroom who were tidying up, seeing the devastation that the attack had left behind, a far cry to the usual order and military cleanliness of the room. Coffee cups were spilt on tables as their owners had dived for cover, there was shattered glass and large splinters of wood where bullets had torn through the walls. Mike realised with a heavy heart that there was a lot of blood, clearly the guardroom had borne the brunt of the attack and perhaps it was luck that only three people had died. Suddenly the welts on his wrists and feet didn't seem so bad after all.

He walked to the main gate and with the low sun still shining bright on his face, he looked at the scene before him. At the main gate, the barrier down, he saw Trooper Smith, the young Trooper they had seen earlier in the day. This time the young Trooper was alert, standing guard in full body armour and helmet, his SA80 carbine held ready across his chest. Mike glanced over at the remains of the booth where he had seen the guard's body. Thankfully the body had been removed, but the glass and blood had remained, yet to be cleaned up. Outside the main gate the road had been cordoned off in both directions, with mine tape stretched across both sides fluttering in the cool breeze. Two more soldiers in full body armour and carrying carbines, stood guard on both sides of the cordon. A crowd of perhaps twenty people had gathered, some had mobile phones out recording what was going on and some were filming themselves, no doubt ready to post their latest adventure or news story online when the internet came back on.

Mike's gaze settled on the red phone box and then up to the post office, the windows shattered and crazed. He remembered the two teenagers who had been stood there filming when the rounds came at him. He turned, walking back toward the Trooper, slowly stretching his arms out, trying to relieve his protesting muscles after his arrest. Mike stood in front of him, casually leaning against the guard booth, his feet crunching on the broken glass. "Up there at the post office," he said, pointing in its direction before continuing, "there were two young lads. It looked to me like they were injured. Do you know if anyone has brought them in? Are they okay?"

The Trooper looked past Mike to where he was pointing before looking back at him. "Sir, the two boys were taken with the rest of the casualties to the medical centre on camp. From what I saw there were just cuts from the glass, no bullet wounds." Mike responded with a nod then turned to look back at the road before asking, "I take it there's still no response on the emergency services? No ambulances or police here? Guess that's why all the casualties are at the med centre?"

Mike already knew the answer, but he wanted to hear it again.

"No, sir, no one's picking up the phones, so far as I know. We've three dead, two wounded, all being treated at the med centre. The on-duty doctor has sent someone in a car to Weymouth Hospital to see if we can flag down an ambulance but that's all we can do."

Mike turned to face the Trooper again, replying, "Three dead? I know the two guards were killed, but who was the third?"

"One of the guys from the guard force. We were just sitting down to watch a movie when the gunfire..." Mike could hear his voice trail off and the Trooper's gaze began to wander, his thoughts becoming clouded. Clearly this lad had known the dead soldier and Mike didn't want to push him any further.

He put his hand on the young lad's shoulder and said in a soft voice, "Hey, it's okay, it's okay, I understand. I'm sorry to have asked."

The Trooper looked up, nodding in thanks, before his jaw hardened and his serious look returned. Ever the professional, he resumed his duties, looking out over the main gate.

Mike turned to cross the road. As he did so he saw Chris emerge from the side road, walking at a brisk pace toward the guardroom. He looked up and saw Mike, his face instantly splitting into a huge grin.

Mike crossed the road toward him and they embraced. Chris was clearly happy to see his friend again. After what seemed like a longer than usual hug, Mike had to fight to release his friend's bear-like grip. "Hey, what's up? Bit late for a bromance isn't it?"

"I thought you were dead!" he replied, his voice almost choking up. Chris quickly explained that after the gunfire they had all come running out of the office to see what was going on. Seeing Mike missing, Chris had asked the secretary where his friend had gone. She'd told him of Mike's message about going outside of the camp gates which was exactly where the gunfire had been. Then Chris told him of the hammer blow when he had heard three people were killed and two injured, and his friend was missing. Upon hearing all the casualties were being held in the med centre, Chris had spent the past two hours bullying and shouting his way inside, trying to find Mike. Eventually he'd been chatting to Sergeant Mahony who had been sent to collect evidence from two witnesses, which were the same two teenagers Mike had seen in the gunfight by the post office. Ironically it was their mobile footage that had not only acquitted Mike but also showed Chris what Mike had been through. It was at Chris's request Sergeant Mahony had been sent to the guardroom.

"If you were over at the med centre then how the hell did you know I was being held at the guardroom?" Mike asked, puzzled.

"Because luckily for you Trooper Smith recognised you from earlier." Mike followed Chris's outstretched arm as it pointed over to the young Trooper he had spoken to earlier. "He came running over to find me, to let me know the man I had been with earlier had been accused of being one of the terrorists. Apparently, you kept shouting my name out to anyone who'd listen. I was going to go myself when Sergeant Mahony volunteered to go, just in case you were the third victim lying on the slab. Where is he, by the way? I take it he found you?"

"Yes, he found me all right, and he did get me out, in his own weird way. Next time, though, I'd settle for a stick of dynamite or maybe a cake with a file?"

Chris looked confused, waiting for Mike to explain. Eventually his friend just broke into a grin. "Come on, I'll tell you later. In the meantime, I've got to speak to the CO."

"Well, that's just as well because the CO has seen the phone footage and heard about what you've done. He's called a meeting with all the department leaders and wants to hear it from the horse's mouth, he's demanding we go straight there."

"Good – you lead the way, dear sir, and I'll happily follow."

Chris looked his friend up and down, taking note of his appearance. Mike had dried blood on his hands, his hair was all on end and sticky, his face dirty and bruised and his clothes were covered in dirt. After a quick ten-second appraisal he asked, "Wouldn't you rather get yourself cleaned up first? You're not exactly looking tip-top?"

Mike clapped his friend on the shoulder and said, "Time and tide, mate, time and tide," before turning to walk, his friend following by his side. Both men walked at a brisk pace down through the camp and back toward the headquarters building they'd visited earlier. As they walked, Mike filled Chris in on the events of the past few hours, telling him about the phone box, the strange man who attacked him, the attack on the camp and his detention right up to when Sergeant Mahony had him released. As he was finishing Chris asked, "And you've really no idea why this guy just attacked you?"

Mike's face became strained as he answered, deep in thought. "I've got an idea as to why, but I'll tell you when we get in with the CO, speaking of which, has Brigadier Rawlinson turned up yet?"

Chris looked at his friend with a quizzical look on his face. "No, why would he turn up here?"

"I'll tell you in a second." With that, both men became quiet as they approached the headquarters building. Mike was expecting there to be a flurry of activity around the camp but even with everything that had gone on, he had counted no more than twenty people walking or running around the vicinity.

Again, Mike found himself sitting in the waiting room of the Colonel's office, but this time his friend was next to him. He was aware of the secretary's eyes boring into him as she took in his appearance. Clearly, he'd left looking like some kind of normal and now here he was after everything that had gone on, looking like some homeless guy Chris had dragged in off the street. He had been tempted to go to the washrooms to try to clean up, but the last time he had left the office he nearly didn't make it back. Besides, knowing what he knew he just wanted to pass on the message and then wait for the Brigadier to arrive.

After no more than a minute the CO's door opened, and a man stood in the doorway wearing the rank of a Captain and ushered them both in. Mike noticed the Captain give a disapproving look as he took in the state of his appearance, but

Mike could do nothing about that so instead smiled and winked at the Captain as he passed. They entered a wide-open office with a large oak desk at one end with the other end dominated by a ten-seater round conference table. Two large windows were open that allowed light to spill into the room and even though it was almost 18:30 the sunlight spilling through was more than enough to ensure the room was well lit. A gentle cooling breeze passed through the office and Mike shivered slightly at the temperature drop as he walked in. Of the ten seats available at the conference table, seven were taken, and Mike saw the CO sat down, deep in conversation with a Major. The others at the table all looked at Mike with an amused merriment, Mike feeling conscious of the fact he was dirty. He did stink, he really should have taken a shower, but he quickly pushed all thoughts of vanity aside because he was here to deliver a message and that was all that mattered.

After a few moments the CO looked up and motioned for Mike and Chris to sit in one of the empty chairs. Mike sat down with Chris next to him looking round the room again as he took a deep breath, conscious of how he must look to these people. Finally, the Captain, who Mike guessed was the adjutant – the Colonel's right-hand man – sat down last. It was the Colonel who started off as he addressed the room, his face stern and his tone solemn.

"Good afternoon, ladies and gentlemen, I appreciate you all being here now. I understand it's summer leave and some of you had plans. But given what's gone on earlier I know you'll understand. I know some of you are not head of your departments and we are trying to contact them, but for now we will go with what we have got. So, I've called everyone in this afternoon to brief you all on the events that happened today and for us to try to figure out what's going on. Is this the worst of it or can we expect more attacks?" The CO paused as he looked at Mike then continued, his tone calm and authoritative. "The gentleman that has just joined us was on camp today as a guest of Major Richards. His name is Mr Mike Faulkes." The CO paused again as Mike looked around the room nodding to everyone assembled. He quickly noted as the CO continued speaking that there were two Sergeant Majors, three Captains and a Major all looking at the hobo in the room. As if almost reading the room the CO continued, "Now you'll have to excuse his appearance, he has only just recently returned from the guardroom after helping with their inquiries there. For those of you that haven't made the connection yet, Mr Faulkes was the gentleman in the footage we saw earlier fighting off one of the gunmen."

Some of those at the table nodded their heads in acknowledgement, as Mike looked to his friend who just sat looking back at him. Mike was trying the read the room, to think about how best to relay the message he had. If he got this wrong, he'd be bounced out of the room quickly. He sat, waiting for his moment.

"Now for those that don't yet know, unfortunately we've had three people killed in action and a further five wounded." The Colonel looked across to the Captain who Mike had winked at earlier before asking, "Adj, do you have any updates from the med centre?" 'Adj' was the nickname most Colonels had for their adjutants – Mike had been right, and he quietly congratulated himself.

Mike saw the adjutant look across to him quickly before replying, "Umm, Colonel, I appreciate this man is here to talk about the events earlier, but is this really something that we want to discuss in front of him?"

The CO looked to Mike for a second, his gaze questioning as he replied, "No, it's okay Adj, what you're all not aware of is that this is the man that Major Richards had mentioned to us last week, to work in the ATDU. If you remember, we've already granted him the security clearance he needs. Besides, after what I saw earlier, I think he deserves the right to sit in on this. He stays for now."

Nodding, the adjutant continued, "Very well, Colonel, anyone that was involved in the incident has been brought to our med centre. So far, of the five wounded thankfully three of those are minor, two were glass cuts and one was a lady that had collapsed due to shock. The two that are more serious suffered gunshot wounds but are stable, and Captain Phillips, who's assumed the role of chief medical officer, assures me that – providing we get them to hospital within the next four hours – they should be okay. We've asked that anyone in the area with blood type 'A negative' report to the med centre to donate blood, as that's what both casualties require. However, we still have a med centre full of people that we need to get to the hospital. So far, all attempts to contact the emergency services using the phones and radios have failed and as a last resort we've sent a driver to Weymouth Hospital to try to get the message to them. Hopefully we should get some kind of response within the hour."

The Colonel nodded in thanks as he then continued, his voice loud, "So now we all know what the butcher's bill is. Now, I want to know who attacked us and why. We're still waiting for the police to turn up, take control of the scene, but until that happens, I'm not going to sit here letting the grass grow under us. At present Captain Reynolds and her team have secured the scene and are taking witness statements ready to handover to the police. Captain Reynolds, do you have anything to add?"

Mike looked over to the second Captain, noting her RMP beret on the desk in front of her. She brushed some wisps of brown hair from the front of her face as she looked sternly around the table, her eyes fixing on Mike. "At present, Colonel, we're still looking into why the CCTV and phone systems are down. I've currently got WO2 Yackers from the Signals wing helping us, but we think the problems are more widespread."

Mike noted that one of the Sergeant Majors who looked up had the name Yackers on his name tape, so he was the man in charge of the Signals wing, he thought to himself. He made a note in his head to remember his name as he poured himself a glass of water from the bottle on the desk. His mouth had gone dry again as the RMP Captain continued.

"I've got one of my most senior Sergeants at the guardroom who's leading the investigation there. I believe, Mr Faulkes, you've already met him?"

Mike was midway through a sip of water when he quickly countered, "Yes – Sergeant Mahony – interesting character." He looked up to the Captain, seeing the glint in her eye. Clearly Sergeant Mahony had briefed her before the meeting on his earlier encounter. She smiled and said, "Sergeant Mahony has taken charge of the scene at the main gate and has a cordon in place. So far, we've recovered shell casings, tyre prints and a pistol which has been bagged for forensics. Access to the camp via the main gate will be limited for now and the main road going through Bovington will cause problems as we are having to divert traffic around the scene. Obviously, we've got limited resources here and a small team, but we're making the best of it and I'm confident the police will turn up in the next hour or so to take the scene off our hands."

"Thank you, Captain Reynolds." The Colonel looked toward Warrant Officer Yackers, his eyes narrowing. "Communications? Do we know why we have no comms or CCTV yet, or why the defence intranet is down?"

The Sergeant Major cleared his throat before replying in a broad Yorkshire voice.

"Last reports were that all of Dorset is experiencing phone and internet issues regardless of their network, so that may not be related to today's attack. Instead, it could just be poor timing for us which would explain the civilian networks also being down. As for the military intranet, I've tried all landline numbers and VHF and HF comms and nothing's going out or coming in. I've even tried to raise the police using their own HF radio frequencies. Something's stopping the signals dead. If I had to guess, I'd say there's some kind of interference causing it. Whether or not it's intentional, though, I can't say. I've not experienced both the civilian and military systems going out at once. We're still investigating, though, and will keep at it."

"At this rate we'll be back to bloody signal flags and carrier pigeons!"

The Colonel looked over to the person who had just spoken out – a large barrel-chested man with a deep booming voice. Quietly confident, Mike knew he was looking at the Garrison Sergeant Major, or GSM as he was called, probably one of the most influential men on the camp. It was the GSM who had nodded to Mike when finding out about the phone footage. "Okay, so regards security GSM how are we looking, are both camps secure?"

"Both camps are secure, sir. We've increased the guard force on the front gates and all civilian guards have been stood down and replaced with armed soldiers in full body armour and helmets. The alert level on the camp is now at Red and the Quick Reaction Force has been bolstered with the standby QRF. We did have some problems, I'm afraid, in trying get hold of duty personnel, what with the phones being down, and with it being summer leave, but as it stands, we currently have full manning on all gates. The problem is though, there's not enough manpower to rotate the guard force through to rest, and until the police arrive, I need every swinging dick on the gates. I've got my NCOs grabbing people as they see them, but the camp's empty as you know, sir. The recruit barracks at Stanley has fifteen recruits who haven't gone yet, so I'm getting them brought here shortly and Major Richards has some of his guys here from the ATDU who I was hoping to utilise, with his permission?"

All eyes were now on Chris as he raised his eyebrows in return. Mike watched his friend closely, seeing the familiar look as Chris rubbed his nose with his fingers as he thought of how he should respond. Mike knew the GSM had asked for the manpower, making it sound like a request, but he knew full well that if Chris refused, the CO would simply step in and take them from him. If a GSM or RSM asked for something in the army, it was rarely refused. Chris took a breath as he looked over to the CO. "Colonel, I take it we are suspending all training and trials for the time being, until this matter is resolved?"

"Yes, I think the priority for now will be on keeping the camp secure until this has been resolved."

Chris turned to the GSM who was still waiting for the answer. "In that case, GSM, I'll turn my guys over to you. But can I please ask that they be given an hour to get back to their rooms and get some extra kit for doing the duty tonight? Some of them won't have any warm kit or wash kit."

The GSM nodded in acknowledgement as he replied testily, "Don't worry *sir*, I'll make sure your lads and lasses get time to dap away and get their make-up bags."

Mike looked at his friend as he saw Chris's cheeks colour slightly at the barb. *Do these two have history?* he wondered. Chris smiled and sat back, choosing not to rise to the bait. To break the silence the CO continued, his eyes scanning the faces around the table.

"Good, so security is now taken care of. I think we'll keep the camp at a heightened state of alert for the time being, as long as we have the manpower to do so." Mike saw everyone nod in agreement.

The Colonel now looked over to Mike.

"So, this is now where you come in, Mr Faulkes."

All eyes turned to Mike as the Colonel addressed him. "At this moment you're our star witness. We've seen the phone footage, you were outside the camp and had an interaction with one of the gunmen. What happened? Did you suspect them? Why did you tackle one to the ground?"

Okay finally, Mike thought, as he swallowed. He reached forward to pour another glass of water, offering Chris one in the process before he sat back, taking a sip. Everyone was patiently waiting for him to speak. The last thing he needed was a dry throat, especially now as his most important moment was about to begin. He looked at the Colonel and as seriously as he could said, "Colonel, I know why they attacked the camp, I know why you're having communication problems on the camp and I'm afraid to say I also know this won't be the last of it. There are more attacks to come."

Mike could see everyone at the table stiffen slightly as he said this, and people seemed to sit up straighter. He dared not look at his friend Chris, whose eyes he could feel burning through him.

Mike took a deep breath, calmed his nerves, and then prepared to put his head into the tiger's mouth.

9

The Eagle

Colonel Yuri Golgolvin's eyes opened slowly to the sunlight that had beamed through the viewing window onto his face. Like a spotlight focusing its beam on his cheek, it kept up its relentless assault, forcing him to sit up, his back against the fuselage, trying to get some measure of comfort. He knew he would not get any sleep, even though he tried. His mind was just too focused on what was to come. The smells within the fuselage were a mixture of aviation and diesel fuel, weapon oil, sweat and flatulence. Annoyed at his discomfort, he stood up and began to walk his way forward along the cargo bay, testing his footing cautiously, leaning against the pallets of equipment, as the floor was littered with the bodies of his sleeping men.

He heard a curse and muttered shout, as his foot connected with someone's arm, but it was soon forgotten as the soldier fell back into his deep sleep. Golgolvin smiled. At least someone was able to sleep, though he saw some of his men were awake, going through the routines that soldiers did before a battle. Some were gathered in small groups, laughing and chatting to each other, others were checking and rechecking their equipment and weapons, whilst some merely sat, headphones in, listening to music or watching a movie on a small screen, their faces glowing like devils in the fading light. He smirked to himself as he thought of that description. *Devils in the night* – yes, that's exactly what his men were and he knew soon their enemies would see for themselves that these men had earned and deserved that name.

Golgolvin's eyes were drawn to a flashlight at the far end of the fuselage, dancing in the dim light, and he watched as it came closer, lighting the vehicles, the equipment and men that were scattered all over. As it got closer, he shielded one eye from habit, his gun eye, and cursed as the owner shone the light into his face, his hand knocking it away irritably. He saw in front of him one of the crew chiefs of the aircraft, dressed in full combat gear and wearing a headset. He leaned forward, pulling his ear defence temporarily away from one ear as the loadmaster attempted to shout over the incessant noise of the engines to be heard.

"Sir, you're wanted in the cockpit!"

Golgolvin merely nodded, as he prompted the loadmaster to lead the way, thankful now of the torch shining his path.

With the loadmaster in front, both men walked through the cavernous hold of the Antonov AN124, one hand resting on the fuselage and the other on the cargo as they walked past more sleeping bodies. Golgolvin looked up at the size of the plane as they walked, marvelling at how something so big could get itself into the air. He remembered quickly the brief that the ground crew had given him and his men before they had boarded. It was a four-engine monster, weighing in at one hundred and eighty-one tonnes, but the most impressive thing was the weight it could carry, almost one hundred and fifty tonnes. At that weight the plane could carry nearly three of the newer T-14 Armata tanks and it was rumoured that this very aircraft had helped to carry some of the best singers and equipment around the world on their tours. Gladly, though, he thought to himself, the plane was back to its real purpose – as a strategic heavy lift transporter, and he and the three hundred men of his battalion were the passengers. They were on their own world tour, with only one destination, and the music they were to play would be sung by their own vehicles and weapons. And how the audience would roar.

He chuckled to himself at his thoughts, as they came to the front of the plane, where there was more space. Leaving the loadmaster behind, he began to climb the long ladder leading to the upper deck area, with steady hands and looking up as he had been taught, towards the small hatchway. Once on the upper deck, he had to duck his head as he walked through the narrow aisle that led into the cockpit area, passing a rough wool curtain that separated the cockpit from the rest of the aircraft. It was here that he always appreciated the size of the plane as he walked into the long, office-spaced cockpit. The cockpit layout allowed for six flight crew with two pilots up front. Behind them, seated on either side of the cockpit, were the four other flight crew. These seats, however, faced sideways, allowing the crew to operate and watch the huge array of equipment and dials that were mounted, running the whole length of the cockpit.

The last seat on the left was usually reserved for the radio man but on this flight it was empty as they had no need for this member of the crew. Golgolvin steadied himself with one hand on the back seat as he removed his ear defenders with his other hand. As he did this, the noise of the cockpit came bursting through, the steady whine of the engines and a mechanical humming noise as the air conditioner and hydraulic pumps worked to help keep the massive plane in the air. The noise was short-lived though, as he then picked up the headset from the back of the chair, careful so as not to accidentally press any of the buttons. He placed it on his head, adjusting it for comfort as he moved the mike boom to his mouth. Once happy, he looked to the front of the cockpit, seeing only the backs of the pilots.

"Major, you wanted to speak to me?"

The right-hand pilot looked round and, seeing Golgolvin, nodded and adjusted his own boom mike to put it closer to his mouth before replying. "Good evening, Colonel, you wanted to be informed when we were about to cross the threshold. We're about five minutes out. Would you like to come look at the view?"

Curious as to what the pilots wanted him to see, he moved forward, resting his hands on the two other seats either side of him, making sure to drag the headset cable with him. It stretched across the back of the navigator, who, uncomplaining, lifted it up and over his head, to rest on the desk in front of him as he continued to closely monitor his displays, plotting and checking the course of the aircraft minute by minute. One of the most important parts of the mission was about to begin and they could ill afford any mistakes.

Golgolvin stood between the pilots' seats, looking out of the forward cockpit windows, the sun dipping low in the sky to the west as he watched what he thought was one of the most amazing sunsets he'd ever seen as it slowly bowed its head and made its exit, dipping below the horizon, the vibrant colours of red and gold flashing across the sea below them. Although a military man born and bred, Colonel Golgolvin had learnt that while his job called for violence and destruction, that didn't mean he couldn't appreciate peace and beauty, and what he witnessed with the going down of the sun was beautiful. He felt a surge of nostalgia as one of his childhood memories came to the fore. He remembered as a boy, sitting in his parents' house beside a

Siberian lake with his father, watching the sun set as they fished. He smiled at the thought of his father – he would be proud of his son today, now the Colonel of an elite parachute regiment, on a mission that would bring honour and pride to his family's name.

He clapped the pilot on the shoulder in thanks, grinning as he then asked, "Nothing new to report? No changes?"

"No, Colonel, so far, so good. We're about twenty miles north of the Scottish FIR (Flight Information Region), our friends in the back are doing all the talking at the moment. I'm just listening in and following the instructions. It's not quite as exciting as when we used to do this with the bombers back in 2016. But if this works, we'll never have to worry about that again."

Golgolvin nodded and grinned as he said his goodbye and turned to leave. He removed the headset and replaced it on the chair, before moving back through the curtain and into the corridor again. Instead of turning right towards the hatchway leading to the lower deck, he now continued into another area. In peacetime it would be used as the passenger deck, allowing up to eighty-eight people to sit in relative comfort above the huge cargo area. Today, half of the seats were removed, allowing another large area that was now full of extra equipment and electronics. Along one wall of the fuselage a bank of computer screens sat, with three people busily working, typing into keyboards and monitoring the displays watching the flight's progress. The Colonel had not attempted to try to guess what it all did. All he knew – all he needed to know – was that at that moment, everything, the whole plan, depended on the three operators who were sat there. When they had boarded the plane five hours ago, he had been under strict instructions that only he was allowed into this area, and that he was not to interfere in any way with the men there. Their mission was to get his men safely to their destination. There was a fourth seat that was empty for the Colonel. He sat down, placing another headset on, allowing him to now talk to the other three.

"So how goes it? Any updates? We're still flying so I'm guessing what you're doing is working?"

Without taking his eyes from the screen the operator closest to him responded flatly.

"Apologies, Colonel, just give me a second."

Golgolvin felt an instant spike of anger, not used to being dismissed in such a way. He was tempted to pull the wiry man out of the chair but quickly held his temper in check – he needed these three to be level-headed. That was the reason they were cocooned up here, out of the way of his own men. The next hour was extremely important, not only to them but to the other planes that were following. He sat back and waited as he looked around the passenger deck, thinking how much smaller it looked compared to the lower decks, but less crowded. He was still happy to be below, though, cramped as it was – he was with his own men, his own kind, but he felt a certain degree of disgust that these men were up here in relative comfort whilst his own men were confined below.

After a minute the operator stopped what he was doing and turned to face him.

"Hello, Colonel, I'm Major Pavitch, Electronics Wing Officer, and yes, it's all going well."

"I'm curious, but how exactly is this all working? How are you able to get us to our target?"

Major Pavitch creased his eyebrows together. "You mean no-one has told you?"

Golgolvin said nothing but raised his eyebrows in response, and the Major continued flatly, "So far, our flight plan has us filed to fly from Reykjavik to Heathrow, which will hopefully allow us entry to UK airspace shortly. We're logged into the NATS system as an Air Iceland flight, a cargo 747, so if any other pilots do see us in the meantime from a distance that's what they'll think." Golgolvin now remembered seeing the strange paint scheme as they had boarded earlier. Now it all made sense as the Major added, "The sun should be setting now, so as we start to fly over land, people on the ground won't see what or who we really are."

"How are you able to convince the people on the radio you are who you say you are? Do you speak Icelandic?"

The Major smiled as he replied, "No, Colonel, for that we have a little trick. One that I'm happy to demonstrate in one minute. Would you like to listen in?"

His anger now tempered, and his curiosity piqued, he nodded as the Major continued. "Okay, Colonel, you'll be able to hear, but whatever you say on the microphone will only come through to my headset. Please, though, don't say anything until after I've finished."

Golgolvin nodded as he watched Major Pavitch now begin to type away onto the keyboard quickly, the sound in the headset being replaced by the sounds of a busy channel. He could hear the constant chatter of the pilots in English, a language he himself had studied when he was younger. The pilots were talking quickly but he managed to understand the majority of what was being said.

"Speedbird One-Eight-Nine, Prestwick Centre, continue on course IFR to Newark, heading two-nine-zero, altitude three-two thousand. Over."

"Continue on course IFR to Newark, heading two-nine-zero and altitude three-two thousand for Speedbird One-Eight-Nine. Out."

"Delta Air One-Six-Seven, descend and maintain flight level two-six thousand."

"Two-six thousand for Delta Air One-Six-Seven."

Golgolvin sat listening in for a minute as various aircraft received orders on their flight paths, amazed at the speed at which the pilots were able to talk to each other. He felt a tap on his arm, and he looked up into the excited face of the Major as he pointed to his radio headset and mouthed, "This is us!"

Suddenly, he heard a broad English accent with a hint of Icelandic in it. *"Good evening, Prestwick Centre, this is Icelandic Air One-Three-Seven, IFR to Heathrow, flight level three-four thousand, heading one-six-zero, speed two-four-five. Over."*

Golgolvin was impressed at the accent but also confused, as when he had heard the voice coming over the headset he'd looked over to the operators and saw none of them were speaking. Who was speaking to Prestwick Centre? He thought for a moment and was about to ask the Major when another voice came on the radio.

"Good evening, Icelandic Air One-Three-Seven, squawk three-three-four-zero."

He watched the Major typing away before hearing, *"Squawk three-three-four-zero, Icelandic Air One-Three-Seven."*

The operator farthest from him now began speaking into his headset, as the Major turned back to him and began to explain. "Captain Petrov there is speaking to the flight crew up front, relaying the orders we're receiving from air traffic control. If ATC want a heading change or altitude change, he tells them and then they follow the instruction."

"Why not just have the pilots speak directly to ATC?"

The Major shook his head, replying, "Too risky, Colonel. Most of our pilots cannot speak English without hiding their accent, so they would all sound the same. Imagine saying you're an Icelandic or American plane and the controller hears the same Slav accent as the previous planes. It would make them suspicious, which is what we don't want right now."

Golgolvin nodded, remembering his own English, although good, still had the same distinct tone.

The Major said, "My job is to talk to the controllers, which I'm able to do using my computer. We've got it set up whereby I can type the message and the computer will use its programming to mimic whatever accent I choose and speak the message. But it also injects the background noise of the cockpit of a plane, so the controller receiving the message believes he's chatting to a pilot."

"How did you manage that?"

"We've spent the past year recording all the pilots' radio chatter as they flew in and out of the UK. We programmed the recordings into the computer, and it's learned from them. Now, any accent in the world, we can produce, authentically. When we first trialled it without the background noise, it sounded too clean, too perfect, but add a little background noise, a muted conversation, or a laugh, and people believe it."

Golgolvin was about to speak, when his headset burst into life again as the Prestwick controller spoke.

"Icelandic Air One-Three-Seven, Prestwick Centre, radar contact identified, fly IFR heading as filed, maintain flight level three-four thousand."

The Major quickly typed away again at the keyboard.

Fly IFR heading as filed, maintain flight level three-four thousand, Icelandic Air One-Three-Seven.

As soon as the message was sent, the Major smiled and looked at him. "That was the hardest bit, but we're in, we're now flying in UK airspace."

Golgolvin closed his eyes momentarily in silent thanks before asking, "What does the other Captain do in the middle?" He Pointed to the third operator, sat watching two large computer screens, one showing what looked to be a giant radar display.

"Ah, that's Captain Ulenavitch. He's our co-ordination officer, monitoring the other Eagle and Kestrel flights on the radar and keeping in communication with them. We're the first ones into the UK so he'll be passing that back to command on Eagle-Four shortly."

He cocked his head questioningly. "Kestrel flights?"

Major Pavitch gazed at him briefly, before pressing a switch on his console, the display in front of him changing. "Here, Colonel, let me show you."

He leaned forward curiously, as his eyes followed to where the Major pointed on the display.

"So here, Colonel, you can see our location, just thirty miles north of the Shetland Islands and just entering UK airspace, and if I just zoom out..."

The map display zoomed out, showing the North Atlantic area with Iceland to the top of the screen and Scotland to the south. The screen looked busy, with lots of radar targets all showing the other aircraft in the area, displaying the flight data for each one. He wondered just how many of those were their own aircraft. As if able to see what Golgolvin was thinking, the Major quickly added, "Of course, Colonel, some of these are irrelevant so I'll just tone out the clutter."

Within a few seconds most of the targets disappeared, leaving just thirty radar targets – all of them were roughly following the same course and all equally separated by about twenty miles. He'd known that they would be the lead aircraft and that there were more aircraft following them in, but he had no idea as to how many, or which were their own targets, as command had deemed operational secrecy important above all else. He now felt a certain surge of pride at seeing them all there, each with their own missions and tasks, and the thought of being the lead callsign made him smile.

"Our smaller aircraft – the fighters, Mig-31's – we've called them Kestrels. All the Eagle flights are the transport aircraft, like us, that is except Eagle-Four – that's the command and control aircraft."

Golgolvin raised his eyebrows to ask, "MiG-31's? Why not our newer next genera-tion fighters like the Su-57?"

"They're in short supply right now, besides, our flight profile required us to fly out over the northern hemisphere and back down through the Atlantic. The range was too much for the Su-57, but the MiG-31 is perfect, with its range of over four thousand five hundred miles. If we'd flown over the shortest route, say Norway for instance, then NATO would have alerted the UK and followed us in all the way, losing us the element of surprise. This way, no one is suspicious as we are coming in along the transatlantic routes, hence we can pose as commercial traffic."

Without taking his eyes off the display he asked, "So how many Eagles are there?"

"We have six Eagles in total and twenty-four Kestrels. All the Eagles will have the same communications and computer set-ups that we have here, so they should be able to fool their way in. But the Kestrels are too small to fit the equipment onboard, so they rely on the Eagle flight operators to talk to air traffic control for them. All the Kestrel pilots have to do is follow the orders from the Eagle controllers. It'll be dark soon, so the Kestrels can then start to follow the Eagle call signs in. With a bit of luck, our fighters should be able to fly down the length of the UK unopposed, and all with the blessing of the British Air Traffic Controllers."

"And how are you getting this feed? How are you able to see the other flights with your own radar systems switched off?"

The Major smiled. "Ah, so you did notice that then. Well, as you're no doubt aware, if we were to turn on our own radar, then the British defences would know who we were immediately, as they constantly scan for our signatures. So, we keep ours switched off and use theirs." The Major saw the look of confusion on the Colonel's face, as smiling, he continued, "You see, we're currently hacked into the British NATS system in Swanwick, getting their own radar feed. Unknown to them, we're watching and using their own radar."

"So *that's* how we're doing it!" Golgolvin sat back, smiling. *At last, the bigger picture,* he thought, as up to that moment he knew his target and more importantly where it was, but he hadn't known how he was to get there. And the thought of flying through hundreds of miles of the enemy's airspace unopposed had worried him. He hadn't wanted to simply throw the lives of his men away in a spectacular fireball as they were shot out of the sky, unable to fight back. He and his men had spent the past six months training for this mission, there had been so many combat drops and so much training, they'd even had a full-sized mock-up of their target built into the wastelands of Eastern Russia, away from prying eyes. He'd lost six good men in training accidents, but it was a worthwhile price to pay, for now he knew his men were as tough and as mean as they were ever going to be. He'd been the only man in the unit who had known the true location of where they were going. As they'd boarded the plane that morning, the men had still believed that they were going back to Ukraine to fight, and once everyone was onboard, he had told them their true target as they sat on the airfield getting ready to take off.

He remembered with pride that not one of them had shown fear as he gave his speech in the cargo bay of the aircraft. Instead, the faces of his men looked back at him with fierce determination and joy. He had told them how they finally had a chance to repay all the suffering and misery that this enemy had heaped on the motherland. How its leaders had watched the fall of the old Russia, rubbing their hands with glee. How its people, lured by greed, had poured into the motherland, robbing it of its youth and future, whilst flooding it with drugs and criminal gangs. Then when Russia had finally had enough and began to rise again and tried to defend itself, by removing the Nazi regime in Ukraine, this country had been instrumental in getting heavier weapons there. It had helped the evil regime of Ukraine kill their countrymen and fellow soldiers in their thousands. Now, though, its time had come, finally it would not be able to hide behind the protection of others anymore. Finally, his men would get to strike at the very heart of the enemy and let them know just how long the claws of the Russian Bear could be. Finally, they'd be striking out at the United Kingdom.

Eagle-Four

Two hundred miles north of Eagle-One sat Colonel Igor Bresavik on Eagle-Four, monitoring the progress of his planes as they began to enter UK airspace. With a drying throat, he had spent the last twenty minutes watching the progress of Eagle-One from his command chair. Shown as a small dot on a display, it had slowly made its way south. From his seat, he had the ability to monitor and listen to all fifteen of his operators on board his aircraft, plus all the pilots, and if required he could speak to the operators on board the other Eagle aircraft. For now, though, he'd filtered all the other communications out, and was listening intently to the operator on Eagle-One chatting to the air traffic controller. He'd hoped and prayed for this phase of the mission to work. For up till now no one had dared test the technology for fear of giving away its secrets. Instead, they had relied on the assurances of the people they had brought it from. Everything was reliant on it all working now, being used as intended.

So far though, everything had gone to plan, but now, this part of the operation was down to him. If it failed, then the disgrace and shame would be his alone to bear. He had already made plans for his family to be relocated to another country should the worst happen. The thoughts of his own son having to repay his father's disgrace and debt were too strong to contemplate. He shook those dark thoughts from his head and instead focused on the task at hand. He would make this work, he had to.

Over his headset, he heard the acknowledgement from the operator on Eagle-One over the radio – they were in. One of his own operator's voices came over the headset louder than the first. *"Sir, we've received confirmation – Eagle-One is now in enemy airspace. Eagle-Two will be at the threshold in fifteen minutes. All other Eagles and Kestrels are proceeding as planned."* He looked to his left to the operator three screens down, who was looking back at him, waiting for a response. Rather than waste time switching the channel to reply to him, he simply raised a thumb to show the operator he understood. He gazed up to give his eyes a quick respite, rubbing them quickly, allowing them to adjust to the lights of the interior of the plane again. Keeping his headset on, in case he was needed, he stood up and leaned on the back of his chair, shaking some life into his legs as he tried to remember how long he'd been sat there. Had it been five hours already?

He looked around the cabin of the Ilyushin Il-80 command and control plane, observing his team, a determined look on his face as he watched for any signs of a problem. This part of the mission called for stealth, to sneak in as a wolf in sheep's clothing. At least the aircraft he was on, the Il-80, looked like an airliner, after being converted from the civilian variant, the Il-86. The only telltale sign of its true nature was the bulge located behind the cockpit, housing the sophisticated arrays of antennas and electronics, allowing him to control and talk to all his aircraft assets within a two-thousand-mile radius. What was it that the NATO planners had called this aircraft? Maxdome? The Colonel smiled to himself as he wondered why they chose that name. He chuckled as he thought at first how strange it had been to see the plane on the tarmac, painted in the colours of a well-known Japanese airline. Silly up close, but at a distance, with a fleeting glance, good enough to convince a passing pilot. Not that it mattered much more, the sunlight was rapidly fading and soon the plane and its secrets would be hidden from view, the navigation lights being the only telltale sign of its presence.

He looked over to one of the flight crew who stood waiting for orders at the front of the plane and he motioned for a drink. He couldn't do anything more yet with regards to the mission now, but he could do something about his dry throat. He walked along the cabin, looking down the fuselage at the fifteen other screens, all with an operator sat in front of them, watching and relaying information to the fighters that were following in set formations behind them. He watched his men and women, checking for any irregularities, any issues that his trained eye could pick up on. He had another five standby operators sitting around the aircraft ready to step in if needed, to relieve someone if they were not fit for the task. Also, if a quick break or use of the toilet was required, then all an operator had to do was simply call someone over, give a quick handover and the changeover would be complete, but Igor knew, at this phase of the mission, his team would not be distracted now. The operators, like him, wanted to ensure this part of the mission succeeded.

Satisfied with what he saw, he turned to face the crewmember now walking towards him, carrying a cup of black steaming coffee in hand. Grateful for the drink, he sipped slowly and closed his eyes, affording himself a moment's grace from the world he was in. He checked his watch, noting that Eagle-Two was now eleven minutes from the threshold, then went back to watching the radar display in front of him. Nothing was going to stop them now. Smiling to himself, he knew Operation Fools Mate was a go.

10

The Carrot and the Stick

CO's Office, Bovington Camp

"Colonel, before I begin, may I ask that everyone here hands in their mobile phones, to be kept outside while we chat?"

A collective murmur began around the table as everyone wanted to know why. The Colonel looked down the table, his hands raised to keep everyone quiet, before turning back to Mike, his face questioning. "Okay, Mr Faulkes, I'd like to know why you want us to do that?"

"Colonel, what I'm about to discuss with you is for this room only. You've asked me to explain what happened outside the wire earlier and my thoughts on the guys who attacked us. I'll explain everything. But I'll only do that if our phones are left outside with your secretary. Besides, as I'm sure you're all aware by now they're not working anyway."

The adjutant stood up, hands resting on the table as he glared at Mike, his voice cold and acidic. "Colonel, I really must protest, this man just waltzes into your office looking like a hobo and is now questioning our honour and integrity by insinuating we will somehow record this meeting. What on earth would be so important? It's bloody insulting."

Mike looked up the table, his eyes meeting all the nodding heads as he replied flatly, "Gentlemen and ladies, please, you misunderstand my meaning. I am not insinuating that you will be recording the meeting. I am, however, insinuating that your phones *will* be recording what we talk about. There is no question of honour or integrity, merely a question of operational security. If this were a classified meeting, then you would have left your phones out of the meeting through habit. I'm merely asking for the same courtesy now."

Mike saw the GSM and the RMP officer Captain Reynolds nod their head in agreement as he looked back to the Colonel who thankfully also agreed.

"Okay Mr Faulkes, so what you're saying is that we treat this meeting as if it were classified and leave all electronic devices outside. Am I right in saying that?"

"Exactly, Colonel. After I've said my piece, I promise you'll understand why."

The CO turned to the GSM.

"GSM, kindly collect everyone's mobile devices please and see that they get taken outside."

With some muttered complaints everybody stood and took out their mobiles, sliding them down the table to the large barrel-chested GSM. Without saying a word, he collected them up in his beret before quickly disappearing outside, depositing them with the CO's secretary. Only after the GSM had returned and was seated and the office door closed did the Colonel reply.

"Okay, Mr Faulkes, you now have our full and undivided attention. Let's hear it."

Okay, thought Mike, *first let's dangle the carrot.*

Mike turned to face the Sergeant Major in charge of the Signals wing.

"Sergeant Major Yackers are you aware that the red phone box outside of camp is in full working order and that it can be used to make calls to landline numbers only?"

The Sergeant Major shook his head slowly. "I'm sorry, Mr Faulkes, but you're mistaken, we've tried all the landlines and they're not working."

"When you say tried all the landlines, you mean the ones on camp? Not the phone box?" Mike cocked his head inquisitively.

Looking amused and as if explaining to a child, the Sergeant Major replied, "No, we haven't checked *that* phone box, but all the landlines in the area are out. Every single telephone line on camp and the surrounding area is *not* working. We've checked. Therefore, if our landlines are not working it stands to reason that the phone box wouldn't work either. Trust me, Mr Faulkes, I do know my job."

Mike held up a hand in submission. "I'm not saying you don't know your job, Sergeant Major, but were you aware that since 2011 all the landlines in this camp and all the other camps – in fact, almost all UK households – are no longer physical landlines? They're all connected by a wire to a socket in a wall. That then goes to an exchange point, but at the exchange point they're converted onto a VoIP (Voice over Internet Protocol) system. Every single *landline* as you call it, is nothing more than a connected Wi-Fi phone. Now that you've lost the internet, the defence intranet and the mobile phone networks, it stands to reason that they won't work. Meanwhile, the good old-fashioned copper telephone wired system is still working, albeit there's not many of those old numbers still left in existence."

Mike saw the Sergeant Major's jaw harden as he thought this through. Mike continued, adding, "And I know it's still working because I made a telephone call – well, actually, *two* telephone calls no more than two minutes before the attack. That was why the gunman approached me. They were watching the camp using a mobile phone when they saw me in the phone box. I think that they were as surprised as you are now to discover a form of communication that was still working. The gunman came over to investigate when I confronted him."

"You confronted him?" Captain Reynolds asked, surprised. "I thought they attacked you?"

Mike looked back at her, shaking his head. "No, I never said that, but I'll come back to that in a second. Firstly though, going back to you, Sergeant Major, if the phone box *is* working couldn't you hack into it with some good old-fashioned Don 10 cable? Perhaps even pipe the feed over the fence and into this office, giving the camp and the Colonel some way to communicate? To maybe call a hospital?"

The Sergeant Major jumped up quickly as the realisation of what Mike was saying finally sunk in. "Sir, with your permission, I'm going to go check this out myself. If what Mr Faulkes is saying is true, and the phone box is working, then we *can* get a phone in here."

"Of course, Sergeant Major, let's hope Mr Faulkes hasn't just made a regrettable mistake."

Mike watched on as the Sergeant Major hurriedly, scooped up his beret and notebook and was running out of the door. It was the RMP Captain who spoke next.

"Mr Faulkes, getting back to what you just said, did you say that you confronted the gunman before the attack?"

Mike nodded, looking up to address the room again. "That's correct, I noticed two men sat in a silver four-by-four watching me as I walked into the phone box. What was strange about them was one of them was speaking into a mobile phone. That's what piqued my interest – how was he able to use a phone when everyone else had problems with theirs? Then whilst I was on the phone the second man came up to the phone box and started banging on the door appearing very agitated. He wouldn't speak to me, of course, but from his tone and demeanour I could see he wanted me out of there. After I'd finished, as I was leaving, I began questioning him, asking why he needed to use a phone box and why he didn't use his friend's mobile phone."

"Hang on," said the adjutant irritably, "are you saying that you provoked the man? That *you* started all of this? Three dead people and a camp attacked because you had an issue with someone interrupting your call? How did you know that his friend's phone was working? What if it wasn't and he had a call to make himself?" The tone was accusing and began to send a sharp spike of anger up Mikes back.

"No, that's *not* what caused this and that's *not* what I said," Mike replied, trying to hide the frustration in his voice. "Those men firing automatic weapons at unarmed people caused this. I did get the impression, though, that he didn't understand me. I wondered if perhaps he didn't speak English, as his face didn't register what I was saying. It was only after I pointed to his friend that he became aggressive and started to attack me. As for his friend's phone, I've seen enough people having conversations on phones to know his body language meant he was chatting to someone on the other end. Also, the other thing that didn't add up and was suspicious to me were their jackets. It was twenty-nine degrees today, and both men were sat there in heavy jackets, fully zipped up. That was another thing that made me look at them again."

"So, your thinking is that it was the phone box and not you that they were looking at?" Chris asked.

"No, I think they were there to watch the camp, to observe what was going on. The fact that I was able to use the phone box distracted them. They were merely coming to investigate why it was working when I got in the way. I think the gunman panicked and thought he could simply get rid of me, but things escalated quickly. The only reason the second guy started firing on the camp was because the gate guard came running over to help me. The second guy saw his partner was going to be captured so extracted him by opening fire. I bet if I hadn't used the phone box, they'd be out there now, still waiting, and watching us."

The Colonel looked at Mike, his eyebrows creased, asking, "Why do you think terrorists would be watching the camp like that, especially so heavily armed?"

"Oh, come on, Colonel!" the adjutant interjected. "This man is a civilian, he shouldn't even be in here let alone giving us all his opinion. You've brought him in to tell us what happened and now we know. It was started over a phone call. Let's get rid of him, move on and get back onto more important military matters. We don't need a civilian in here telling us how to do our jobs."

The Colonel sat looking at the Captain with an amused look on his face. Clearly, he'd heard his adjutant rant before.

It was Chris who jumped to Mike's defence. He leaned forward across the table, the anger in his tone simmering just below the surface. "Captain Norris, this man has conducted more operational tours in the army than most of the people in this room. Perhaps that's why you feel the constant need to try to attack or tarnish him, perhaps there's a little bit of envy there. I don't know. What I do know is that he was invited here by request of the Colonel to explain what had happened. As you have already pointed out he is a civilian, which means he is under no obligation to obey orders from any of us. Yet without any thought for himself, he has come here to help, immediately I might add, after being held and interrogated by our own side for two hours. I think a little bit of respect for Mr Faulkes is in order, instead of your incessant attempt at what appears to be just blatant character assassination!"

The adjutant's face turned red and Mike almost chuckled, watching the man's mouth open and close, not knowing what to say. It was the Colonel, though, who acted the peacekeeper as he now stepped in, interrupting them both.

"Thank you, Major Richards and Captain Norris, for both of your views. I do, however, agree with the good Major here, Adj, I understand what you're saying, but so far, the only person giving me any answers is Mr Faulkes. So, for now he's staying, so if you both don't mind maybe we can get back to the matter at hand?"

The Colonel waited patiently for both men to settle back down before turning back to Mike. "So, Mr Faulkes, like I asked before, why do you think these terrorists were watching the camp?"

Mike looked at the door hoping to see either Peter Rawlinson or the Signals Sergeant Major stood there. Annoyingly it remained empty. He was still going to have to play for time while he waited for the carrot to arrive.

"Colonel, firstly, they were not terrorists – terrorists would not have been armed as they were."

"Really? What do you mean by that?" the Colonel asked quizzically.

"Getting firearms into the UK has always been next to impossible thanks to our strong border checks and police forces. Most UK terrorist groups don't even get to use firearms, choosing either low-grade homemade explosives, knives or fake suicide vests. And even if the terrorist organisation can get their hands on firearms, they're usually old cold war-era stock, such as Makarov pistols and AK-47s or Skorpion machine pistols. When I saw those gunmen earlier, I recognised the pistols they were using, but I couldn't remember where I'd seen the submachine guns before. I've been thinking about it all afternoon. And it wasn't until I was sat back out there in your reception area that I remembered its name. They were using Kalashnikov AK-12s with folding stocks and MP-443 Grach pistols. That's next-generation stuff, not available to buy over the counter. The AK-12 for instance is still relatively new and only now being issued to FSB agents. But not only did they have two of them, but they were also equipped with tactical assault vests, fully fitted with all the trimmings, even having smoke and fragmentation grenades. That's not the sort of stuff you simply buy from any criminal street gang or bring into the country in your carry-on luggage."

Mike saw almost everyone at the table nodding, as if to agree with his thinking. He quickly took another sip of water as he continued, "The other thing I'd like to draw your attention to is the fact that they had the camp gate pinned down. The QRF were stuck in the guardroom, probably trying to get their weapons out of the rack, which we all know would have been padlocked. And let's not forget also that each man on the gate had no more than what – ten rounds per man? The gunmen had the tactical advantage with more firepower and certainly more ammunition. As heavily armed as they were, they could have come through the gate, killed everyone there and gone through the camp like a dose of salts, killing a lot more people than they did." Mike saw the GSM give a disapproving look as he said that last part.

"Instead, they broke contact and withdrew, showing a level of tactical thinking and discipline that terrorists just wouldn't have. Whatever their mission was, getting into a fight wasn't it, but at the same time they had the firepower to carry off an assault if they had to. I think there's more to this than you think."

The CO leaned back, his arms folded behind his head as he mulled over what Mike had just said. The RMP Captain now said, "Okay, so if they're not terrorists, are you thinking these operators were state sponsored perhaps? You mentioned the FSB, could it be that you're thinking this was some kind of espionage being conducted on UK soil? Or perhaps you blundered into some clandestine operation? Is that what you're getting at?"

Chris looked thoughtfully over and remarked, "I'll be honest, I'm struggling to believe that anyone would be so bold as to sanction any operation, regardless of the outcome that would require *that* level of aggression. Remember the fallout after the Salisbury poisonings."

Mike was about to answer when suddenly a commotion in the reception area made them all look up. Standing there in the doorway sweating and out of breath stood the Signals Sergeant Major, a big triumphant smile all over his face.

Before the Colonel could say anything, the Sergeant Major said excitedly, "Sir, the phone box it's *working*! Mr Faulkes was correct!"

The room erupted into smiles, and Chris stood up to pat his friend on the back. "Well done, mate, well bloody done!"

The Sergeant Major continued, "I've got my guys laying out the Don 10 cable now, they'll be ready to patch into the phone box in five minutes, then we'll get the line brought into your office."

Mike sat there poised, the carrot had indeed been delivered, but shortly he'd have to use the stick. And that was going to be the hard part. He sat watching on as everyone at the table started to talk over each other.

The Colonel stood up to make his voice heard as he quietened everyone down. He looked over to the still-smiling figure in the doorway. "Excellent, Sergeant Major. First, I want you to call the emergency services, get the ambulances here right now and let's get these wounded away immediately."

Mike sat there shaking his head. "I'm sorry, Colonel, but I've tried that already. Once I knew the mobiles were out, I tried the emergency services to test the line. I think it only works if we call a genuine landline to landline number. Don't forget the emergency services are using the same VoIP system as you are, therefore, you won't get through – we'll need a landline number first to call."

Sergeant Major Yackers interrupted him, full of pride. "I've already done it, sir, I've got through to Dorchester hospital and the ambulances are on their way now. I've sent one of my guys over to the med centre to tell the doc they're enroute. We couldn't get a message over to the police yet though."

Mike looked at the Sergeant Major in surprise. "How did you manage that? I thought the hospitals were also on the same VoIP system as you are?"

Still grinning he replied, "They are, but my wife works in the old library building next door to the hospital. They're still using an old landline that was installed back in 1940 which she's forever complaining about. I used to call her back in the day before she got a mobile, so I knew the number off the top of my head. I simply called her using the old number and asked her to run next door and get one of the A and E doctors. She's been fully briefed, and the ambulances are on the way."

Mike gave a congratulatory nod as the Colonel beamed. "Well done, Sergeant Major, well done, the first bit of good news all bloody day!"

Chris leaned over and whispered into his friend's ear, "Fucking hell mate, what a way to make an impression. First, the attack and now saving the day with that phone box. Are you going to drive home later, or fly home with that cape billowing behind you?"

Mike just looked on, grimacing – unfortunately, he knew it would be neither yet. There was still more to come.

Everyone remained seated as another two soldiers entered the room. Mike recognised them as the two Signallers that the Colonel had shouted at when he first waited in the reception area. Both were now sweating heavily, as they manhandled a huge cable drum into the middle of the room and set it with a loud thud on the table. They began unwinding the cable and walked over to one of the large windows and threw out one end, with one of the Signallers shouting out to an unseen colleague below. Once they were happy with what was going on, they uncoiled some more of the cable before cutting off a suitable amount, then produced a rather crude-looking olive-green telephone, and connected the device to the remaining two ends of line. Mike watched as one man listened on the line, grinning in triumph as he heard the dial tone whilst the other picked up the remaining cable drum and walked out. Sergeant Major Yackers still stood in the doorway, patting him on the back as he went.

Once he was happy it was all set up, the remaining Signaller placed the field telephone on the desk in front of the Colonel, and then produced a green speaker, and using a multi-tool, spliced the cable and connected the speaker to the phone. After he checked all the connections were secure, he lifted the handset, and the dial tone was heard through the speaker. Satisfied that everything was in working order, he left the room, getting a pat on the back from one very happy Signals Sergeant Major.

"Sir, I've taken the liberty of having a speaker connected, so you won't need to keep the handset held up to your ear. It's not perfect but it will allow you to listen in on what's being said."

The CO looked up, thanking the Sergeant Major as he resumed his seat at the table.

Mike looked around the room then to his friend Chris, before taking a deep breath. Now it was time for the stick.

After everyone had sat back down, and without waiting for a prompt, Mike began. "Colonel, you asked to know my thoughts on why the camp was attacked today and what those gunmen were doing?" The Colonel looked at Mike expectantly, waiting for the answer. "Well, I can go one better than that. I can also answer why your phone systems are down, why the internet isn't working, why your CCTV systems are down and why the MoD intranet is down."

Mike paused to take another sip of water, looking around the room as he did so, seeing he had everyone's attention now. The phone line and calling the ambulances had now put him in good standing, as he hoped it would. The next part would be difficult, but now he had an ace up his sleeve, ready to play.

"Colonel, did you ever get to work with Brigadier Peter Rawlinson?"

The Colonel sat a bit straighter at the mention of Peter's name.

"I did. How do you know of Brigadier Rawlinson? And what bearing does that have on what you've just mentioned?"

"In 2001, he was the CO of the 24th Tank Regiment. *Our* regiment." Mike pointed to himself and Chris before continuing. "In 2003 we were all sent off to take part in the invasion of Iraq and that's where I got to work closely with him during my time there."

The Colonel had now leant forward, showing nothing with his poker face, his elbows on the table and head resting on his hands, listening intently as Mike continued.

"Brigadier Rawlinson, against all army rules, became good friends with the soldiers under his command. It was frowned upon, of course, for such a high-ranking officer to have attachments to junior ranks and did put some people's noses out of joint, but Peter being Peter, he didn't care."

Mike saw the look of disgust on the adjutant's face as he talked. Clearly the House-hold Cavalry didn't do that sort of thing, he thought to himself before continuing.

"After everyone had left the army back in 2014, Peter – sorry – Brigadier Rawlinson, would still meet up with us, sometimes as individuals, sometimes as a group. But we always kept in touch. When my wife Kate met his wife Elizabeth, they got on like a house on fire, and that's when we all became very close friends. In 2016 at one of our many weekends away, at their house, our wives were busy chatting, and Peter took me into his office with something troubling him, wanting my opinion. He'd told me in confidence of a report he had been asked to compile in 2012 before he'd left the army. He'd always been known as a free thinker and had some creative and some would say radical and imaginative ways on the use of troops and strategy. Some of his ideas were seen as unconventional, bending the rules in a way no one else had thought of before. If you remember, he had been made Brigadier of the 143 Wessex Brigade which, at the time only existed on paper. He built that up, on his own initiative into an effective operational unit that's been used to great effect since, as I'm sure you're aware." Mike saw the CO nod at him in understanding. "The Civil Service think tank in Whitehall had asked the MoD to come up with some possible scenarios for future attacks on the UK with which the government could then plan a means of defence. There were five plans all drawn up, all compiled by senior serving officers of the military, of which Peter's plan was one of them..."

"What has this got to do with the attack that took place today though, and the loss of comms?"

The Colonel, still resting with his head on his hands, raised his eyebrows at Mike as if to emphasise the point.

"I'll get to that very shortly, Colonel, I promise, but to continue, of the five reports drawn up, Peter told me the first four were scrutinised, evaluated and filed away. They were simple but detailed plans that outlined a standard first strike on the UK, fol-lowed by NATO mobilisation and retaliation. In two of the reports, nuclear weapons were highlighted and again all the options were the standard NATO response. I know you're all aware of it, it's called Article Five, an attack on one partner was an attack on all. It was all very vanilla and by the book, as Peter had called it. His report, however, was called Operation Fools Mate."

"That's a chess move, isn't it?" Chris asked.

The GSM looked up, intervening. "Yes, it's one of the quickest ways to win at a chess game. It involves two moves and it requires your opponent to literally make all the wrong moves. Good name for an operation, provided of course you can get your opponent to do what you want..."

Everyone at the table looked to the GSM open-mouthed. Clearly, they did not see him as a chess player.

Mike nodded as he continued, "Brigadier Rawlinson's report, Operation Fools Mate, was buried, and never made it out of the Civil Service, it was never talked about again and never saw the light of day, which was something that concerned him."

"Why did he think the report was buried? Perhaps it was just not as good or realistic as he thought?"

Mike turned to look at Captain Reynolds before responding, raising a finger to emphasise.

"Perhaps, but Peter thought it could also have been because the report *was* plausible and *was* entirely possible, and that maybe the people in government didn't want this information to be out there. Imagine, a blueprint of just how to exploit our country's weaknesses, out there for all to see. Maybe the government realised that as things stood, the plan could work. But there was another twist to the story that added fuel to the fire, which was why Peter had wanted to speak to me."

By now the Colonel had sat back upright.

"When the reports were compiled and submitted to the government in 2012, they arrived at the offices of the Ministry of Defence via MoD Abbey Wood in Bristol, not Whitehall as some would believe. Abbey Wood was run then by the Civil Service, and not wanting to lose face within government, they secretly changed the name of the authors on the reports so that it would seem as if the senior members of the Civil Service planning team had thought them up. Meanwhile, the genuine authors, all still serving members of the military, were sworn to secrecy as they were all still signed up to the Official Secrets Act. Effectively they were all told to shut up, and never mention it again."

"Sounds just like the Civil Service," mused the Colonel.

"Each report had a different author. Brigadier Rawlinson's report, which had now been passed off as a Civil Service report, was signed off by a Christopher Ward. Nothing strange in that, you would think, but the Brigadier had then found out in

2016 via sources in the MoD that Christopher Ward had died in a car crash back in 2012, no more than two days after all the reports had been submitted. The report into his death concluded that he had been drink driving and drove himself into a wall – he was found to have been six times over the limit."

"Okay, so apart from the poor timing of this chap's death, where are you going with this?" The Colonel asked as he looked on, intrigued.

"When the Brigadier had a look at the investigation using contacts he still had within the police force, he found out some background information on Christopher Ward. Christopher was teetotal and had never touched a drop of alcohol since 2002."

Interrupting Mike, the GSM blurted out, "We all say we're going to be bloody tee total; it doesn't mean on the night we won't have one or two." Some of the people at the table smirked clearly agreeing.

Mike shook his head in disagreement as he looked at the GSM, replying, "No, because in 2002 Christopher Ward's wife and son were knocked down by a drunk driver. His son was only six years old and killed, whilst his wife suffered severe spinal injuries that put her into a wheelchair for the rest of her life." Mike saw the smirks quickly disappear from the faces as he continued to speak. "Since that day, Christopher never touched a drop of alcohol – he was teetotal, hated the stuff. In fact, he was quite a vocal campaigner against it. Then, while the ink is still drying on his signature on a report, he supposedly leaves his disabled wife at home alone, a woman he's spent years caring for, and goes and gets absolutely wasted and drives himself into a wall. Neither the Brigadier nor I really believed that he would have done that."

"So, a report that was never seen, never filed, never mentioned, goes missing, never to be seen again, and the person who supposedly compiled the report dies in suspicious circumstances."

Mike looked over to the Engineer Captain. Finally, she had now decided to enter the conversation. Mike saw that her name was Captain Baker. He smiled as he replied, "Correct, and that's why Peter was convinced the report was important, important enough to hide and more importantly, to kill for."

"This is all starting to sound a bit too much Ian Fleming for my liking," interjected the adjutant.

"Okay," said the Colonel, ignoring the adjutant's sniping remarks, "Brigadier Rawlinson obviously told you what was in the report, but again I'm going to ask what that has to do with today?"

Mike was thinking ahead, trying to tread very carefully now. He had them, but he could lose it all so quickly. He thought back to what Peter had told him all those years ago.

"So, the report or plan was to be broken down into four phases – Phase One is more complicated to explain now, so I'll just skip to Phase Two. Phase Two would begin with a major cyberwar offensive on the UK mainland that would overload our cyberwarfare protection. GCHQ, MI5, MI6 and the NCA would all be overloaded, unable to stop multiple attacks happening at once. Everything was to get hit; air traffic control systems, the NHS systems, banking systems, financial markets, all the mobile phone networks, internet service providers, all government departments, everything. There'd be no emails, no phones, no way of communicating at all between anyone. Even the emergency network would go down. Like you said yourself earlier, GSM, we'd be left with carrier pigeons and signal flags."

No one spoke as Mike continued, "Phase Two also consisted of using ships to block the ports of Portsmouth and Southampton. I know everyone has seen the news earlier today, so I don't need to divulge any more on that. But why these two ports? Simple – Portsmouth houses the Royal Navy's carrier task group and is the only port deep enough for its carriers to get into. By blocking it, you now keep one of the carriers out of the port and the other carrier penned in. Right now, the *Queen Elizabeth* is sat there, the most expensive UK runway in the world – a sitting duck. That's not including all her logistical ships and destroyers all now unable to leave. Meanwhile, the *Prince of Wales* has no other deep-water port on the south coast and has no support either – she's now stuck with the only option of going north when she wants to go to port. As for blocking Southampton, they'd be blocking one of the south coast's deep-water ports, and would also be blocking Marchwood, the MoD's main logistical hub for loading and unloading all of our military hardware. As you all know, that's where any armour is brought in and out of the UK. Now that's out of action, so, if the UK wanted to bring any armour reserve in from say Canada, Germany or the Baltic states, they can't. Now it's a case of the only armour you have left in the UK is in Catterick, Warminster, Tidworth, Lulworth and here..."

"Now hang on, Mike," this time it was Chris talking, "are you saying that this is happening now? That somehow, someone has got hold of Brigadier Rawlinson's report and is using it to attack us?"

Mike stumbled with his words as he thought quickly.

"No, I mean yes... What I mean is we both think that someone has the report and is using it against us. However, the report wasn't about an attack on the UK...It was about an *invasion* of the UK..."

11

The Calm Before

Mike felt the atmosphere change in the room, saw everyone at the table stiffen and sit up straighter, as if his words had been cattle prods, jolting them all from the stifling heat of the day.

"Mr Faulkes, look, I know it's been a long day, but really? Can you seriously sit there and say you think that right now we're on the cusp of some sort of invasion?"

Mike looked over to the final Major who up to now hadn't spoken, guessing he was the Squadron Leader of the Recruit Training Squadron located down the road in Stanley Barracks. His name tape read *Noakes*. Mike responded quickly. "Hello, Major Noakes, I appreciate it all seems far-fetched, but what would you do right now, right this second, if you looked out that window and saw a whole Brigade of paratroopers landing in the camp? How exactly would you, or could you, stop them? Who would you call to warn about it? The phones aren't working, so how would you get the message out?" Mike saw the Major look out of the window as he contemplated what Mike was saying to him. Mike stood up, pacing the room, waving his arms in frustration as he continued, "Right now, right this very second, we are all powerless to do anything. All your tanks are sat in the hangars, there's no ammunition readily available, all the equipment needed for them is locked away and more importantly all the crews are away on summer leave. They're about as much use to you now as the ships were in Pearl Harbour when the Japanese attacked, and that's probably not a bad analogy given what I'm saying."

The Colonel looked up at Mike as he heard the mention of Pearl Harbour, his eyes betraying something that Mike couldn't yet understand. Mike sat back down as

Captain Baker then intervened, "But didn't you say that we're protected by Article Five? So really all of this is rather irrelevant, isn't it? An attack on us, is an attack on NATO, therefore it doesn't matter what we do with our tanks or our armed forces. We're protected by the threat of other NATO members coming to help us, so I'm struggling to understand why this plan you're worried about would work."

The Colonel looked to the Captain and then back to Mike, adding, "Yes, you mentioned Article Five already. You said that of all the written plans, four depended on it. But then you also said that the Brigadier had managed to somehow mitigate this in his plan – how?"

"Because Article Five becomes null and void if the country invading us is also a member of NATO. Two member states of NATO *can* go to war with each other, and NATO would not, and could not intervene. How could it? Whose side would they go with? That sort of thing would tear the very fabric of what NATO stands for in two."

The adjutant stood up confidently. "Well, that settles that then, Russia is not, and never will be, a member of NATO. This whole idea has just become one big fantasy rollercoaster. Article Five is there for a reason, that's why we don't have our armed forces in a constant state of readiness, there's no need. Perhaps now you're out of the army, you should just keep it that way, maybe think of something less tiring to focus your energy on?"

Mike turned to face the adjutant, leaning on the table as he did so, his face radiating calm despite the barb. "I'll admit I don't know the full picture yet, and I'm not sure exactly who's using this plan against us. You mentioned Russia, but I didn't. All I'm making you aware of is that this is far too coincidental. Any one of these events happening on their own and I wouldn't be suspicious. But all together within hours of each other? And not to mention the impact it would have – and don't forget – technically whoever is using this plan has no idea that the author is still alive. They believe the plan died with Christopher Ward, so we at least have that to our advantage."

Mike said nothing as the adjutant strode over to the window, staring out. The CO, meanwhile, sat there looking at Mike deep in thought. "Mr Faulkes, you said a minute ago *we*, as in *we* thought this, and *we* thought that. Who was this *we* you are referring to?"

Mike was about to answer when in the distance they could hear the unmistakable sound of approaching sirens. Everyone stopped to look out of the window as the sound grew louder and louder until it stopped abruptly as the vehicles reached the camp. The ambulances from Dorchester Hospital had finally arrived at the front gate, with blue lights flashing rhythmically. Everyone smiled at each other, happy with the little victory as the five vehicles were driven quickly towards the med centre. No doubt, the doc would be relieved to see them and as everyone sat back down around the table Mike could see again the smiles and sense of relief on all their faces. Even the adjutant managed a grin. No one liked the thought of injured people having to wait longer than they had to for help.

Mike picked up from before. "The *we*, Colonel, is myself and Brigadier Rawlinson. He was the person I spoke to on the phone earlier. I told him about the sinkings in the ports, the emergency lines being down, and what was happening here. He said he'd be down here in two hours to meet you, but first he had to meet a friend, somewhere more important than here."

"*Somewhere more important than here?*" the Colonel enquired.

Mike realised now was the time to play his ace. "Well, Colonel, let's find out. You've got the phone in front of you – call him yourself. I've got the number right here to his landline. With a bit of luck, we'll get through to his wife Elizabeth. He was supposed to be here over an hour ago, I'd like to know where he is myself."

The Colonel nodded. "Okay, Mr Faulkes, but I warn you, if I find out this is some sort of joke, or you're wasting my time..."

Mike nodded, knowing only full well what would happen, as standing up he then walked out to where the secretary sat, asking to borrow a pen and smiling at her as he retrieved his phone from the pile, quickly jotting down the Brigadier's number that he had called earlier. Returning to the office, he stood beside the Colonel as he read out the number to punch into the old-style keypad. After a few seconds the Colonel handed the receiver to Mike.

"Here you go, Mr Faulkes. It's ringing."

Mike felt his heart almost skip a beat as the phone was picked up at the other end, the last thing he needed was for the phone not to work or for no one to be home.

"Hello, who is this?" The voice of Elizabeth came through loud and clear on the speaker.

Mike nearly jumped for joy as he answered, holding the mouthpiece close to his face. "Hello, Elizabeth, it's Mike again. I don't suppose Peter is still there, is he?"

"Ah, Mike, thank God. I was hoping you'd call back."

Mike didn't know how much Elizabeth knew, so he was guarded with his response. "Look, Elizabeth, I'm sat with some new friends of mine and you're on loudspeaker so the whole room can hear you. They'd like to speak to Peter about that same thing as well. However, he said he'd be down to meet me and was supposed to be here an hour ago. Do you happen to know where he went earlier?"

"Mike, these new friends of yours that are listening in, are they all from your old line of work?"

Mike looked up, surprised at the question as he answered, "They are."

"Well, I can't tell you where Peter went to as I don't know how secure this line is, but I can tell you this – he left two hours ago in a helicopter that was sent for him that was painted green. He left me a telephone number for you to call and has told me you may be having difficulty explaining to your new friends about what's to come. Therefore, he's asked that you call the number as soon as possible, but before you go can I get your number there in case I have to call you back?"

Mike looked up at Sergeant Major Yackers, who, seeing the prompt, produced a piece of paper with the number of the phone box on it. He'd scribbled the number down when out at it earlier.

Mike smiled in thanks as he took it, reading out the number slowly to Elizabeth, hearing her jot it down, repeating it to herself. Once she'd read it back to him, he took a paper and pen and jotted down the number that Peter had left for him. He read the number back, just to confirm it was correct before adding, "Look, Elizabeth, things may get a bit hectic soon. I just want to say you take care of yourself up there, okay?."

He could imagine her smiling as she said, "Don't worry about me, I've got my own little private army."

Smiling, Mike remembered that Patch, Tony and Alan were living there. Of course she'd be all right.

"Okay. Well, I've got to get going. All the best, okay?"

"You too, Mike, you stay lucky. Peter told me where you are, I just hope *they* listen to you."

Upon hearing the conversation through the speaker, Mike saw everyone look at each other as the phone went dead.

"Picked up by a military helicopter? Where has he been taken to?" Chris enquired thoughtfully.

Captain Baker looked over to Chris, her eyebrows raised. "Why do you think it was a military helicopter?"

Chris frowned as he replied, "Green, Mrs Rawlinson said the helicopter was painted green. She thought the line wasn't secure so just dropped in the colour so as not to give too much away."

"Smart woman," remarked the GSM in admiration. "I wish some of my ex-girlfriends had been that smart."

Smiling, but with a bit of malice in his eyes, Chris replied, "Perhaps they were smart, GSM, hence they're not with you now."

The CO quickly interjected, not wanting to get dragged off topic. "Look, as much as I'm sure you'd like to discuss the GSM's love life, I'm more concerned with where the hell did the Brigadier go to? And to send a military helicopter, something's up here. Let's ring that other number if you please, Mr Faulkes."

Mike dialled in the next set of numbers, wondering himself where Peter had ended up.

After only two rings the phone was answered. A cold officious voice said, "Hello?"

"Hi, it's Mike Faulkes here, can I speak to Brigadier Rawlinson please?"

"How did you know the Brigadier was here?"

"I've just spoken to his wife, who told me to call this number."

"Give me your telephone number please."

Mike read out the number again off the paper in front of him. The caller confirmed the number before replying, "Right, I'd like you to keep this phone line clear and wait for further instructions."

With that, the line went dead. Chris looked over at the CO and Mike, frowning. "Bloody strange telephone manner there. No introductions, no explanation – who the hell were we just talking to?"

Mike looked equally puzzled as he replaced the phone on its cradle and sat back down, before remarking, "Well, whoever it was they're located with the Brigadier. I guess we just wait for them to call back."

The adjutant returned from the window and stood by the Colonel. His voice was low, but the tone strained. "Colonel, surely you're not going to speak to the Brigadier about what this man has mentioned today? I agree that the phone box was a great idea, but even a broken watch can be correct twice a day. The story he's just mentioned sounds pure fantasy, almost borderline unbelievable – if I was reading a book, I'd be impressed. But, let's say that you do manage to speak to him, what on earth will you say? He may be retired but I also happen to know he has connections, powerful connections, who could still damage your career if he thinks you've gone soft. I mean, are you really saying you believe any of this?"

"Are you really saying Adj that you don't? That you think all the events today are coincidental? Why did someone just whisk him away in a helicopter? And who were we just speaking to then?"

The adjutant said nothing in response as the Colonel looked up the table to everyone sat there.

"What do you all think here? You've all heard the same as me, do you think there's some truth to it? If you have any thoughts, please share them."

Captain Reynolds was the first to speak. "As you know, Colonel, I can never afford the luxury of what ifs or hunches in an investigation. I have to go with the facts, but the facts are that so far this camp has experienced an attack the likes of which has not been seen on UK soil for at least thirty years. I think even then we'd have to go back to the Northern Ireland Troubles to find something equal. Let's not forget as well that this is a Training Squadron and the main training centre for the Royal Armoured Corps. It can't be random and *if* it was a terrorist attack, why here? There are softer targets to hit. After what Mr Faulkes has just told us, I'm thinking terrorism is not the cause and this could be part of a bigger plan. But again, an invasion of the UK? It just seems so... far-fetched."

The adjutant and engineer Captain both nodded agreeably, but importantly Mike saw that others were shaking their heads and looking at each other. Some people at least thought it possible.

Captain Baker then remarked, "I'm not buying it. I'm sorry, Colonel, but I just can't see how it's possible. I'm sure there's going to be a rational explanation for all of this."

The Colonel nodded as he turned to his adjutant. "What about you, Adj? You've made your thoughts clear already, but I want an official opinion."

The adjutant looked around the room as he spoke, his eyes settling on Mike. "Colonel, I think this whole thing is just one man's fantasy, coupled with pure coincidence. He's been sat there listening to all of us chat, against my better wishes, and just thought this whole thing up on the spot. I mean he's been out of the army for what? Eleven years? And now look at him, Lord of the table, with even a Colonel hanging on his every word!" Mike saw the CO grimace as the adjutant continued. "No wonder he's loving this, granted three people are dead, and granted we've not been attacked before like this, but do you really believe that *our* country, *our* intelligence services, *our* government has just simply sleepwalked itself into being attacked? I find it insulting to all those in higher office and request this man be arrested for attempting to waste our time."

The adjutant sat back confidently, a look of triumph on his face as he considered Mike's guilt an open-and-shut case.

Mike narrowed his eyes as he leant towards the adjutant, his tone measured. "Adjutant, if I might ask, what would I hope to gain from this meeting? I've got better things to do with my time than sit at this table trying to convince you all of the shitstorm that's brewing around you. My friend here offered me a job earlier, I'm thinking I'd like to accept. So why would my first matter of business be to come here, and risk my reputation, my honour and my integrity to fabricate a fantasy story? If I were lying, then tomorrow I'd be made to look a fool, I'd have ruined any future employment with this camp, but more importantly I'd have sacrificed my friendship." Mike looked to Chris before continuing. "My friend took a chance bringing me into this camp today, and I wouldn't repay that by tarnishing his reputation by him being associated with a raving fruit bat. The facts are the facts. Kick me out, I'll just go home and plan my next move for what I know is coming, leaving you to your own fate. But trust me, *something* is coming and tomorrow will be different if you do nothing and just sit there throwing insults."

An uneasy silence descended on the room as everyone looked at Mike in thought, finally broken by the Colonel, who turned to face Chris.

"Major Richards, you know this man better than us, as he has already mentioned, you brought him here. What are your thoughts? Should we be concerned?"

Chris had picked up a pen and was tapping it into his hand as he looked at Mike thoughtfully. "Colonel, I've known this man for almost all of my army career. We joined almost at the same time and both of us have followed the same career path, both being promoted within months of each other. We've been on operations together, been through some tough times together, and been involved in heavy combat together. I can safely say I know this man better than my own brother. I've seen him in times of stress and fatigue think clearly and act decisively. Something that others also saw, that meant Mike was one of the most respected and finest soldiers I ever had the pleasure to serve with. I've never known him to lie and even though it might have upset the people in the room, Mike would always tell people how it was, *not* what they wanted to hear. So, with regards to what he's telling us today, like you said already, Colonel, he's been able to answer more questions than anyone else at this table. And he does know Brigadier Rawlinson, they do spend time together, so that also begs the question why would he jeopardise that relationship? I can see no reason why he would sacrifice his honour, integrity and friendships over what the adjutant has described as an *ego* boost. I'd pay attention to what Mike says and heed his warnings. If he says this could happen or is happening, I'd listen."

The Colonel nodded as he turned to look at Major Noakes.

"Well, what about it, Major Noakes? Let's have your tuppence worth."

"I'll agree, Colonel that there's things happening here that are very strange, but an attack on the UK? Now? I'm sorry, I just don't see it. For a start, like the Adj mentioned, why no warning from our intelligence agencies? Why no warning from anyone? Surely you can't just expect an enemy force to appear on our shores – we'd track their aircraft coming in, their navy sailing down. You just don't do that in a matter of hours. If this were happening as Mr Faulkes has predicted, and let's say for argument's sake that Article Five had been neutered, then how on earth would you get an armed invasion force so close to our shores, without us first knowing about it and attacking it?"

All faces turned to Mike, waiting for him to answer. He took another sip of water, before replying.

"The Brigadier had thought outside of the box. Like you say already, Major Noakes, we'd track and follow all the naval and military air activity within UK airspace and waters. But what if it wasn't identified as military aircraft or seen as naval traffic? Let's start with the flights. For a start, do you know how many flights right this second are currently flying through UK airspace? How many cargo planes, private planes, passenger planes are flying right now above our heads? And how many of them are civilian? Imagine now you look up at the sky and see a plane at about thirty thousand feet. You can't make out its details, but you see it's a plane from the contrails in the sky. Naturally you'd pull out your mobile and look at an app on your phone and it would give you the flight details like aircraft type, heading, destination and such. But how do you know that's what you're looking at? Your app would say perhaps it's a Boeing 737. But again, how do you know that? You can't see from the ground what it is any more than a radar station hundreds of miles away would see it as anything more than a blip.

"The Brigadier had learnt from friends within the air force that an enemy air force could fly in using the commercial routes, with commercially approved flight plans. And even if they weren't approved, remember that Phase Two called for infiltration of the UK's NATS network and air traffic control systems. Flight plans could be changed, altered or even updated, on the go. The radar operators looking at a blip on a screen would only see what the computer wanted them to see, relying on the filed flight plan held on the NATS database. What would look to be a simple flight from Iceland to Paris, could instead be a fully loaded military transport plane, loaded with soldiers, happily flying across the UK with no one any the wiser, until, of course, it gets to its intended target. And by then it's too late, it's there above its target and there's not a damn thing you can do to stop it. Same for fighter aircraft, again flying across UK airspace with everyone thinking it's a commercial plane. It's already over its target ready to strike by the time you're aware."

Mike paused to let his words sink in. He realised it was almost information overload, but he needed to answer their questions. If they believed him then there was half a chance this could work. The GSM ran a hand through his hair and looked up. "Fucking hell, could it really be that simple to do?"

"You mentioned the fighter jets, Mike, but wouldn't people on the ground see them as such? Wouldn't that set alarm bells ringing?"

Mike turned to his friend and said, "Yes, mate, it would, but what could you do? Again, the phones don't work, so how would you respond? How would you get the word out? By the time we'd know about it, it would be too late. Besides, daylight will be fading soon. Anyone on the ground looking up would only see the navigation lights on the planes, if they were able to see anything at all. From that height you still wouldn't know what it was.

"I take it the same applies to the marine traffic, ships loaded with troops and weapons sailing through our waters posing as freighters or tankers. Again, undetected until they arrive at their port of destination?" the Colonel now asked, with eyebrows raised.

"Exactly, Colonel, remember the Germans used the same techniques to get their army into Denmark in 1940. Cargo ships that were fully loaded with SS battalions sat docked in Copenhagen port ready to go. They had arrived days before Germany planned to invade. When the Germans began invading, they simply unloaded the troops in the very ports they wanted to capture."

Mike looked back to Major Noakes. "So, Major, that's *how* an enemy force using Fools Mate could get in under the radar, so to speak. Hopefully that answers your question?"

Major Noakes sat there silently nodding his head as he muttered, "Bloody sneaky, if someone pulled that off. I hope to God your wrong though. Why the hell a report like this would be ignored is anyone's guess!"

Mike was about to answer when the Colonel asked, "Mr Faulkes, you mentioned these different phases, so are you suggesting that if you believe Phase Two is being conducted now, then this Phase Three could begin tonight? Is that the sort of timeframe we could be working to?"

"Perhaps, Colonel," Mike replied thoughtfully. "I'll be honest though, I'm hoping that when that phone rings you should be able to talk to the Brigadier. At least he can give you more answers than I can. I appreciate it's been a long day and not the sort of information you wanted to hear, and I hope to God I'm wrong. But when we spoke, he didn't seem to think I was overreacting, and it was that important that he wanted to come down here and warn you all about Phase Three."

The Colonel cocked his head inquisitively. "Why would he want to come down here to speak to us? What's Phase Three?"

"The capture or destruction of this base..."

Everyone looked up as Mike said the words, the GSM looking over to the Colonel as the information began to sink in, hardly able to believe what Mike had just said.

The Colonel was open-mouthed and then, recovering, he asked, "I beg your pardon, Mr Faulkes, the capture or destruction of this base? How?"

"I'm sorry, Colonel, but again that's something I don't know. All I can tell you is that for Fools Mate to work, the UK's armoured forces were to be destroyed at their bases. Lulworth, Tidworth, Warminster, Bovington, and Catterick were all to be either captured or destroyed. Hence the ports of Marchwood, Southampton and Portsmouth were to be denied their use as there'd be no way of getting armour back into the UK quick enough to reinforce our losses to stop any invasion force. One thing the war in Ukraine showed was just how important the tank was. Remember, before the Ukraine invasion everyone was talking of the tank having had its day in the sun and being obsolete. There were plans to phase them out by 2030, to be replaced by lighter vehicles, drones, and handheld anti-tank weapons. Now everyone can't get enough of them, even the Challenger 3 programmes have all been sped up." Mike looked over to his friend as he said that last part.

"So, if what your saying is true, then this base could come under attack, a very serious attack, tonight?"

"It could do, Colonel, yes," Mike replied, his tone quiet and serious.

The Colonel stood up and walked to the window, looking out at the camp in the dying light. He watched as some of the soldiers walked around in front of the offices, on their way to the cookhouse for their evening meal. He turned to face the group, his voice louder than before. "Did you all know that when I was at Sandhurst as a fresh-faced young officer cadet, I had to write a report about the attack on Pearl Harbour? It's something they get all young officer cadets to do. My roommate had to write about Gettysburg, but for some reason, some unknown reason, I was given Pearl. I spent weeks researching it; how the attack had been planned and organised; how the Japanese had secretly sailed to within three hundred miles of Pearl Harbour; how the American intelligence agencies had tried to figure out what the Japanese would do, even though they talked of peace. But do you know what the biggest thing that stuck in my mind was from that report I composed, the thing that I remember most? It wasn't the success of the attack, or the consequences of it, everyone knows that. No, it was Admiral Husband E Kimmel, the man in charge of the Pacific fleet and overall commander of Pearl Harbour, the man who everyone forgot."

"Colonel?" the adjutant enquired, looking puzzled.

The Colonel turned to face him, holding up a hand. "Hear me out, Adj, please."

After taking a deep breath he continued, "Admiral Kimmel was a good leader, well respected and known for his good tactical judgement. He was marked by his superiors as one to watch or, so people in the navy had thought, and was destined for greater things, even possibly a career in politics after the military. He'd been promoted to Commander-in-Chief of the Pacific fleet after his predecessor had been demoted for complaining about the lack of preparation in respect of fighting the Japanese. He came into Pearl Harbour like a breath of fresh air, organising the defences, training the ships in gunnery practice, and was credited with the fact that the Pacific fleet was brought up to speed and became more battle ready far earlier than had been anticipated. He knew the war with the Japanese was coming, he'd warned about it, he'd talked about it, and now he was preparing the Pacific fleet for it."

Everyone in the room was watching the Colonel, wondering where he was going with his thoughts, as he spoke calmly and slowly. "Three days before the attack on Pearl Harbour, Kimmel had received serious intelligence about hostilities with the Japanese and an attack on Hawaii. But, he'd also received a message from the US government that ordered him to release fifty per cent of his planes over to the islands of Wake and Midway. He assumed, against his better judgement, that they were the true targets. He ignored his own judgement, his own assessment and trusted those at the top to know what they were doing. He was sure that the intelligence services were briefing the president and his staff and that by being told to send his planes to Midway and Wake, they had more information than he did. Why would they ask him to weaken the defences of Pearl Harbour, if there was a risk it could be attacked? he thought. So even after receiving his own intelligence reports, he ignored the threats to his base and sent the planes away. That weekend, shore leave was granted and the men stood down and everyone prepared to have a great weekend..."

The Colonel paused, looking at Mike briefly before he continued addressing the room. "A moment ago, Mr Faulkes, you used the analogy of Pearl Harbour to describe the camp's current defensive state, which I think is fitting given what I'm trying to say now."

Mike looked at the Colonel as if reading his intentions, replying, "You're questioning what you believe and what you know. You want to think that what I've said is nonsense and just dismiss it, go home and forget all about it. But then deep down you're also thinking what if what I've said is true, what if it really is happening. What if tomorrow you wake up and someone else is sat in this office at that desk. What if you could have somehow stopped it?"

"Exactly that, Mr Faulkes," the CO replied, looking at him and pointing his finger. "This morning, before all the problems with the internet and phones, I received an email from the MoD telling me to begin stripping another six of my training tanks for spares, ready to send them to the Baltic states. There's a severe shortage of spares in the system and no replacements..."

Mike suddenly remembered his earlier conversation with Chris in the turret of the tank. Things really had been bad for the Armoured Corp.

The Colonel walked back over to his desk, "Did you know that on the morning of the attack at Pearl harbour, Kimmel was planning to play an early round of golf with one of his senior officers? Japanese fighters were already en route to his dockyards and airfields after having been spotted on radar. Midget submarines were trying to enter the harbour to attack the ships. Yet with all of this going on, Kimmel was still preparing to tee off on the first hole. All that preparation and training for his ships, aircraft and sailors would amount to nothing. His planes were lined up in neat little rows – sitting targets – their guns locked away, no ammunition readily available. His battleships all sat with guns locked in place and crews relaxing on beaches or asleep in their bunks. I always remembered thinking what would I have done; would I ever have been caught napping like that? I always made a point to remember that report I'd written as an example of how not to get caught with your pants down. I'd vowed I'd never allow myself to get into that sort of situation."

He stopped and pointed to a golf bag sat by his desk. "After this briefing, myself and the GSM were to go to the local golf course and play a few holes. I say *play*, but really the GSM would wipe the floor with me. Isn't that right, GSM?"

"Bloody right, Colonel!" he replied gruffly, hiding a smirk.

The Colonel added, "But after all you've just told me, Mr Faulkes, what *If* there is imminent danger? I could become Kimmel. What if I'm going against my better judgement, like you say, going to bed hoping you're wrong. What if tomorrow history judges me as the man that knew and did nothing?"

The Colonel sat back down, leaning forward with his elbows on the table and his hands clasped together, his chin resting on them. He gazed at Mike as he looked deep in thought, then said,

"Are you my Moros, or perhaps my Elpis?"

"Colonel?" Mike questioned.

It was Major Noakes who answered knowingly, "It's Greek mythology, Mr Faulkes. Moros was the impending spirit of doom and Elpis was—"

"The spirit of hope," Mike interrupted. "I was aware of the meaning, Major."

As if realising he'd suddenly shared too much with the group, the Colonel snapped himself from his thoughts, looking up with a sudden vibrant energy, his eyes fierce.

"Gentlemen, however history judges me, I'd rather be the overcautious fool any day than the man caught asleep at the wheel. GSM!"

"Sir!" The GSM now stood up, as the Colonel began to bark out his orders.

"I want you to get your merry band of blood hounds over to the cookhouses, all the messes and all the accommodation blocks and all the married quarters. I want everyone in full combats with helmets and body armour and reporting downstairs in front of the offices in one hour. All leave is now cancelled. No one is to leave the camp. Also, tell the guards on the gate to stop all military personnel from leaving. I don't care what the excuse is, they're to turn around and get into uniform. I want as much manpower as you can muster. Include the recruits at Stanley Barracks, get them up here, leave only minimum manning on the gates please. I'll also need two further men to act as runners for the time being, get them outside the office as quick as you can please."

With a quick "Sir!" the GSM was off and out the door. Striding through the reception area he turned to the three soldiers sat there waiting for orders and barked at them, "Come on, lads, time to earn your pay!"

The adjutant stood by the doorway as he watched the GSM disappear. He turned to say something, but the Colonel beat him to it. "Ah Adjutant, I need you to kindly do the same for me over at the officers' mess. Get everyone out of there and in uniform with helmets and body armour. I've no doubt there will be lots of questions and I'm hoping to have some answers within an hour. Tell them to expect a full orders group back here at the offices."

Without any further ado the adjutant walked out, his face betraying his disgust. Clearly, he wasn't happy with what had been said that afternoon.

Sergeant Major Yackers stood up, as if already expecting the orders to come, as the Colonel looked towards him. "Ah, Sergeant Major, I'd like you to go and get the quartermaster please, I understand you're good friends with him?"

"I am, sir. I know where his house is just outside of camp. What do you want me to tell him?"

The Colonel pointed a finger to emphasise the importance of what he was about to say. "I want you to tell him he's to round up his guys, from wherever they are and get into the camp in full uniform, again carrying helmets and body armour. I want the armoury opened and any ammunition stores opened ready to be issued. I want the keys to all the vehicle parks and hangars out of the guardroom, and in one hour, both he and you reporting back here. Happy?"

The Sergeant Major kept a stern look as he saluted. "Happy, sir, I'm on it now." With that he turned and left the room.

The CO now turned to Captain Reynolds. "I want you to collapse the cordon immediately, get your people back inside and open the road."

"But sir," she protested, "I've got an active murder investigation being conducted, you can't simply expect me to just drop it and collapse a crime scene. At least give me another twenty-four hours to get what I can from it!"

"I'm sorry, Captain, I'm more than happy to note your complaints, but the cordon is costing us too much manpower, and besides, being left out on the road like that they are too tempting a target. I'm deeming that camp security takes priority. The investigation will have to be suspended for now."

With a look of anger, Captain Reynolds glared at Mike as she picked up her beret from the desk and stormed out.

Mike stood up as the Colonel now addressed those left in the room.

"I'd like you all to return to your departments and grab whoever you can that are still around, then get them here within the hour. Again, full uniform, body armour and helmets. I'll want to know how many vehicles you have fit and ready to go and how many crews you can muster. I appreciate this isn't how the day started, but I need you all to remain focused and ready for anything. Questions?"

Everyone except Chris nodded. Instead, he looked over at Mike, asking, "Colonel, what about Mr Faulkes?"

The Colonel smiled as he looked at him. "Sorry, Chris, but if you don't mind, I'd like to steal your friend for a while." Chris smirked as he heard the CO use his first name. The Colonel quickly turned to Mike before asking, "That is, of course, Mr Faulkes, if you don't mind?"

Mike grinned back, pleased that people were now listening to him as he extended his hand to shake the Colonel's. "Of course not, Colonel, but please call me Mike. *Mr Faulkes* makes me sound like a bank manager."

The energy around the camp seemed to be contagious over the next twenty minutes as people sensed something was amiss. Normally, everyone would mill around a camp over the summer period, but Mike could see from the window of the Colonel's office people running between buildings, dressed in all manner of attire with a new sense of purpose as the orders began to filter through. Mike had taken the opportunity to go into one of the toilet washrooms and try to clean himself up a bit. He noticed the face looking back at him seemed to have aged slightly since that morning, but using some warm water he was able to clean the dried blood off his clothes and looked semi-presentable again as he walked back through to the CO's office and took a seat. Mike heard the GSM before he saw him as he walked back into the reception area, followed by another two soldiers.

"You and you sit there. Anything the Colonel wants, and I mean *anything*, and you both do it. You understand?" he growled.

"SIR!" came the response.

The GSM walked through, standing to attention as the Colonel was seated back behind his desk.

"Relax, GSM, for now at least we can wait until everyone's assembled. We can't do anything else." The CO pointed to one of the chairs.

The GSM removed his beret and sat down next to Mike, nodding as he did so.

"Sir, I've still got most of my soldiers getting the stragglers, but we should now have everyone on the camp getting into uniform. I've got to be honest, a lot of them wanted to know why. I didn't know what to tell them so just shouted at them to hurry up. The recruits aren't the problem, they'll do whatever we tell them to do, but the more senior guys, they'll want to know what the plan is. I've got to be honest *I'd* like to know what the plan is."

The Colonel looked out of the window. "I know, GSM, I'm hoping in the next few minutes for that phone to ring and we can all find out if this is a waste of time or not. For now, though, I'd rather have everyone hanging around outside, especially if we need to move quickly. Hell, if I must, I'll just shout orders out of the window."

The GSM smiled as he said, "No, sir, if there's any shouting to do that's *my* job!"

Smiling back, the Colonel pulled a bottle of Talisker whisky, single malt, from a drawer in his desk and produced three glasses, filling each with a generous measure. He offered one each to the two men who nodded their thanks as they each took one. As they raised their glasses and sipped on the drink the GSM looked over at Mike.

"One thing I've been meaning to ask you, how did you know about the phone box working? Was that in the plan that you told us about?"

Mike winced as the whisky warmed his throat. He shot the Colonel a look of approval as he placed the glass on the table before telling them all about his old friend, now working as a phone engineer. After he'd finished it was the GSM who spoke. "So, whoever had the plan hadn't factored in our own phone company's upgrades being crap and slow. They hadn't considered the possibility of the landlines still being in use, which was why those gunmen were as surprised as we were."

Mike nodded as he took another sip of the whisky. Perhaps it could dull the pain in his cheek, he thought hopefully, despite knowing he'd need at least another bottle for that.

The CO sipped his drink as he asked, "I take it that the Brigadier kept an old landline in his office then for that reason?"

"No, he hadn't factored any of this in either, he just felt that regardless of what the future held, it was also a good idea to have a backup phone in case the mobile networks ever went down. Don't forget even something like a solar flare could wipe out the world's mobile network. If that ever happened, the Brigadier probably wanted to be one of the few people in the world still able to order a pizza."

With a tense shrill the telephone on the desk suddenly began to ring, everyone's heads turning at once, the tension in the room suddenly increasing a notch. The CO looked on as Mike now stood and reached over to the phone, lifting it from its cradle.

"Hello?"

"Mike, it's Peter, you still in the phone box?"

Mike's eyes closed briefly in silent thanks that finally he had Peter on the phone. He looked at the CO and said, "Peter, firstly you're on speaker phone, we've piped the phone-box feed into the office of the big man you mentioned earlier. He's listening in now."

All three men in the office could hear in the background that Peter was somewhere very busy. There were muted conversations and raised voices going off and it sounded as if Peter was on the trading floor of the stock exchange on a busy day.

"Okay. Well, listen. Firstly, forget trying to talk in code on this phone, there's no time for that now and we need to be clear from the start. So, you're telling me that you've piped the feed from the phone box into Colonel Williams' office and he's listening in and can hear me now. Is that correct?"

The Colonel, without waiting for Mike to answer, now took the phone from him. "Hello Brigadier. That's correct, Colonel Williams speaking."

The relief in Peter's voice was plain to hear as he replied, "That's great news, that could save us a lot of time. Well done, Mike." Mike looked at the GSM as Peter continued, "Right, Colonel, I appreciate you don't know me and that you don't know where I am. So, I'm now going to pass the phone over to someone in a second who will verify to you that this call is genuine, and we are who we say we are. Wait one…"

The Colonel sat with a look of wonderment on his face as he heard the muffled noises over the loudspeaker as the phone was passed over to another.

"John, you there?" The Colonel looked up to the other two in the room as for the first time that afternoon he heard his first name. He recognised the voice immediately as one of his friends, Major Sam Tristan-Phelps.

"Sam, that you?" The Colonel asked.

"It is. Listen, before we continue, time's tight so I'm not going to mess about. Do you remember on your twenty-fourth birthday when we were in Canada, we both went up to Edmonton? I took you to that strip club called Stilettos and we both came back from there with two of the strippers?"

The Colonel looked up, his cheeks flushing, as he realised the speaker phone was allowing Mike and the GSM to listen in. Realising it was too late to stop his friend, he merely swallowed the lump in his throat, replying with, "I do."

"The two ladies were called Crystal and Dakota. I fell asleep drunk and you were the lucky bastard that got to enjoy the rest of the night with them. In the morning, we found out that they'd stolen both our wallets. When we got back to camp we cooked up a story about being mugged. Now you know that you're talking to me. Do you agree? Or should I share another story as proof?"

Mike and the GSM shared a look and smiled. Clearly the CO had an interesting past, but that would wait for another time. The CO looked out the window, probably to hide his embarrassment as he lowered his voice and said, "No, I'm happy it's you, Sam, now what the fuck is going on?"

Mike wondered what other stories the Major was willing to share.

"Do you remember where I've been working this past year?"

"Yes, you're the aide to the Chief of the Defence Staff."

"Good, because that's who I'm about to pass you over to now. Just wait one please."

The Colonel looked at the others in disbelief. The GSM looked at Mike enquiringly and whispered, "The Chief of the Defence Staff? That's General Catmur isn't it?"

In response Mike merely shrugged his shoulders, not knowing what to say. He was as surprised as anyone as to how Peter had ended up there.

After a few seconds the speaker phone blared again. "Okay, Colonel, standby for the CDS." There were muffled noises again as the phone was passed between hands before a loud authoritative voice boomed through.

"Colonel Williams? It's the CDS here."

"Good evening, CDS, how can I help?"

His voice was cold and calm with military precision and clearly no time for pleas-antries as he replied, "Colonel, I'm ordering you to immediate combat readiness, I want your camp alert level raised to red immediately, all leave is now cancelled. You are to get all military personnel back to camp, I don't care how. I want all your vehicles armed and ready for immediate deployment for war-fighting operations. Do you understand?"

The Colonel had stood up as the CDS said this, looking to the GSM and Mike, his face draining of colour. Even though Mike had warned him of what was happening, the cold hard reality of the most senior military commander telling him was now like a hammer blow to his chest.

With no time to reflect, the CDS shot back forcefully, "Colonel, do you understand?"

The Colonel quickly gathered himself as he replied, "I understand, sir. I must ask, though, is this an exercise or a real-world situation?"

"No, I'm sorry, old boy, but this is no exercise, it's real world. Now, there's written orders being flown down to you by helicopter, they'll be with you in the next ten minutes and will explain more clearly what your missions and tasks will be. In the meantime, I want you to be prepared to evacuate and withdraw from both camps no later than 21:00 hours. *No one* is to be left in those camps after this time. Any equipment that cannot be taken with you is to be destroyed immediately. No exceptions."

The GSM was open-mouthed as he heard the orders. Almost in disbelief the Colonel now asked, "But, sir, what about Lulworth? No one's spoken to them since all this began. How are they to be warned? What are they to do?"

The voice on the end of the phone was speaking to someone in the background, again distorted and muffled. Whatever was going on there it sounded like organised chaos. Finally, the CDS came back on.

"At present you are one of the only camps in the southwest that we've been able to talk to directly. When the helicopter gets to you it's yours to use as you see fit. I'd recommend you send a senior man with it over to Lulworth, try to get them to do the same as you have with the phone box that's there and then get the senior officer to call us. I believe you have the number?"

"We do, sir, Is there anything else?"

"Yes, I believe you have someone there who knows Brigadier Rawlinson? A Mr Faulkes?"

The CO looked over to Mike as he replied, "Yes, sir, I can hear you."

"Good. Colonel, whatever this man has told you, you are to take as factual and you are to consider his information genuine in all regards to Operation Fools Mate. Mr Faulkes, if you haven't already highlighted the threat to the camp then I suggest you do so after we've spoken."

"Already done, General, the Colonel's seen fit to bring the camp to alert status already." Mike was pleased that they were already ahead of the curve.

"Good. Well, in that case I'll leave you all to it. I appreciate you're out on a limb down there, and we're doing all we can to get the comms back online. You'll have your orders shortly. I cannot reiterate the importance enough though; you *must* be out of the area by 21:00. Right, Colonel, I've got to go, I'll pass you back over to Major T-P. Good luck!"

The line went quiet before the familiar voice of Major Tristan-Phelps came through the speaker.

"John, sorry about all this, it's absolute bedlam as you can imagine. I've just been told to quickly bring you up to speed on what we know so far. Can you just confirm, did Mr Faulkes tell you everything about what he knows?"

As Mike was listening, he watched as WO2 Yackers came in with another man who Mike assumed to be the quartermaster tech. The QM(T) had a look of confusion on his face as he entered the room, looking at the GSM and mouthing silently, "What the fuck?"

The GSM simply pointed to his lips, indicating for silence as the Major continued speaking. The two men were quickly followed in by the adjutant, red-faced and breathing heavily, carrying the Colonel's body armour and helmet whilst also carrying his own. He set the equipment down on the table with a loud bang as he took a seat, listening in.

The Colonel looked to the new additions as he spoke. "Mike's told me all about Phase Two of the operation and some of Phase Three, mentioning that Lulworth, Tidworth, Bovington and Catterick are to be targeted, but we don't know any other details. Are you able to help?"

They all looked to the door again as this time Chris, Major Reynolds, Captain Baker and Major Noakes all entered, carrying their body armour and helmets. Chris was in the process of chatting to the RMP Captain, but his voice died out when he saw everyone assembled in the room with serious looks on their faces as they listened to the small tinny voice on the speaker.

"John, have you seen the news about London? If not, I suggest you put it on now. I won't talk about it over the phone, but we've had multiple attacks across our air network. We've lost Swanwick and with it almost our entire UK-wide radar coverage. You're to treat UK airspace as compromised and certainly unfriendly for now."

The new additions in the room all looked shocked, almost unbelieving at hearing the news as the voice continued, "There's over forty ships currently transiting through the English Channel that we are suspicious of, coastguards reporting that eight cargo ships that were due to dock in Southampton have since changed course and are now heading towards Weymouth at full speed and we've got another seven heading for Poole. None of them are answering on the radio and they're not responding to any visual signals. We believe now that they have hostile intent and that they're going to attempt landing troops and equipment in your area shortly. We believe they're going to try to capture or overwhelm the Lulworth and Bovington camps."

"How close to Weymouth are they?" The Colonel's face was now a mask of seriousness.

There was a slight delay, as if the Major was reading the answer, before replying.

"The last report we had was that they'd be in Portland Harbour no later than 20:00, which means they could docking in as little as twenty-five minutes, hence your orders are to have you out of there no later than 21:00. Any time after this and you're in danger of being overrun. I'm sorry it's not good news, but I've got to get going, you need the time now more than I do. Good luck, old friend."

And with that the phone went dead...

12

Into The Fire

Peter knew they were landing as he heard the pitch of the Merlin helicopter's twin engines change and the rotors beat more heavily against the air, as the helicopter began to flare, to pitch up to bleed off its airspeed. He sat with Patch next to him, electing in the end to bring him, thankful of the company if ever they needed to get back to the farm. He'd left only ten minutes ago and as he'd kissed his wife goodbye, he'd given her a piece of paper and instructions on what to do should anyone call that needed to speak to him. He was aware that he'd promised Mike he'd be there, but he also knew that the man he was going to meet was more important and was necessary in getting the warning out. He'd smiled at Elizabeth and blew her a kiss as the rear ramp of the helicopter had closed before lifting him away to his new destination. Patch had said nothing during the flight, simply sat there, his back to the fuselage as they had both watched the English countryside flash by the window. The height and speed of the helicopter had told him that the meeting was urgent, and he sat back thinking about how best to begin the conversation. On his lap was the folder containing the report, all fourteen pages of it, a second copy that he had kept secretly after submitting the original.

They felt the rush of air as the loadmaster opened the rear ramp, whilst the helicopter was still in the sky and looked rearwards at the lush green countryside, watching fields full of animals and horses all grazing away oblivious to the noise of the helicopter overhead. Clearly, they were used to the comings and goings of helicopters in the area, the high-ranking dignitaries and visitors to the Chief of the Defence Staff's country estate a common occurrence.

The loadmaster walked to the rear of the helicopter and stood on the ramp, one hand supporting himself, as he kept relaying to the pilot information on what he could see on the ground. The view momentarily disappeared in a cloud of grass and dust as the helicopter lowered and hovered mere feet from the ground, before they felt the distinct soft thump as the wheels finally connected with the grass. Then, with the engines beginning to whine down, the helicopter settled on its gear as the power was decreased. Instinctively, both men unbuckled their seatbelts and stood up, watching the loadmaster as he walked out of the back of the helicopter, dragging the umbilical cable with him, keeping his headset still connected to the aircraft, allowing him to talk to the pilots.

Once happy with what the pilots had told him, the loadmaster gave them the thumbs-up signal to get off and pointed towards the safest direction for them to run to. They felt the familiar hot blast as the engine exhausts hit them, followed by the distinct smell of aviation fuel as they jogged off the ramp and, fighting against the powerful wash from the rotors, into the direction of a man who was stood in uniform, patiently waiting for them.

Peter approached the man and was about to speak, when he heard the engine pitch of the helicopter change and turned to see it was already about to take off again, with the loadmaster stood on the ramp. He wisely waited a few seconds, as the noise increased and the helicopter lifted off, the downwash from the rotors blasting all three men as they fought against it, backs turned to the helicopter out of habit, as dust and small stones hit their legs and arms. Thankfully, after only a second, the noise and wind died down and they heard the helicopter recede as it flew off on to its next mission. Afterwards, the silence seemed somehow alien to Peter as the stranger offered his hand to greet the newcomers.

Peter accepted the hand and smiled as he shook it in greeting. "Good afternoon, I'm Brigadier Peter Rawlinson and I believe the CDS is expecting me?"

The stranger replied, his tone courteous but clipped.

"Good afternoon, gentlemen, my name's Major Tristan Phelps. I'm the secretary to the CDS. I'm here to escort you to the General's office. If you'd both like to follow me."

Both men looked at each other as they began to follow the Major across the grass and over a large sweeping gravel drive, towards a set of wide steps that led to the vast Georgian-style country house. At the top of the steps were a set of double doors that were flanked by large white stone columns that added to its grandeur. They walked through the doors and into a large open hallway, with a white marbled floor and staircase that led to the upper floors. It was a grand entrance and Peter knew it had awed many a guest as it had him the first time he'd walked through the entrance, but he'd been here many times since and now the effect was lost on him. The Major turned to Peter and said, "Ah, Brigadier, perhaps your man here would be more comfortable in the kitchen area whilst you meet with the CDS? I can have food and drink brought to him."

Patch said nothing as the Brigadier gave him the quick once-over and smiled. Patch hadn't cleaned up after working on the horses, and in all the rush to get here Peter had forgotten that fact. Now there he stood, covered in horsehair and hay, and in boots covered in muck that had left a trail on the pristine marbled floor.

He nodded and said, "What do you think, Patch, do you mind waiting for me in the kitchen?"

Patch looked around him at the hall, then back at him, replying with, "If you don't mind, boss, I'd be happy to wait outside. The sun's still shining, and I think it's a bit too stuffy in here for me." He then turned to the Major. "I'd still like that drink and food, though, sir, if you don't mind?"

The Major nodded, choosing to ignore the barb. "Of course, I'll get it out to you right away." He then turned to Peter, his hand directing him. "If you don't mind, Brigadier, this way."

Leaving Patch where he stood, Peter followed the Major through an archway that led to a long hall, with large windows on one side and a collection of oil paintings on the other. Peter had seen them before and knew they depicted some of the British Empire's finest moments as he followed the Major, his shoes tapping on the stone floor. He already knew where they were going and how to get there, but decided to keep quiet and let the Major lead him in. At the end of the hall was another doorway that led through to a large open drawing room, with a large fireplace dominating one wall. The last time Peter had been here it had been on a cold winter evening and the fire had been lit, roaring away and illuminating the room as the guests had mingled and chatted away merrily. Now it was eerily quiet – the only sound was the rhythmic ticking of the grandfather clock sat at the far end. Peter noted the time was ten minutes too fast, checking his own watch to be sure. It was always the silly little details that he noticed first, he thought, as he walked across the room which was fitted with a plush blue carpet and paintings that adorned the walls. The furniture in the room was a mixture of English oak and cedar and Peter knew it was all original, as the General's wife had a habit of purchasing very expensive antiques. A habit he was happy that Elizabeth did not follow. Peter continued onwards as the Major walked over to the far wall where a large set of double oak doors were closed. He knocked once and waited, then the voice of the person inside replied, "Come!"

With a slightly dramatic flourish, the Major opened both doors at once, bursting through.

"Sir, may I present Brigadier Peter Rawlinson."

Peter followed the Major through the double doors and into another large, high-ceilinged room; an office with a large window that dominated the far end. In front of the window sat a huge oak desk, adorned with papers and folders and a lamp and telephone. In the middle of one wall sat an impressive fireplace, flanked by two Chesterfield armchairs, and above the fireplace hung a large oil painting depicting a cavalry charge at Waterloo. The cavalry's sabres were drawn, and the horses' mouths were foam-filled and wild-eyed with nostrils flaring; truly shocking if you were on the receiving end of such a charge. The General was perched on the edge of the desk, wearing a cream-coloured polo shirt and light-blue trousers. He was reading a piece of paper with a set of glasses on the end of his nose. He stood up as Peter entered, his face stern and focused as he looked to the Major, removing the glasses. "Thank you, T-P, there's no need for the theatrics, Peter's an old friend. Do we have an ETA on our other guests?"

As Peter stood there, the General motioned him over to sit by the fireplace as the Major replied, "Not yet, sir, The helicopter left only three minutes ago, so it should be back with everyone onboard in about forty-five minutes."

"Okay. Well, when they all arrive, I want them to wait in the conference room, and please make sure that they all have drinks ready for them."

"Certainly, sir, I'll get the house staff on it immediately."

"Now if you don't mind, I'd like to be left alone with the Brigadier. Close the doors on the way out please."

Peter walked over to his friend and clapped him on his arm, as both men nodded in greeting before sitting down in the armchairs facing across from each other. The

General reached behind him to a decanter and poured two drinks into the tumblers, before handing one to Peter who nodded his thanks. He waited for Peter to take a sip of the drink, before leaning forwards, eyebrows raised. "So, Peter, I'm afraid the pleasantries will have to wait for now. If you have an answer as to what's going on here now? I'd like to hear it please."

Peter placed his drink on the side table next to the armchair then leant forward, handing the folder to the General.

"James, I'd rather you read it than me explain, it'll be quicker."

With curiosity etched on his face, the General put his drink aside as he took the folder and extracted the file. He put his glasses back on and sat back to read as Peter picked up his drink and waited for the questions that he was sure were to follow.

As his friend read the report, Peter also sat back, sipping his drink slowly and looking around the room, admiring his friend's taste in military memorabilia. On the far wall hung a collection of swords; one ceremonial, which belonged to the General and was worn with his ceremonial dress. But the other two were in display cabinets mounted below the General's sword. One had belonged to a French cavalry officer who had died at Waterloo; its blade was bent and nicked in places. The other sword had once belonged to a German cavalry officer who had died early on in World War One; a bullet had bent the blade tip, as the unlucky owner had led a disastrous charge on horseback against British machine guns. James had acquired them through his various sources in the antiques world and had hung them there not as some sort of grisly trophy of a battle won, but as a reminder that there's always two sides to a war, the winners and the losers. The trick in life was to not become the loser, and every time the General looked to the swords it was to remind him that his own sword was never guaranteed to remain at the top. However, so long as he was the CDS it was his job to make sure it did, to ensure that even in peacetime his country's armed forces were always ready for war, and that in the years to come his sword wasn't going to be just another example of failure sat in an enemy officer's collection, mounted on the wall. Peter had laughed at first when his friend had told him. However, he also understood the motivation behind it. A testament to what failure could look like.

He gazed back at his friend as the CDS asked without looking up, "When did you write this?"

"March 2012, it was part of the Anvil files. There were five reports written, what you're looking at is the fifth report."

"Really? I was asked to write one of the Anvil reports, I wrote the fourth one although you'd never have known, the author was put down as some bloody senior civil servant. I hadn't known there were five written and I certainly haven't read any of this before." He looked up at Peter as he continued, "Who else has seen this? Who did you pass it on to?"

Peter leant forward, his eyes narrowing. "James, this report was kept out of the Anvil files and never submitted. I thought at the time that it was just because it was perhaps too outlandish, or too cavalier to contemplate. Either way I was ordered not to ask any further questions and to forget I'd even written about it. But I decided I'd keep a copy regardless. And that is what you're holding in your hand now, the only official copy of Operation Fools Mate."

"So, this was never submitted and never commented on by the Civil Service?"

"No, it was submitted, the Civil Service gave it an author, but two days after being submitted, he was killed in very suspicious circumstances."

"I see, hence why you wisely kept quiet." James turned a page on the report and continued to read as Peter talked.

"I wasn't sure if it was our side keeping the report quiet because it was too plausible, or if it was perhaps someone on the other side doing it because they wanted the report to be kept hidden. Either way, that folder was locked in my safe just in case."

"Just in case of what? Someone using it?" The General cocked his head inquisitively, smirking as he carried on reading.

Peter said nothing as he watched the General continue to read, but this time he noticed that as his friend did so, he slowly began to tense and sit up straighter. He looked up at Peter momentarily and then carried on reading. This time a finger was placed on the paper, following the lines as if that would somehow help the General understand better. Peter noticed the General was reading much faster now, as he flipped through the pages, quickly scanning the rest of the folder. He looked up after he finished, horror on his face. "Good God! Did you really write this back in 2012?"

"Yes."

The General stood up and quickly went behind his desk, the folder still in his hands, pressing a bell located near the telephone.

"And no one in office has seen it? No one in our government has even commented on it?"

"No, like I said, the original was buried."

"This could be the missing piece." A faraway look appeared in the General's eyes as he continued talking to himself. "Yes, that would make everything all fall into place. Everything would fit."

"Tumat by any chance?" Peter raised an eyebrow questioningly.

The General looked up at Peter, his thoughts drifting back to the room. "I'm sorry, my friend. I promise I'll explain it all shortly, but there's things we need to do first."

The General looked out of the window at the fields of the estate beyond. Before turning, he glanced over at the swords, his jaw hardening. Peter didn't need to be a clairvoyant to know what the General was thinking as he'd spent the past hour contemplating the same dark thoughts. The double doors now opened, with the Major walking to the desk and standing to attention. His head turned to Peter and then back to the General as he saw how serious they both looked.

"T-P, I need this report photocopied eight times. Plus, I want you to activate the Wonderland protocol immediately."

The Major's face creased in confusion. What had panicked the General so, he wondered. Keeping his thoughts hidden he replied with, "Certainly, sir, I'll do it now. Is everything okay?"

The General had a faraway look in his eye as he stood there, then quickly realising how it looked in front of his aide, he composed himself and smiled, his voice calm as he looked back to the Major. "Yes, everything's fine. I want Wonderland up and running, though, within the hour. Get everyone back in with no exceptions, all leave is now to be cancelled for all the staff."

The Major's mouth opened as he realised what he was being asked to do. "Sir with the phones down, we'll struggle to get people back in within an hour."

The General nodded as he said urgently, "Yes, regards the staff, let's get the two police guards outside on their bikes to go door-to-door and notify them. Most of the staff live locally so that shouldn't be too hard to do for them."

The Major quickly took the report from the General, turned and semi-jogged out the room, leaving the doors open. Peter sat pondering what had been meant by the word *Wonderland*. What trick did the General yet have to play? Remembering what had been said earlier Peter quickly asked, "James, what about your guests coming in on the helicopter to the party, won't you have to warn them off?"

"Guests? Oh, you mean *those* guests. No old friend, after I'd spoken to you and found out myself just how bad the communications network were being affected, I'd activated the Defence Council into coming here. We all call it a Seven-meeting due to the seven members of the council. You see, the phones may not be working but thankfully we've still got the VHF communications working. Every member of the Seven now has a backup radio watch on at their homes twenty-four-seven, for just such an emergency as today, hence that helicopter you came in on earlier has now been sent out to pick them all up. The Defence Secretary is on his way in. He wasn't happy about it though, but I think he'll understand the importance once we meet. I thought that your report would explain what was happening, though, I didn't realise it would be the bloody catalyst for what was happening. They'll be here shortly, and we can both show them what you've just shown me. Plus, there's other factors at play, ones you can't have known of yet, which is why I want you in the room with us."

The General walked back to the fireplace, leaning against it as he looked at his friend. "Peter, we've got some time until they get here, so apart from what's written in that report I'd like you to tell me everything you know about the operation. How did you get the idea? How did you know to call me on the landline? And how did you know all about Tumat?"

Peter stood up, took a breath and then began to tell his friend all about Operation Fools Mate.

Thirty minutes later, and Peter found himself in the large open briefing room that would normally be set up for one of the General's frequently held dinner parties, also doubling up as a dance floor. But today, it was arranged for its true purpose, with a large rectangular table and twelve chairs setup in the middle of the room. On the far wall stood a large eighty-two inch flat-screen TV, its display showing the MoD logo and the words *Defence Council Meeting*. On the table were glasses of water and each of the positions had a name place denoting who was to sit where. In front of the General's chair sat eight copies of Peter's report, printed no less than ten minutes ago. The General was stood talking to Major T-P at the far end of the room. With nothing to do but wait, Peter walked up to one of the folders and picked it up, noting it seemed to have less pages than his own folder. He quickly glanced through the other eight folders and noticed that the first four pages of the report were missing from all of them, the part he had always referred to as Phase One. He looked to his friend, his mouth pinching in irritation as he spoke. "James, sorry to be a stickler, but these reports are all missing their first four pages."

The General nodded at the Major, who turned to walk out of the room, the General waiting for him to leave before replying.

"Yes, I know, Peter. It's not a cock-up. I just don't want the Defence Secretary to see those details yet."

Peter looked on confused, as his friend continued, "You remember Sir Charles Lynwood, Chief of Defence Intelligence and Tony Kew, my Vice CDS?"

Peter nodded and the General said, "Sir Charles, Tony and myself have been discussing our new friends in Tumat a lot over these past few months, privately of course, and it would appear that from Sir Charles's various sources that our new Prime Minister and the American President have become very chummy with this President Iylanovitch. There's been a lot of talk of secret trade deals and negotiations behind very closed doors, all very hush-hush and making us suspicious. Sir Charles and his American counterparts in the CIA have been watching Tumat for some time and they're not liking what they're seeing."

"And what did our PM say when you discussed it with him?"

"That's just it, we haven't discussed it. The mere fact that we know of these meetings could drop both myself, Tony and Sir Charles into some very hot water." Peters face creased into a frown as his friend added, "We've all been under very strict orders right from the start not to go sneaking into the affairs of Tumat. Even a mere mention of the country with any hint of suspicion invokes the PM's wrath. I've been waiting for the PM and Defence Secretary to bring up the subject with the Seven, but they never have. So far, the PM's inner circle is remaining tight-lipped about this new country, and I don't know who knows what." The General shrugged as he continued, "Has the PM briefed the Defence Secretary on his plans? I don't know, but I can't take the chance if he has. If we want to at least get the other members of the Seven to see your report, then for now, Phase One must be kept out of it."

Peter nodded in understanding, before asking, "So even as the CDS, even *you've* not been briefed by the PM on Tumat or *any* of these meetings?"

"No, not even a sniff."

"But what about privately? You're the CDS, surely you've had private meetings with the PM?" Peter asked, surprised.

"No, for the first time in a long time I've been kept out of the loop. Every time I've tried to schedule a private meeting with the PM he's been too busy to see me. His chief advisor has been keeping us apart, I think deliberately."

Peter shook his head in disbelief. What on earth had the government been playing at? Keeping its plans secret from its own armed forces. What would they hope to gain from that?

The General pointed a finger at Peter to emphasise what he was about to say. "Which is why when the Defence Secretary comes in shortly, you need to let me handle the meeting. By all means discuss the concept of the operation, talk about the plans and the other phases, but *do not* mention Tumat, keep that part to yourself. If you do mention Tumat early on, then I fear the Defence Secretary will pull the plug on the meeting, as I can't guarantee what he knows or more importantly what he's hiding. If he is part of the PM's inner circle, then he'll be keen to whitewash the whole thing and then we're left with nothing. And you know what these bloody politicians are like, they're all bathed in Teflon at birth."

Both men were interrupted by the sound of the helicopter approaching the estate, followed by Major T-P standing in the doorway. "Sir, as you've no doubt heard, the helicopter has arrived, also Wonderland is now up and running and the remainder of the staff are all coming back into work now."

"Thank you, T-P." He noticed the Major still stood staring back at him before he enquired, "Is there something else?"

The General felt the Major's eyes study him from head to toe before he replied, "Sir, might I suggest you get into uniform, perhaps I could have it brought here for you?"

"Oh bollocks!" exclaimed the General as he realised he was still wearing his trousers and polo shirt. "Yes please, T-P, have someone bring me my uniform. I'll change after the meeting, there's no time now."

"Sir."

With that, the Major turned and left, his footsteps echoing down the hall as Peter remained looking towards the now empty door. Keeping his voice hushed, he asked, "James, what's Wonderland?"

He saw his friend's face break into a smirk.

"I'll show you that later, Alice, when we *both* tumble down the rabbit hole."

Five minutes later and Peter was sat at the back of the room on a chair with a small desk, away from the main table as he watched the members of the Seven – the Defence Council for the UK government – arrive. Some he recognised from the dinner parties, others he knew from his own time in the military. All of them were in uniform and some of the council members were chatting amongst themselves quietly as they came in and took their seats at the table, whilst others were looking around the room, their eyes settling on Peter, wondering what he was doing there and what his purpose was at the meeting. Sat near the head of the table was James, who Peter knew throughout the meeting would now be referred to only by his title of CDS. With other Generals in the room it would soon become confusing if everyone were to be called General. The CDS stood as the members arrived.

As everyone took their places, Peter noted that all the Chiefs of Staff had a Major or equivalent rank sitting to their right, no doubt acting as secretaries or assistants to the more senior officers. The seat at the head of the table was left empty, reserved for the Defence Minister and Secretary of State the Rt Hon Jeffery Dickinson MP on whom everyone now waited for.

As they waited for the MP, Peter took the time to scan the room, to see the people he would be briefing shortly. He looked over to the person next to the CDS, wearing the uniform of the RAF. He recognised her as the Chief of the Air Staff (CAS), Air Chief Marshall Penny Moore, one of the first in a long line of women to have qualified as a fighter pilot. Next to Penny sat her secretary wearing the rank of Squadron Leader. Next to the Squadron Leader, sat in the dress uniform of the Royal Navy was the First Sea Lord and Chief of the Naval Staff (1SL/CNS) Admiral Sir Tony Phillips. Sir Tony was a highly decorated sailor who had been the first Commander of the carrier HMS *Queen Elizabeth* when she was commissioned in 2016. Next to the First Sea Lord was his secretary wearing the rank of Commander and next to him sat the Chief of the General Staff (CGS), General William Boswell, a former infantry officer - Peter remembered he tolerated no nonsense and was always forthright in giving his opinion. Next to William sat another Major and next to him sat the Chief of Defence Intelligence (CDI) General Sir Charles Lynwood, a former special forces soldier who was once the Commanding Officer of the Special Reconnaissance Regiment. Unlike some of the other Generals, he kept himself 'match fit', as he liked to call it, and even at the age of fifty-six still ran ultra marathons. Peter noted he did not have anyone acting as his secretary – instead, an empty chair sat next to him. Peter guessed perhaps they couldn't find the person they needed in time for the meeting and the CDI had elected to come on his own. Finally, next to the CDI sat the Vice Chief of Defence Staff (Vice CDS), General Tony Kew, who again, like the CDI had no secretary.

The chatter died down and everyone stood as Jeffery Dickinson, the Defence Secretary entered the room. Peter noted he was wearing a dinner jacket complete with dickie bow and guessed he'd been pulled from a formal engagement to attend the meeting. He smiled to everyone before seeing Peter and a brief look of confusion crossed his face. Ever the politician though, he quickly hid his doubt as he took his seat, motioning for everyone else to sit down with a wave of his hand.

His head turned towards the CDS next to him. "Appraising his attire he enquired, "Wash day, perhaps, CDS?" raising an eyebrow.

No one laughed as the CDS replied, "Excuse my dress sir, but I didn't have the time to get changed."

The Defence Secretary nodded as he looked back. "Okay well, no matter. Between ourselves we should look like quite the contrast, don't you think?" He glanced at his watch before continuing in a displeased tone, "Right, I'm already going to be late for the Prime Minister's fundraising gala this evening, so let's take a look at what's got us all in a fizz, shall we?"

The CDS nodded, ignoring the criticism in the Defence Secretary's voice. He looked around the room and began. "Thank you all for coming in at such short notice, but I think you'll all agree that with the events ongoing today, and from what I've just discovered, it will certainly warrant this meeting being called. Now you'll all notice a new addition to our meeting. I'd like to introduce you to Brigadier Peter Rawlinson, retired of course, but still the same sharp mind that those who knew him of old will remember. Some of you have served with him before and some of you have met him here at the house at one our parties. But aside from his charming conversation that's not why I have brought him into this meeting."

Peter acknowledged everyone as all eyes in the room turned to him. Then the CDS continued, his voice booming. "Peter's here because he's the one who earlier had brought to my attention the seriousness of what's been happening today. For those that don't know, aside from the two incidents at Portsmouth and Southampton, we've recently found out that all forms of mobile communications are down, including the internet and more importantly the emergency service networks. So now the question is how bad will this get? Is the worst over or is this the beginning of something bigger?"

He looked up the table towards the Chief of Defence Intelligence Sir Charles Lynwood, as he asked, "So, Sir Charles, what news from you?"

Sir Charles looked down at his laptop, now open and powered on in front of him. After a few clicks the TV on the far wall came to life and the display changed, showing the bullet points of what Sir Charles was about to say. He cleared his throat as he began. "What we know so far is that as of 06:45 hours this morning, the UK began to experience the beginnings of what we now know to be a highly sophisticated and co-ordinated attack on our systems. Without getting too bogged down with the details, this type of attack is known as a DoS or Denial of Service. Its aim was to disrupt and destroy key infrastructure systems, more hostile from the ones that GCHQ usually see. First to go were our mobile networks, with civilian operators reporting massive outages across the length and breadth of the UK, then it was our land-based internet, with all feeds offline, and now in the past few hours we've had various government systems being disrupted. Our air traffic control network, education databases, police systems and banking and military systems are all offline. Whatever this attack is, it doesn't seem contained. It's everywhere at once. And that concerns me."

"How has the attack spread so quickly to all our systems?"

Sir Charles looked up from his laptop at the CAS. "We're not sure at this time, we were looking into the possibility that once the attack had infiltrated the mobile networks that it was able to somehow hijack the 5G network using people's phones as the carrier. The emergency services in the UK all use 5G in their communications networks and to transfer data between hospitals and ambulances. So once the 5G network had been compromised it could get into our hospitals. From there it multiplied everywhere, using hospital systems and departments to spread further into the government's systems."

"But how did the military networks get infiltrated? And how is it that we have lost all our phone systems?" This time it was the Defence Secretary who spoke, his hands clasped together on the desk in front of him.

"Regarding both those points, I'm afraid at the moment we don't have an answer." Sir Charles looked up to the Defence Secretary almost apologetically.

"Well, Sir Charles when *can* we expect an answer? You are after all, Chief of Intelligence are you not?" The tone in the Defence Secretary's voice was condescending.

Sir Charles cleared his throat again before speaking. "My apologies, Defence Secretary, but the last communication that I had with GCHQ was over four hours ago. I had assumed that since no one had called me that there were no further updates and the situation had been contained. It was only after the CDS called me on the VHF radio that I was informed of just how grave the situation is. But I'm afraid that right at this moment I'm in the same situation as you – In the dark."

"So, at this moment in time, we have no way of communicating with GCHQ and no way of knowing what they are doing to stop this attack or how to prevent it from escalating?"

Sir Charles shook his head. "No, sir, but when we landed here, I'd cleared it with the CDS to get us a helicopter in from Brize Norton. We still have VHF comms with some of the bases around here in range, so once that lands later I'll personally get onboard and fly to Cheltenham. I'll have the answers you need before the night's out."

The Defence Secretary nodded, satisfied with Sir Charles's answer.

The CDS now looked up to the First Sea Lord Sir Tony Phillips. "Well, Sir Tony, I appreciate communications are poor at present, but do you have any further updates on the two ships that were sunk this morning?"

The Admiral looked over to the Commander sat next him and nodded. As if on cue, the Commander opened up his laptop and punched a few keys, the display on the TV changing to an aerial view of Portsmouth Harbour, showing the container ship seen earlier on the news. All heads in the room turned to look at the display as the Admiral leant forward, his elbows resting on the table as he began to talk.

"The reports I received earlier from Southampton and Portsmouth concern me. Clearly this was not accidental. Both ships were boarded and searched by members of the SBS. They found no crew members onboard but did find evidence that suggests both ships had been set up to allow them to be fully automated." As the Admiral talked, the images displayed on the TV began to scroll through, showing both scenes at Portsmouth and Southampton taken from multiple angles.

"What do you mean *automated?*" the Defence Secretary queried.

"The boarding parties found a sophisticated camera system on the bridge and all the controls were linked through to a computer-controlled station, meaning whoever controlled those ships did so remotely, never having to set foot on them." As he spoke, the images on screen now displayed the photos taken from the boarding party. Everyone could see the multiple cameras located around the bridge and a series of computers connected to the bridge controls. Waiting for the pictures to scroll through, the Admiral took a sip of water before continuing.

"We've also investigated as to how both ships sank, looking at the numerous camera feeds and from seeing what limited access we had to the hull, using divers, we think that shaped charges were used to blow out the hulls and watertight bulkheads, which maximised flooding, allowing them to sink as quickly as they did." This time the clear pictures were replaced with grainy ones, a blue-green hue to them, clearly taken underwater. But even though poor quality, everyone could see the jagged, twisted holes in the hull, the metal torn outward, blackened and charred from the explosives used. The Admiral looked up at the screen, waiting for the pictures to scroll through again, before adding, "This level of sophistication tells me that this was more than just a terrorist attack. It reminds me of the fire ships back in the day of sail. I cannot help but think that this was part of a bigger operation, which would make sense, as it's going to be a hell of a job to remove them."

The Defence Secretary picked up a pen, poised to write his response as he asked, "What's your estimates, Sir Tony, on getting them removed and the ports reopened? The PM will need to know."

"Already I'm receiving initial estimates of six to eight months for the salvage work, *at the very least.*"

"Six to eight months!" the Defence Secretary replied, his voice betraying his surprise. "Do you have any idea how much trade will have to be diverted and how much revenue will be lost with those ports now being closed? That's not to mention how many redundancies could be on the cards with unemployed dock workers. I've already spoken to the PM, reassuring him to have the ports reopened in six to eight weeks. Damn it, Sir Tony, you're going to have to do a lot better than that!"

The Admiral continued speaking, keeping his voice calm and measured. "But to salvage the ships will take time. The containers that we've managed to look at so far all show signs of being filled with concrete and scrap metal, not the easiest of combinations to unload. And the containers' locking pins all look to have been welded together, so we won't be able to lift them off to lighten the ships without undertaking some major engineering work. And even without taking into consideration the sabotaged cargo, the ships themselves have a draft of between sixty to eighty thousand tonnes. Normally the situation would require that we patch the holes and pump out the water, allowing us to refloat the vessels, but these ships have sustained serious structural damage from the explosive charges, plus we don't yet know if any of the charges failed to go off. Any attempt by us to refloat them quickly and we could have them break apart where they lie. Add to that the environmental damage if the fuel tanks were to rupture whilst we salvage them, and you could be looking at much of the south coast of the UK having a major environmental disaster. But as bad as that sounds that's not what worries me the most."

The Defence Secretary leant back, dropping his pen to the table, an acidic tone in his voice.

"Of course that's not what worries you, Sir Tony. Why worry about what the voters will think. But remember that you *all* want those budgets increased for those lovely, shiny new boats. And that funding comes from the taxpayers and to pay tax, people need jobs. So, I'll reiterate the priority *will* be to open those ports."

The Admiral remained impassive as he continued. "I'm sorry, Secretary, but the priority now for me is not getting both ports reopened, my priority is getting Portsmouth reopened. We should put all our resources into there first."

The Defence Secretary cocked his head curiously, asking, "And why on earth should we do that? Southampton has the bigger port and the biggest revenue, surely that should be our priority?"

The Admiral nodded to his aide who began to flick back through the photos on screen until the aerial view of Portsmouth was displayed again. Using a laser pointer, he highlighted the area behind the sunken ship. "His Majesty's Naval Base, Portsmouth, home to our carrier fleet and type 45 destroyers. There's HMS *Queen Elizabeth*, fifty percent of our carrier force and her support ships as well as four of our Type 45 destroyers and two Type 23 frigates all at their docks. All of them were due to deploy in a week as part of the Black Sea fleet to monitor the situation in Ukraine and to be a deterrent in the area. They're already fully loaded with supplies and arms and now all that firepower has been made redundant, stuck in the port for the next six to eight months. Meanwhile, the *Prince of Wales* and her task force are due back in a week and now have nowhere to go, the only other deep-water port able to accommodate her is Rosyth. And she'll need at least two months in dock, she's already overdue a much-needed refit. So, for the next two months we'll have no carrier task force able to put to sea, with one of our carriers and her fleet's logistic support now stuck in Portsmouth, along with three quarters of our Type 45 destroyers, Whilst the other carrier will be in Scotland, far from her home port and in need of a refit. From a navy point of view, sir, it's not what we'd call an ideal scenario."

It was the CDS who answered. "Okay, Sir Tony, thank you for the update," as he now stood up, indicating he had something urgent to say to the room.

"The events today do seem to be connected, I think we can all agree on that, but how? In what way is this all being played out? But before we investigate further, before we begin to dissect and digest the facts, I'd like you all to do something for me."

The CDS picked up the folders in front of him and passed them down the table, speaking as he did so. "Now you've never known me to waste your time and I can assure you that today is no different. In front of you all are folders containing a report for an operation that I would like you to read. We're going to do something that we haven't done in a while in this room – a little wargaming. However, I want you to discount the fact that we are part of NATO. As you read the report, imagine our country is on its own, no NATO and no allies. Once you've read it, I'd like you to share your thoughts on its plausibility. I appreciate it's not the usual format for our meetings but for now please study the report. It's only eight pages long and please save the questions, if any, until after everyone has finished reading."

Peter saw some confused looks around the table at the vagueness of what the CDS had just asked. But without any complaints they merely opened the folders and began reading. The only one who did not do so was the Defence Secretary, who merely stared at the CDS as he sat back down.

"Hang on, CDS, I appreciate the urgency of us meeting here this evening to discuss the matters at hand and after what I've just heard we seem to have more questions than answers. How is reading this report and playing a game going to help? The PM will want answers and I'm already an hour late for a black-tie event. Do you really expect me to tell him the Seven met this evening and sat around having a good read and finished off playing a bloody board game?" His tone was curt and accusing.

The CDS sat back in his chair, clearly unimpressed by the Minister's tone as he replied,

"Sir, this is an ultra-top-secret document, and I can assure you this is pertinent and important. I need you to read it so that we can decide on our next course of action."

"Next course of action?" The look on the Defence Secretary's face was almost unbelieving.

The CDS leaned forward, his voice lowered.

"Please, sir, just read the report. I promise it will all make sense once you have."

With loftiness and disdain, the Defence Secretary reached over, taking the folder, turning over the first page and began to read.

Peter watched on over the next few minutes as everyone continued to read. Some showed looks of confusion, others raised eyebrows as they began to digest the information from the report. Charles Lynwood was the first to finish, calmly closing the report and looking around at the others.

Next to finish was the First Sea Lord, who appeared deep in thought, passing the report to his aide beside him to glance over, as he, too, now looked around the room.

One by one, everyone finished reading the report, closing their folders and looking to the CDS who had sat back, pen in hand, tapping it against his mouth in thought. Some of them looked confused, as if a joke was about to be revealed. Others began muttering with their junior officers, highlighting parts of the report that they felt needed discussing further.

Finally, the last to finish reading was the Defence Secretary. Closing his report, he looked to the CDS, frowning.

"Interesting reading, CDS, but do you mind telling me why you've written a report on the events happening today?"

Ignoring him, the CDS stood up, hands planted on the desk in front of him as he addressed the others.

"Before I continue, I need to know now, has anyone in this room seen this report before or anything like it? Has anyone ever mentioned to you something similar to this in the past?"

Silence answered his question as the CDS continued staring at the Defence Secretary. "Sir, the report you've just read was not written today but was written in 2012 by Brigadier Rawlinson."

"That's impossible! How could you have known what was going to happen today? How did he know?" The Defence Secretary looked over at Peter then back to the CDS in disbelief.

Everyone turned to look at Peter, some open-mouthed, others clearly disbelieving, as the CDS continued speaking slowly and calmly. "Back in 2012 the Civil Service had approached senior military commanders to write a series of reports which were to be known as the Anvil reports. These reports were designed to try to forecast how an enemy force could attack and subdue the UK in the future, the idea being that if we knew what the hammer blow would be, we could be the anvil to take the strike to come."

The Defence Secretary nodded as he listened. "I remember those being written, it was the basis on which the MoD would focus its future spending. I think it was called the Army 2020 plan. But as I recall there were only *four* reports and those *were* written by the Civil Service."

The CDS looked down at the Defence Secretary, shaking his head. "No, Minister, I'm afraid that those reports were written by the *military*, as I myself was asked to write one. I wrote the fourth report. I submitted it only for my name to be scrubbed off the bottom and replaced by a different name."

The Defence Secretary replied flatly, "Okay so the reports were stolen from the military, a good idea taken from one department and passed off and submitted by another. Welcome to the world of politics, CDS, it happens every day in my line of work. So, this fifth report? How did it come to get misplaced?"

The CDS raised his eyebrows in response and then looked over to Peter and nodded as Peter now stood up to continue. "The report wasn't misplaced Defence Secretary, it was buried. I thought at the time it was due to being simply too far-fetched to be considered. However, I've since found out that the Civil Service author who was named, was killed two days after the report was submitted. I assumed that the UK security services had filed it away as ultra-top-secret and left it at that. I didn't find out about the author's death until 2016. By then it was too late to discuss further as I was retired and out of the loop, so to speak."

Peter remained standing, expecting more questions to follow.

The First Sea Lord looked to the CDS, his face creased with worry and his tone unbelieving. "Was this really written in 2012? Could someone be using this report now? Is that what you're saying James?"

By now the reports were being passed around the junior officers and aides, all reading through what the senior chiefs were now discussing.

The CDS looked around the room, addressing everyone. "Before we answer that question, I want to know do you think it's possible? From what you've just read, do you believe that it could work? Remember NATO is now out of the equation. It's just us, on our own."

The CDS turned to the Chief of the Air Staff. "Penny? What do you think? From the air perspective, could what you've just read be plausible?"

She looked at the folder, thinking, then looked to Peter before answering. "I mean, it's a novel way of getting aircraft through our airspace undetected, hiding them in plain sight, so to speak. I'd never considered or heard of anything like it before, but I mean the level of sophistication required, you don't just simply file a flight plan. You'd need to be hacked into multiple systems all at once to do this. And that would require a highly sophisticated cyberwar attack..." Her voice trailed off as she suddenly realised what she'd just said.

"A highly sophisticated cyberwar attack like the one we're currently experiencing now?" Peter cocked his head to emphasise the idea.

She nodded.

"But then of course you've got the radar signatures. You'd be reporting a commercial airliner coming in, but the radar operator would see that the return would be of a smaller aircraft, such as a fighter. Unless you've got stealth tech, you cannot fool the radar. It just wouldn't work."

"Actually, you can." Everyone looked at Peter. "I'm sorry to interrupt you, Penny, but you can fool radar."

"Okay, Peter, do you mind explaining to me how, because I'd like to know," she asked.

"Please forgive me, Penny, if I'm already covering something you no doubt know very well. In the days of World War Two, radar consisted of the operator watching the radar return and assessing what altitude and bearing the incoming contact was at, all very rudimentary and basic. But as these systems evolved, so did the information it gave. Suddenly, radar could detect much more than just the aircraft speed, height and heading. Because radar had become more precise, the radar return would also now pick up smaller targets such as flights of birds, rain clouds, land masses, off-shore wind farms and ships to name but a few examples. Now, some operators *could* distinguish between a flight of birds and an enemy contact through experience and personal knowledge of the system, whilst other more inexperienced operators could not. Knowing that the big weakness in the system was now human, radar designers sought to eliminate this, and as early as the 1970s radar systems began to rely more on computers to remove the clutter before the operator ever got to see it. Now, the only thing seen on modern radar screens is the actual aircraft flying. Everything else is digitally processed and removed if it's deemed as unnecessary and that's all done by computer."

As if expecting the answer already, she interrupted. "Yes Peter, I'm well aware of quantum radar, computers that do all the leg work, but what you're suggesting is that one of our radar systems could be hacked into. An unlikely concept as we have independent radar sites located all over the UK and all guarded by our own armed police and military. To think someone could simply hack into one would take a large amount of work and involve a level of espionage that even James Bond would struggle with. You'd need to hack into at least four of them to make any kind of dent within our air defence network, and it would not go unnoticed. By attempting to infiltrate the sites, they'd have warned us about their intentions long before their planes had even got off the ground."

She sat back shaking her head as Peter quickly countered, "Actually Penny, there's twenty-three independent radar sites covering the UK, something that is widely advertised all over the internet. In fact, if you were to Google them, you'll find out their exact locations dotted around the UK and all these radar feeds go to the Swanwick Centre in Hampshire. Granted, you'd need someone on the inside at Swanwick to plant the tech, allowing them to access the programming, but that's not impossible given what we know about foreign intelligence services. Instead of hacking into four sites that are guarded, you'd hack into one site that has regular military and civilian contractors visiting. Then you'd programme the system to filter out certain returns. The computer would think it was simply filtering out a flock of seagulls, or the latest wind-farm site and the operator wouldn't even know about it. Now you have access to all twenty-three radar sites, and you also have access to the NATS database, allowing you to alter and change flight plans at any time."

The CDS looked up to the CAS inquiringly. "Well Penny, is he right? Could it be done?"

She sat back, deep in thought, looking at Peter, and then finally she replied, "I didn't think about it like that. Instead of fool the radar, fool the computer." Suddenly as if dismissing the notion, she shook her head and looked at the CDS. "But what about the ASACS (Air Surveillance and Control System) at RAF Boulmer? They'd see on their own screens what Swanwick had missed. They'd still pick up the aircraft regardless of Swanwick being hacked into."

Peter shook his head in response. "I'm sorry, Penny, but the ASACS at RAF Boulmer gets its feed direct from Swanwick. They'd both be fooled by the same system, relying on it to be secure."

The CAS sat back and nodded in thought, before replying, "I'd have to confirm all of this with 19 Squadron, but I can't rule out the possibility of that working." Her tone was inquisitive as she thought through what had just been said.

The CDS continued. "Okay, so we've agreed at least that the air plan is plausible." He now turned to the First Sea Lord. "What do you think about the sea power aspect, Sir Tony? Would the incidents at the ports today cause that much trouble? Could this all be part of a bigger plan?"

Sir Tony looked at Peter thoughtfully before remarking, "To sneak in an invasion force right under our noses, of course that's possible – unless we boarded every tanker or freighter in English waters you wouldn't know what or who they're carrying. The English Channel has at any time hundreds of ships sailing those waters, so you could hide in plain sight. But surely our intelligence services would pick up on the mass mobilisation and hostile intent of another nation? And again, the level of planning and detail. And why would NATO not assist us? That's the bit I don't understand? What are you keeping from us?" The Admirals looked quizzically at the CDS.

He merely held up a hand and replied, "All in good time, Admiral, all in good time."

The disbelieving voice of the Defence Secretary interrupted. "Look, I'm sorry, but before we go any further, can I just ask, and I appreciate that I'm not as militarily minded as everyone else here, but how is this plan supposed to work if this invasion force consists of only one hundred and fifty thousand soldiers? That seems a little light, doesn't it, given we have a large population and an army with reserve forces that can match those numbers."

"We can discuss the numbers in a moment, sir," the CDS countered, adding, "Peter, could you explain using the large screen how this plan of yours would work, from a land warfare perspective I mean?"

Standing up, Peter walked to the main screen. Looking over to the CDS he asked, "Could I get someone to bring up a map of the UK please."

The display now flicked on to show a large map of the United Kingdom. Peter walked over to the table and picked up a laser pointer, before highlighting areas of the map he wanted to talk about.

"So, the key to all of this, is surprise, speed and most importantly, the destruction of armour. For this to work effectively, the invasion force would have to seize or destroy our armoured forces within the first forty-eight hours. Here we have Catterick in the north, and Tidworth, Warminster, Bovington and Lulworth all to the south, all areas where the UK's fighting forces of tanks are kept. In the initial stages of my plan these camps were to be seized or destroyed by overwhelming force, to keep the tanks and armoured vehicles stored in them away from the battlefield. I had planned to have forces coming ashore at Weymouth and Poole Harbour in the south and Newcastle upon Tyne in the north. This allowed the attacker access to main routes to travel quickly to the bases. Now if the invading force could get ashore quickly and seize these bases and capture or destroy our main battle tanks, then it would leave them at a considerable advantage. As now, the defenders, us, would be restricted in the type of warfare that we could conduct. With no armour to counter theirs, and no force manoeuvre group, we would be on the back foot relying solely on anti-tank weapons and lighter armour. We would lose the initiative for any further battles to come and would have to react solely in a defensive posture."

"Oh come on!" the CAS interjected. "We've all seen how poorly the Russian armour has performed in Syria and Ukraine. Are you telling me that if we lost our tank force that we wouldn't still be able to destroy their armour? Our anti-tank weapons are the best in the world, and have you forgotten all about the Apache? There's a reason it's called the tank killer."

Peter looked back, a serious expression on his face. "We've all proven by now that attack helicopters only work so long as their airfields and bases remain protected. Plus, they're high-maintenance items, and right now we don't have enough. From memory I believe we have twelve still operational in the UK right now. The rest are currently broken, awaiting parts that no one seems to want to pay for. Within a week of high-intensity warfare, most of our Apaches will be still sat broken on the tarmac, requiring spares as the enemy tanks drive past them. And as for our anti-tank capability, we still have not yet fully replaced the missiles and launchers sent overseas to the Baltic States or to Ukraine. We don't have enough to counter the threat, so if this were to happen, we would not have the luxury of time nor the industry to replenish our losses."

"Why those ports in the south?" the First Sea Lord asked. "Surely you would have been better off using Portsmouth or Southampton to land your enemy forces?"

"Geography and resources, Sir Tony. If you Look at Weymouth, it's protected on three sides by the island outcrop of Portland Bill, with a large causeway running to the northwest along Chesil Beach so it's well protected against land attack. Plus, it's got refinery facilities and fuel tank storage to allow replenishment of the attacker's ships. As for Poole Harbour, it's deep enough and has port-handling facilities to be able to handle large ships and has good road networks out of the area, so transportation can be mainly wheeled. But it also has its own oil-pumping station and refinery located here at Wych, currently pumping one hundred thousand barrels a day. With that amount of daily supply coming in from the oilfields, refuelling your tanks and armoured vehicles would never be a problem so long as the refinery remained operational."

The CDS then turned to the Chief of the General Staff (CGS) General William Boswell.

"What do you think, Will? Regarding the land warfare side of this, what are your thoughts?"

The CGS sat up straight as he replied confidently, "At present our army is spread around the four corners of the globe, manpower is at its lowest as you know. I believe the last number we had officially was eighty-two thousand soldiers combat fit and ready with a force reserve of thirty-two thousand. However, unofficially, that number of total troops is possibly as low as seventy-eight thousand with a force reserve of probably twenty-four thousand. You know how slow the recruiting figures can be to catch up. What with the Baltic states requesting more manpower and equipment, and our ongoing commitment to Ukraine, we're spread pretty thinly, probably with about fifty-five per cent of our combat forces overseas. So right now, we've got perhaps somewhere in the region of thirty-four thousand soldiers on the UK mainland." He paused as he looked at his notes that he'd hastily written down after reading the report. "As for our armour reserves, aside from what's currently overseas, in the UK, we've got fifteen tanks in the Bovington Lulworth area, they're mainly used for training of recruits and testing the Challenger 3 upgrades. And then there's another eight in the Tidworth area, with five in Warminster. Catterick has the lion's share now, having sixty tanks." The CGS saw the Defence Secretary look up at the numbers. As if to pre-empt the question to come, he quickly added,

"Catterick's got more at the moment due to the 20th Armoured Brigade getting itself ready to deploy to Estonia and Poland."

He saw the Defence Secretary nod in understanding as he continued speaking.

"So, overall, we've not got large numbers of troops located here, but then we've never considered if someone were to just come kicking our door down as such. Of course, we'd have more time usually to recall armour that was overseas if the threat was there, but with Southampton blocked, we'd have to look for a more northern route to get the tanks back."

"So, could it be done, would the risk be there?" the CDS asked, his eyebrows raised questioningly.

Nodding as he spoke, the CGS answered. "If a quick attack like this were allowed to happen as the Brigadier has just explained, and if we lost our armoured reserve early on in the war and didn't have time to activate the reserves or replenish our losses, and if for whatever reason that you have yet to tell us NATO simply stood by and refused to intervene, *and* we were caught in our camps unprepared, then yes, an invasion like this could work. That's a lot of *ifs*, though, CDS. But what I can say though, with great conviction is thank God for Article Five, and thank God that we *are* part of NATO."

The CDS nodded as he looked down the table to General Tony Kew, the Vice CDS and his second in command. In the event of anything happening to the CDS, Tony would step in to take charge. "What are your thoughts on all of this, Tony?"

Tony looked at him, frowning. "Is it possible? Yes. Is it plausible? No. Why would someone invade us, they'd be inviting their own destruction themselves. Unless of course you've got something else to share with us?"

The CDS said nothing as he finally turned to the Chief of Defence Intelligence, Sir Charles Lynwood. "Sir Charles, in regard to what you've just read what are your thoughts please?"

Sir Charles drummed his fingers on the table, looking at the CDS, deep in thought as he contemplated what he was about to say.

"Are you suggesting, James, that there is a strong possibility that the report as we've read it, this Operation Fools Mate, could be in play and that the report that was written by Brigadier Rawlinson in 2012 was somehow leaked out to another audience, one that was not supposed to see it? And that these agents who had received the report have killed who they thought was the original author in order to keep it quiet? I need to understand fully what you're implying before I voice my own thoughts and analysis."

The CDS looked to the Defence Secretary, knowing that if he committed to this, if he was wrong, then his career would be over in a matter of minutes. The people in this room were responsible for the defence of the country, not taken to rash or quick decisions, but what if this time they had been caught out, what if this time something too big or too ugly to contemplate was about to happen? He took a deep breath and replied, "That's exactly what I think and furthermore, knowing what I know, and what you know, I believe there's a strong possibility this operation is underway right now."

Sir Charles's face showed a look of relief as he replied, "Well, then, the risk is worth it, as what I'm about to tell you could just cost me my career..."

13

Revelations

Peter sat and watched as everyone round the table stiffened in response, all of them registering shock and surprise. All except for the CDS, who leant back stone-faced in his seat and looked at Peter with a knowing look in his eyes. Had he known all along about what Sir Charles was going to discuss? Peter thought to himself. Is this the reason part of the report had been kept back? He watched on with curiosity as the Chief of Intelligence opened his laptop and began quickly typing into it. Within a few seconds it had connected to the large TV in the room, now showing a large map of Russia. He leant forward and began to address the room. "Everyone here is aware, I take it, of the new Republic of Tumat, created last year and recognised at the United Nations in February of this year?"

Everyone around the table nodded, and Peter watched the Defence Secretary's face for any sign that he was uncomfortable with what was being said. His face remained impassive as the CDI continued. "Geographically it's the largest of the Russian states, with a land mass consisting of about eleven per cent of the total square footage of Russia." Using a laser pointer, he highlighted a large central area of the map as he continued. "Due to Tumat's size, Russia is now almost split into two, with a small land bridge to the south, the only thing connecting what we are now calling East and West Russia. Not long after Tumat had separated from Russia, a small scientific team from the US were secretly sent there to investigate the areas to the north of the country."

The picture now changed to a close-up of Tumat and to highlight its size and scale a picture of the United Kingdom was superimposed over it. Peter noted that Tumat was almost four times the size of the UK. Sir Charles continued whilst using the laser to highlight the areas he was talking about. "As you can all see, Tumat has large open areas in the north ranging in the hundreds of thousands of hectares. All of which have been unspoilt and untapped for resources. The US scientific team wanted to see just what Tumat had to offer, if it were to be accepted in the wider world as a country. Their new President, Iylanovitch, was keen to cement friendships with the west and gave the US scientists unlimited access to go where they wanted, free to sample all the land they could. In total, the scientific team spent two weeks taking core samples from various sites before bringing the results home with them to the US. What they had found in their studies were kept out of the public domain and only the highest levels of the US office were informed of the findings."

Sir Charles paused to take a sip of water. As he did so, the Defence Secretary enquired, "Sir Charles, I'm guessing that although they were destined for the highest levels of US office, and you being in the position you are, you already know what these findings were?"

Placing the glass back on the table he said, "The scientists found that the samples taken contained extremely high levels of Silver, Palladium, Lithium, Cobalt, Gold and Neodymium.

"Neodymium?" General Boswell asked.

Sir Charles looked up at him, nodding. "It's used in the manufacture of electric motors, magnets and such. The demand for these minerals worldwide is already at an all-time high. When you consider all the plans for electric vehicles, renewable energies, and more sustainable fuels, the prices of these metals themselves – well, you've got the potential for Tumat to be a very rich country in a small amount of time. The Americans, having realised this, and keeping their findings secret, began courting President Iylanovitch, hoping to secure future agreements to mine in these areas before anyone else could. These deals would be worth trillions and would also secure the future of the United States economy."

"So," the Defence Secretary interjected, "America is courting with the President, in fact now I know what you've told me I'll be sure to mention to the PM that we should do the same. Perhaps even a state visit for the PM to visit him in Tumat." The Defence Secretary began to quickly making notes as to what had just been said.

Peter noted that the CDS was watching the Defence Secretary's reactions closely as the information was being divulged to him. Nothing that he had seen so far gave any indication of the MP knowing any more than was being said, and he had shown the same level of interest as everyone else in the room to Sir Charles's brief.

Sir Charles nodded as he continued speaking. "Well, America has already gone one better than that, Minister. Firstly, they've lobbied the UN to get Tumat officially recognised, promising all kinds of sweet deals behind the scenes. You'll all remember that no less than six months after it separated from Russia, the UN officially recognised Tumat as a Sovereign state. It took six years for Kosovo to even begin to be recognised, so for Tumat to do it in six months was always going to raise suspicions."

"Granted it was quick..." Sir Charles looked over to the CAS as she said, "But we didn't want Russia to think that we'd sit back and watch them do to Tumat what they're doing to Ukraine. It wouldn't have been long before the Russians would have perhaps thought to invade, to impose their will through force."

Sir Charles nodded, replying, "Perhaps, Penny, but don't you all think it was strange that Russia didn't do that? You've just lost one of your biggest states, full of resources that's resulted in your country almost being carved in half. They've already gone to war for less, and yet the Russian President did nothing. He just sat back and watched as Tumat grew on the world stage. Doesn't anyone else here think that's odd?"

Sir Tony was quick to reply. "Well, all I can say is that I for one am glad of it. One more piece of his own private empire breaking away. Hopefully more of the Russian states wake up to that man's rhetoric and lies and do the same."

"I'm afraid, Sir Tony, that it's not that simple," Sir Charles continued, "both myself and my counterparts in US intelligence have had our doubts for some time about this new country offering up riches beyond our wildest dreams, located in the backyard of Russia – it all seems too good to be true. The US President had decreed that there is to be no further intelligence gathering on Tumat, as he's keen not to offend its new leader, and also to try to keep his own interests in the country quiet. We all remember the Bush/Blair controversy over the Iraq war for oil revenue. Hence all the warning signs being put out by both the UK and American intelligence agencies against this new country are being ignored and swept under the carpet. And I'm afraid there's yet one more twist to this story—"

"If you could just hold it there, please, Sir Tony," the CDS interrupted respectfully. "I'd like Peter to just explain what Phase One of his plan entailed. I was going to simply give you the paperwork to read, but I think you really should hear this from the horse's mouth."

"Phase One?" the Defence Secretary asked, confused.

"Yes, sir. You see, when we discussed the plan a moment ago, the file you read had only contained Phases Two to Four. We'd kept Phase One, the initial phase, out of it, deliberately. That's the part of the operation that would help explain how NATO were to be made redundant and powerless to help. You all asked how this would be possible, and now I'd like Peter to explain it to you." He pointed to the open room, "If you wouldn't mind, Peter, there's a good chap."

Peter stood up and walked over to the table, his hands behind his back, looking as passive as possible. He cleared his throat and began, "Our country is one of the few remaining democracies that still holds a monarchy as its head of state whilst also having its people elect a government with a serving Prime Minister as leader. The monarchy and the government go lockstep, hand in hand, denoting powers and control over the country and have existed, as such, for hundreds of years since the days of Charles the Second. However, this marriage, this perfect union, is far from so. History has shown us many examples whereby the monarchy has come under attack from both the government and its own people. During World War One, not long after the Russian Revolution of 1917, the monarchy, fearing the same winds of change in the UK, were forced to change their name from Saxe-Coburg-Gotha to Windsor, to be seen as more British and with the people. Then in the 1960s the Labour government with its austerity plans sought to shut down the monarchy and use its funding and land for other projects and schemes designed with the people in mind. Then in the early nineties, the public opinion of the royal family was at its all-time low with the Princess Diana tragedy, unpopular family members and the incidents reported on in the press with one of the princes. And, more recently, the fractious relationship between the public and the family over its recent scandals, of which I don't think we need to mention any further. Most of the commonwealth countries are now removing the King's head from their currencies and government buildings, and with the recent lack of funding from government for public services, people are beginning to talk more openly about a United Kingdom without a monarchy."

"There *will* always be a monarchy." The First Sea Lord scowled.

Peter held his hands up, a sign of surrender. "Please, Sir Tony, I'm not suggesting otherwise, I'm just merely stating how some of the public feel, which is important given what I'm going to say next."

Sir Tony sat back; his arms folded defiantly as Peter said, "Phase One of my plan involved seeding the British government early on with a low-level operator. Someone junior enough who could rise through the ranks of power in Downing Street and be influential, but with the funding and power of a hostile nation behind him or her and able to pull strings behind the scenes. Now we all know that historically British politicians don't have the best track record for keeping themselves out of the press for various misdemeanours, so I think for a hostile nation to be able to get leverage over someone would be easy enough.

"Oh, come on, Brigadier. Granted we're not all squeaky clean, but don't you think our own security services would pick up on that? A clandestine security force approaching one of our own MPs? We are all vetted annually." The Defence Secretary's voice barely hid his annoyance.

"Of course you're right, Defence Secretary. MPs would be vetted and scrutinised by our own security services, the microscope is on them all the time. But what about your own staff? Your advisors, your most trusted people that are around you twenty-four hours a day, seven days a week, always telling you what to wear to look good for the camera, what to say on this subject or that, which baby to hold at the nursery. What party strapline you should talk about today. What about those people? What if one of those people, those that know your innermost secrets were to be the one pulling the strings, the one working for a hostile power?"

A reserved look crossed the Defence Secretary's face as he replied, "Well, I don't know about those people, that's the job of my chief advisor Sonya to sort out. It's her job to security-check them."

A look of triumph crossed Peter's face. "There you have it, you rely on the people around you to check *on* the people around you. The sheep protecting the sheep. And there's the first weak link and the door to get someone into higher levels of Cabinet to now do what you want. Remember this was never going to be quick. My plan called for a slow infiltration, taking years, slowly moving higher and higher up the chain of Cabinet and building trust with the politicians there. How long has your own chief advisor worked for you?"

The CDS interrupted before the Secretary could answer. "Okay, Peter, let's say that for argument's sake this has happened and although some of us have doubts, a hostile, unknown power has managed to get someone embedded into our higher office of power." The CDS looked towards the Defence Secretary as if to highlight who had the doubts.

"Then the next step would be to infiltrate NATO. At first, I thought about the possibility of trying to get one of the existing partners turned – could a hostile power infiltrate another country's election? Perhaps be able to use vote rigging to get the party they wanted elected? But I quickly realised that with all the news coverage on these things that any form of election tampering would be scrutinised and any hint or rumour of fraud and the winning party would be disavowed. We all remember seeing the Belarusian elections on the news and how quickly they were labelled as a farce. No, for this to work, the hostile power would need to blind NATO, to convince them the country trying to join was sincere. And what better way to do that than for the republic or country to become a breakaway from the parent, similar to what we have seen in the past with Latvia and Estonia to name but two—"

General William Boswell quickly interjected. "But Peter, those countries had to first go through rigorous vetting processes and checks that took years to implement. NATO didn't simply just open its doors and let them in. First, they had to go through the Membership Action Plan which took four years to complete, and during which the countries were heavily scrutinised by all other NATO members. Then and only then, after passing all these checks, did they get offered the Ascension Protocol granting membership. But your report was written in 2012 which rules out any country that has joined NATO before this date. Since then, the only countries that have been granted membership were North Montenegro in 2017, North Macedonia in 2019 and Finland and Sweden in 2023 and 2024. Are you suggesting that if these events today are linked to your report, that one of these new members are somehow involved? Or may now have hostile intent?"

Peter shook his head as he replied, his tone confident, "No, William, I'm not. For starters all those countries are democratic and as I've mentioned before, are too well governed, too established. And besides as you have already so clearly described, they have been under scrutiny for all this time. No, my plan called for a country to get accepted quickly, to forego all the checks, to almost be too good to be true, to offer something so good that it cannot be refused. I believe that country is indeed Tumat, the US President's new friend."

The Defence Secretary sat forward, his interest piqued. "And how do you come to that conclusion?"

Peter now pulled his chair closer to the table and sat down, to be closer to the members of the Seven. He settled himself comfortably in his chair, confident now that he had their full attention. "Well, ever since Georgia and Ukraine, the west has always been nervous about letting their intentions for NATO's expansion out of the bag, so to speak. Georgia was happy to shout about possible NATO membership in 2010, and what did Russia do? They invaded and occupied key areas of Georgia, crushing any thoughts of this happening quickly. I might also add that Georgia is still not a member of NATO. Then we move on to Ukraine, again a country courted by the EU, recently separated from Russia and as soon as its aspirations to join NATO become clear, Russia invaded, thus preventing any further NATO membership from going ahead. How can NATO accept an occupied country like Georgia or Ukraine? You're only opening yourself up to further conflict, as Russia has made its policy towards countries wanting to join more than clear. Now, that brings us towards Tumat, a country that has recently split from Russia, that's full of huge, as of yet, undiscovered resources, and, as if by magic, is situated slap-bang in the middle of the Russian continent. Why would the NATO checks be forgone? Simple, the risk of Russia reinvading would be too high. They've already shown previous form for doing so. And all that potential future income and trade would be gone, not to mention any thoughts of expanding NATO eastwards. Because of its location, Tumat would also put NATO closer to China, checking their own expansion westwards and politically having an ally in that area would be good for us. No, Tumat would be too good an offer to turn down and I expect the western leaders would be urged, if not strong-armed, by the US into accepting it into the fold.

The Defence Secretary sat back, his pen tapping his lips, deep in thought.

"So, Brigadier, you're suggesting that *Russia* could be behind all of this and that Tumat's independence *was* orchestrated as part of this plan all along? Its independence, its new President, all an act to allow Tumat NATO membership? To slip in undetected, so to speak?"

"I am, and before you ask why Russia would sacrifice one of its own states, think on this. The Russian nation has been built on sacrifice, it's ingrained into their way of thinking: to win you must first sacrifice. Napoleon's invasion in 1812, the Russian Army pulled back, destroying their own villages and towns, even their own capital city and gifting vast swathes of Russian land to the French forces. Thousands of their own people died as a result, but the French Grand Army suffered also, as they were denied any food or shelter as it was all burned to a cinder. After weeks of starvation and freezing weather conditions, Napoleon was forced to retreat, his army in tatters, whilst the Russians went on to win. The same tactic was employed in World War Two when the Nazis invaded. Again, the Russians sacrificed territory and a percentage of its population to affect the overall win. I believe the same holds true today. The Russian President has sacrificed one of their own states to affect the win against us. If they pull this off, it could result in the NATO alliance being split and humiliated, and more importantly the UK removed as a member. That's a big win for them in my book and one which I felt could possibly happen hence my report."

The Seven Chiefs of Staff began muttering amongst themselves and their other officers as they digested what Peter had just said. After less than a minute, it was the Defence Secretary who held his hands up to silence the room. Peter watched him with interest, remembering his earlier conversation with James. He was sure that whatever had been discussed with the PM, this man was not part of it, choosing instead to listen intently, the arrogance from earlier gone as he thought through the implications.

"Please, everyone settle down, we've still got much more to discuss."

He was interrupted by a loud knock on the door. Everyone turned to look as the double doors opened and a man in a suit, wearing an earpiece came into the room, dressed in the uniform of the Security Services, clearly part of the Defence Secretary's security detail. The bulge under his suit jacket and the slight sheen of sweat on his forehead gave away the fact he was armed and wearing body armour under the suit. He looked up as the man approached and began talking quietly into his ear, loud enough, though, for the room to hear.

"Sir, apologies on disturbing you, but Sonya outside has asked me come in and to remind you about the PM's fundraiser event. It's already 6pm and if you want us to make it at all, we need to leave in the next five minutes, otherwise we'll be too late to go."

The MP looked quickly at his watch and then exclaimed, "Bugger, I'd forgotten the time." He looked to the CDS, seeing his stern face staring back. He was about to get up, then, as if having second thoughts, he looked back at Peter in contemplation. After a few seconds he looked back at his bodyguard.

"Matthew, thank you for letting me know. Please tell Sonya that I'm going to delay getting to the event as we've still got important things to discuss here. See if she can try to raise the PM's staff to let them know – oh, and send my apologies will you."

The bodyguard hesitated, as if to say something, before deciding against it. With a simple, "Certainly, sir," he turned and walked away from the Defence Secretary and closed the doors.

With the doors closed, the Defence Secretary turned back to Peter. "Okay Brigadier, for argument's sake let's say that Tumat has managed to get into NATO and that Russia is behind this. What did you have planned to happen next? How would you instigate an attack on the UK and prevent NATO from responding?"

"Well, Minister, as I have already mentioned, we are one of the few countries that still have a monarchy and democracy. Our members of the Armed Forces are sworn to protect by oath the Crown and the Government of the King. If ever the two were to become separated who then would our Armed Forces take orders from? The King or the Prime Minister?"

"That would never happen!" the Defence Secretary said with a smile, "The constitution and the Crown's own powers forbid it."

"What if a false flag operation occurred, whereby it was made to look like the King, using his own powers of judgement, deemed parliament incompetent and used members of the military to arrest them in an attempted coup? And in doing so, ends up killing the Prime Minister and all members of government?"

The Defence Secretary stiffened at hearing this, his face hardening. "Why would you even suggest such a thing? How could you think of that in your report?"

"My apologies sir, I know it's hard to hear, but you must understand my job was to think of a creative way to attack the UK. What better way to start an attack than sow distrust between the government, the Royal Family and its people? Plus, it would be required to set the scene for what was to come."

"And what would that be?" The Defence Secretary's eyes narrowed.

"The invasion of the United Kingdom, the part of the plan you've all discussed and read already. Forces from another NATO member, in this case, Tumat, would now invade under the pretence that they had been asked earlier on by our own government, who suspected the Royal Family and the Armed Forces of attempting a coup to take power from within the UK. The assassination of the PM and the government would play into this theory, meaning the evidence could be overlooked. The people, some of whom are already suspicious of the monarchy, could very well believe this narrative. Then once on British soil, the enemy forces would subdue what was left of the army in a short space of time, which, let's not forget, is sworn in its allegiance to protect the Crown. Then, with no one to stand against the occupying army, it's free to assume the mantel of a peacekeeping force. Now allowing what's left of the new government to take charge, whilst dismantling what remains of the British Army. This is where the plant, the person seeded earlier into the government all those years ago, takes charge. They assume the mantel of PM, and stand everyone down, reassuring the public, and now are free to fabricate any truth you care to mention. You now have the complete control of the United Kingdom, and Article Five is now null and void as both countries are members of NATO and assisting in an internal matter, but now Russia owns us."

The shocked faces around the table all stared at Peter. Some had looks of rage, not at Peter but at the thought of another country having access to such a plan.

The Defence Secretary turned to the CDS. "Could that work? Could that be plausible?"

It was the First Sea Lord Sir Tony who now stood up, his face red with rage. "I for one think this... plan, as outrageous as it sounds, needs to be given serious thought. I think we should lodge an immediate complaint with our partners in NATO. Nothing, absolutely *nothing*, should be allowed to threaten our country or *our* King like this. I demand we veto any attempt to get this... Tumat into NATO. The risk is just too great, *too great!*"

The Defence Secretary held up his hand to quieten the Sea Lord down and urged him to sit. "Yes, Sir Tony, yes, of course we will do that, but first I've got an urgent question for the Brigadier."

Sir Tony looked around the room, gaining some restraint as he adjusted his shirt after his outburst, looking at the CDS as he sat down. He was known for his fiery temper and the threat of an invasion was just too much of a challenge for him.

Peter leant forward. "Yes, Defence Secretary, what's your question?"

"If we are being led to believe that this plan of yours could be underway and that the events today are all connected to it, how could that be, if the main star of the show, Tumat, is still not a member of NATO? How, or why would they now only be using part of your plan? Do you have an answer to that?"

Peter was about to answer when the CDS stood up, interrupting him. "Peter, I'll take it from here if you don't mind." The CDS, still standing, looked directly at Sir Charles, his eyes bright with intent as he nodded. "And now, Sir Charles, the missing piece if you please..."

Sir Charles looked around the room, getting eye contact with all the members of the Seven as he said in a calm, low voice, "It is to be announced by the American President tomorrow morning at the anniversary celebrations for Tumat that thirty days ago, Tumat was officially recognised and signed in as a full member of NATO."

14

Eyes Closed

Eagle-Four

Colonel Bresavik was snapped from his thoughts by the voice bursting through his headset, the tone urgent. "Sir, we have a problem."

He looked along the cockpit to his team and saw the operator furthest from him had his hand raised to get his attention. keying in the correct radio channel from his chair's console, he barked out,

"What is it? Report!" He was in no mood for pleasantries.

"Sir, Kestrel-Six are not responding to our communications. I have him on radar about eighty miles west of us, approaching UK airspace."

He quickly looked down to his display, bringing up the radar picture showing all the aircraft flying in from that area of airspace. He quickly found the blip corresponding to Kestrel-Six displaying the aircraft as a Boeing 767 flying inbound from New York to Heathrow. After a few more taps on his keyboard the information on the display changed, showing the true nature of the aircraft.

"Okay, I've got him, flying in at thirty-two thousand feet and heading one-six-zero. It looks like Eagle-Three is their handler, get them to try to contact him and quickly!"

The operator responded, his tone apologetic. "I've tried that already, sir, Eagle-Three can't get through to them either."

"Have you checked your equipment is functioning? Are we transmitting on the correct frequencies?"

"Yes sir, both myself and the operator on Eagle-Three have checked and double-checked. We're transmitting and receiving."

"And when did you last have comms with Kestrel-Six?"

"Fifteen minutes ago, sir, when he last checked in."

"Shit!"

He rubbed his face with his hands as he thought of ways to fix the problem. Usually when an aircraft lost communications, he could send another aircraft to conduct a fly past, to visually communicate with the pilot and bring the lost aircraft back into the fold. However, with all their planes now visible on the UK radar scope, they were all being watched and had to remain on their assigned headings. The Colonel was limited as to what he could do, and he knew it. Stealth and surprise had been the key objective from the start and as if to compound the problem he now faced, he noticed from the details on his screen that the payload that Kestrel-Six was carrying was one of Russia's most prized possessions, a Kinzhal hypersonic missile. There were only twelve of these planes flying tonight and now he'd lost communications with one.

He looked back to the operator who was still waiting for a response.

"What were his last instructions from Prestwick centre?"

"He was to fly and maintain the heading he's on, but I'm expecting ATC to give him a course change shortly."

"Okay, tell Eagle-Three to continue as planned and to acknowledge the ATC instructions for Kestrel-Six."

"Yes, sir, and what about Kestrel-Six?"

"For now, those idiots are on their own," he replied acidly. "He knows where we're going and what his target is, and if he doesn't, he can bloody swim home!"

"Sir!"

He sat back, trying to control his frustration. They'd planned for this event, but to have it happen so early in the mission infuriated him. He looked to the Captain to his right sat at another console, flicking to another voice channel so he could now talk directly to him.

"Captain Davikov, give me an update."

Hearing the Colonel's voice in his headset, he sat up slightly.

"Colonel, we have Eagle-One and Eagle-Two now in UK airspace, and Kestrels-One, Eight, Five, and Nine about to cross the threshold."

"Captain, where *exactly* are Eagle-One and Two? Simply telling me that they are in UK airspace does not help me. Give me their exact positions."

"Sorry, sir, Eagle-One is currently flying over Fort William and Eagle-Two is approaching the northern coast of Scotland in the area of Ullapool."

Without acknowledging the Captain, he switched the channel on his headset, double-checking the frequency being displayed on his screen, the new frequency allowing him to talk to his most senior controller currently sat in Eagle- One and already now flying over the Scottish mainland

"Eagle-One, this is Crowsnest."

After a second of static in his headset, the familiar voice of Major Pavitch his second in command, burst through his headset.

"Crowsnest, Eagle-One, send."

Knowing their communications were encrypted and no one would be listening, he continued, his tone angry.

"Sasha, we may have a problem. Kestrel-Six is not responding on comms and will be required shortly to conduct a course change."

"Understood," the voice acknowledged calmly.

The Colonel paused a second before replying, "When that happens, when they don't comply with the British controllers, I'm expecting them to launch their fighters to intercept and escort the flight in."

"And when they do, they'll shit their fascist pants when they see what's waiting for them!" The Major's voice sounded humorous at the thought.

The Colonel smiled, his anger abating, happy to break the strain of the past five hours of flying. He'd requested that Major Pavitch remain on Eagle-Four with him during the mission, but Command had deemed the Major's expertise should be placed on the lead aircraft. Now the Colonel was missing the input, knowledge and humour that the Major had shared with him throughout their two years of working together.

"Yes, they'll probably shit their pants, but they'll also be aware that an airliner has managed to turn itself into a fighter bomber and will launch further flights that will complicate things. We're still sixty minutes away from starting operations – you're the closest there, what are your thoughts? Should we launch early, or carry on as planned? I'd like to know what you think."

There was a pause and a slight hiss of static over the airways as he waited for his second in command to respond. The Colonel noticed that whilst he waited, the coffee that he'd asked for earlier sat there untouched and cold. He motioned to another flight crew member for a fresh cup as the headset crackled to life.

"For now, I think we should continue as planned. Some of the fighters are still too out of range to launch. Besides, even if they do suspect Kestrel-Six, they'll think it's nothing more than an airliner with faulty radio equipment. Standard practice will be to escort it in, not shoot it down. They'll waste time trying to identify it, and when they do, we can jam their communications and take them down. The British will waste time wondering what happened, plus, we've still got our little surprise to play if needed."

The Colonel nodded as he listened. He'd been thinking the same, but always liked to have a second opinion from Major Pavitch, respecting his ideas and thoughts. More confident now in his decision he relaxed slightly as he replied, "Yes, I agree my friend, continue as planned and let's react to what the British do when the time comes. Good luck and see you when we land. Crowsnest out."

He heard the click as the line was closed and looked up as a second cup of coffee was handed to him. He smiled again as he thought what the next hour could bring. Without looking down and from muscle memory, his fingers flicked the switches as he changed the frequency on his headset and looked back to Captain Davikov.

"Captain what's our own ETA to the threshold?"

The Captain looked back at him earnestly. "We will be crossing the threshold in fifteen minutes, sir."

"Good, keep me updated. Let me know the moment ATC start to query Kestrel-Six."

"Yes, sir."

He sat back, and trying to find some level of comfort, shifted slightly in his seat, his back muscles protesting at their lack of use. Finally finding a position more suitable, he settled in, drinking his coffee as he continued to watch his plane's progress on the map.

Kestrel-Six

Eighty miles west of Eagle-Four, onboard Kestrel-Six, Captain Mikhail Vasiliev and his navigator Lieutenant Nikolai Egorov were desperately trying to fix the problem they had with the radio in the cockpit of their MiG-31BM using the limited light available. The fading sunlight was not helping the navigator, who had removed his harness and was sat facing rearwards. He was trying to work in the cockpit's cramped conditions, and saw with dismay the cable that had come loose during the flight that was just out of his reach, a mere six inches from his hand, teasing him. The cable looked to have been fitted incorrectly, probably in the days leading up to the mission when the engineers and technicians had pored over their regiment's aircraft, retrofitting all the electronics and computers needed to make the mission work. Thinking that the homeland lacked the resources, they had been surprised at the number of new technologies that had appeared suddenly. Clearly the Russian scientists had been busy behind the scenes, and the pilots had watched with satisfaction and pride as outdated and broken equipment had finally been replaced with newer, more modern systems. However, it was this rush to retrofit their own aircraft that had now caused the problem at hand. Frustratingly Nikolai realised that if the aircraft was on the ground with the canopy up he could easily fix the problem, but at thirty-two thousand feet in the environment he was in, that was now impossible to do. Cursing in Russian he removed his gloves and aviator watch and rolled his sleeve up as he tried everything he could think of to make his arm thinner, in an effort to jam his arm into the gap. He managed to get in further, up to his wrist, the metal edges of the seat cutting into him as he felt his flesh tear and the blood flow freely down his arm. The cold temperatures of the cockpit had numbed his exposed hands, allowing the pain to be lessened. It was more his pride that was hurt though, as he realised with a growing dread that his arm was never going to fit. He pulled his arm out angrily, his voice bitter and angry. "*Fuck*! I'm sorry, Mikhail, but I just can't reach it. Fucking technicians! Some stupid, careless, traitorous Chetnik bastard has cost us the mission."

"Fuck! You sure you can't get to it? Have you taken off your gloves?" the pilot replied, trying to hide his alarm.

Nikolai replied dejectedly, "Yes, and I've rolled up my flight suit. I need arms like a Chinese gymnast to get to that fucking cable." He then added in a more sombre tone, "Should I take off my oxygen mask and try to get at it from a different angle?"

Mikhail quickly countered, "No! Don't do that, you'll pass out and I'll never be able to get the weapon released from up here."

"Okay, what if we fired up the computer? At least it will give us an idea of where everyone else is."

All modern military aircraft used a vast range of complex sensors, systems and computers to help identify targets and build up what they would call the 'battlefield picture'. The problem with these systems was that when turned on, they themselves would give off an electronic signature that could be detected by the enemy. NATO had already documented and stored all the Russian aircrafts' EW (Electronic Warfare) signatures into their own computers, so if the pilots turned on their systems they would immediately show up on the British radar as hostile. It was for this very reason that for the past four hours, they had been flying blind with their own radar systems and Baget 55-06 targeting computer switched off. Instead, they had relied on the Eagle controllers to give them their heading and altitude to fly to. With the radio no longer working, they had now lost the ability to know what heading and altitude the ATC wanted them to fly to.

Worse still, with their own systems switched off, they would not be able to see the location of other aircraft around them or see if anyone had attempted to engage them. As if realising the fear, Mikhail looked out to the darkening sky, expecting the streak of an enemy missile at any second. For a fighter pilot, the feeling of being unable to see tactically ahead of you, unaware of what was going on around you, was alien to him. *Calm yourself, Mikhail, calm yourself,* he thought, *fear is the enemy now, calm down.* He controlled his breathing and tried to clear the fearful thoughts from his head. Still listening to the navigator swearing and cursing, he quickly replied, "Okay, Nikolai, we'll carry on as planned for the moment. Let's give it twenty minutes and if we haven't been blown out of the sky by then, then I'll switch on our active radar and computer to give us a better picture of what's going on."

"But if we do that, won't the British see us on their own screens?"

"Perhaps, but I'm hoping if we leave the system in passive mode then they might not detect us. All I need is a quick radar fix from the computer. But if we do nothing and keep flying as we are, we'll either get blown out of the sky, collide with another aircraft or run out of fuel – which do you prefer?"

Looking out at the Atlantic Ocean below, both pilots knew their chances of survival would be next to zero if they had to eject from where they were. There would be no rescue party coming to save them. Sighing to himself and refitting the glove over his now bleeding arm, Nikolai replied apprehensively, "Okay, Mikhail, you're the pilot, you know what you're doing."

Mikhail looked over at the screens in front of him, looking over the gauges, checking their course and heading. As he did so he checked the fuel gauge, noting that they had no more than two more hours of fuel remaining. He had been briefed that after their attack they were not to head home, but instead the whole regiment would rendezvous at a new airfield, its location already known to him. He hoped that whatever happened over the next sixty minutes that the plan was still in play. Otherwise he'd be landing at an enemy airport, and the thought of being captured, of being paraded on the TV like a trophy, was worse to him than the fear of being shot down.

Eagle-Four

Colonel Bresavik was still watching the screens, wishing somehow that the rogue plane would quickly fix whatever issue it had and return to formation. He heard the static in his headset as the voice of Captain Davikov boomed through.

"Sir, we are approaching the threshold now, and about to enter British airspace."

"Thank you, Captain. I think I'd like to hear this for myself."

He flicked the channel that allowed him to monitor the air traffic control frequencies, his headset bursting to life as he did so. He quickly lowered the volume as a loud American voice came over the net; brash, confident, arrogant. Everything that the Colonel despised about the Americans and the west. By contrast, the voice of the controller sounded clipped and reserved, very conservative and pompous; so very British. The Colonel smiled and enjoyed the thought that some of the aircraft he was now hearing were his own wolves now safely in amongst the sheep, waiting to strike. Now, though, it was their turn, and he felt a sense of national pride in what was happening. For the first time ever, an air force – *his* air force – was going to slip right through the defence screen of another country, undetected. He wondered if in years to come citizens of the new Russian Republic of Britain would read about his exploits, how he and his men had been the first ones. He was dragged from his patriotic fever as he heard, "Good evening, Prestwick Centre, this is Tokyo Air Two-Six-One, with you, IFR to Paris, flight level three-four thousand, heading one-six-zero, speed two-four-zero. Over." He noted with pride the slight accent in the computer-generated voice denoting someone from Japan. The software that China had supplied was indeed working as promised. He listened in as the controller unknowingly chatted to the fictional pilot and after a few brief exchanges he heard the words he wanted to hear.

"Tokyo Air Two-Six-One, Prestwick Centre, radar contact identified, fly IFR as filed, maintain flight level three-four thousand."

He clapped his hands together as now they had the blessing of the British, free to fly through their airspace. He kept quiet as he heard their own response with the same oriental tone: "Fly IFR heading as filed, maintain flight level three-four-zero for Tokyo Air Two-Six-One."

He looked around at the smiles of relief from his colleagues. All had understood the importance of what had just happened. His thoughts of joy were short-lived though as another thought crossed his mind. Kestrel-Six was still out there flying blind. Before he dealt with that problem though, there was something else more immediate that could wait no longer that he wished to address. He stood up and took off his headset, signalling to the Captain that he would be off the air for a few minutes. The Il-86 did not have a holding tank like most modern airliners, the weight being deemed as unnecessary. Instead, it had a toilet tank that could be emptied when necessary whilst in flight. The Russian thinking being why carry your toilet waste around with you unnecessarily when you can dump it out into the air, to land on the ground below. Colonel Bresavik had only told one person of their mission tonight – his brother, Vadeym, who had been severely injured fighting in Ukraine, losing both his legs. The injuries were the result of British-made anti-tank weapons fired at his tank company as he'd fought those damned Ukrainian Nazis. All of Vadeym's company had been killed or injured thanks to these British weapons. Upon hearing the secret news that his brother was involved in this mission, Vadeym had one simple request, one that his brother was only too happy to do now. Colonel Bresavik was on his way to the toilet; he was off to shit on the heads of the British.

Ten minutes later, after completing his own personal mission, Colonel Bresavik returned to his control chair, feeling lighter and more alive, as he picked up the headset stowed on the back of the chair. He adjusted it for comfort, moving the boom mike closer to his mouth before keying in the channel to chat to the Captain, already expecting the news to come.

"Okay, Captain, I'm back on. What have I missed?"

"Sir, ATC have now requested that Kestrel-Six change course, the operators on Eagle-Three have responded, but with no way to talk to Kestrel-Six, they're still on the original heading. It won't be long before British ATC get suspicious of their intentions, sir."

The Colonel nodded in understanding, quickly picking up a pen and a notepad as he replied, "And our other aircraft?"

"Eagle-Three is about to cross the threshold along with Kestrel-Two, Three, Four, One-Zero, and One-Two."

Writing down what had been said, he quickly made some mental notes before asking, "So including Kestrel-One, Five, Eight and Nine, we now have nine fighters in UK airspace? And of these only six are carrying Kinzhals?"

"Yes, sir."

Damn it! That's not enough, he thought angrily to himself.

"How long before *all* of our aircraft are across the threshold and into firing range?"

There was a pause as the Captain worked out the calculations in his head. "As it stands sir, if all aircraft maintain heading and speed, we should all be safely inside the threshold to launch in twenty-four minutes."

He tapped the pen against the table and his foot on the floor as he thought about how close they were to launching. *Twenty-four minutes... Just twenty-four minutes. God grant me that... Please, just give me those twenty-four minutes.*

He checked his watch, it was nearly 19:00, time to send an update to Command. He changed the channel on the panel in front of him and quickly wrote down on the paper what he was going to say. So far, the operation was proceeding as planned, Kestrel-Six was not yet a problem. He took a breath, pushed the pressel to talk on the radio and began to send his report.

Defence Council Meeting, Chief of Defence Staff's Residence

Peter watched the shocked and surprised faces of the senior members of the defence staff as they absorbed the news on Tumat's new membership within NATO.

Unsurprisingly, the only faces not registering surprise or shock were those of Sir Charles and the CDS, whom Peter suspected had known all along. They both sat there, a picture of calm as everyone else looked around the room.

"Did you know of this?" The accusing tone of the First Sea Lord shot back as he glared at the Defence Secretary.

The Defence Secretary leant forwards, his face betraying the shock at the sudden news as he stammered in reply, "No, Sir Tony, I bloody did not! I can assure you if I had known about this, I'd have brought it to *all* your attentions sooner." The Minister looked down to where Sir Charles sat, slowly sipping his glass of water.

"Sir Charles, how long have you known of this information? How long ago were you told of Tumat's membership into NATO?"

The CDI placed his glass back down on the table, quickly glancing at the CDS before replying, "Secretary, I was made aware of it only last week, thanks to my own sources high up in US intelligence. I had to tread carefully with the information we had, as I was reliably informed that this was only known to the highest offices of the UK and US government. I approached the CDS about it and we both agreed to keep quiet. Besides, the agreement was to be announced tomorrow so the secret we were to keep would soon be public knowledge."

The Defence Secretary's head snapped round, his face reddening. "CDS? Care to elaborate? Why keep this from *me*?"

"With all due respect, Secretary of State, I've kept *nothing* from you. The Prime Minister has. Sir Charles and I had already tried to meet with you and the PM to warn you of our fears over Tumat, but your offices said you were always too busy to speak to us. I assumed the PM had briefed you about the deal with the American President and with your offices ignoring us, that reinforced my suspicions. However, now I can see that I was wrong. Besides, the deal had been signed, we were already too late. It was only when I read the Brigadier's report today, knowing Tumat was already in NATO and seeing the events on the news, that I realised how serious and how time-critical this was, hence I requested the Seven meeting this afternoon."

"And if you knew how serious this was why did you wait so long before telling us?" The Defence Secretary's tone was accusing.

"Because if I had simply given you that report, plus my warning about an invasion would you have believed me? I needed you all to see for yourselves, to hear *all* the evidence and make your own assessments."

The Vice CDS General Tony Kew cleared his throat to speak, before responding. "All of our intelligence assessments on the Russian forces in Ukraine show an enemy that's struggling to resupply and equip its soldiers in that theatre. This plan calls for logistical support not yet seen from them. Converting civilian ships into assault ships is no easy task. And where would they get the technology from to re-equip and modernise their ageing aircraft and tanks? What I'm seeing on the battlefields of Ukraine does not tally up with a modern assault force ready to begin invading the UK. Are you certain of this, CDS?"

The CDS looked over to Sir Charles. "Best to show them all what you briefed me on yesterday. I think now's as good a time as any."

Sir Charles nodded and began using his laptop, bringing the main screen in the room back to life. Everyone looked over as a satellite image showed an aerial view of a dockyard, with the cranes and shipping containers on display. Ten ships sat in the docks, with another four at anchor waiting to enter.

"What you're all looking at now is the Iranian port of Amirabad on the coast of the Caspian Sea. Since 2024 this port and the four other Iranian ports on that stretch of coastline have reported no new cargo shipments coming in or out. The Iranians were citing equipment failures and industrial action of the port staff as the main reasons for the closures. However, the image you're looking at was taken four months ago and as you can see, the port is fully operational and we believe is loading ammunition, hardware, and more importantly technology such as microchips, processors and drone tech that the Russian military so desperately needs. China also has reported no new shipments to Russia, choosing instead to keep America on side, but if I can just show you this..."

The display changed to another satellite image showing a mountainous area with a railway line disappearing into a tunnel. Construction vehicles were dotted around the image, their yellow and orange bodies clearly visible against the drab grey of the rocks.

"This is the area of Xinjiang national park in north-western China on the Russian and Chinese border. The area is very mountainous and the terrain too hilly to allow any form of heavy road transport through the passes. The railway you see there did not exist until two years ago, having only recently being constructed. The Chinese claimed it was built to carry tourists and visitors into the national park area, giving their workers freedom of space and fresh air. Interestingly though, despite the Chinese claims, there's no station terminating at the end of the line, instead it continues into this tunnel and under the mountains. This photo was taken when construction was almost finished at the latter end of 2023."

The picture changed as a new image showed a railway line disappearing into a tunnel. This time what appeared to be a large freight train was emerging from the tunnel, its carriages shown clearly from the picture.

"This is the area twenty miles north where the tunnel begins, on the Russian side, around the region of Altai. Again, this railway was newly constructed, only being finished at the latter end of 2023. It serves no purpose, has no station and we believe it's the same railway, linking mainland China with mainland Russia. This photo was taken in January 2024."

The Defence Secretary studied the images as Sir Charles highlighted the areas with a laser pointer, before finally asking, "Why no new images, why nothing more recent?"

The image changed to another picture, one that was blurry and scratched, as if someone had taken a knife to the image and had manically slashed away. "This was the last piece of intel that our satellite was able to take in February 2024. As you can see the image was not of the quality that we were expecting. We had our technical labs look at it and it would appear that the Chinese and Russians are using ground-mounted focused lasers in these areas to blind our satellites. It scratches the optics and causes the damage you see here. The camera lens is now damaged in such a way that causes the satellite to be now rendered useless. So far, we've lost three of our sky birds to these new attacks and are trying to develop a new type of filter to protect them, but at the moment we've been forced to keep the rest of our satellites away from these locations."

General Kew's eyes narrowed as he looked at the images. "You're saying then that China and Iran have been supplying Russia with the technology and hardware to replace and modernise their forces. Whilst denying this politically of course and taking the time and resources to try to hide it from us. And that what we are seeing in Ukraine, the poor condition of the Russian war machine and lack of effort could be more of a deception, a ruse?"

"That's exactly what I'm saying. For the past two years now Russia has gone dark, we've lost most of our human intelligence assets ever since the Russian President had his Stalinist purge in 2023. Whether he meant to or not, when he labelled most of his senior circle as traitorous, and had them all executed or imprisoned, he managed to take out some of our most well-placed agents and some American ones too. In doing so, he also created such a suspicious and hostile circle around him that any attempts now to introduce anyone or attempt to turn anyone within that circle are met with immediate failure. Six have reported to me that they've lost more assets this past year than the past twenty years of operating in the area."

"What about the shipping? Could they get the shipping converted to carry tanks, troops and logistics and such?" the First Sea Lord said.

The picture on the display changed, showing a large company logo – a large red-letter M with blue-and-white stars flying around its base. Underneath the logo was the company's tag line; *Mosflot The Titan of the Seas*. Once the logo was displayed, Sir Charles began. "Mosflot, one of Russia's largest commercial freight companies, boasting some of the largest ships in the world. At one time one of the largest commercial shipping companies in the world. Various intelligence agencies have always suspected it of being a front for Russian dirty money and being used to transport arms and illegal goods around the world. Its CEO and owner is a very good friend and ally of the Russian President and we believe is part of his most trusted inner circle."

"In 2022 with the sanctions against Russia, all of Mosflots ships were ordered back to Russian ports, but in 2023 the whole of their fleet was seen moving east to the area of the port of Vladivostok." The picture on the display changed to a map of the east coast of Russia, Sir Charles highlighting with the laser a peninsular that jutted out into the Pacific Ocean. "We believed at the time that the Russians were sending them there to be scrapped, preferring to use the ships' machinery and steel to produce tanks for their war effort. But with the latest threat to our satellites we couldn't overfly the area to prove this. However, in late 2024 we were able to get the following image out from a dockyard worker."

The screen changed to display a rushed image from what looked like a camera phone, part of the lens was obscured by something. The picture looked like it had been taken from a gantry high above, possibly from a ship's loading crane. In the image they could clearly see one of the cargo ships, with a large rectangular piece of its hull removed and what appeared to be a ramp and doors being fitted into place. The Mosflot logo could be seen clearly on the ship's side. In the distance they could see another cargo ship, its white hull was halfway through being repainted a light blue.

Sir Tony stood up and walked over to the screen to study the picture closely. After a few seconds he remarked, "She looks like she's getting some kind of landing-craft style ramp fitted. And that ship in the distance looks remarkably similar to what we saw in Portsmouth and Southampton."

Sir Charles highlighted the section of hull they were looking at with the laser pointer. "We've had the photo analysed by the RAF and Navy for scale and they estimate the ramp you're looking at is approximately one hundred and twenty feet across and over sixty feet high, the thickness of which would allow vehicles of up to seven hundred tonnes on board, which is plenty, given the heaviest armoured vehicle they have right now would weigh no more than a modern battle tank, say seventy tonnes maximum."

"And where are these ships now?" asked Sir Tony as he walked back to his seat.

Sir Charles lifted his hands in resignation. "We don't know, the last time we had their location was when that picture was taken. Since then, the operative who took the picture has gone quiet, probably either scared off, or worse."

Peter was under no illusion as to the person's fate. He looked to the room confidently as he spoke. "So they could be repainted and right now sailing through the English Channel and no one here would be any the wiser?"

Sir Charles pursed his lips together, replying, "Yes, that could very well be the case."

The Defence Secretary looked away from the screen as he said, "So we're deaf and blind in Russia, but what about the Americans or the rest of NATO, what do they have to say? Have they said anything to us? Any inklings of any of this happening?"

Sir Charles shook his head apologetically. "I'm sorry, sir, but since Tumat left the Russian republic, the Americans and NATO have focused all their efforts into trying to win them onside. The focus has shifted, with some now no longer seeing Russia as the threat it once was, especially with Russia doing so poorly in Ukraine. Most NATO planners are now looking into China and India as the emerging future threats. I think if Tumat were to be a smokescreen it's bloody well worked, and if the Brigadier's plan is in play, then no-one else has seen or thought of it either."

The Defence Secretary stood up and walked over to the big screen, gazing at the picture of the cargo ships. Then he turned to look at Peter, his gaze lingering as if his mind was going through the options. He turned to the CDS, his face showing his indecision, "CDS, look, I need more than this if I'm going to issue a nationwide alert. I need evidence, *hard* evidence and at the moment, what you're giving me sounds plausible, but there are no hard facts. I agree that the events today are inexplicable, but I'll still need to speak to the PM about this. I need him here and I need his input."

General Catmur rose, adjusted his uniform and stood to face the people around the table. "Given what we have seen and heard today, is there anyone here who would disagree as to the validity of Operations Fools Mate and its plausibility?"

No one spoke. The room remained deathly quiet as the Chiefs of Staff sat with cold, serious faces. The CDS waited ten seconds before he turned to the Defence Secretary, his face firm and his tone grave. "Sir, in that case, I must inform you, the Secretary of State for Defence that I, as Chief of the Defence Staff, believe this threat to be credible and that this country is under threat of an invasion from a hostile power. I also believe that our Prime Minister is under threat of attack or harm. Therefore, as CDS I am strongly urging you, as the Minister of the hour, to issue the necessary alert."

The Defence Secretary sat looking up, nodding as he heard the words spoken. He stood up, his jaw hardening and his face set as he breathed out heavily, replying with, "Very well, CDS, now you leave me no choice." He looked over to his bodyguard, standing by the door and gruffly said, "Codeword Platinum." The bodyguard immediately sprang to life, talking into his radio microphone attached to his wrist. His voice was lowered but his tone urgent as he walked out and into the corridor, his footsteps echoing off the hall floor.

The Defence Secretary watched him leave the room, before turning back to the CDS. "Okay, CDS, let's get the Wonderland protocol up and running, hold off on the general alert for now, but let's have our eyes and ears fully opened for anything suspicious that looks like this plan may be underway."

He then turned to Peter and asked, "Brigadier, this plan starts in the air, so as I understand it we're looking for any unauthorised excursions into our airspace, is that correct?"

"It is, Secretary of State, but I still believe our own radar network will be compromised – we should bear that in mind when relying on what we're seeing."

"Thank you, but I'm pretty confident in our own defence capabilities." His tone was dismissive. He turned to the CDS. "So let's start with looking at air incursions, anything out of the ordinary, let RAF Boulmer know. Meanwhile, we can wait here for Wonderland to be ready."

"Wonderland is already active, Defence Secretary, I saw fit to get it up and running before the meeting. It's fully staffed now and operational." Leaving a look of awe on the Defence Secretary, the CDS looked up and addressed the rest of the room. "People, let's make our way over to Wonderland, the PM should be with us within the hour and we need something more concrete for the Defence Secretary to brief him on."

Everyone began to make their way out of the room. With Peter not too sure what to expect, he stood and walked over to his friend. "James, where do you want me in all this?"

The CDS quickly looked to the Defence Secretary who gave a slight nod of his head before he continued. "You, my friend, are coming with us. Right now you're the only one who knows everything that's going on, and between us we are going to try to stop this bloody plan from happening."

"You realise, of course, that we're wasting time with all these discussions and meetings – every minute we waste is one more minute our forces face destruction. You know the targets, you know where will be hit. The threat is real, James."

Pulling his friend closer he lowered his voice. "Look, I hear you, but without the PM's say-so nothing happens. So, keep it cool, keep your mouth closed and let's play this smart, we've already got this far."

Seeing the frustration on Peter's face, the CDS ushered Peter towards the door, as he said, "Now I told you we'd go to Wonderland, now let's see if I can impress you for a change."

15

The Storm

Eagle-Four

The voice burst through the Colonel's headset as he listened in on the ATC chatter directed at Kestrel-Six which on the British radar screens was showing up as Sinari Air One-Three-Two.

"Attention Sinari Air One-Three-Two, this is Prestwick Centre, you must expedite your turn to heading one-nine-zero immediately. Please acknowledge. Over." The voice of the controller was firmer and more resolute this time; gone was the friendly, welcoming demeanour that they had been listening to these past two hours.

"What do you want us to do, sir? Eagle-Three are asking if they should continue to answer up as Sinari One-Three-Two?"

The Colonel scrolled out the map display to show the north coast of Scotland and Northern England, assessing where all his aircraft were. He'd needed another twenty-four minutes and so far, had managed to buy himself ten. All the Eagle callsigns were now heading down the west coast of Scotland, safely inside UK airspace and en route to their own targets. To the north, another two hundred miles away, flew the final ten fighters, with Kestrel-Six amongst them. He quickly checked the callsigns of the fighters nearest to Kestrel-Six, noting with satisfaction that they were both equipped with the new R-37 Vympel air-to-air missile. The missile was one of a new breed that could reach hypersonic speeds of Mach five and had a range of eighty miles.

Noting the callsigns of these two aircraft he replied tersely to the operator, "Tell Eagle-Three to cut communications for Sinari One-Three-Two. Let the British eat static. Eagle-Three is to continue as planned on their own mission."

"Yes, sir."

He continued listening in to the ATC controller now talking to nothing but fresh air as they tried to raise the fictitious aircraft, his thoughts now turning back to the mission. He knew that it was only a matter of time before the RAF responded and it took no more than four minutes before his Captain interrupted his thoughts, his voice tense.

"Sir, we've heard on the guard net, fighters are now being scrambled from Lossiemouth. Time to intercept Kestrel-Six is five minutes."

"Five minutes?" he mused. "They must be going supersonic already. Impressive that they're in such a hurry to die."

"Sir, what would you like us to do?" the Captain said.

The Colonel smiled and sighed, happy now that the tension had at last been relieved. Now the decision was taken out of his hands – with the launched fighters, the game was finally afoot.

"Do we have the frequency for the RAF planes?"

There was a pause as the Captain checked his display. "Yes, sir, it's one-two-seven decimal five hundred, but we can't talk to them directly as their channel is encrypted."

"I'm well aware of that, Captain," the Colonel responded curtly. "When the RAF planes are within two hundred miles of Kestrel-Six, I want you to divert all communications power and jam that frequency until I say otherwise. Tell all the Eagles that Crowsnest will be offline until we deal with the current threat."

"Okay sir."

He changed channels, speaking to the pilots in the closest planes currently flying to Kestrel-Six.

"Kestrels One-Nine and Two-Zero, this is Crowsnest"

"Kestrel One-Nine."

"Kestrel Two-Zero."

Happy to hear the acknowledgement from both aircraft he stood up, preferring not to sit for what he was about to order them to do...

Jackal-One

Meanwhile, screaming westwards at a height of forty-one thousand feet and accelerating towards Mach 1.5, Flight Lieutenant Edwards was quickly checking with his controllers as to why both aircraft had been scrambled. Less than five minutes before, both pilots had been watching TV in their ready room and were about to enjoy a cup of tea, when the alert to launch the Quick Reaction Alert (QRA) had come through. With the klaxons and bells blaring through the base, both pilots had run from the room shouting the word "SCRAMBLE!" whilst hitting the green button to sound the alarms, alerting everyone as to what was happening. They had both ran to the two separate dispersal hangars that were side by side, each with a fully fuelled and fully armed RAF Typhoon sat ready to go. The flight crews for both aircraft had arrived at the same time, leaving their ground crew to quickly go through the prestart procedures. Edwards had raced up the steps to the cockpit of his aircraft, donning his flight rig and helmet at the top. With quick precision he'd climbed into the cockpit and more from muscle memory than thinking, had begun to connect his suit and helmet to the internals of the aircraft as the cockpit canopy had closed around him, sealing him from the outside world. With a quick press of a few buttons, he'd started the Auxiliary Power Unit and both engines, as the avionics and screens flicked to life in front of him.

In less than thirty seconds both Typhoons were accelerating down the runway in close formation as they took off into the evening sky, heading west as the controller began to vector them towards their target.

"Jackal-One and Two, this is Blackdog Controller, climb to flight level four-one thousand. Best speed is decimal nine for now, mission is to interrogate aircraft designated Zulu Zero-Zero-One, vector to bandit is two-seven-zero."

Acknowledging their instructions, the pilots throttled up, feeling the sensation of the acceleration as their aircraft's engines were pushed to eighty per cent throttle as they'd climbed to forty-one thousand feet. Within two minutes the planes had reached their designated altitude, the cloudless sky turning a hue of purple as the night now began to creep into the horizon. Not that the pilots could enjoy the view – their focus now was on the task at hand as they received permission to push the aircraft up to speeds of Mach 1.5

Edwards felt himself pushed backwards into the seat as the two EJ200 engines powered up to full throttle, watching the airspeed climbing quickly as he contacted the control room.

"Blackdog Controller, Jackal-One, any further information on Zulu Zero-Zero-One?"

"Jackal flight, this is Blackdog Controller, Zulu Zero-Zero-One is type Boeing 767, commercial flight from New York to Heathrow. We have the aircraft on comms. However, it's refusing to comply to ATC requests. Intentions unknown at this time. Zulu Zero-Zero-One currently on heading one-six-zero at flight level three-two thousand. Range to bandit is three-two-zero miles."

"Roger, understood. Is it passenger or cargo aircraft?"

Edwards had a marker pen in hand, writing the information on the notepad stuck to the leg of his flight suit as the controller continued, "Jackal flight, Blackdog Controller continuing, it's a passenger plane, and new information for you, aircraft is now *not, repeat not* responding to ATC on comms. Lost comms procedure to now apply."

Edwards scribbled down the notes as he responded, "Roger, understood, lost comms procedure apply."

Quickly checking that the flight data in his helmet display was correct, he flicked his radio over to the chatnet, a radio frequency to allow him to talk freely to his wingman, Flight Lieutenant Leyland, who was flying the second Typhoon off to his starboard side, no more than a hundred metres away, the fighter's navigation lights blinking in in the twilight.

"Ley, did you copy all that?"

"Yeah, I got it all, Ed, how do you want to play this one?"

"It's lost comms procedure – I'll take lead, you shadow, ready to fly down the port side. Let's get a visual on the cockpit if we can, see if we can see what's going on in there, before the light goes out totally."

"OKay, Ed, understood."

Both pilots began to mentally prepare themselves for what they might have to face, or do, as they flew towards Zulu Zero-Zero-One. At the speed they were flying and, on that heading, they had four minutes until they were set to intercept the target. And unknown to them, those four minutes would be the longest of their lives.

Kestrel-Six

Mikhail's mind was playing tricks on him as he was certain that twice already he'd convinced himself that he'd seen the flash of an aircraft's navigation lights on a course to intercept them. *Damn this fucking radio silence*, he thought to himself. He looked at his flight watch, he'd already flown blind for ten minutes longer than he should have done. *The other aircraft must be in UK airspace now*, he concluded. He'd given it enough time. He finally broke the silence as he said, "Okay, Nikolai, let's fire up the targeting computer, passive mode only."

"Okay, computers booting up now, passive mode only." Both pilots could hear in their headsets the chirps, clicks and audible tones that came alive, signifying the plane's systems were beginning to waken. With the system in passive mode, it would search for any enemy threat radar that was active, whilst at the same time keeping itself quiet, meaning for the first time in the whole of the flight they would be able to see just what was out there in front of them.

"Mikhail, I have multiple contacts north and south of us, ranges between forty and one hundred and fifty miles, all on roughly the same speed and heading as us with no electronic signatures detected yet. Those contacts must be the rest of our formation, don't you think?"

"Yes, I think so, what heading are they all following?"

"It looks like they are all heading on course one-nine-zero. Do you think that we should turn to one-nine-zero as well? Maybe we can still bluff our way in.?" he replied optimistically.

"Yes, let's give it a go. Still nothing on the threat radar?"

"No, I'm looking out to two hundred and fifty miles. Nothing on the scope, we might have just got away with this."

Breathing a sigh of relief, Mikhail altered the course of the autopilot to turn right to the new heading. Perhaps things were going to work after all.

Eagle-Four

The air Captain looked over to the Colonel. "Colonel, we're showing a computer startup on Kestrel-Six. It's passive mode only, but we may be able to send a message to them on the targeting matrix."

One of the great things about the MiG-31's Baget computer was that it could talk to the aircraft around it independently of the radios, creating a targeting network, allowing a flight of MiG-31's to control the airspace by sharing all their target tracking data. Each aircraft's Baget computer could assess and track up to twenty-four aircraft at once and target six within a two-hundred-mile area. This enabled four aircraft, working together, to track up to ninety-six aircraft and target twenty-four within a flight radius of eight hundred miles, the idea being that there would no longer be the need for a controller aircraft, which Eagle-Four was currently serving as. Now that Kestrel-Six had turned on its computer, Eagle-Four could now send a message to them, warning them of the incoming threat.

Not wanting to waste any time, the Colonel shot back,

"Quickly, send them this message: enemy aircraft inbound, do *not* engage. Tell them to leave their computer on passive mode only. Allow the enemy aircraft to close to within eighty miles. Once at eighty miles they are to paint the target."

After a few seconds the air Captain responded. "Message sent, sir. But won't that put them at extreme risk though? After all they are carrying a Kinzhal."

"Those fools are the reason we are having to fight early, besides, that's why we have reserves, Captain. Now inform Kestrels One-Nine and Two-Zero that Kestrel-Six will be lighting the target for them. They are authorised to fire once they have a target in range of their missiles."

He stood and watched as the team in front of him began to rapidly fire off his orders. *Now*, he thought, *let's see if these new missiles are as good as the designers boasted about.*

On board Kestrel-Six, Nikolai watched in shock as the message flashed up on his screen. Suddenly realising the danger, he quickly reported, "Shit! Mikhail, I've just received a flash message on the target matrix, we've got two enemy fighters inbound to us; but we are to do nothing except let them close to eighty miles. Once at eighty miles we are to paint the target."

A look of confusion creased his face as he thought aloud, "Paint the target? But we're not carrying anything to take them out?"

Suddenly realising what the plan was, he exclaimed, "Fuck, Nikolai, I think we're being used as bait."

"They wouldn't do that would they?" he asked, already knowing the answer. He continued dejectedly, "You mean we've just flown five fucking hours in this cockpit to get shot down before even getting to see England? What a load of shit!"

"Relax, my friend, I've no intention of dying just yet. We'll paint the target for them as ordered, you just be ready on the countermeasures. We've got this."

"Yeah, yeah, there you go again with the optimism. Just remember though, I've not been to London yet and promised my mother I'd get a photo in Buckingham Palace, lying in the King's bed."

"We'll get you that photo, Nikolai, I promise, except you won't be lying in it, you'll be fucking one of those pretty younghand maidens we we're always seeing with the Queen!"

Both pilots laughed and they felt the mood lighten as they both realised they were powerless to do anything but follow their orders. They continued to fly through the darkening sky, Nikolai staring intently at the radar screen on one of the three multi-function displays in front of him. After only forty seconds he reported, "Okay, I see them. We don't have them on radar yet but I'm picking up their EW signal. Looks like they're scanning for us – two targets, range two hundred and ninety miles, on course to intercept us. Speed looks like Mach 1.5. Should be within eighty miles in ninety seconds."

"Why aren't we picking them up on radar at that range?"

"They could be F35's or Typhoons, both have a reduced radar signature. Either way, we should pick them up when they get to two hundred miles."

Jackal-One

Unaware of the danger, the RAF Typhoons continued to close the distance as Edwards kept scanning his radar screen, the display superimposed onto his helmet visor. He could see another two aircraft on screen, but knew both were commercial aircraft. One was sixty miles to his south, and one was ninety miles to his north. He checked they were still both on their original headings and that they were both well below his own altitude. Happy that there were no further threats in the immediate area, he began to check over his weapons systems to clarify all were in the green and good to go. He kept visualising what he would do, what actions to take if certain scenarios were to play out. He knew that right now the senior controller would be using the red telephone, the line that went straight to Downing Street to inform the government of what was going on. He secretly hoped that this was just another lost pilot or aircraft with radio issues, needing a steer and an escort. All pilots understood what it meant to scramble, but it was one thing to be taking off to attack a hostile enemy and another to think of shooting down a fully loaded civilian passenger plane. Suddenly a new blip appeared on his radar, interrupting his thoughts. He checked its heading and speed, confirming it was Zulu Zero-Zero-One.

"Blackdog this is Jackal-One, I now have radar contact on Zulu Zero-Zero-One, range two-four-zero miles, ETA two minutes, over."

"Jackal-One, Blackdog Controller, roger. We have a threat update—"

Edwards, out of instinct, tapped his headset as he heard Blackdog's message being cut short.

"Blackdog Control, Jackal-One, say again your threat update. Over."

Static was all he heard in reply as he repeated the message.

"Blackdog, Blackdog, this is Jackal-One, say again your last message. Over."

Without needing to be prompted he heard his wingman over the radio also try to contact control.

"Blackdog Control, this is Jackal-Two, comms check. Over."

Again, nothing but static in response. *Not now,* he thought to himself. *Of all the fucking times to lose comms with control this is not the time.* He quickly flicked his radio over to the chatnet.

"Ley, did you receive anything or are you just getting the same static?"

He looked over at his wingman, still in close formation as his voice came over his headset.

"Nothing either, but I heard you loud and clear. We're sending and receiving. I think the problem's at Blackdog's end."

He looked at the radar contact, now only two hundred miles away and closing fast.

"Okay let's continue as planned. I'll try to get a visual using PIRATE. Can you continue to monitor comms and try to raise Blackdog on the alternate frequency. In the meantime, let's just play it safe and give ourselves separation of half a mile. I like to have room to think."

"Roger, Ed, understood."

Both aircraft slowly separated to half a mile, giving each other the room to manoeuvre should anything try to surprise them, but close enough to support each other as Edwards now began scanning his aircraft's camera-tracking system. Called PIRATE for short, the Passive Infra-Red Airborne Track Equipment would use extremely long-range sensors and cameras, slaved to a computer, to build a picture of exactly what aircraft they were heading for. Edwards already had the target on radar, the visual picture would just be to confirm what he already knew. Still to far away for PIRATE to identify, he checked his instruments one final time and prepared himself as the distance began to quickly close...

Eagle-Four

The air Captain looked triumphantly at the Colonel. "Sir, we have the frequency locked out; the enemy aircraft will not be able to talk to their controllers now."

"Good, keep it that way, I want continuous jamming for the next two minutes."

He turned to the Electronics Warfare Officer at the far end of the aircraft towards the rear, changing his channel to talk.

"EW officer, if we upload a package, will it affect our jamming capabilities at the moment?"

Watching his body language, he saw the man stiffen as he realised after hours of nothing but watching instruments and displays he was finally being put to use.

"Colonel, the jamming is using all of our transmitter power at the moment. If we attempt to upload anything we may burn out the transmitter or degrade the jamming."

"Very well, I want you to prepare a package, I want ten Tu-95's to appear out to the north east, have them fly high and slow inbound to Scotland, let's say on a heading of two-one-zero. I want it ready to send in four minutes."

"Yes, sir, it'll be ready in three."

He watched as the airman quickly jotted down on the panel in front of him everything he had just heard and then began to type quickly into the computer keyboard in front of him. Satisfied that his orders were being carried out, he switched back to the air-net to listen to his pilots. Now the vital part would begin.

Jackal-One

Edwards was watching the screens in front of him, still waiting for PIRATE to gain a better understanding of the target to his front. He patiently waited for the computer to build a picture of what the aircraft would look like when his wingman came through on the radio.

"Ed, I'm receiving a threat alert from our south, southwest. I'm getting EW warnings from Praetorian that don't make any sense to me."

The DASS (Defensive Aids Sub System) or 'Praetorian' was the onboard computer which constantly monitored and assessed for threats to the aircraft. Using sensors located across the airframe, it could detect threats from lasers, missiles, enemy radar systems, and jammers, like the one being directed at it now. Unknown to the Russians, their jamming was now giving away the position of Eagle-Four.

"What? Where's it coming from?" Edwards asked, his disbelief clear.

"It says one hundred and fifty miles to our southwest. It's coming from one of the commercial aircraft – that's not making any sense?"

What the hell is going on? thought Edwards. He was about to respond when suddenly an audible alert sounded through his headset. Finally, PIRATE had compiled the image. He looked to the display in his visor that showed an alert on the aircraft they were approaching. His eyes widened as, fully expecting to see the information of a Boeing 767 it instead flashed up as red, the display reading, *MiG-31-THREAT HOSTILE.*

"What the... SHIT! THAT'S NOT A 767, IT'S A MiG-31!" he exclaimed.

Kestrel-Six

On board Kestrel-Six, Nikolai was watching his radar screen as the two inbound enemy fighters closed with them. Despite the Typhoons being harder to pick out on the radar, the MiG-31already had a good lock on them, thanks to the Typhoons coming in with all their own electronic systems active, not knowing of the threat that faced them. It would be the equivalent of two gunfighters at night stalking each other; one was quiet and waiting in the shadows, whilst the other was loud and stood in the spotlight, announcing his presence and location. Despite being told to wait until they were eighty miles away, Nikolai and Mikhail had already decided that they would paint the target at one hundred and fifty miles. To let the Typhoons get any closer would mean their own chances of surviving the engagement would be little to none.

Nikolai's finger rested on the toggle switch that would make their own systems go from passive to active. A strange sense of empowerment came over him as he began to realise that the two enemy pilots' lives were literally his to take. He waited until both targets were at one hundred and fifty miles and activated the switch. Within less than a second their own audible threat alert began to sound as the Typhoons now finally saw the threat they posed and began to target them back.

Jackal-One

For a moment Edwards was numbed into shock, his brain suffering sensory over-load as his headset filled with noises and alarms and his multi-function displays in front of him flashed red – the colour of danger. He'd trained for this very moment, hundreds of hours of training in the skies above Europe and America, dogfighting with fellow NATO pilots. But, even so, the cold, hard reality of knowing there was a real threat still caused him to delay for that fraction of a second. The cold robotic voice of the aircraft's defensive computer began to blare through his headset.

"Caution – radar warning. Caution – radar warning. Caution – Missile! Missile! Missile!"

The Praetorian system on the Typhoon came alive, as within milliseconds, far faster than the pilot could think, the system had detected another aircraft's radar locking onto it. Using the data it had already acquired from the PIRATE system, the weapons computer locked on to Kestrel-Six, determining the aircraft type and range, and selected the most suitable missile to use. Deciding the range was too great to use the ASRAAM (Advanced Short-Range Air-to Air-Missile) the computer instead select-ed the Meteor BVRAAM (Beyond Visual Range Air-to-Air Missile). Now all Edwards had to do was press the trigger on his flight controls and the weapon would fire. But before his brain could register the fact that he was under threat, or that a missile was ready to fire, the aircraft's missile warning system began to alarm as it detected the launch of the two R-37 missiles, one to the north of them from Kestrel One-Nine, and one to the south from Kestrel Two-Zero.

Praetorian took over control of the aircraft's electronic counter-measures as it attempted to jam and interfere with the radar lock that Kestrel-Six now had on it.

"JESUS CHRIST!" was all Edwards managed to exclaim as from instinct he threw over the stick, banking the fighter up and over at Mach 1.5. The G-forces crushed him into the seat as his G-suit rapidly inflated to keep his blood pressure stable, trying to stop him from going into what the pilots would call G-LOC – a temporary blackout. He began to rapidly throw the fighter into a series of tight turns, trying to disrupt the lock of the enemy missile as he tried to take back control of the situation, transmitting to his wingman.

"TWO, ONE! DEFENSIVE!"

He knew his wingman would be taking his own evasive action. For now, all Edwards could do was avoid the incoming missile and stay alive.

Meanwhile, seventy miles to the north, the R-37 missile fired from Kestrel One-Nine began to rapidly accelerate towards Jackal-One, its seeker head already identifying its target, as it kept track of the course corrections required to hit it. The missile was at its full speed of Mach 5 within five seconds, meaning the seventy miles' distance to its target would be covered in less than sixty seconds. Small fins on the missile would help keep it on course as the distance closed. Designed originally to chase down the SR-71 Blackbird travelling at Mach 4, Jackal-One had no hope of trying to outrun it, as both aircraft and missile – the hunter and the prey – now headed towards each other at a closing speed of Mach 6.5.

On board Jackal-One, Edwards began to refocus and control his breathing as his brain began to quickly recognise what was happening to him as his years of training took over. Still throwing the Typhoon through the skies, he transmitted over the air, knowing Blackdog wouldn't reply, but wanting to send anyway. There was always the possibility that someone else was listening in and help could be sent.

"Blackdog, Jackal-One, Defensive! Defensive! Launch the alert fighters, launch the alert fighters!"

Once the message was sent, he concentrated on the immediate threat: where were the bandits and who was firing at them? He'd no idea where his wingman was, but hoped he'd followed him into the tight banking turns and was still with him.

Edwards saw the two missiles incoming on radar from different directions, yet the threat radar was warning him that the enemy was off to his west. He saw he still had a missile lock on Zulu Zero-Zero-One, but that hadn't been the aircraft that fired at him. He wasted another few seconds in hesitation, as he tried to make sense of what was happening, listening in as the aircraft's Praetorian system came to life. Over his headset came the cold, calm female voice again, giving him a running commentary on the inbounds.

"*Missile now twenty miles. Evade! Evade! Evade!*"

"Jesus! That's quick!" he said, realising he was fast running out of time and options. He decided first to engage the aircraft targeting him, then he could deal with the missiles.

"Jackal One, Fox Three!" he shouted over the radio, hoping his wingman could hear as he pressed the firing switch. He felt the missile drop away and fire, the tail igniting into the darkened sky and shooting past as it accelerated off to find its target.

As soon as the missile left its pylon, he threw the fighter over onto its back, and pulled hard over into a dive, his G-suit saving him from the crushing G-forces as he took a deep breath and held it, his eyes feeling as if on stalks as the blood drained from them, white spots dancing past his eyes. He blinked hard to refocus, watching the clouds screaming up towards the cockpit. He was hoping to try to evade the incoming missiles by diving lower, perhaps even getting below them. The warnings continued to ring loudly in his ears. He heard his wingman transmitting over the radio, attempting to raise Blackdog and declaring he was defensive as well, confirming Edwards' worst fears. Both fighters had been targeted. He saw the clouds tearing past the cockpit as he dove the fighter towards the ocean, his plane picking up more speed as he scanned the horizon for the telltale streak of flame from the missile tail. According to Praetorian's warnings screeching in his ears, both were now less than ten miles away and closing fast.

Praetorian automatically began to dispense chaff and flares, briefly lighting up the darkening sky as the aircraft began to compute how close the missile was, as finally he saw the flash on the horizon as the missile streaked up towards him. His eyes opened wide in shock when he realised instead of coming from above, the missile had been below them, and now he was diving towards it. He was out of time and the missile was on a perfect head-on trajectory with him, accelerating towards him from below. *Time,* he thought to himself, *if only I had more time.* The Praetorian system tried its best – as quick as it was, it was still too slow to respond to the missile closing in at over three thousand five hundred miles per hour. The missile homed in, time slowing down for Edwards as his heightened senses could feel and see everything at once. He could feel the aircraft begin its roll to the left, then a quick flash as the missile exploded just ahead of the aircraft, hearing the crash as the debris hit the airframe, feeling the cold icy rush of air as the cockpit canopy disintegrated in front of him – and then nothing. His eyes went dark and the inky blackness of the sky seemed to envelop him. *So, this was what it's like to die.* His last conscious thought. The whole incident from the radar locking on, to the missile hitting his aircraft had all taken no more than forty seconds.

Kestrel-Six

"Threat warning!" Nikolai shouted in alarm as suddenly the instrumentation in front of him came alive as Edwards' Meteor missile now began to home in towards them at Mach 4, using the information still being received by Edwards' Typhoon.

"Missile inbound! Twelve o'clock on the nose, range one hundred and thirty miles."

Mikhail breathed heavily through his mask as the adrenaline began to flow, feeling more alive as he shot back, "Status on targets?"

He wanted nothing more than to begin evasive manoeuvres, but also knew that they were painting the target for the other aircraft. He couldn't just stop and break off the attack yet, he needed to make sure the Typhoons were destroyed. Judging the range to the incoming missile to be acceptable he ignored the threat, keeping the fighter bomber on the same heading and speed.

Nikolai punched the air excitedly as he watched one of the Typhoons break apart from the missile hit and begin to plummet to the ground, its radar signature slowly fading. The other one was also fading fast as it began its earthward spiral, and he watched the altitude decrease rapidly on its signature. It continued below one thousand feet and the blip disappeared, lost thirty miles north of Scotland, never to be seen again.

"Mikhail, we've got them both, both targets destroyed!"

Mikhail was about to throw the aircraft into a dive, stopping himself suddenly as he remembered the missile was now on its own, no longer receiving data from the Typhoon. Without further updates from the launching fighter on its target, the incoming missile could now be deceived.

"Right! Shut down the computer, full power to electronic counter measures. Wait till the missile is fifty miles away."

In the nose of the MiG-31 sat the powerful electronics array, its suite of Electronic Counter Measures (ECM) designed to counteract and confuse the seeker head of the incoming missile, blinding it with a more powerful signal and causing it to lose sight of its target. The trouble was, to do this, the MiG-31 had to remain flying towards the threat, so Mikhail still couldn't try to evade it. Ignoring all the warnings in his head, and fighting the urge to dive or break off, Mikhail kept the plane flying straight and level, as Nikolai began to relay the missile's progress to him.

"Okay, missile tracking clean, still inbound, range now one hundred miles. ECM is powered up."

Mikhail stared straight ahead, looking out at the orange glow on the horizon as the sun began to finally set, knowing he wouldn't see the missile until the last possible second. He kept a firm hand on the controls, ready to throw the aircraft over if necessary. There was always the chance this wouldn't work.

"Range now eighty miles! Missile is still tracking us; we now have radar warning."

So now the missile had them targeted on radar – *Good, now it could be blinded*, he thought to himself.

Nikolai's voice began to rise excitedly from the back as the missile came ever closer.

"Seventy miles... Sixty miles!"

"Standby to jam!" Mikhail shot back, his voice raised, adrenaline coursing through him.

"Fifty miles! Jamming!" Nikolai shouted in warning.

Mikhail stared ahead, waiting as Nikolai kept reporting the track of the missile. He decided he'd wait until the missile was twenty miles out – if by then it showed no sign of deviating off course then he'd be forced to throw the fighter bomber into evasive manoeuvres.

"Missile now at forty miles, jamming is active, ECM on high-power frequencies, still no deviation," Nikolai reported as they both waited.

Come on... come on! Mikhail was saying over and over in his head, praying the missile would lose sight of them. In anticipation he flexed his fingers at the controls, ready to begin the manoeuvres as Nikolai kept reporting.

"Thirty miles... Wait! Deviation! We have deviation! Missile now veering off course!"

Mikhail kept quiet, scanning ahead for the inbound missile, waiting to be certain as Nikolai announced excitedly,

"Missile now veering off course and losing altitude. Range ten miles. You should see it now, eleven o'clock high.

Mikhail peered up to where his weapons officer was indicating, shaking his head.

"I can't see... FUCK! THERE IT IS!" he exclaimed as the missile dove from above and into view. It was off course, about two miles away from them, travelling fast, but importantly it was heading down and away from them. Mikhail held his breath, expecting at any second to see it turn towards them – perhaps this was a ruse that western missiles would do – make them think they'd missed, then reacquire the target.

He watched on, his fears subsiding, as instead of turning, the missile exploded harmlessly into the air, lighting up the sky and showering the area around it with hot molten metal that fell towards the earth in a shower of sparks.

Both erupted into shouts and cheers, bouncing in their pilots' seats, overcome with joy at having survived the engagement.

"Those damn R-37 missiles were quick! Seventy miles in under forty seconds. Damn, I wish we had a few of those babies on board. Fuck the RAF and their fighters. Here come the 143rd Air Regiment!" Nikolai proudly proclaimed.

Relieved at the outcome, no doubt helped by the fact they had not let the RAF Typhoons come too close, Mikhail smiled as his weapons officer excitedly began singing an old Russian song about a man and his dog who together defeat a wolf that had terrorised a village. With his friend singing away he was now more confident than before, happy now to have helped with the first kills of the night. If everything went to plan, there would be more, many more, and finally their homeland could breathe as they went together to slaughter the wolf that was terrorising their own village.

Eagle-Four

Colonel Bresavik watched the demise of the two RAF fighters as the radar signatures slowly faded, denoting they were breaking apart and falling below the radar coverage. He'd watched the inbound missile tracking Kestrel-Six with bated breath, certain to lose them, smiling in triumph as instead of a strike the missile had missed.

Thankful for the outcome he turned to his air officer. "Well done, Captain, pass on my congratulations to Kestrels One-Nine and Two-Zero – first blood belongs to us. The night is young, though, and I feel there's more game yet to hunt."

Smiling proudly, the Captain turned to him and replied, "Thank you, Colonel, it's an honour to be here with you on this historical evening."

The Colonel walked over to the man, grasping his shoulder respectfully, the stress of the previous four hours washing away now that finally they had taken out two of the RAF's latest generation of jets. For years, Russians had been told to fear the west, to fear their technology, but now using their greatest asset, deception, they had overcome the technology, and as the British were going to bed, they were themselves coming to repay the sins of the past. Careful not to become too distracted, or overconfident, the Colonel shook the thoughts of victory from his head – he needed to remain focused on the mission and there was still much to do. He turned to the electronics warfare officer, checking he was on the channel to speak to him.

"EW officer, cease jamming the frequency and begin to send the package. Let's see if our money was well spent."

ASACS - RAF Boulmer - Northumberland

The senior controller of 19 Squadron was looking up from his desk, at the large screen on the wall in front of him showing the airspace to the north of Scotland. Below him were a bank of twelve workstations, all manned with operators. The Air Operation Centre was a hive of activity and noise as the RAF controllers and staff talked to each other and to 78 Squadron in Swanwick who themselves were co-located with the air traffic controllers. Between the three departments, they all controlled both the civilian and military traffic coming into and going out of UK airspace. The senior controller was chatting to the air operations manager who everyone referred to as Flight, who was stood hunched over a monitor, looking at the display.

"Flight, any updates on Jackal yet?"

Flight stood up from the monitor, a look of concern on his face. "Not yet, sir, we're still tracking them on radar inbound on Zulu Zero-Zero-One, they should be in visual range shortly. We'll keep trying comms, perhaps the issues affecting Zulu Zero-Zero-One's comms are affecting theirs too?"

The senior controller shook his head. "I doubt it, Flight. At that altitude we should still be able to talk to one of them. What's the status on the standby QRA team in Lossiemouth – are they ready to go now? I've got the Air Chief Marshall on the line wanting them launched immediately."

"Not yet, sir, there's been a technical issue with one of the aircraft. They're replacing it now and should be at QRA status in five minutes."

"Not good enough!" the senior controller fumed. "Tell them next time to check and double-check those reserve ships would you. If Jackal do need assistance, I'm sure they won't be too pleased to have to bloody wait."

A surprised gasp sounded from one of the air controllers, causing the colleagues around her to look in her direction. She quickly raised her hand to get the attention of the Flight. Seeing her urgency, he rushed over to her screen before quickly looking up to the senior controller, the shock plain to see on his face. "Sir, we've lost radar contact with Jackal flight!"

"Which one, Flight? For Christ's sake, there are two out there, help me out will you?"

"Sir, *both* of them – radar contact lost with Jackal-One and Two. Last track we have showed Jackal-Two breaking up mid-flight and Jackal-One descending rapidly. We've lost radar contact as he's now below one thousand feet."

"Launch QRA immediately. I want them supersonic as soon as they're airborne. Break windows if they have to but get them as quick as you can to Jackals' last-known position. Tell them threat level is red and mission is to intercept, not interrogate. Get hold of pilot search and rescue in Lossiemouth, give them the last-known position of our downed aircraft."

"Sir!"

Flight picked up the radio telephone to talk to RAF Lossiemouth but before he could speak, his mouth opened in shock as on the large display to the northeast four large blips appeared. He was about to say something when another operator shouted, "Bandit! Bandit! Bandit! Tracking multiple aircraft inbound, count six, make that eight, now ten aircraft, tracking inbound, course two-one-zero, altitude three-zero thousand feet and speed three-zero-zero knots. Threat level is high, I assess them to be Tu-95 Bears."

The senior controller stood open-mouthed for a few seconds before barking out, "Divert the QRA out to them immediately. Get Lossiemouth on the radio, I want them stood by with every available fighter. *Now!*"

Flight talked into the radio telephone, his voice urgent. Quickly speaking to the controller there he relayed the message, waiting for the acknowledgement before hanging up.

"Okay, sir, QRA fighters will be in the air immediately, and the duty controller is rallying the troops, but it's going to be difficult, sir, with some of the personnel away on leave."

"I know, Flight, I know, but I don't care if people are wearing bloody hulu shirts, I want those planes ready to go. I don't like how this is playing out. Losing Jackal flight and now this... Something's up."

He reached over to the red radio telephone next to his desk, the one telephone that had a direct line straight to Downing Street, relying on radio waves instead of phone lines. Without needing to dial he picked it up and pressed the button and waited as the phone began to ring.

I don't like this one bit, he thought, as the phone continued to ring...

16

Wonderland

Wonderland Operations Centre (WOC)

It was rare for Peter to be speechless, something his wife had always joked about with him in the past. But as the lift doors opened, his jaw hung slack in surprise as he stared into the large room that opened before him. *Wonderland*, as his friend James had called it, was indeed a wonder and as he looked around, he began to understand just how Alice had felt. After their meeting earlier, he had walked through the beautiful home of his friend with the others, as they had come to a long corridor which Peter remembered had abruptly ended. James had always joked that it was a family tradition to leave the corridor untouched. However, as they approached the end of the corridor, the far wall had slid across to reveal an elevator, large enough to accommodate twenty people. He tried to hide his curiosity as they all got into the lift, the doors closing smoothly and quickly behind them. There were no buttons in the lift, just a camera watching them, its red light blinking as Peter felt the lift begin to descend. After fifteen seconds Peter felt the lift stop, then begin to move sideways, as if on rails. The sudden motion caused some of the occupants to reach out to steady themselves, as like being in an underground train with no windows they rumbled along an unseen track. Peter looked over to James who said nothing, his poker face on full display as the lift continued to rumble along the tunnel, picking up speed, until after only two minutes they all felt the lift begin to slow, the doors reopening into the room where they now stood.

Peter left the lift first and walked into a cavernous room, measuring two hundred feet by two hundred feet and at least one eighty feet in height, with three huge screens mounted on the wall at the far end, each screen hung side by side. Below the screens were five rows of desks, with a computer and operator at each station. Peter counted ten stations on each row, making a total of fifty operators, all wearing headsets and all either animatedly talking to each other or busy typing on keyboards. Peter could see from the collection of uniforms that there were members of the army, RAF and navy there, as well as the police force, border force, and some people dressed in civilian suits. Peter guessed that those in suits were part of the Civil Service departments, the other functioning arms of government. Besides the banks of workstations were stood junior soldiers, mainly Lance Corporals, looking like the ball collectors seen at a tennis match, patiently waiting for orders. From what Peter could see these runners were there to carry out whatever task the operator would need for them.

To the left of the room was a galleried landing, with wall-to-ceiling glass partitions and behind the glass Peter could see a briefing room, like the room they had just left, with a central table, telephone system and display near the wall. The vast chamber reminded Peter of mission control at NASA and as they had walked in, he noticed the floor gently sloped towards the screens at the far end, so where they were stood now gave an uninterrupted view of every aspect of the room. On the right side of the room was a set of blast doors which were closed, and above the doors, Peter could see a galleried landing accessed by a staircase that was off to his right side. The landing ran around the outside of the room and led to a large raised balcony on the left which led to a second set of offices sitting above them, allowing whoever was there to monitor everything that was going on.

Not knowing where to look first, Peter walked awkwardly into the middle of the room, feeling like a toddler on his first day of nursery as he looked at the workstations. He could see that each workstation had a sign above it, informing the unwary, like himself, which department each operator worked for. Peter looked up, reading aloud some of the signs, "Air Ops South, Air Ops North, Police Ops Central Command, Police Ops Northern Command, Police Ops Southern Command." The operators ignored him and his curious gaze as the other members of the Defence Council and the Secretary of State filed past, making their way into the room, and walked left towards the conference room, as Peter stood in awe. It was only James who stopped by him to explain what he was looking at. Peter noted he'd now changed into full uniform, wearing the multi-terrain-pattern combats that most soldiers wore during normal daytime duties. "Peter, welcome to the WOC, standing for Wonderland Operations

Centre, or as some like to call it simply Wonderland, the beating heart of the UK in times of national emergencies."

Peter was about to say something when he was interrupted by the arrival of Major Tristan-Phelps, who had also now changed into combat uniform. The Major stood to attention next to them, both glancing at Peter before reporting, "Sir, Wonderland is up and running, we have communications confirmed with Downing Street, Whitehall and GCHQ. We are talking to RAF Boulmer and Dover Coastguard, but so far there's nothing new to report. We are monitoring all ships and aircraft for any unexplained activity but so far, it's all quiet."

"Thank you, T-P, keep an open line to RAF Boulmer, we may have some orders to go up and investigate a few flights shortly."

Peter watched the Major walk back to the centre of the room, joined by another two people in RAF uniforms, as the orders began to filter down to the operators manning the consoles. He turned to his friend and stammered, "But I don't understand...I thought London, the Cabinet, COBRA, were all London based. Why here in the middle of nowhere?" The look of confusion on his face clear to see.

"Because like you've just mentioned, all of those places in times of war or emergency are too well known. What's the first thing the news reports on in an emergency? The PM's bloody meetings at Cabinet Office Briefing Room A, COBR(A). No, it was always going to have to be replaced and the location moved. Plus, all the old government places in times of war, Churchill's old War Rooms in London, all the secret nuclear bunkers around London, they're all tourist attractions now. We couldn't use them in times of crisis, so secretly the MoD and government came up with this, Project Wonderland. If the PM comes under threat and we deem London unsafe, then there's a helicopter ready to fly him and his team out here to us, as you quite eloquently mentioned, in *the middle of nowhere*."

Peter looked on incredulously as he replied, "But James, it's built on *your* family land, it's under *your* house. What are you going to do when you retire, they can't just fill all this in? You're going to have to relinquish the house, you realise that?"

A knowing look crossed James's face as he nodded. "It's not under my house, Peter. You did feel the sideways movement of the lift?"

"I did," Peter replied, wondering what his friend was going to say next.

"What if I told you that in that small amount of time we travelled four miles through a specially built transit tunnel, and that now we're actually two hundred feet underground in the middle of fields and countryside."

"Really?" Peter asked, amazed. "But that still changes nothing. Your house is still connected to this place. Surely when you leave the post of CDS, you can't remain living there, can you?"

James smiled, replying, "My friend, we've been well compensated for the loss of the house, it's a draughty, expensive old thing, and for me and my family it would be time for a change I think, when I do eventually retire. Besides, it was my idea. I put the notion forward to do this before being made CDS. When I give up my post, the house now becomes part of the new incoming CDS's residence. Going forward all new CDS's will move here, and I like to think my family has now done its bit, helped to keep the lights on at home and all that. It's a bit like the PM's residence at Chequers – that never belongs to the PM – except here we have access to all the working arms of the UK government and I might add, we are *not* advertised all over the bloody internet."

"But how did you keep all this a secret? How on earth did you build it? I've never seen any construction traffic at yours in all the time I've known you."

Checking the other Defence Council Members were still preoccupied, James said, "2020 – Covid had everything in the UK and the world locked down. Everyone was forced to stay at home. That meant no dog walkers, no ramblers, no visitors to the house. The usual prying eyes that you would get daily were now hidden behind closed doors and windows. So I, along with Sir Charles and his friends at MI5 had a construction team, trusted with these sort of government projects sent in to do the work. Do you remember in 2020 there was a concrete shortage in the UK, in between all the lockdowns and Covid 19 measures? Everyone thought it was because the construction industry had used all the supplies in going back to work suddenly?"

Peter nodded.

"All of it was a lie. The truth was that we'd used all the UK's current supply in building this place. Once we had the initial tunnel built, and all the heavy plant machinery was below ground and out of sight, then it became easier. We could work night and day, out of sight to those above ground. We've still got all the construction equipment, the bulldozers, the diggers, all buried on the bottom floor. It's far too risky to bring it all up now, so we've had it all entombed in concrete."

Peter shook his head admirably; it had been no easy project to have built all of this and to have done so without arousing suspicion. It had been one hell of a feat.

James continued with the tour, pointing to the blast doors.

"The lift we came in only goes to the house. However, over there, behind those doors is another lift and staircase that goes down another four floors, to the workspaces, offices and living areas, available to house four thousand people if we had to, in relatively modest accommodation. Here in the Ops room is where the decisions get made and the government continues to function."

James swept his arm around the room as he continued. "The offices behind us on the gantry are where the PM and his staff will go when they arrive. And we have those offices up there to the left above the conference room. The workstations in front of you are all connected to the UK's police, fire, ambulance and coastguard operations centres as well as the control centres of the MoD, army, navy and RAF. From here, we should be able to run the country in the event of a national emergency if we had to."

Peter looked down at the workstations, watching the operators working. "How many personnel do you need to run all this?"

"We have two hundred and fifty personnel to operate the ops centre, all living within a ten-mile radius, hence we can call everyone in at a moment's notice to activate this place. It's a mixed bag of military, Civil Service and civilian personnel, all of whom work together to paint a picture of what's happening around the UK."

"But how are you still communicating with everyone? All the internet and phones are down, except for radio comms. So how are you getting the information in or out?"

"Remember all those smart motorway upgrades, fifty mile per hour speed limits and miles and miles of roadworks?" James raised an eyebrow questioningly then added, "Whilst the Highways Agency were conducting the work, the MoD secretly piggybacked the laying of hundreds of miles of fibre-optic cables from the control centres around the UK to here at Wonderland. Anyone seeing the work was simply told, that it was all part of the smart motorway upgrade. The truth was, we were able to lay our own separate fibre-optic cables down the whole stretch of the UK motorway network, connecting everything to our systems here. Because they're separated from the civilian and our other military networks, we shouldn't have to worry about this bloody ongoing cyberattack, which is now the reason we can still maintain data connections and voice communications with certain departments. Sir Charles won't be flying to GCHQ, he's on a video call with them now in the office behind us. I just didn't want the Defence Secretary to know Wonderland was up and running until now."

Peter shook his head thoughtfully as he remembered his friend had also been a great poker player, keeping his cards very close to his chest.

James was distracted as the Vice CDS opened the glass door to the conference room, beckoning to him urgently. He turned to his friend. "Okay, Peter, looks like they're ready for us."

"One more thing before we go in though," Peter said. In response James merely raised an eyebrow. "Project Wonderland? Sounds a bit fairy tale to me. Why the name?"

James smirked as they walked, and he replied proudly, "Simple. Firstly, like you say, it all sounds 'fairy tale', certainly not what another hostile country would be looking for if they tried to locate us and secondly, my granddaughter picked the name."

With his friend leading the way, they both walked into the conference room, the glass door closing behind them. Peter heard a soft noise of air escaping as the door sealed behind them. Immediately the noise and din outside disappeared and the room became quiet. The video display on the far wall came alive and Peter saw the face of the Foreign Secretary, Yvette Chongaya, whom he recognised from the media coverage of the elections last year. From the backdrop it looked like she was in London. Peter recognised the distinct landmarks and skyline in the distance.

"Evening, Jeffery, so what's up and why the urgency?" Her tone clearly implied she was not happy to be there.

"You not at Checkers for the fundraiser this evening?" Jeffery quizzed.

"No, otherwise I wouldn't be here talking to you." The tone was condescending, and she quickly added, "The PM needed someone he trusts to be in Downing Street as the designated survivor. Plus, I've got some papers that need to be finished for his speech tomorrow. You know how it is. Besides, may I ask why *you're* not there? I thought it was a three-line whip, every member of the Cabinet was to be there. You're all dressed up with no party to go to."

Forgetting he was still dressed in his tuxedo, Jeffery smiled as he quickly countered, "Well, something has come up. Something important." Not wanting to waste any more time he quickly added, "Look, Yvette, I need you to know that I've called Platinum, I'm expecting the PM to be on his way here to us shortly."

Her mouth dropped open as she took in what the Defence Secretary had just said. Quickly realising how she looked, she composed herself and her jaw hardened, a flash of anger crossing her eyes as she shot back, "You did *what?* Why would you? You have *no* authority to order that."

Before he could speak, the Foreign Secretary continued. "Do you have any idea of how this will look when the PM is bundled out of his own fundraiser at his home by his security detail? How the hell is the party supposed to get funding when we pull a stunt like that? Not to mention what the press will make it of it. Why on earth would you call a Platinum alert, Jeffery?"

Jeffery opened his mouth to reply but was interrupted again when she quickly added, her tone condescending, "Also, have you heard of ministerial ranking, Jeffery? I believe you're fifth on the list. There's four other people ranked above you, including me, therefore any decision to call Platinum must be passed up through the chain. Did you forget that? So why the hell have you called it? Honestly, the PM will have your balls in a jar for this."

The CDS was about to speak up, when the Defence Secretary held his hand up to stop him as he sought to answer the Foreign Secretary. Peter watched the Defence Secretary's face colour slightly, though whether that was anger or embarrassment, he wasn't sure. Peter thought it was best to stay out of the way as he watched the heated exchange. The chastising from the Foreign Secretary was over as she raised her eyebrows waiting for Jeffery to respond. He kept his voice calm and measured as he explained.

"Look, Yvette, firstly, I have every right to call Platinum. As a member of the Cabinet, it was set up for all Secretaries of State to be able to instigate the protective measures of the country – you should know that, and if you don't then perhaps you should read the reports your office churns out before you sign them. Secondly, Platinum is there in case we deemed there to be a hostile threat to either our monarch or serving PM. So, your ministerial ranking is irrelevant. Information has been brought to my attention on both counts – there is a threat to the King and a threat to the PM and our country. And it's for this reason I've instigated Platinum."

She scowled as she replied acidly, "What information? What threat?"

"I have seen evidence that suggests all the events today are related and that we are currently under threat from a hostile power and that tomorrow our country will come under attack with the aim to remove both the government and monarchy. The threat is real and the defence chiefs here all agree with me. We must start preparing now."

She looked across on the screen to where the CDS now sat. "CDS, what's the meaning of this? Why hasn't the PM been briefed on any of this instead of Jeffery here? Why have you not asked for a Cabinet meeting?"

The CDS stood up as he replied, "I'm sorry, Foreign Secretary, but there just was not enough time. We had only managed to piece everything together this afternoon, what with the phones being down and this being such a time-critical event, we needed to action it immediately."

"Time-critical event... Action it now... You military types love your power words, don't you? Well, send this report over to me now, I'll have a look at it and I'll deem whether it's important or not. In the meantime, I'm revoking the Platinum alert. The PM can be briefed about this tomorrow morning."

The CDS looked to the Defence Secretary who, understanding the prompt, stood up. "I'm sorry, Yvette, but you can't see the report in time, we can't email it because it's ultra top secret and you can't rescind the Platinum alert – only the PM has the power to do that. Whether you like it or not, it is happening with or without your permission." Her face flashed red as he continued, "Like you've said, it's my balls in the jar, so it's my call to make. Either get on board or get off the bus."

She was about to respond when someone entered the room offscreen. She looked up quickly and spat out, "I thought I told you I was *not* to be disturbed."

Everyone in the conference room looked up, as they all heard the unknown person offscreen reply formally with, "Red phone, red phone."

Her face froze as she heard the words. Quickly she looked back to the screen and replied curtly, "I've got to go. Ask the PM to call me back when he gets there." The screen went dark as the signal at her end was abruptly cut.

The Chief of Air Staff stood up expectantly as she looked over to the CDS. "CDS, with your permission I'd like to go find out what's going on." The CDS looked over to the Defence Secretary who merely nodded in response. Taking his cue, the CDS turned to the room and said, "Okay, everyone, I think it's best if now you all take charge of your departments, we've done enough talking for now. Brief them on what we know so far and then let's start looking to see if there's any truth to this thing. We're looking for anything out of the ordinary, anything that makes you want to take a second look." As the Defence Chiefs filed out of the room, the CDS turned to the First Sea Lord, "Sir Tony, we should have communications with Plymouth, let's see if we can get something ready to go at a moment's notice, anti-ship capabilities, helicopter or destroyer perhaps? Appreciate it's short notice but I'd rather have and not need, than need and not have."

Sir Tony replied gruffly, "I'll make sure that you have surface fleet and submarine," as he walked out, leaving the CDS, Peter and the Defence Secretary alone. Peter watched as all six of the Defence Council members walked over to the control desks, the various operators looking up as their respective bosses began to brief them on the events so far.

James motioned for Peter to leave the room with them as both stood to leave, following the Defence Minister out into the loud and hectic ops room. Peter followed them both over to a master control desk and as they surveyed the scene in front of them, Peter asked, "James, what's a *red phone* message?"

James looked up to reply but it was the Defence Secretary who spoke first. "The red phone is the secure line from RAF Boulmer to Downing Street. It's also connected here and at the Chequers estate, in the event Downing Street doesn't pick up quickly enough. If the RAF controllers deem there to be a threat entering UK airspace, they call the red phone to inform the PM if he's there, or to inform his deputy, which in this case is Yvette - sorry, I mean the Foreign secretary. Usually it's a rogue aircraft that's inadvertently got itself lost, but if the threat were real, if the RAF thought there was a threat to the UK, then they would ask for permission to shoot it down."

Nodding in understanding Peter looked to one of the large screens that now came to life. On its display the radar image of the northern coast of Scotland was shown, and about fifty miles north of the coastline was a small dot with the symbol 'Z001' alongside it. He guessed he was now looking at the feed from RAF Boulmer and Swanwick. As if to answer, Penny now came up to them as she reported, "Okay, the air chief has reported an unresponsive aircraft, now onscreen as call sign Zulu Zero-Zero-One. Boulmer has scrambled the QRA fighters to investigate and get a visual, they're about four minutes away. With your permission I'd like to recommend we launch a secondary QRA flight to start to get eyes on some of the other aircraft approaching our airspace, just to confirm what we are seeing on radar is what's actually out there. I'm conscious of what Peter's told us already, and I just want to confirm facts."

Without waiting for the CDS to reply, the Defence Secretary jumped in with, "Agreed, CAS, let's make that happen. I'd feel better knowing we've got human eyes looking at what's above our heads at the moment."

Peter watched her walk away to pass on the orders to her team, as the CDS turned to the Defence Secretary, his irritated look barely concealed. "Sir, I would appreciate it if you'd let me give the orders to my team. Just as you have a pecking order in the Cabinet, so do we in the military. It was my permission she was seeking, not yours, unless of course you'd like to put on a uniform?" His tone was light, but his displeasure was clear, and the Defence Secretary smiled apologetically in response.

"Of course, CDS, my apologies, you're right of course. Besides, I think a uniform would be more comfortable right now than this bloody tux."

Seeing his discomfort, the CDS asked, "You're about the same size and weight as my son, would you like someone to bring down one of his suits? We don't yet know how long this will go on for and you might be here a while yet." He saw the indecision on the minister's face and he added, "The PM's not expected to get here for another twenty minutes, you've got plenty of time to get changed in the offices behind us."

Nodding his head imperceivably the Minister agreed. "Okay, CDS, if you don't mind, then thank you."

James looked to one of the runners standing by the operators who instantly reacted, briskly walking up to the CDS. He stood to attention; Peter could see that he was a Lance Corporal of the RAF regiment and after a few brief words from the CDS in his ear he turned and disappeared into the lift.

Over the next few minutes, everyone in the ops room was watching the progress, as two new targets appeared off to the right of the screen. Peter could see the symbols clearly as the names of the fighters were displayed. Jackal-One and Jackal-Two. He watched impressed by the speed at which the two fighters travelled across the map from the east to the west. Something didn't look right on the screen though. He could only see the target aircraft and two friendly fighters. Where were the other planes? He looked over to the CAS and for a brief second was about to use her first name, when seeing she was surrounded by her subordinates, he stopped himself. How you spoke to people at dinner parties and how you spoke to them in a work environment were two different things, he quickly reminded himself.

"Excuse me, Air Chief Marshall?"

The CAS looked away from the screen, initially confused by Peter's formal tone of address, but she quickly realised why he'd said it, as his eyes darted to the airmen next to her. "Yes?" she enquired, "what is it Brigadier?"

"Why are we only seeing the three aircraft, Zulu Zero-Zero-One and the two QRA fighters? Where's the usual civilian air traffic that's incoming?"

"It's been filtered out of our overlay so as not to confuse us with this intercept. Why?"

His expression was strained as he replied, "I think rather than confuse you, it could help you, as right now you're blinded by the fact you're dealing with one plane. Potentially there's more threats, won't you want to know where they are?"

She thought for a second before quickly turning to the nearest controller. "Get the original track up, I want to see all the aircraft in the area."

The display changed quickly, showing a more cluttered display with another thirty targets now on the screen. Peter walked closer to the display, seeing the planes' headings and altitudes. The planes heading north out of UK airspace he ignored. But the ones heading south, into the UK he paid interest to. After a few seconds of studying the screen, he quickly turned to the CAS.

"Do the pilots visually check on the planes as they fly past them or will the pilots be concentrating on this Zulu Zero-Zero-One only?"

"No, why would they? The mission is to interrogate the target, all they'll be looking at and concentrating on will be the target aircraft."

"Bear in mind that in about one minute they're going to be flying between two aircraft, one forty miles to the south, and one seventy miles to the north. I'm no fighter pilot, but as a former tank commander I was always taught to check my arcs, to see what's left and right of me, as that's usually where the danger would come from. If they are only concentrating on what's in front of them, aren't they in danger of flying into a kill box?"

"You're assuming that those two targets are hostile," the CAS replied doubtfully.

"And your assuming they're not. How much fuel or time would it cost to simply divert them to check, or at least warn them of the possibility? When you were flying fast jets up there, wouldn't you want to know?"

The CAS looked thoughtfully at the screen for a few seconds, watching the progress of the two fighters, thinking back to the times she'd grumble about the lack of information fed to her as a pilot. Now she was in danger of doing the same thing to her own pilots. Making her mind up quickly she turned to another operator to her left.

"Get Boulmer to inform Jackal flight of the potential threats north and south of them. Advise Jackal to proceed with extreme caution."

James came and stood by his friend and whispered in a low voice, "You really think those aircraft are hostile?"

Peter turned and whispered, "James, my apologies. I'm not here to try to bark out orders or take charge, but this whole thing, this fucking report, it was all my doing. I'm responsible for this. I should have told you sooner. Instead, I did nothing for years but kept quiet and ignored my instincts, which at the time were screaming at me that something was wrong. Now I'm stood here watching those fighters, my instincts are doing the same. I'm not going to sit back and ignore them any longer. Those pilots need to know."

His friend nodded and was about to reply when one of the controllers quickly turned to the CAS and reported loudly, "Ma'am, we have a problem, Blackdog controller are reporting they've lost comms with Jackal flight. They're checking the equipment, but he thinks the problem is from Jackal's location."

The CAS shot the man a quick look as her voice betrayed the urgency of the request. "Did they pass on the message to them, did they relay the threat warning?"

"Er, negative, ma'am. The message was not sent in time."

She walked over to one of the phones connected directly with Boulmer and began rapidly speaking to the controller.

After a minute of chatting, she hung up and looked to the others, frustrated. "They're trying to get the next batch of QRA fighters ready, but there's a problem with one of the standby aircraft. The controllers assure me they'll be airborne as soon as they're ready."

For the next minute nothing happened, as everyone stood transfixed by the screen, watching the progress of the fighters as they passed between the two planes separated by one hundred miles of airspace.

Peter looked towards the CAS again as he asked, "Penny, with the equipment those planes carry, how close do they have to get before they get a visual identification on the aircraft they're tracking?"

She was about to reply when Peter saw the radar contact of one aircraft split into smaller blips and then disappear from the screen. The second contact began to lose altitude quickly, the display counting down the altitude as the plane headed towards the sea. Peter watched the numbers rapidly counting down, hoping to see them stabilise to show the pilot had somehow recovered. Everyone watched in dread as the plane's last-known altitude was shown as one thousand feet, as it dived below radar coverage, its fate almost certainly sealed.

The CDS, as if not believing what he had seen turned to the CAS, trying to remain calm. "What the hell just happened? Penny, did we just lose them? Were they shot down?"

The CAS stared at the screen for a second, her face full of concentration as if she was trying to will the radar contacts to reappear. She turned to look at Peter briefly, as if in understanding, before replying, her voice raised and tense, "CDS, I think, yes... I think they're gone. We've just lost them."

The ops room went silent, as everyone digested what they'd just witnessed. It was the CAS who quickly responded, shaking everyone from their shock. "Right, let's get Zulu Zero-Zero-One now designated as inbound hostile and let's start taking over control of our airspace. I want to talk to the controller at Boulmer." She was about to pick up the phone when another warning sounded from one of the operators sat in front of her, loud and excited. "Ma'am, we have an air-raid warning red alert from Blackdog control. Hostiles reported inbound from the northwest, range three-hundred miles!"

Hearing the raised voices now echoing across the ops room, the Defence Secretary came out hurriedly in a state of undress, his jacket and bow tie removed, and wearing only his shirt, trousers and socks.

"CDS, what the hell's going on, what have I missed?"

The ops room exploded into a frenzy of activity as people began to respond to the orders given to them. The CAS picked up the phone again to talk to the controller at Boulmer. The CDS had to raise his voice above the noise to be heard, as he began briefing the minister on the past five minutes.

"Good God!" the Minister exclaimed. "We've lost them both? Any chance this was accidental? Could they have hit each other whilst manoeuvring?" Overhearing the minister, Penny responded, still holding the phone in her hand, "Not a chance, sir, both planes were separated by half a mile and both went down at the same time, plus we suspect their communications were being jammed. I'm just trying to get through to the senior controller now." She listened to the phone before slamming down the receiver angrily. "The senior controller is vectoring the next QRA flight into the air, but there's a delay in launching them. When they're airborne where do you want them?"

The CDS looked to the Defence Secretary stating, "Sir, until the PM gets here, you're the senior cabinet minister onsite – what do you want us to do, what are your orders?"

The weight of responsibility plainly showed on his face as he looked around the room, his eyes wide, then watching the big screen as the inbound targets tracked into British airspace. He stepped closer to the CDS, whispering, "I'm a little bit out of my depth here CDS, I'd appreciate a little help for now." The General looked at him with eyes narrowed, seeing the indecision in the man. Nodding in understanding, he stepped away, proclaiming loudly, "The Defence Secretary has just given us authorisation for the defence of our airspace." The relief was plain to see on the Defence Secretary's face as Peter stepped closer to the pair, his voice lowered. "James, these new targets will be a smokescreen, a deception. The real threat is already flying over our shores. You need to look closer to home, forget these and concentrate on the aircraft already flying over Scotland." All three men stood there looking at each other as the CDS's voiced boomed out, "CAS, that new contact – what are they and where are they heading?"

She looked down, reading the information from the display. "We've got them as ten Tu-95 Bears, turboprop bombers, coming in at altitude three-two thousand. No attempt at stealth or jamming. Almost like they're on a parade flight. Course is two-one-zero. If they stay on present course, they'll be flying over Faslane Naval Base."

The CDS turned to the First Sea Lord. "Sir Tony, do we have anything in Faslane right now?"

The First Sea Lord looked at one of the screens before responding, his face puzzled, "Two Astute-class submarines in for repairs, the rest of our sub surface fleet are all out on operations."

The CDS nodded, as finally he made his decision. "CAS, I want the QRA launched against those new targets." He looked at Peter, his voice lowered, "I can't overlook the threat to those submarines. If we're wrong and Faslane is the target..."

Peter nodded in understanding, realising the responsibility that his friend carried. He quickly responded, whispering, "But James, don't forget about those other planes, we *need* to get something up to check on them."

The CDS looked over to Penny. "CAS, speak to Boulmer and Swanwick and inform them that UK airspace is now under military control. I want you to run with it for now with your team until the PM gets here. And CAS, let's get a handle on this, shall we?"

She nodded quickly as she passed her orders to the operators looking up at her.

"Right, I want whatever fighters we can get up in the air out of Lossiemouth, directed to the last-known location of those aircraft. Let's get it moving and quickly. Also, let's get Coningsby brought up to speed, get their QRA ready to deploy. I also want additional aircraft brought up to readiness. Get them armed, fuelled and ready to get off the ground."

The lift doors opened behind them and the young RAF Lance Corporal came back in, now carrying the suit and shoes for the Defence Secretary to quickly change into. The minister nodded a simple thanks as he disappeared with the suit into one of the offices to change. Less than a minute later he came out, looking more composed than before. The suit was a good fit, Peter noted, and no one would ever have known it was borrowed. The minister looked surer-footed, cutting a more composed and purposeful character to the man who had stood before in his socks, trousers and shirt-tails. He stood in the middle of the room watching on screen as two new tracks showed the two fighters from Lossiemouth racing away to intercept the new bandits.

An air of expectancy filled the room as the fighters closed ever nearer to the targets, knowing that RAF Typhoons, designed to dogfight were far superior to the Russian slow-moving bears. The Defence Secretary turned to the CAS and asked expectantly, "At what range will our fighters be able to identify these bombers?"

"They'll have radar range at two hundred and fifty miles and visual range at one hundred and fifty miles using their onboard systems, Minister," she replied, her eyes not leaving the display.

"And these bombers, these Bears, are they the best the Russians have?"

"No, sir, the Bear was a cold-war era aircraft, four-engine turboprops, low and slow we used to say. They do have far better and faster bombers. But in the past, they've always preferred to send the Bears over to test us, to fly near our airspace. We had an incursion of two aircraft only last week – same profile, same approach pattern."

"And have they ever come in like this before? So many and so aggressively?" he asked doubtfully, looking over to Peter as he spoke.

She shook her head, replying, "Never before like this, but then we've never had two of our fighters shot down over UK waters." Her tone was menacing. Clearly the CAS wanted payback. She knew that the chances of survival for both pilots from the earlier encounter were extremely low and that the probability was both pilots were dead. To have had her pilots led like animals to the slaughter had infuriated her. She looked over to Peter who was also staring at the screen. How did it take a civilian to tell her to open her eyes and see the danger? she thought. She needed to focus, to sharpen up and get back in the saddle. If this was going to be a shooting match then she needed to get her game face on – she needed Penny Moore, callsign 'Warhammer' to get back in the game and start thinking like a pilot, not a bloody desk jockey...

17

The Reckoning

Jackal-Five

In the lead Typhoon, callsign Jackal-Five, Flight Lieutenant Jackson was double-and-triple checking his weapon systems as he flew at Mach 2 at an altitude of forty-four thousand feet over the North Sea. He'd been expecting to be airborne five minutes earlier but the delays with his aircraft had kept him on the ground. Now, frustrated and annoyed he tried to concentrate on the task at hand. He'd watched as Jackals-One and Two had taken off, and the next two aircraft were towed into the Q-sheds ready to go, but he had never expected to be scrambled less than ten minutes after the first QRA fighters had launched. What had happened? he thought. Where were Ed and Ley? He'd tried to get more information as both his aircraft became airborne, but Blackdog Control had told them to concentrate on their own mission and that the threat level was now at status red, meaning they were authorised to shoot down any aircraft they deemed threatening without need for further permission. In all his years of flying he had never heard such a threat level over the UK and he wondered what had happened to his colleagues to warrant such a thing. Realising that those thoughts were best left on the ground, he quickly shook any doubts away and began to focus on the mission, his aircraft and his wingman.

He scanned his instruments, checking the displays for any signs of the aircraft heading towards them. He quickly worked out the mental arithmetic, and with the range, speed and flight time, he knew he should be seeing something on his screens in the next five minutes. He settled himself into the seat and began to mentally prepare himself for the possibility of air-to-air combat.

Eagle-Four

Eagle-Four was now flying over Glasgow and still heading south, the Colonel watching on as the second flight of RAF fighters scrambled north to intercept fresh air. He clapped his hands in delight as the new targets had appeared on his display, indicating the Chinese programmers had indeed delivered on their promise. He was tempted to introduce another target package, to cause another alert for the RAF to chase, but cautioned himself against it; he did not want the British to know that Swanwick was compromised yet. If they became suspicious of their own feeds, they could still yet unplug the whole system and that would leave them all blind.

"Air Captain, time till launch threshold?"

"Time to launch now ten minutes, Colonel."

Good, he thought, *very good*, "And progress on Eagles?"

"Eagle-One is now thirty minutes from target, currently flying over Manchester and heading south, Eagles-Two and Three currently flying over Edinburgh, time to target forty minutes, and Eagles-Five and Six are twenty miles north of us, ETA to their targets will be thirty minutes."

Satisfied with the report, he sat back to continue to watch the RAF fighters progress as they flew out to sea, chasing the ghosts on the screen. He flicked over to another channel to the command net allowing him to speak to the Operations Command Centre back in Moscow. They had another five hundred personnel back there, all helping to co-ordinate what was about to happen. Taking a breath and closing his eyes, he quickly thought through what to say before keying the Pressel. "Flash eye, this is Crowsnest, ten minutes to launch, I repeat, ten minutes to launch."

The voice that replied was cold and flat. "Understood, Crowsnest, ten minutes, out."

MV Leyberg

Two hundred miles off the north coast of Scotland, sailing in calm seas, the Freighter MV *Leyberg*, registered out of Hamburg, ploughed along at fifteen knots, her decks heavily loaded with shipping containers. Her destination had her logged as Liverpool sailing from Delhi, but she was already further south from the shipping lanes than she should have been. Her Captain had kept her speed slower than usual and to the watchful eye, a keen sailor may have noticed that her antennae array and mast were far larger than required for commercial shipping. For the past three weeks she had sailed unnoticed through the Indian Ocean, the Suez Canal and up through the Mediterranean before finally sailing around the east coast of England to get to her current destination. For the past three hours she had been sailing slowly in a large circular pattern, careful to avoid other shipping, ready for just this moment. Meanwhile sailing up the east coast of England, eighty miles offshore from Hull, her two sister ships, the MV *Trojan* and MV *Majestic* were doing the same thing, avoiding other shipping and prying eyes and sailing in a circular holding pattern, waiting patiently for orders.

The crews on all three ships, although made to look sloppy and merchantlike, were far from it, and were the best the Russian navy had to offer, as now all three ships' crews sprung into life at the orders of their Captains. The crews began to climb up the stacks of containers using hidden ladders built into the sides, sure-footed and confident, the years at sea being put to good use. With sledgehammers, they knocked the pins from the locks of the uppermost containers that had prevented the container doors from opening accidentally, watching as they fell away into the sea. The actions on each ship were mirrored, as once all the upper containers had the pins removed, one of the crew members leaned over the towering height to give a simple thumbs-up signal to the bridge. With the press of a button on the bridge, all forty containers on the top stack began to open slowly, the lids sliding upwards and outwards, resting at an angle of ninety degrees, revealing four launch tubes per container. Each tube contained a 3M54-1 Kaliber cruise missile, which meant that in less than two minutes each container ship had now been converted from a harmless freighter to a deadly missile platform, carrying one hundred and sixty cruise missiles. Between the three ships, that meant the UK had four hundred and-eighty cruise missiles targeting it, and all within one hundred miles of its coastline. As the containers finished opening, the crew members on the stacks began to quickly and expertly check the launch tubes and missiles for signs of damage or seawater ingress. More crewmen clambered up the ladders, carrying satchels with laptops and tools ready to begin the prefight checks before the missiles could be reported back as ready to fire.

Now it was just a case of waiting...

Jackal-Five

Meanwhile, onboard Jackal-Five, Jackson was checking his instruments, confident that his aircraft's systems should be picking up at least some kind of electronic signature from the enemy aircraft by now. He assessed that the Bears should be three hundred miles away to his north and that by now they should have seen something.

He checked he was on the chat-net before asking, "Six, this is Five, you got anything at all on your screens? I'm showing nothing but fresh air."

The voice that came back was distorted by the oxygen mask as he heard, "Negative Five, my screens show no contact, no contact. Over."

Without wasting any more time he flicked his radio back over to the guard net, to talk to Boulmer.

"Blackdog Control, this is Jackal-Five, can you confirm location of inbound bandits? Over."

The controller came back through, loud and clear, confident in what he was reporting.

"Roger, Jackal-Five, inbound bandits are two-seven-zero miles north of you, heading two-one-zero, and altitude three-one thousand. You should have them now on radar. Over."

"Negative, Blackdog, we have nothing on radar, nothing on EW, can you recheck the position of bandits? Over."

"Jackal-Five, we have checked and double-checked. Bandits are twelve o'clock of you, range now two-six-zero miles and closing. You *should* see them." The voice was insistent.

"Roger, Blackdog, I'll keep on course to intercept." Jackson tried to hide the frustration in his voice. Even if the enemy were jamming the planes, from his systems there would be evidence of the jamming, instead there was nothing. He rechecked his Praetorian system was online and running correctly. Within a few seconds the self-test confirmed everything was fine and all systems normal. All he could do now was close to within one hundred and fifty miles and confirm visually – perhaps there was a small chance the enemy had slipped away to a new course, undetected by the radar operators. With nothing else to do but wait, he kept scanning his instruments and remained alert.

Wonderland Operations Centre (WOC)

Back in the WOC, the progress of the fighters was being watched closely, with the radio messages from the controllers and pilots being fed to the overhead speakers for all to hear. As this was playing out, the CDS looked at his watch, worried, as he realised it was 19:20 hours, nearly twenty minutes since the Defence Secretary had called Platinum. By now they should at least be getting an update from the PM's security detail to say they were on their way. He turned to Major T-P and ushered him over.

"Find the Defence Secretary's close protection team and his assistant Sonya and confirm that the PM is inbound."

He watched as Major T-P walked quickly to the lift, its doors closing quietly behind him.

"CDS!" The voice from above on the gallery made him look up as Sir Charles stood looking down at him. In all the excitement, he'd forgotten that the CDI was still up there, organising with GCHQ the measures to defeat the ongoing cyberattack.

Sir Charles pointed to one of the big screens, remarking, "We need to put one of the news channels on, you're going to want to see this."

Seeing the urgency on Sir Charles's face, he nodded to one of the operators near him, "Put one of the news channels onto one of the other main screens, but keep the volume low please." A few key clicks later and the large screen came to life, showing a podium with President Iylanovitch speaking. Behind him the flag of the republic of Tumat hung from a wall. Sir Charles walked down the steps speaking as he went. "President Iylanovitch has called an immediate press conference. He's announcing his country's NATO membership now, before the US President does. In doing so he's undermining the US President and making a mockery of them."

Everyone except the busy RAF operators looked up, as the picture changed to a close-up camera shot of the Tumat President. Speaking in his own native Russian language, it was the female voice of the interpreter that sounded through the speakers in the room.

"To my fellow friends in NATO that have asked us for help, I say this – we are now finally in your club and able to help you. We all know NATO is not perfect, but perhaps with us onboard now we can help you to become better and more fit for purpose. Let us be the inspiration and the help you need to rid yourselves of the shackles of imperialism that your elitist leaders

have burdened you with. To my new friends who recently met me, I promise now that all the resources of Tumat, a full NATO member, will be yours to help you in the days and weeks to come. Now if you'll please excuse me, there is still much to do."

Ever the showman, he smiled and waved to the assembled press, and with questions being shouted from all sides in many languages, he turned and walked through the door behind him. The volume was muted as everyone from the Council looked at each other.

"That cheeky bastard!" All eyes turned to the Defence Secretary, surprised at his sudden outburst. Ignoring their stares, he added, "I've seen some shabby underhand tricks in politics, but that's a class A effort. Last year that man was on the world stage pleading poverty and begging us to let him join. Now he's in the door, he's confidently telling the world that he's a fully paid-up member of NATO and offering to help it clean itself up, and in doing so he has undermined the US and UK. And what was all that rubbish about the offer to help to end imperialism? Was that a jibe aimed at us?"

"I think he's just setting the scene for what's to come. Article Five will not protect us now, especially if this is made to look like an internal struggle," Peter said solemnly. "James, I really think that PM or no PM we *must* get the message out to the bases. We now know the threat; we know the intention. At least get our armed forces on alert, especially now we know someone is already shooting our planes down."

The CDS looked to the Defence Secretary, whose face was wracked with hesitancy. "Defence Secretary, this needs to be your decision. Only you can give me the power to begin."

Jeffery looked over at the large clock on the far wall showing it was 19:27. *Where the hell is the PM?* he thought. Every time they had practised these scenarios it was with all the Cabinet, assembled perfectly at Downing Street, biscuits and cups of tea in front of them. The CDS would be sat near to the PM briefing him on all the available options as the PM would sit there, composed and in control, measured and confident. The PM would think for a moment and come out with the correct answer to the problem. Statistics would be shown on the big screen, showing the estimated casualty rates and response times and the problem would be solved. Everyone in the Cabinet would smile and congratulate him on a job well done and then they would disperse and go back to their offices, confident in the leadership at the top. But where was the PM now? Off at a fucking party and it was him, Jeffery Dickinson that everyone now looked to. He was brought back from his thoughts as the CDS asked again, his voice louder this time. "Sir! You're the most senior Cabinet Minister here. Until the PM gets here, you're making the decisions. Should I order our forces to high readiness alert? The order *has* to come from a Cabinet member."

Looking around the room the Defence Secretary quickly countered, shaking his head. "No, not yet, CDS. Get me the Foreign Secretary on a video call in the conference room."

He walked off towards the room, shutting the door behind him, leaving the Defence Chiefs stood looking at each other in frustration and worry at his indecision. Behind them the lift doors opened and Major T-P entered the room followed by the Defence Secretary's protection detail and his aide Sonya. Seeing the look of concern on T-P's face, the CDS walked quickly to them.

"Well?" His tone was curt. "Where's the PM?"

Before Major T-P could answer, the close protection officer interjected. "Sir, we're trying on radio comms to raise them at Chequers but at the moment we can't get through." He looked to Major T-P as if to say something else then stopped. Picking up on this, the CDS shot back, irritated, "Well, what is it? Speak, man, I don't have the time to mess around. What's on your mind?"

"Sir, all the CPOs attending the event tonight at Chequers were under strict orders to switch off all personal comms at 7pm."

The CDS looked on, flabbergasted. "Why the hell would they do that?"

The CPO's face was strained as he replied, "When we'd rehearsed the security arrangements last week, we found out our radios would interfere with the PA system significantly, giving off large amounts of feedback over the speakers. The PM's Chief of Staff didn't want any interruptions on the night, so when the PM was due to give his speech at 19:30..."

"Everyone switched off their comms," the CDS finished for him, closing his eyes in disbelief.

"Yes, sir, I'm afraid that for the next twenty minutes at least, there's no way to contact him."

Peter, overhearing this, interjected, "But you've got phone lines, fibre optics, surely something that links us here to Chequers?"

The CDS shook his head sadly. "No, Peter, we don't. They were due to be installed next year..."

"So, we've no way at all of warning them?" Peter looked on in disbelief as the CDS looked back at him deep in thought, before suddenly turning back to the Major.

"T-P, get yourself a sidearm, some body armour and take the protection officer here with you. I want you both to commandeer the helicopter outside the house and get yourself to Chequers, fastest possible speed. Go straight to the PM, no excuses and both tell him to get his ass here now. If he won't come, then you have my permission to drag him kicking and screaming back here. Codeword Platinum has been called. We need a bloody decision and we need it now."

He looked back over to Penny shouting, "CAS! I want authorisation immediately for a flight from here to Chequers, no limits on speed or altitude. I don't care if they have to shut down Heathrow, the helicopter does not get stopped."

She responded with a thumbs up, as still holding the phone she continued speaking to RAF Boulmer, relaying the request.

The CDS looked around him. *Damn*, he thought, everything seemed to be coming at once, all within the last five minutes. He had no idea of knowing just how correct he was – and things were about to get even uglier...

Eagle-Four

Colonel Bresavik looked over at his air Captain, his foot tapping the floor nervously as he asked again for the tenth time, "Time now to launch window?"

"Sir, now five minutes."

At last, he thought, *now is the time*. He flicked his radio over to the command net, allowing him to speak to all the aircraft in his squadron. Now it was too late for the British to do anything. Even if they saw and knew what they were up against, it didn't matter. Their time had come.

"All aircraft, this is Crowsnest. Thunder in five minutes. Thunder in five minutes. Attack plan alpha, attack plan alpha. Prepare. Crowsnest out."

He turned to the Captain again. "Get that message out to Kestrel-Six via their attack computer."

Kestrel-Six

On Kestrel-Six, flying high above the Scottish Highlands, Nikolai watched as the message flashed across his displays as his computer received the instructions. He checked and rechecked the message before reporting, "Mikhail, we have attack orders, attack plan alpha, Thunder begins in five minutes."

Finally, thought Mikhail. Already the excitement from the past twenty minutes had worn away as he refocused his thoughts on the mission. At last, they were about to strike.

From the back seat, Nikolai began to run through the missile's pre-flight tests, checking its internal navigation system was running and that it was talking to the computer. Satisfied with the readings from his display he reported, "Okay Mikhail, missile is online and ready to receive the target."

Mikhail checked over his notes, looking through the target list that he had written before take-off. Scrolling down to the page marked *Alpha*, he carefully inputted the co-ordinates into the Baget computer, checking twice the numbers displayed before hitting the accept button. The computer relayed back that the co-ordinates had been accepted.

"Nikolai, the missile is ready to fire, give me the flight profile for missile release."

Looking at his displays, Nikolai read back, "Profile for missile release, fuel remaining, fifteen thousand pounds... we need to be at Mach 2.5 and an altitude of forty-thousand feet. On a heading of one-six-zero degrees."

"Nikolai, start the count; I'll wait until we are thirty seconds to launch then accelerate to the profile. What does our attack radar show? Anything near us?"

After a quick glance at his screens Nikolai replied, the excitement building in his voice, "Radar and EW are clear, all aircraft in the vicinity are friendly. Airspace is clear and we are ready to fire." Mikhail flexed his hands in his flight gloves and his toes and neck, like a boxer limbering up before a fight as he prepared for what was about to unfold. "Nikolai, give me the countdown to the thirty second mark!"

Wonderland Operations Centre (WOC)

Back in the conference room, the Defence Secretary cut a lonely figure as he looked at the black screen in front of him. The thought of what could be happening outside the room was too much to contemplate. He was startled as the screen flickered to life and the Foreign Secretary came on, her face set and firm.

"Jeffery? Do you have the PM with you yet?"

"Not yet, we've still got him on his way to us. I think he should be here sometime soon – I hope so, because things are starting to spin out of control here. I could really do with his input."

"Okay, calm down, but first, what's this intelligence you were speaking of earlier; you mentioned a report? What are the Defence Chiefs telling you?"

"They're convinced that we're under some sort of attack, some plan that the Russians are using to set off an invasion under the pretence of sending in assistance from Tumat. Something's amiss because we've already lost two of the QRA fighters investigating a rogue aircraft and we're currently monitoring an incursion of Russian aircraft to our northeast airspace over Scotland. We've got fighters out looking in that area but they're not reporting seeing anything. I'm being told two different things from two different sets of people and I don't know what to do."

"Two sets of people?"

"Yes, the CDS has brought in a retired Brigadier, someone he used to work with. He seems to know all about the report, I think he calls it Fools Gambit or something, it's based on a chess move. Anyway, he seems to be under the impression that the Russians have infiltrated our radar network at Swanwick and what we are seeing on our screens is incorrect. And he seems to be right. He warned us of the threat to the QRA fighters and then—"

"Is this man a member of the Defence Council?" she quickly interrupted.

"No, but—"

"Then he has no right to be there, retired Brigadier or not!" she said, leaning towards the camera, adding, "You should discount what he has to say and listen to your bloody Defence Council. Has it occurred to you that he could be playing you and that he could be the reason for what's going on? Hang on... Is he there with you in the WOC?"

"Yes, he's in the ops room," he stammered.

She shook her head slowly, her face red with anger.

"Oh Jeffery, Jeffery, Jeffery, you always were a bloody fool! The PM is on his way to your location – a *secure* location – and you've opened the doors to a stranger to be in there with him. Get rid of him immediately *before* the PM gets there. In fact, if he now knows of Wonderland's location, you'd best detain him." Her tone was furious.

Jeffery stared at her, his eyes narrowing as he felt his old angry feelings begin to rise. He thought back to all the little digs and comments that she had made in the past about him, both off and on the media stage. It had been no secret that they disliked one another. Both had been contenders for the leadership race for party leader along with the new PM, but at the last second a story had emerged, one totally fabricated, about Jeffery being investigated over his tax affairs. The story had no truth to it, but the damage was done. Nobody liked a politician who tried to cheat the tax man, and he had been forced to pull out of the leadership race with his reputation tarnished. He'd found out later via the back channels in parliament that the story had come out of Yvette's office. Whether she knew beforehand or not, he wasn't sure, but he'd been told by the PM to put it down to another dirty chapter of politics. Besides, the PM had said that the job of Defence Secretary had needed to be filled and he was the perfect candidate; loyal, honest and now with a reputation to save. The Cabinet meetings since had always been frosty but professional, but he'd noted that she gladly took any opportunity she'd had to twist the knife. There was no love lost between them and he instantly regretted calling her to ask for her opinion now.

Annoyed with her condescending and bullying tone he quickly countered, "Hang on, Yvette! No, I'm sorry but I disagree, this isn't just some back-alley hawker in off the street, he's highly recommended from the CDS and most of the Defence Chiefs have met him before or know of him. You ask me to trust their judgement and I do – so if they trust him then so do I. And if I'm being honest, he's been correct about the whole bloody thing so far, so perhaps in talking to me you've helped me to galvanise what course of action to take. Thank you, Yvette, as always, your input is *most welcome*."

He couldn't hide the scorn in his voice as he said that last part.

She smiled thinly, leaning confidently back in her chair, her voice full of contempt.

"Jeffery, you're so innocent, so naïve. Why you ever wanted a career in politics, I'll never know. But one thing I do know is that you're *out*, you were never *in*. That's why the PM kept you out of the loop on Tumat. You were too by the book, always wanting to be beyond reproach and better than the rest of us. Well, when you swim in muddy waters it doesn't matter how clean you are to begin with, the mud always sticks."

"What do you mean?"

She laughed humourlessly and she replied, "Tumat is in NATO, did you know about that? I did. The PM saw fit to tell me weeks ago. He didn't tell you, though, did he? That's because you're to be our fall guy when the cuts come next week, our pawn to be sacrificed. You're the one who told the country we would *increase* our defence spending. I'm sorry to tell you this, Jeffery, but with Tumat now in NATO and the threat to our borders now decreasing, we've been planning on cutting the defence budget further. The old bogeymen of the past are long gone. People want free Wi-Fi and better healthcare now, not more guns and bloody bullets. If I were you, I'd stop worrying about this nonsense you're being fed about phoney attacks and worry about writing your resignation speech. Oh, and thank you for helping *me* to get rid of you – by calling Platinum and embarrassing the PM you've galvanised *his* resolve to get rid of you in any case."

Shaking his head at what he'd just heard and trying to keep his temper in check, he took a deep breath before replying, "Yvette, am I missing something or did you not just hear what I told you earlier? We've just reported the loss of two of our aircraft and the possibility of an incoming air raid and all you can do is sit there and throw insults at me and tell me your plans to *cut* the defence budget."

"Jeffery, I've already been informed by my staff that the two aircraft reported as missing have now reported back into the controllers. They've had radio issues and the aircraft that was inbound for the UK is being escorted in with them. This 'incursion' as you call it from the northeast was an RAF training exercise to see how the QRA fighters would react when scrambled to two different threats at the same time. The threat, as you put it, is no longer there. Being the Defence Minister, I'm surprised I'm having to inform you of these things. You're supposed to be monitoring the defence of the country. Maybe things are not spinning out of control like you imagine, perhaps you're the one spinning out of control. Now if you don't mind, I've got your resignation speech to help write. I should have a draft over to you by the morning. Enjoy your evening."

The line was cut abruptly and the screen went black. Jeffery sat motionless, looking at the screen, his temper rising until he could stand it no longer. "BITCH!" he shouted, releasing some of the tension. "FUCKING FUCK!!!!" He sat there for a few moments, his breathing hard as anger coursed through him. To hear how she had described him, how all along this had been a ploy, a political move to chastise him further and bury his political career, had pushed him to the edge. He sat there watching, his anger simmering below the surface, as outside the ops room continued working, oblivious to his rant, the conference room was soundproofed after all. As his breathing calmed down and he composed himself, a thought flashed into his mind. *The two RAF fighters were not shot down? And this was all an exercise? How would she know that?* He quickly stood up and raced out of the door, startling the people gathered around the command console. His face was flushed and his tone angry.

"CDS, I've just spoken to the Foreign Secretary who has told me that the two fighters that disappeared off our screens earlier have now contacted control and are escorting in the rogue plane. And that this incursion off to the northeast is an RAF exercise to test the scramble times of the secondary QRA aircraft?"

Everyone within earshot looked back at him confused, as he quickly added with his voice raised, "Well? Is this true or not? Am I being led down the garden path here by you all? I need to know!"

It was the CAS who quickly replied, "Sir, those planes have been lost, they're no longer flying, and we do not have any eyes on the rogue plane, no one is escorting it in. And as for the incoming raid from the northeast, I can tell you now that there are *no* RAF exercises in play to simulate this. And if there were, they'd be cancelled immediately after the loss of the two fighters. I'm sorry, but the Foreign Secretary is wrong. The threats are still active and incoming. This is a real-world threat."

"And how do you know for sure the fighters were shot down? Could they be simply off radar due to a technical issue? The same one that's affected their radios perhaps?"

She shook her head as she replied confidently, "Not a chance, sir. All our fighters have a distress beacon, it activates automatically if the plane is shot down or crashes and is used to help us to locate the aircraft if we want to recover any sensitive data or equipment from the crash site. Five minutes ago, we began to pick up Jackal-Two's beacon. Its active over the sea twenty miles off the coast. If that plane were still airborne, we would *not* be receiving the data."

Seeing the fury and disbelieving look on the Minister's face, the CDS stepped closer to whisper into his ear. "Sir, I don't know what was said in that room, but you need to know that we work for you, we don't have any agendas or political ambitions. Everyone on our team, *your* team has one goal: the defence of the country. It's you today and could be someone else tomorrow, but our loyalties lie to the current serving Defence Secretary, which right now is *you*, to help *you* make the right decisions for the PM. Do you understand?"

Calming down, his anger abating, the Defence Secretary nodded, suddenly taken aback by how he'd just conducted himself. Yvette had clearly got under his skin again.

Clearing his throat he stammered, "My apologies, CDS, I... I... Gosh, I don't know what to say."

"Then say nothing. But *do* something."

He nodded his head as the CDS enquired, "Now, who has given the Foreign Secretary this information? Who's feeding her the wrong information? That's something that we need to know."

"I don't know. She wouldn't say, but one thing's for sure – she's convinced all this is fabricated and has told me to remove Mr Rawlinson from the room." He folded his arms as he looked Peter up and down. "For now, though, he stays. I'm happy with what I've seen. And if I'm being honest, he's been spot on with calling this from the start."

The Defence Secretary turned to the big screen. "CAS, any updates from the fighters intercepting those incoming aircraft?"

"No, sir, they're still fifty miles away but are reporting there's nothing on the radar or on their systems. They're convinced they're not there."

The Defence Secretary nodded confidently as he replied more assuredly, "So am I. Recall them immediately, see if they have enough fuel left to intercept Zulu Zero-Zero-One. Make them fully aware that Jackals-One and Two are gone. I want them to have eyes wide open going forward."

"But sir, they're only five minutes away from visually confirming, wouldn't you want to wait?"

The Minister thought about what the CDS had just said and what the Foreign Secretary had said to him, and about how he'd been waiting for the PM to arrive to make the decisions – the person whom he thought would be there to do it better than he could. But hearing how the PM had really felt about him and how he was viewed as nothing more than a pawn, had angered him. He felt betrayed, and for the first time in a long time he decided to take charge again. *Fuck it*, he thought, if he was going to go down, he would go down swinging. He looked at the CAS and said confidently, "No, we've wasted enough time playing their game, now we take the initiative. Get them recalled now." Turning to the CDS he added, "I'm issuing an immediate alert to all

UK forces. I want everyone on high readiness alert, let's get everything and everyone awake, alert and ready to go please, CDS."

Kestrel-Six

"Thirty-second warning!" Nikolai said, trying to keep himself calm, even though the adrenaline was beginning to flow again, the tension and excitement rising in the cockpit.

"Right, here we go!" Mikhail responded, as he pushed the throttles forward, feeling his body being pressed back into the seat as the engines roared to life and the plane began accelerating.

He kept a close eye on his speed, watching it climb and then, as he approached Mach 0.9, he pulled gently back on the controls to begin the quick climb up to launch altitude, constantly checking both the readouts on his Heads-Up Display and the skies around him. All the while, the voice of his weapons officer was counting down the time to launch.

"Twenty seconds... Fifteen seconds... Ten seconds..."

He levelled off at forty thousand feet, checked the airspeed remained at Mach 2.5 and his heading was steady on one-six-zero degrees. He noticed a slight crosswind at this altitude that was causing him to slightly deviate off course, compensating slightly with a gentle press of the rudder, amazed that even whilst flying at Mach 2.5 the wind could have such an effect. Happy with how the aircraft was now set up, he reached forward to the weapons release switch, pulling up on the safety guard, reporting, "Safeties are off, ready to release."

"Five... Four... Three... Two... One... Launch!"

Mikhail pressed the trigger on the joystick, instantly feeling the aircraft shudder and become more responsive on the controls at the difference in weight, as the heavy missile fell away from the centre pylon.

"Weapon is away!" he shouted as he gently eased the aircraft over to the right, to clear it further from the rocket ignition of the missile. After a second of freefall, the rocket's motor fired, and it began to accelerate away, leaving the MiG-31 in its wake. Mikhail had been prepared for the flash of light and closed both eyes as the rocket tail flashed in front of them before it disappeared. The rocket began to scream earthwards and within less than five seconds was up to its hypersonic speed of Mach 12. At this speed it was covering 2.5 miles per second which meant the distance to target of three hundred and eighty miles would be covered in less than one hundred and fifty two seconds.

Across the whole of the UK's northern airspace, the pilots of the other eleven MiG-31's, also carrying Kinzhal missiles, had accelerated to attack speed and altitude, and were patiently waiting to hear the radio orders to release their missiles.

Onboard Eagle-Four, as Kestrel-Six fired its missile, the Colonel transmitted on both his own air net and the command net the words everyone had waited so eagerly to hear.

"All callsigns, this is Crowsnest. Thunder... Thunder... Thunder..."

18

Thunder

Chequers: PM's Country Residence

Duncan needed another drink. Smiling courteously at those he passed, he walked across the grand function room to the waiter by the door, as he motioned for another refill in his near-empty glass. He looked over to one of the PM's CPOs stood at the far end of the room and shook his head in frustration – the female operative stood out like a sore thumb, ruining the ambience of the room. *Why couldn't they have waited outside?* he thought angrily. The only threat to the PM tonight would be choking on an hors d'oeuvre and he deemed the security over the top for the night. If the PM couldn't be safe in his own country residence, then where would he be safe?

At least he had managed to get them to switch off their bloody radios for thirty minutes. More than long enough for the PM to be able to deliver his speech without any of the screeching feedback they had experienced last week. He listened in as the PM began to tell the same joke he had earlier rehearsed with Duncan, checking that its sensitivity wouldn't be too offensive for the room. As the PM's Chief of Staff and senior aide, it was his job to scrutinise every single word that came out of the PM's mouth. Every speech written was to be said as read, making no attempt to be cavalier or veering off topic, not at least while he was the Chief of Staff. He'd seen in the past the gaffes and bloopers that former PMs had made and had promised this PM that so long as he did what he advised, he would remain at the top of the tree. As the PM now came to the joke's punchline, he watched the reactions of those in the room, pleased to see almost all were smiling and clapping. He frowned when he noticed the Education Secretary and Chancellor were not clapping and laughing like everyone else. Instead, they were stood side by side, deep in conversation, looking for all intents and purposes like a deliberate snub to the PM. He made a mental note to speak to their aides in the morning, to pass onto both MPs his displeasure at what he had seen.

He took a sip of his drink as he thought about the press conference that would follow tomorrow, to announce the details of Tumat's NATO membership. The timing was critical. He'd spent hours liaising closely with the American President's aide and Chief of Staff, to ensure that both men would go on their own national news channels at the same time, despite the eight-hour time difference. He smiled at that stroke of genius. In the past, the US had always insisted that they were to be the ones to tell the world of any change to the new order, but given that the Americans had needed the UK's drilling rights to explore Tumat, he had negotiated – no, strong-armed them – into allowing the PM and President to tell the world at the same time. He smiled as he remembered the look on the PM's face as he had told him of the prestige – to be stood shoulder to shoulder with one of the most powerful men in the world order, announcing another brick in the wall of the former Soviet Empire was being removed. Speaking of things to be removed, he suddenly wondered, where was the Defence Secretary?

He walked slowly around the room, careful not to arouse suspicion while the PM's speech was ongoing. A veteran amongst fundraisers, he found that a well-placed smile could be very disarming to people as he mingled with the guests. His gaze lingered over the Housing Minister, Fiona Precik, who wore a long, flowing, blue ballgown. She would always be seen with Jeffery, so perhaps she knew where he was. She was stood next to one of the party donors, a media mogul who was known for changing his allegiances to parties quicker than changing his wives, depending, of course, on what he could get from them. Duncan smiled at them both, seeing Fiona quickly whisper into the ear of the man, who laughed before looking away from him. Duncan wasn't stupid, he knew a comment had been aimed at him. He kept up appearances as he continued smiling, his tone sarcastic. "Fiona, how lovely to see you here, may I have a quick word?" She glanced across to the donor, as Duncan gracefully took her arm and led her out of earshot, not wishing to create a scene as the PM was mid-flow on the podium, his voice carrying far and loud over the PA system.

He lowered his head closer, so as not to shout, the smell of her perfume arousing him as he did so. *Classy*, he thought, *very classy*.

"Where is Jeffery?"

A confused look crossed her face as she glanced around the room. "He's not here? He should be, he told me he was going to get here for 6pm."

He continued to stare at her, his voice menacing. "Well, he's not. Kindly find out where he is and why he thinks a three-line whip doesn't apply to him."

She smiled, her eyes fierce as she countered, "Duncan, I'm not one of your doe-eyed flunkies who you can just boss around and take to bed. I'm a member of the Cabinet, a *senior* member of Cabinet, remember, the one you work for. Don't think that just because you've got the ear of the PM that it gives you the right to give me orders. Now why don't you just scurry away and do your own leg work for a change."

Gracefully and with poise, she unhooked her arm from his and walked back over to stand by the side of the media mogul, leaving Duncan standing alone, his face a mask of a smile, hiding the rage he felt.

He looked around the room for one of the more junior MPs, someone to vent at. He was interrupted in his hunt as he heard a distant rumble, a noise like thunder. Some of the other guests heard it, too, and looked at each other in surprise as Duncan gazed out of the window, confused at the darkening evening sky, because there was not a cloud in sight.

Wonderland Operations Centre (WOC)

Back at the ops centre, Penny was seeing the events unfolding on the main screen at the same time as the Blackdog controller in RAF Boulmer. Even though both were over a hundred miles apart, the effect was the same and both wore the same look of shock as they watched the radar contacts of some of the incoming commercial traffic now accelerate and climb to altitudes and speeds that identified them as fighters.

"James!" was all the CAS had time to shout, forgetting the CDS's rank, as in disbelief they heard the electronics warfare officers begin reporting loudly. "Multiple EW signatures, we've got designated targets on screen now."

Quickly the yellow squares on the screen denoting commercial airliners were replaced with red triangles, denoting hostile fighters, now easier to identify amongst all the other aircraft.

"Christ, they're over Scotland already! How many do we have on radar?" The urgency in her voice was hard to conceal.

It was the senior EWO who shouted out in alarm.

"Ma'am, we're counting twenty-four bandits... SHIT! MULTIPLE MISSILE LAUNCHES! VAMPIRE! VAMPIRE! VAMPIRE!"

Everyone looked to the screen as they watched the smaller, faster tracks split away from the fighters and head on their own separate headings as the voice of the EWO continued to report.

"Missiles are tracking away, speeds approaching Mach 12, I make them out to be Killjoys... Hypersonic."

Peter, recognising the codeword *Killjoy*, knew this meant the missiles were Kinzhals, one of Russia's most feared super weapons. Nothing had yet been developed to counter their threat and given the speed they were now flying at and their locations, nothing would catch them.

The CDS turned to the nearest operator. "Quickly, get me the details for Killjoy on the screen." The third screen flashed to life as a picture of the missile appeared for all to see. The CDS had a look of horror as the young operator read aloud the details. "Kinzhal missile, range of three hundred miles, warhead either five hundred kilogrammes or nuclear."

The CDS turned to the CAS, his face unbelieving, but his voice full of hope. "Penny? What can we do? How do we stop them?"

She looked back at him, her face still registering surprise as she replied, shocked, "We can't stop them. They're hypersonic already."

The Defence Secretary stood behind the operator. "Any idea on targets?"

"Not yet, sir, We're tracking fourteen missiles all in flight, four are tracking south and the rest are heading southeast."

Out of desperation, the Defence Secretary looked over to Peter. "You're the man with all the answers, well, come on! Where are they going?"

Peter stared at the track of the missiles. Quickly thinking, he replied, "They won't be nuclear, they don't need to be, it's not part of the plan. Besides, the speed they're travelling at now, when they hit, even if carrying five-hundred kilos of explosives, they'll be ten times as powerful with the kinetic energy alone. If I were a betting man, Minister, I'd say Downing Street and Chequers. They're going for the government; they're going after the PM."

"If those were the targets, how long till impact?" the CDS shot back to the EWO.

"Er, if those are the targets, sir, then time to impact is... twenty seconds."

"God help us." muttered the Defence Secretary.

***

The lead Khinzal fired by Kestrel-Six was already five miles ahead of the other missiles, tracking at an altitude of ten thousand feet. It had kept on its original flight path after launch and was now relying on the latest data and imagery stored in its memory to scan the terrain ahead, plotting its course on its own internal guidance computer. It recognised the roads and towns it passed over, thanks to a highly sophisticated optical system in its nose. Using Oxford as a marker, it adjusted course slightly to head due east, recognising Wheatley, Thame and Longwick in a matter of milliseconds. Finally seeing its target set back at the end of a long horseshoe-shaped drive, it cross-checked the image against its own image stored onboard its targeting computer and confirmed the target before beginning its attack run. The missile began to dive down from ten-thousand feet, allowing gravity to help it accelerate further to maximise the impact. Then, when one mile out, it fired its rocket booster, sacrificing fuel for speed as it slammed into the roof of the building at over Mach 12.5.

Chequers: PM's Country Residence

At the party, Duncan was still looking out of the window for the thunder he had heard when the missile hit. His brain had no time to register shock or surprise as the roof collapsed onto the party. Tonnes of rubble came crashing down, crushing everything and destroying anything in its wake as the missile continued, finally burying itself in the basement of the grand estate building. Then, as the explosive warhead detonated, it blew apart the building's walls and the foundations, causing the floors to cave in. But the power of the explosion was merely the *amuse-bouche*, served before the main course as the kinetic energy of the missile, equivalent to ten tonnes of explosives, sent out a shockwave that blew away the outer walls, reducing the estate house to a pile of red-bricked rubble and dust in an instant.

Outside the house, on the driveway, thirty cars were parked, all patiently waiting for the guests to leave. Some had drivers inside, reading a book or watching a movie, oblivious to the danger they were in. Some had the briefest of seconds to look up as the shockwave continued outwards from the house, tossing the cars like children's toys and scattering them over the outer walls and into the fields around the estate. Some exploded as their fuel tanks were punctured, setting off fires in the fields, whilst others sat, now mangled wrecks, twisted beyond all recognition and covered in the red dust that now drifted down from the sky. Across the estate, the smoke and dust drifted on the breeze as the only sound to be heard was that of the car alarms going off. And then one by one, the few who survived, began to scream...

Three of the missiles heading south were now flying over what locals called the Black Country, the forward optics scanning continuously. They were originally designed to be the reserve missiles, in case any of the other planes had been shot down or lost, but now, with a full complement ready to be fired, they had been given another target, one that the Russians no longer had a use for. The missiles were separated by a three-second flight time difference, which at the speeds they were flying meant that every missile was ten miles apart. The first missile was approaching Swindon. Recognising the topographical features of the town, it corrected its heading, beginning a slow turn to the right to line up on its target. It flew over Stonehenge in a blur, the people below looking up in wonder as the thunderous noise flashed overhead. Even at ten thousand feet, its rocket motor caused people below to instinctively duck their heads in shock. It now began to approach Romsey and Nursling, recognising the motorway and with another small course correction it began to follow the motorway through Southampton, past the airport and then finally spotting its target, sat on the northern edge of the M27. It quickly checked the targeting data, confirming the target and then began its deadly descent, ready to attack.

National Air Traffic Services, Swanick

Inside the large three-storey complex of the NATS headquarters building, over two hundred air-traffic controllers sat, directing the aircraft on their displays to land at the nearest airports. Without understanding why or how serious the situation had become, they had been ordered to clear the skies above the UK and to cancel all flight plans and begin landing aircraft safely where they were. Already, Bristol airport, Birmingham and Manchester were reporting they were full and smaller regional airports like Cardiff and Luton were being asked to accommodate some of the larger, heavier aircraft they would not usually see. With everyone watching the monitors, no one had time to register the flash as the missile smashed through the roof of the building and impacted into the ground, the force throwing people and equipment up and out through the roof. The shockwave reverberated out, crushing people and destroying the computer stations, as the five hundred kilo warhead exploded, detonating the building's backup generator tanks and creating a fireball that covered most of the room in burning diesel fuel. The windows exploded, covering those in the car park outside with broken glass, and every car parked there was dented and smashed, covered in rubble, all windows cracked and broken and alarms and lights flashing.

A second missile flew down to add its own deadly kinetic energy, slamming into the northern end of the building, exploding in the cathedral, where the sensitive electronics and vast databanks of computers had been stored. The destructive forces blew out large sections of the steel beams that held the building together as part of the roof caved in on itself, releasing a vast cloud of steam vapours as the building's complex heating system came apart. Burning fuel poured out of the obliterated walls and into the car park like lava, igniting some of the cars. Those that were smashed and trapped beneath the rubble, still alive, screamed as the fiery mass reached them, setting clothing and hair alight.

The third missile began its attack and tracked into the fiery hell. But the missile struggled to identify the target as it was now covered in a hot steam cloud and thick black smoke from the fires, confusing the onboard sensors. The missile's flight computer thought that the fault was with its own targeting software and so it rebooted itself. But in doing so, the missile now lost its positioning data and the ability to understand where it was. Travelling towards the ground and losing its bearings, the missile attempted to pull up out of the dive in order to be able to reacquire its position and reattack, but its speed was too fast, and the controls too slow to respond, and instead the missile slammed into the soft banks of Fareham Lake, the mud helping to absorb the massive energy, muting the shockwave. As it buried itself deep, the waters and mud sloshed back with a gurgle to cover its position. However, the other two missiles had done more than enough damage and now pilots all over the country were facing the growing fear and realisation that for once, there was no longer anyone in ATC responding to them. For once, they truly were on their own.

Downing Street, London

Wang Foo swore as he tried for the third time to get a picture of the famous shiny black door. He'd seen it on television so many times and finally as a member of the South Korean press delegation, he'd been allowed into the press area of Downing Street. They had been told to set up the night before, ready for the Prime Minister's announcement early the next morning, but every time he tried to focus the camera and check the lighting angles, another visitor would arrive and the door would open. Outside the door, uncaring, sat the newest and most loveable of Downing Street's visitors. With the official title of 'Chief Mouser', Bruce the cat was there, meowing at the visitors, warranting a quick stroke as they walked past. He'd only recently been rehomed there, replacing Larry, who had died last year. He didn't care about what was going on in the world and Wang smiled as he saw the cat ceremoniously wash his face for the fourth time that evening.

Seeing the door close again, he quickly put his eye to the camera viewfinder. *Finally*, he thought, *now I'll get that shot if it kills me.* He focused on the door, the silver number ten reflecting back at him, as he began to unknowingly record the last few seconds of his life. He watched through the camera as Bruce looked up to the sky, startled, and ran as fast as he could down the road. Wang took his eye away from the lens, confused as he watched the cat disappear. *What spooked him?* he wondered, as a noise like thunder came from above.

Ten of the Kinzhal missiles were now screaming towards London, all were travelling at Mach 12 but were inbound from different flight paths and altitudes. The operational planners had prepared for this, so as to prevent the risk of some of the missiles colliding with each other during the attack phase. Now they were all safely separated and flying on their own preprogrammed flight paths, scanning the terrain and mapping it against their own computers. The first three missiles were all programmed to strike one target, whilst the other seven were destined to strike the larger target, the one that would really hurt the British the most.

The first of the three missiles arrived, flying over the capital, using the famous London landmarks to plot its position and target. Using the Thames as a guide, its powerful camera and sensor identified Buckingham Palace, then moving off to the east it followed St James's Park, until it eventually identified its target. Double-checking the targets images against its own, it then began to dive down from ten thousand feet, mirroring the same attack pattern as the missile that had hit Chequers, as it slammed through the roofs of the building complex of 10 Downing Street, punching through to the basement level of the house before exploding.

Outside, Wang had just enough time to register the explosion as the door, the one he had waited so patiently to film, now came blasting off its hinges, propelled by explosive forces too large to comprehend. As if by a sadistic twist of fate, the armoured door hit Wang in the face, killing him instantly and pulverising his body as the façade of the house now blasted outwards. The shockwave hit the people outside, picking them up and propelling them through the building opposite at speeds of over two thousand miles an hour, instantly shredding flesh and bone as their bodies tore through the steel and concrete and glass. The shockwave continued through the building, following the paths of the bodies as every wall and window was blown outwards, sending desks, office furniture and workers into the streets below. Vehicles in the streets were blown over and hundreds were killed and injured as debris and rubble tore through between the buildings.

The missile's warhead detonated in the cellar, igniting the broken gas lines, adding to the destruction as the immense shockwave was followed a second later by a fireball, igniting anything in its path. The structure of the building, already compromised by the shockwave, finally succumbed to the fireball and with a tremendous crash, the roof and walls slid down into the street. A cloud of dust covered everything in the area and fires burned out of control in the rubble as the masses of paperwork that the offices held now began to catch alight and blow along the famous street into the area of Whitehall.

Within seconds of the attack the police and security teams, trying to overcome their shock, were attempting to take charge, to check for casualties and for further danger. Usually, the police would be easily identifiable by the yellow hi-vis vests that they wore, but now all were covered in the same thick grey dust, making identification as to who was in charge difficult, as people began to shout and scream for help. Just as they were starting to take stock, everyone looked up – the same threatening noise of thunder – this time people knew what to expect, and forgetting any thoughts of heroism everyone ran for their lives.

The second missile came in using the same flight profile as the first, identifying 10 Downing Street, but this time the target was the Cabinet Offices, striking the northern end of the building with the same destructive results. The building was already weakened from the first impact, and as the second missile hit, the northern end of the building collapsed in on itself, spewing rubble into the streets of Whitehall as the blast wave flattened everything in its path. The memorials in Whitehall, heavy bronze and marble statues, were picked up and flung into the buildings as if made of paper. The busy street was packed with tourists and pedestrians who were cleared like wheat in the wind, as the blast wave smashed into them. It tossed people from their feet and into the air, their bodies smashed against the buildings, leaving only red smears on the broken concrete, as trees were felled, and the blast wave tore through the capital.

The third missile was closely following behind and within two seconds was plummeting into the Cabinet Office, hitting the southern side of the building and burying deep within its lower levels. The walls of the building were already compromised, the supporting walls gone, as the whole building now fell into the street with a roar and a crash. Plumes of smoke rose above the maelstrom, as Londoners – those that survived – looked on in bewilderment and terror. For the first time since the Blitz, London was again under attack from the air.

Those still working at the Houses of Parliament had heard the explosions and felt the tremor of the shockwaves, as they looked out of the windows across to the direction of 10 Downing Street. They watched in grim fascination as the thick black and grey smoke began to rise above the skyline of London and they could hear sirens and screams as people began to realise the severity of the attack. From instinct some took out their phones and tried to call their loved ones or to check the latest news to try to make sense of it, all forgetting that for the past seven hours nothing had worked; there was no mobile signal and no functioning internet. At this time of evening, most of the workers in the Parliament building were cleaners or cooks, getting the vast building ready for the following day's activities. In the bar and canteen areas, a few more junior ministers sat, chatting about the day and what latest news topics took their fancy. In the upper offices some of the Cabinet Ministers' junior staff worked, keeping files organised or replying to the non-urgent emails that each MP would receive daily. Since the internet was not working, though, and all the Cabinet members were away at the Chequers fundraiser, those left behind had taken the time to socialise, to go through into the other offices, chatting to the other juniors and to hopefully get the latest gossip or rumour to help further their own ambitions.

Within seconds of hearing the explosions and feeling the tremors of the shock-waves passing through the building, the tannoy system chirped to life, stopping people in their tracks as it robotically announced, "*Attention. Please calmly evacuate the building by the nearest exit. Attention. Please calmly evacuate the building by the nearest exit.*" The warning was on a loop and continued to repeat itself. With a sense of purpose, people stopped what they were doing and began to pick up coats and belongings and make their way out of one of the many security gates. The building was large, and unfortunately for most, the order to evacuate was too late; far too late.

The remaining seven missiles en route to London all had one target to hit. The Russian High Command had deemed that seven were necessary as the building they were to strike was large and had recently undergone window renovations, making them armoured and bulletproof. Plus, the British needed to see it burn, to watch their beloved capital fall apart before their eyes, so it was for this reason that the Russian President had personally demanded they take it out.

It was time for the Houses of Parliament, Big Ben and the House of Lords to fall.

With cold precision, the first missile slammed into the centre of the parliament buildings, scything straight through the Westminster tower, causing it to slowly crash over into itself. The warhead failed to detonate, but the shockwave blasted outwards, crushing the walls and sending shrapnel hurtling through to the House of Lord's chamber.

The second missile had approached at the wrong altitude with its glide path shallower than the first missile. Approaching the target at speed, its optics failed to see the tourist attraction of the London Eye as its booster motor fired. The missile body impacted with the steel structure of the wheel, with enough force to crumple the supports of the structure, causing damage that the designers of the attraction had never envisaged. People could only watch in horror from the riverbanks, as slowly the huge colossus tipped over into the murky brown waters of the Thames, metal screeching and tearing. The faces of the people in the glass-and-steel gondolas stared in abject horror as they plunged towards the water, screaming. Some of the people in the lower gondolas had the least height to fall and suffered less injuries, so were able to smash open the doors to swim free. Others, however, were not so lucky. Those that survived the plunge and were severely injured from the fall were last seen trying to desperately smash the glass with broken limbs as the dark waters of the river closed over the windows. The boats on the river raced to help rescue those struggling in the water. One boat captain had seen people trapped in one of the sinking gondolas trying to get out, so in desperation had rammed the glass windows with his ship's bow, breaking it with the intention to help them escape, but watching in grim horror as, unable to stop the mass of his ship in time, it then continued over the gondola, pushing it deeper into the depths, the screams cutting abruptly.

As the terror in the river continued, another three of the missiles tore through the Parliament building. The famous tower of Big Ben collapsed, as a missile smashed through one of its four clock faces and exploded below, destroying the structure's supports. The tower toppled forward as the two famous bells fell out, crashing onto the streets below, their demise sounded by the metallic 'bong' as the bells hit the concrete, coming to rest distorted and bent out of shape against a smashed double-decker bus. The Speaker's House of Parliament, a chamber where the Ministers sat, took a direct hit from another missile and in an instant, hundreds of years of history and prestige were gone, reduced to ash and rubble, as the walls blew outwards and the weight of the roof came crashing down. Another missile slammed through the House of Lords, destroying all the chambers and offices surrounding the iconic hall where the Lords and Baronesses would sit and vote on the new laws of the land. As the final missile slammed home, the iconic parliament building was no more. The roof had collapsed and all the floors were gone, replaced by a huge mass of rubble and steel and broken wood, with fires quickly taking hold and spreading throughout the mess. The outer wall, with its armoured supports and huge bulletproof windows had stubbornly remained standing, but like a skeleton without a body, it now had no purpose and stood as a gravestone to all those who had just died. Now finally, the Empire that was the United Kingdom, that had lasted for hundreds of years, had fallen to its knees.

Wonderland Operations Centre (WOC)

Nobody knew what to say. The ops centre was deathly silent as everyone stood, some shaking in shock, others sobbing as they had watched the breaking news stories now displayed on the screen. They had been powerless to act, as the missiles had been tracked into Central London, but with no exact co-ordinates they had been left helpless to predict the targets, forced to wait until the news story broke minutes later. The devastation had been gut wrenching to see; this had happened on their watch and everyone felt an intense pain deep inside that few in command had ever felt before – the feeling of a battle lost. Already the civilian side of the ops centre had instigated the Emergency Action Plans, well-rehearsed in peacetime and now coming to life. The emergency services on the scene were attempting to locate as many casualties as they could, ignoring the bodies for now and instead concentrating on those whose chances of survival remained relatively high. The Chief Constable of the UK police forces looked over to the CDS, his face grim as he asked, "James, is this over now? Or is there more to come? Should I tell my people in London that we do not have full control on this yet?"

James looked over to the Defence Secretary who sat in shocked silence, eyes wide as he watched the events unfolding on the screen. Realising he wouldn't get anything from the minister for now, he looked to Peter who was slowly shaking his head in reply. Nodding in understanding, he said, "David, I'm sorry, but I don't think this is over. Can you manage with what you have for now? Give us ten minutes to get ourselves shaken out?"

The Police Chief nodded solemnly as he spoke to his team. "Get onto Gold Commander, tell her we've got additional assets coming in to help from the surrounding forces. For now they're to assume there's more threats to life, evacuate as best they can and clear the area of Westminster."

Peter walked over to the CDS, whispering, "James, don't forget the threat to the Royal Family. If this is playing out as per their plan, then whoever is behind it will now use them as the excuse."

His friend nodded, then looked up at the big screen before replying, his voice loudly echoing through the ops centre. "Everybody, listen in." All heads turned to him as he continued. "Our two priorities now are the evacuation of the Royal Family to safe locations, and activation of all our military sites – if it's green and armed I want it awake and angry. Everything else is secondary for now."

The General's words had the desired effect as everyone now became galvanised back into action, the shock from the missile strikes subsiding. Now was not the time to mourn, they realised, there would be plenty of time for that later.

The Police Chief looked over. "CDS, I've got units en route to the palace, but the streets are gridlocked with traffic and it's going to take time. Can't we just send a helicopter instead to pick them up? It'll be faster."

An RAF Captain looked up from his terminal and answered for him. "Sir, we've lost all radar coverage across the UK and all of ATC is down. Blackdog control is reporting Swanwick is gone, it's taken a direct hit from three missiles. Trying to arrange safe passage for a helicopter out of London might be too risky until we have a clear understanding of what's going on in the skies."

Penny walked over to stand by the CDS as she added, "I agree with the Captain. Until we can confirm what is friendly and what's not, I think we should use ground-based units only to evacuate."

The CDS looked at them both as he responded, his tone firm, "Okay, Chief Constable. For now, we'll use ground units to get them out as best we can, see if we can't use the Guards Division at the palace to assist. CAS, let's get control back in the skies please."

Penny responded quickly, looking over to the RAF Captain. "Tell Blackdog I want an AWACS Sentry plane up from Brize Norton immediately, and get fighter cover for it. We need to find the location of those fighters. Tell them the skies are currently hostile and see if RAF Boulmer can stand in for Swanwick, act as a temporary ATC. Those civilian planes will need help to get down." She stopped as a report was handed to her, her eyes scanning the page quickly before she replied, her tone dour.

"James, we're hearing from Major T-P on the radio. It's not good. They're flying over Chequers now; it's gone."

The Defence Secretary stood, eyes narrowed as he blurted out, his voice rising, "What do you mean it's gone, it can't be gone. What about the Cabinet? What about the fucking PM?"

Looking down at the floor, she continued, her voice low. "Sir, it looks like they've taken a direct missile hit. It's all gone, the whole house is in flames. Major T-P wants to know if you want him to land to check for survivors?"

Quickly thinking he replied, "No, let's get him back here as soon as possible, we've got other things to worry about now."

The Defence Secretary stood up raging, "What do you mean 'other things to worry about'? The only thing to worry about is finding the PM. He's our leader! We're not just going to leave him out there alone stuck in the rubble. Land the helicopter and get the PM! At least see if he's alive. Get the helicopter to land and check. THAT'S A FUCKING ORDER, CDS!" He walked towards the CDS, his fists clenched and body taut. Peter thought he might try to punch the General but at the last second, he stopped himself, standing almost nose to nose, his eyes darting left and right, the indecision clear to see. Not the picture he'd want in the press.

The two men stood facing each other, neither wanting to back down until eventually the CDS said softly, "Sir, the Major's flying in a Wildcat helicopter, with only the pilot and the CPO for company. Three men, with no heavy equipment. Even if they had the time, and even if by some miracle the PM managed to survive, if they landed now and searched through the rubble it could take them days to get to the PM. That's *valuable time* that we no longer have. We've spent the past three hours talking all of this through, and now it's happening, the enemy are here. We've been looking out of the window at the garden, whilst all this time the enemy have been coming down the chimney. Now our priorities have changed, I need that helicopter to get a message to the bases in the southwest. They're all out of contact at the moment and have no idea of the threats coming for them. If we waste time trying to find people that we know are already dead, we may doom our own Royal Family and military forces to destruction. You remember what Peter said about the next phase of this operation, there's an invasion on the way and someone will seek to blame the government. Our job, our goal tonight is to stop that from happening and protect our country. The next forty-eight hours will be critical. Now go into the office and have five minutes and compose yourself, because right now, you may be the only serving government minister left alive and we need a leader."

The MP's eyes narrowed as a bewildered look spread across his face. "What?"

Relaxing slightly the CDS continued, keeping his voice low. "You just saw the devastation in London. Downing Street is gone, Parliament gone, Chequers gone. The chances of anyone surviving any of those attacks are minimal, and in all probability all of the current Cabinet members are either dead or incapacitated. Until we get another government up and running, you are the acting PM, you are in charge. So go and have five minutes alone to sort yourself out, but when you come out of that room, I, *we*, want to see our Prime Minister."

The minister looked around the room at everyone, as the realisation of what the General had said to him struck home. With a stern face he turned and walked to the conference room to be alone and to compose himself. The CDS watched on, waiting until the the Defence Secretary had closed the conference-room door before turning, his eyes searching the room until they settled on the person he was looking for; his Vice CDS.

Tony was animatedly talking to three junior officers. "Tony," he interrupted, "get hold of NATO if you can, tell them what's happening over here, and that we need their assistance."

"The phones and internet are still down, James, I don't have any way to communicate outside of the UK at the moment." His colleague's face showed his frustration.

Nodding in understanding he then shouted, "Sir Charles, any news on when GCHQ can crack this virus? When can we expect communications to be restored?"

Looking up from his own team of people he was speaking to, Sir Charles answered, his tone solemn, "I'm sorry, CDS, we've got our top team on it. The virus or programming looks to be some new type of artificial intelligence. It's able to integrate into our systems and almost rewrite its code, meaning it's going to be some time before we crack it. Until we do, I'm afraid all communications in and out of the UK are blocked."

"But how much time, Sir Charles? How long for?" he asked with desperation in his voice.

Shrugging his shoulders, his face showing resignation, he replied, "I'm sorry, James, I really don't know – perhaps two to three days?"

"Two to three days? At this rate we will be back to bloody carrier pigeons!" he replied sardonically.

Penny, overhearing the exchange, suddenly turned. "Carrier pigeons? CDS, That's not a bad idea."

Looking confused he responded, "CAS, I wasn't being serious!"

Approaching closer she said quickly, "James, let's use the modern-day equivalent. Get an aircraft to deliver a message to NATO headquarters now. We still have comms via fibre optics with Lossiemouth and Coningsby, one of our Typhoons could be in Brussels Headquarters in what? Thirty minutes?"

His face registered surprise as he realised what the CAS was suggesting. "Penny, that's a great idea, why didn't we think of that before! Let's get Coningsby to send it, closer to the coast. I'll get something across to you in a second."

The CDS was in the process of writing down the message when a soldier came racing into the room, running up to the CDS with a piece of paper in hand. "Sir!"

Damn, it's never-ending, he thought. Quickly taking the paper, he read the first few lines then looked up to Peter enquiringly. "Do you know a fellow by the name Mike Faulkes?"

"Yes, why?" he replied, then suddenly exclaimed, "Of course! He's at Bovington! Shit, I'd forgotten all about Mike with everything going on. He called me on a landline earlier, they've got a phone box working outside the gate. If we have the number, we can warn them."

The CDS looked up to the young soldier. "When did this come through? When did he ring?"

"I received this from your secretary, sir. She told me one of your staff in your office received the call twenty-five minutes ago. He's waiting to hear back from you. Numbers at the bottom."

He glanced down, seeing the number, before turning to one of the ops-centre staff, an army Corporal in charge of communications. Handing him the paper he said, "Corporal, can we get this number dialled into our systems here?"

The Corporal quickly typed it into the computer, shaking his head.

"Afraid not, sir. Looks like this is an old analogue number, you'll need another analogue landline to talk to it."

He chewed his bottom lip as he thought, then said, "Back at the house, in my office is an old analogue landline, can you direct the feed down to here perhaps?"

The soldier narrowed his eyes, thinking the problem through before replying.

"That's a good five miles of cabling, sir, and it would need to be piped through the tunnels—"

Sensing the answer to be no, Peter quickly interjected, "But you won't need to do that, Corporal, you've already got fibre-optic cables running underground down to here. Surely all you have to do is convert the signal at source, put a digital-to-analogue converter in the General's office at the house..."

The Corporal nodded in agreement as he replied thoughtfully, "And then pipe the feed down here using the existing cabling. Great idea, sir, yes, that could work... It'll take us about ten minutes to set up, though. Leave it with us, sir."

The Corporal quickly pointed to another two soldiers and all three jumped up and out of the room. As they did so, Major T-P arrived back followed by the CPO. Both wore grim and forlorn looks.

"I'm sorry, sir, we were just too late. We saw the explosion from ten miles away. But, by the time we got there... If we had only managed to get there sooner—."

"You'd all be dead," the CDS interrupted. He placed a hand on his shoulder, looking him in the eyes. He'd seen survivor's guilt before. "This isn't the time, T-P, not here and not now. Now I need you focused. Go and get yourself a drink, then be ready to fly again. I'm going to be sending you out as my own version of Paul Revere."

"Okay, sir, okay," he replied, his voice regaining composure and looking up curiously. "Paul Revere?"

Smiling, the CDS replied, "He's the American messenger on horseback in 1775 famous for shouting out 'the redcoats are coming', except this time you are going to be shouting for us 'the reds are coming'. The Colonel at Bovington Camp – Colonel Williams – he's a friend of yours, is he not?"

"Yes, a good friend, I've known him since we met at Sandhurst. Why?"

Because shortly we'll have a phone in here and be able to call them, and here's what I want you to say..."

Eagle-One

Colonel Golgolvin walked amongst his men on the lower cargo deck, as the bright lights began to blink on, his eyes squinting as he adjusted to the sudden change. His younger officers and NCOs now began to earn their pay as they shouted and kicked and cajoled the men into action, walking up and down the fuselage, wakening those from their slumber, their voices carrying over the noise of the engines.

"Come on. UP, MEN! Thirty minutes to drop! You've had enough beauty sleep, now it's time to earn your pay! Thirty minutes... You, Pasha... what do you want – an invite? Breakfast in bed? Get your lazy ass up!"

He smiled as he listened to the NCOs, using language more befitting a brothel than a paratrooper unit, reminding him of his younger days as a fresh-faced recruit. Now twenty-four years later, he was no recruit and this was his paratrooper unit to lead. All around him his men prepared weapons, stowed away kit and began to get themselves ready for the mission. He walked back to where his own equipment lay, hung on the side of the aircraft's fuselage, and expertly cast his fingers over the equipment, checking his static line parachute, ensuring the D-ring was not damaged or bent and that the metal cable running to the parachute container was not frayed. He stopped short of lifting the parachute container to check inside, as he'd not packed his own. Instead, he had trusted another to do this. Before boarding the plane, he had ordered that each man in the unit would hand their own packed parachute to another, for one of their own comrades to use. In doing so he wanted the trust and faith they had in each other to be firmly cemented. They had looked at him in confusion as he gave the order, stating, "The man to your left and the man to your right, you must now trust with your own life as they must trust you with theirs. What better way to start that trust, to *prove* that trust, before battle, than to jump with the parachute that he himself has packed for *you!*" He remembered the pride on the face of the young private, one of the most junior members of the unit, as he had walked up to him to take his parachute, trading it for his own. The message had been clear for all his soldiers to see: *If I can trust the most junior and inexperienced man in the unit, then so should you all.*

Satisfied that his parachute and harness were all in good order, he turned his attention to his assault vest and rig, quickly checking the magazines were correctly stowed and all the flaps were fastened down with the Velcro straps. It would be no good upon landing to find his ammunition was gone. He'd remembered reading about the Normandy landings, when most of the US airborne forces had landed with no equipment, it being torn from them by the violent airstream as they jumped from the aircraft. Always believing history was there to teach and learn from the mistakes of others, he'd made a point of double-checking his own troop's equipment, ensuring all the straps on his men's equipment were triple-sewn to prevent the same thing happening. It had caused holy hell with the regiment's ten seamstresses but it had been worth the extra cigarettes it had cost his officers.

After checking his assault rig and weapons, he checked his watch – it was now twenty-five minutes until time to drop. He used the time to exercise his legs and arms, limbering them up using techniques taught to him years ago by his instructors. After sitting in the plane for so long he did not want to jump, only to end up injuring himself when landing hard. So as with all jumps in the past, he spent valuable time warming up his muscles, readying his body for the physical impact it would absorb. Starting slowly, he rotated his shoulders, building up into larger and wider circles, then, checking that he had enough room around him, he outstretched his arms and began to rotate them until they were swinging in large circles, faster and faster as his blood began to pump freely. He watched as others around him began their own series of exercises, all part of each person's individual routine before a jump. After completing four exercises for his arms, he began to work on his legs, squatting and jumping and feeling them stretch further, the muscles protesting at the sudden workload. *Good,* he thought, *better to hurt now than later.*

He stretched off his back and neck, rotating his head as he arched his back, seeing the white spots dance before his eyes as the movement invoked a small amount of dizziness. Satisfied his muscles were sufficiently stretched off and limbered up, he began to don his body armour and assault vest. The weight of the rig felt strangely comforting to him, as without it he always felt naked and unprotected. Checking and adjusting the straps, ensuring it was tight, but not too tight he then checked and holstered his MP-443 Grach pistol into his chest rig. He then picked up his AK-12 assault rifle and checked the magazine was seated correctly and secure before slipping the weapon's sling over his chest and attaching it to the plastic clip on his chest rig, allowing it to hang freely when not in use. When he jumped, he would make sure that the weapon was secured to his side, helping to keep it away from the parachute harness but also allowing him to roll freely away out of a hard landing if he had to. Pulling a small stick of camouflage cream from his pocket, he applied the cream, dark lines streaking across his face, giving a menacing, threatening look, as the whites of his eyes now shone fiercely. He placed his helmet on, checking that the headgear for his own personal radio was secure and comfortable as he did up his chinstrap.

Feeling and looking more like a paratrooper ready for combat, he walked to the front of the aircraft, passing his men as they stood dressed in combat gear, with faces darkened and eyes focused as they prepared themselves for the fight to come. He watched the loadmasters of the aircraft as he passed, as they climbed like lice over the vehicles, methodically checking the parachute-deployment systems for the sleds. On the first three of the sleds were three 2S25 Sprut-SD tanks – light, air-portable and fielding a one hundred and twenty-five millimetre gun. The oversized barrel sat inside a small two-man turret and was capable of firing the same ammunition as the larger T-90 tanks. Although not the prettiest of vehicles, the Sprut had been designed for just this purpose, to be able to land with the airborne forces of the VDV, Russia's paratrooper forces, and give them an anti-armour capability, its 125mm gun being more than adequate for what the British had to offer.

He continued forward, now passing two of the brand-new Kamaz K-4386 Typhoon vehicles. These oversized four-by-fours had a large armoured body on four large wheels and a turret hatch to access the roof-mounted thirty millimetre cannon sat within its own cupola. The vehicles gave the Colonel an extra level of mobility and firepower that his forces had lacked in the past. He was looking forward to seeing how they performed in combat and hoped they had been worth the additional weight. He climbed awkwardly up to the second deck, more slowly than the first time, his body armour and weapons slowing his progress as he carefully climbed. Once on the second deck, he walked into the cockpit, the lights now dimly on as the evening sky was beginning to darken. The two operators at the rearmost consoles glanced up at seeing him enter and were initially taken aback at the sight of the Colonel ready for war, only having seen him earlier in light order. His face cold and hard, he stared past them through the cockpit windows to the darkened sky, looking at the dark-green terrain slowly rolling by at twenty thousand feet. *Damn*, he thought, he'd hoped it would have been darker. These long summer nights were keeping the light levels far too high for a combat drop. They should have planned for this, he thought. Now he and his men would be jumping in twilight conditions, still visible from the ground.

No matter, the British would not be expecting them. The last intelligence reports he had read, mentioned they had stood all their forces down for the summer – the bases and camps would be almost empty – ripe for the plucking. So even with the disadvantage of the light level, the advantage of them being away for the summer made up for the shortfall. Never had he thought in his career would he be about to conduct combat operations this deep inside the UK. He picked up the headset from the empty operator's station and began talking to the pilot.

"Major, any news or updates for me?"

"No, Colonel, we're already receiving the beacon's signal as planned. When we are ten minutes to jump, I'll turn the cargo lights to red before we begin descending to three hundred feet. I Just want to confirm, though, that you want me to drop the vehicles on our first run and then I'm dropping you in three sticks of one hundred men, all at three hundred feet, is that correct?"

Thinking the numbers through quickly, he replied, "Yes, that's correct, the drop zone isn't long enough for all of us to drop together and I want the vehicles down first rather than have a fourteen-tonne tank come down on my head." He smiled as he added, "We paratroopers are tough, but not that tough."

The Major smiled in reply, before his face became serious again. "And Colonel, the altitude of three hundred feet – you're happy with that, that's not too low for you?"

"Too low? We're normally used to jumping out at two hundred."

The pilot looked stunned as he shot back, "But Colonel, at three hundred feet, if your parachute fails, how do you have time to pull the spare?"

He smiled as he replied, "Oh, that's simple, Major... we don't carry the spare!"

Leaving the pilot and his team shocked and thankful that they were staying in the aircraft, he turned and walked back through to the passenger compartment where Major Pavitch and his team were working. All were still positioned where he had left them, watching and chatting on the radio. Deciding not to disturb them, he simply patted the Major on the shoulder and gave him the thumbs-up sign, smiling. The Major was forced to do a double take at seeing the green monster with a black face grinning at him, and upon recognising the Colonel, he smiled and held up his own thumb in recognition. The Colonel left the cabin thinking, *no more smiles*, now it was game time.

He carefully climbed back down to the lower decks; his men in full combat gear waiting patiently for him. Everyone stood to attention as he passed, looking him proudly in the eye and wanting him to see they were not afraid. He nodded to each man as he gave them a once-over, happy with what he saw before him. They were all grouped in their combat jump formations, organised before the plane had been loaded.

He walked to the rear of the aircraft beside the huge ramp where his parachute hung ready to be used. With great care he removed it from the fuselage and stepped into the harness, legs first, the straps nice and tight but not too high, before slipping the harness over his body armour and rig. Once it was on tight, he adjusted the leg straps, knowing that the uncomfortable feeling would not be for long. Jumping at three hundred feet, he would only be in the air for fifteen seconds, vulnerable to enemy fire during that time, but counting on the team on the ground to be doing its job of keeping the drop zone secure. If everything was going to plan then the enemy should have no idea they were coming, but long ago he'd learned to never to trust a plan. With his parachute harness on, he adjusted and clipped together the strap around his waist, feeling the extra weight almost pulling him backward as he carefully turned around and leaned against the back of the fuselage, helping to take the weight off his legs. He adjusted the sling on his assault rifle, making sure the folding stock was tucked away so as not to strike up and smash him in the ribs as he landed. He had seen good friends invalided out of the VDV this way. Content that his equipment, parachute and weapons were ready, he now began to think through the plan again, to prepare himself mentally for what he would see on the ground, to think of anything they could have missed or not prepared for.

He knew his men were ready, they had practised and trained for this mission for many months, but with the short time to go before the jump he tried to focus on anything to keep his mind active. He thought about the drop zone, he had memorised its location and how large it was. Usually, he would have preferred an area large enough to land his whole unit together, but this time he had to compromise, sacrificing the space for the location, as this particular drop zone was no less than a mile from the target. Therefore, they would be landing in four separate jumps if he included the equipment drop, but once on the ground they could be moving against the target in fifteen minutes if all went well. He just wished it had been darker...

The interior lights suddenly went red, bathing everyone in a demonic glow as he heard the shouted warning pass down the plane, "Ten minutes! Ten minutes!"

Now he felt the fuselage dip to a downwards angle – finally they were descending, finally it was time...

UK - Somewhere in Dorset

Leaning against the four-by-four, Sergeant Artem Feodor took a long deep drag of his cigarette, disappointed at the lack of taste and flavour. *These fucking British cigarettes*, he thought disappointingly, and with disgust he spat it out on the ground before quickly stamping on the cherry-red end as it hit the dry grass. He was here to protect the drop zone, not burn it out. What he wouldn't give for a good packet of

Belomorkanals, he thought longingly. Hopefully some of the troops coming in had brought some with them. Looking skywards, he quickly checked his watch before glancing at the suitcase-sized radio beacon on the bonnet of the vehicle. Seeing it was time, he picked up the heavy case and began the long walk into the middle of the large field that they were parked in. During the day, the huge five-hundred metre by nine-hundred metre field was used as a landing strip by the local glider club, but tonight they were using it themselves as a drop zone for Eagle-One. After a while the Sergeant stopped and, after looking around, was satisfied that he was in the centre of the field. He placed the case on the ground, opened it and connected a large antennae array that he made sure was facing north. Then, happy with its location, he flicked the toggle switch to power the beacon on, checking the battery light and signal light had both illuminated. Using the beacon's display he checked it was transmitting and, once satisfied, began the long walk back to the four-by-four.

In the four-by-four's passenger seat operating the radio, sat Captain Aleksei Lunyou, in charge of the small eight-man FSB team that had infiltrated the UK three weeks ago. The other six members of his team were elsewhere carrying out other tasks and missions and it had been Lunyou who had gladly volunteered for this mission to secure and paint the drop zone for the incoming aircraft. He knew the threat would be low and nothing like his previous missions in Ukraine or Syria. In fact, this afternoon's little shoot-out with the British had been quite enjoyable and he and his comrade had laughed as they drove away, watching the Brits scuttle around like roaches. *If they think this afternoon was bad, then wait until they see what's coming for them later tonight,* he mused to himself.

A static hiss came through the earpiece followed by the message, "Wolf, this is Eagle-One, rain to begin in twenty minutes over." He banged on the roof of the four-by-four whilst whistling to get the attention of the Sergeant before pointing to the beacon. The Sergeant simply gave the thumbs-up signal to indicate all was working and continued to walk back. Lunyou picked up the handset, replying, "Eagle-One, this is Wolf, rain in twenty minutes. Sheep pen is empty, and the wolf is awake." He'd just sent the code that the drop zone was secure and the beacon was active – now nothing would stop them from coming in.

As he walked, Feodor produced yet another cigarette, lit it and inhaled deeply. *Still the same rubbish*, he thought, as his cheek and jaw ached in protest as he inhaled. He winced in pain as his fingers touched the swelling and bruised eye on his left side as he thought about the fucker who had done this to him. He had been caught off guard as the man had used some kind of jiu-jitsu or karate to disable him, similar in style to their own sambo that the Russian forces were taught. Had he not been caught off guard, he was certain he would have killed the man. The satisfaction he could have felt snapping his neck like a twig left him feeling angry again. He had hoped at first to have shot him as he unloaded a whole magazine at him, but as they drove away, he watched the man run towards them brandishing his own fucking pistol. The embarrassment of it hurt more than the wounds. When all this was over, the Sergeant had planned to go on a little hunting expedition, to find the bastard and toy with him – if, that is, the bastard managed to live through what was coming. The thought of it warmed him again and for a moment he smiled, forgetting the pain and the taste of the poor cigarettes. He was distracted from his thoughts when he saw movement off to his right side. "Oh, fuck, what does this prick want?" he muttered under his breath, as he watched the overweight figure of a sweating red-faced man come striding towards the parked four-by-four.

Lunyou was watching his Sergeant's progress as he ambled back to the vehicle, smiling as he thought about the Englishman who had humiliated him. He had only told his Sergeant to go and find out why the phone box had been working, as he was told all communications for the enemy had been shut down. Still on the phone to one of his other teams, he had suddenly looked up and seen both men fighting hard. Even then, his money had been on his Sergeant, a tough veteran of many conflicts, and even more bar fights and public brawls. Seeing him getting beaten, and then having his own weapon taken off him had surprised Lunyou. He saw the body language of his Sergeant change and became instantly alert to someone approaching from behind the four-by-four. He hid the radio receiver and stepped out of the vehicle, closing the door behind him as the stranger came into view.

"You there! What on earth do you think you're doing here? This is private property. This land belongs to the glider club. You're trespassing!"

The man was wearing a flat cap, jeans, wellingtons and a faded pink polo shirt stretched over a large belly. Aged about mid-to-late fifties, he had an air of English arrogance about him, thought Lunyou. He looked over to where the man had come from and saw a silver BMW Estate parked over by the two hangar buildings at the far end of the field. As the man continued to rant at him, he observed the car, noting the only other occupant was the dog in the back. A big dog, Lunyou noted, as even from this distance he could see the BMW jolt on its suspension as the dog, visibly excited by its owner, began to jump about, barking. Lunyou turned back to face the man, who now stepped closer, his face reddening as he began to get louder and more animated. "Didn't you hear me? I said, I'll call the police. Now get off here. NOW!"

Lunyou watched on, fascinated, as the man's face went from anger to shock and then creased into pain, his hands scrambling behind him as he tried to pull at fresh air, realising that something was wrong, but not totally comprehending what. Behind him stood Sergeant Feodor, bloody knife in hand, poised to strike again if need be, but the two strikes had been good, as the knife had entered into the man's left and right lungs, causing them to collapse. As he struggled to breathe, his legs buckled beneath him and he fell forward to the grass, his lips moving but no sound escaping as his lungs filled with blood and slowly drowned him. It was a silent kill, designed to keep him quiet. However, the dog in the car was a different matter. Sensing its owner was in trouble, it now began barking ferociously, with the car rocking manically as the dog fought to get out.

The Sergeant knelt down and wiped the knife's blade on the dying man's shirt before searching his pockets for the set of car keys. He stood up and handed them to Lunyou, who, sighing, turned and walked towards the car, seeing as he got closer that the dog was a black-and-tan German shepherd. It's eyes were wide, and it's jaws flecked with saliva, coating the rear window of the car with spittle as it growled and barked at him. He was tempted to let the dog loose, but quickly shook the thought, as he knew he couldn't take the chance that it wouldn't attack him or his moody Sergeant. He loved dogs; he had fond memories of when he'd grown up with them as a boy on his grandad's farm in Northern Russia. But this was not his farm, and he was no longer a boy. With a heavy heart and a sad face, he pulled out his pistol and began to fit the silencer.

19

The Acorn

12th June 2012

Why do they always choose these shitty places to meet? he thought to himself. He adjusted his damp coat again, trying to keep it from touching the dirty lino floor of the roadside diner he was sitting in. Through the dirty windows he could see it was still raining hard, matching his mood. *Yet another typical summer downpour in the UK,* he thought. He cast a disapproving eye over the diner, one of the many cheap and cheerful that were found criss-crossing the countryside alongside the A-roads of the UK. The floor was yellowed and cracked, the lino looking like it had been many months since it had seen anything resembling a brush, mop or bucket. The large menu that sat above the counter looked like it had been designed in the 1970s, its once garish colours now faded, showing the three meals of the day, all looking equally unappetising and certain to assist the customer in coronary overload. The kitchen behind the counter looked cold and dark, with one of the overhead lights randomly flicking off and on, crying out for a bulb replacement. He wondered how on earth these places were able to make any money.

The hefty chef stood at the far end of the kitchen area, large knife in hand and cutting some type of meat. He dared not guess the hygiene rating, given the state of the worktop he was working on. The overweight waitress, who looked to have been pretty once upon a time, was behind the counter, applying another slick of lipstick, the third time in the past ten minutes, he noted. If she paid as much attention to the cleanliness of the place as she did her own tired and saggy features, this place might be more appealing, he thought. He'd already tried to get her attention twice to ask her to clear away the mess in front of him. All of the tables around him were cluttered with dirty plates and cups, some looking like they still had yesterday's meals on them, and at the far end of the diner, in one of the other booths, sat a huge hulk of a man, one of the many truckers who visited these places. The trucker was calmly drinking from a chipped cup and smoking a cigarette, using one of the dirty plates as an ashtray. *Disgusting*, he thought, and felt instantly dirty just from being in the room with these people. The sooner he concluded his business here and left, the better.

He removed yet another wet wipe from his coat pocket and for the fifth time in as many minutes wiped his hands for fear of touching the table. He looked at his watch, his frustration beginning to show. He'd been told to meet at the diner at 14:30 and it was now 14:45. *Why are they always late?* he thought angrily. Every time they met him, they were late. So tardy and unprofessional. *Not like the movies at all*, he growled to himself. They'd called him late last night at home, telling him to meet at the same place he had met them only two days ago. He usually only met them once every six weeks, but after giving them the folder, he had now found himself being summoned again. Clearly, they had liked what they had read – that had been his intention all along – and now as he sat there, he finally felt ready to walk away. He had a promising career in politics waiting for him and the sooner he shook off leeches like this the better. After another five minutes of waiting, he was tempted to get up and leave, he'd already driven two hours out of London to get here and knew that even if he left now, he'd still end up getting back late and hitting the rush-hour traffic, not good considering he had another appointment at 17:30. He'd probably be late for his next meeting. Should he call them, he thought, find out where they were? No, he'd been told to never do that. They always called him.

He looked down at the table, undecided as to what to do. The bell above the door jerked him from his thoughts and he looked up to see the man he was to meet, enter, stamping his feet and shaking the rain from his jacket. Sergei was not a large man, perhaps five feet six at best, but his character and demeanour easily filled the doorway, and he always gave off an aura of power, his eyes fierce and his brain sharp. He didn't know much about Sergei on a personal level, except what he had gleaned from the small talk in their meetings. He knew he was Polish, which explained the Slavic drawl, and that he worked for a conglomerate of wealthy Saudi businessmen in the defence industry. Sergei's job was to get insider information for them to help woo governments, to help them devise ways to make their own products more appealing.

What better way to get contracts, Sergei had reasoned, than if you already knew what the customer country was looking for to begin with.

He'd been meeting with Sergei now these past two years, after being passed over to him from a local loan shark. The gambling debts he had accrued had been monstrous, falling foul of an illegal gambling den and owing the wrong people a massive amount of money. The loans had been easy to accrue, but the repayments began to quickly spiral out of control, and it had been with trepidation and dread that he came home and found them waiting for him when he fell behind on the payments. Fully expecting a violent outcome, it had been their suggestion to work it off, to help their good friend Sergei and that's how he now found himself two years and many meetings later, sat in this shit hole of a diner, wet, cold and hungry.

Seeing the moody expression on his face, Sergei broke into a smile. *Honestly*, he thought, *I swear he enjoys doing this to me. Every time he's late.* Keeping his temper in check, he smiled and pointed to the seat opposite. Sergei approached, looking at the table and tutting at the mess he saw. Looking over at the waitress disapprovingly, Sergei said something that he couldn't understand. *Was that Russian? Well good luck with that.* Regardless of the language, she wouldn't come over. He sat with a look of surprise and anger on his face, when with renewed gusto, the waitress now walked over to the booth behind them, clearing it quickly and adding a quick spray of disinfectant. Sergei slipped into the newly cleaned booth as the waitress returned from the counter and placed a fresh cup of coffee in a brand-new-looking cup. Sergei nodded in thanks, and looked back and motioned for him to come join him at the newly cleaned table. With mute anger and staring back at the waitress, he stood and joined Sergei, placing his suitcase on the floor.

"Was that Russian I heard you just speak to that waitress?"

"No, Polish. I thought she looked Polish and it looks like I was correct in that observation."

Nodding in understanding, but not believing a word, he countered, "Sergei, you're late. I've been waiting fifteen minutes..."

Sergei merely grunted in understanding as he picked up a spoon and slowly stirred two lumps of sugar into his coffee, looking down at the table.

"And you would have waited another fifteen minutes, would you not?" His manner was infuriating.

His anger rising, he shot back, "Look, I don't know what you think this is, but I'm not some lapdog that you simply tell to sit and wait."

Looking up quickly and holding his hands up in resignation Sergei interjected, "Of course, of course... my apologies for being late. I was delayed somewhat by your country's glorious traffic and even better weather."

Calming down somewhat, he watched as Sergei clicked his fingers and pointed to him. Within seconds the waitress now reappeared, carrying another new cup, full of freshly poured tea, the steam rising off it. Sergei smiled again, seeing the look of confusion on his face as he answered, "I believe that Earl Grey is your drink of choice, with a slice of lemon?"

"How did you know that?" he asked, trying to hide his surprise.

Laughing, Sergei replied, "We know a lot more about you than you think. Now, before we go into all that small talk about our drinking habits and the weather, let's get straight to business, shall we? The folder you gave us a few days ago, its contents were... interesting, and I've had time to show it around to some of my colleagues and they agree."

"Okay, great, so you all found it interesting. Does that mean it's worth something to you?" His eyebrows raised questioningly.

Slowly raising the cup to his mouth, Sergei took a sip of coffee, smiling at the taste, and then he said, "Tell me more about this file, how did it find its way into *your* possession?"

Picking his cup up to drink and finding the tea surprisingly good, he began, "It's a simple Civil Service exercise. We've asked some of our senior planners to come up with these plans to review our country's defence needs over the next ten years. There are five independent reports, each by a different author and who have no idea of the existence of the others. I was told that I'm to oversee all the reports, to collate and review them before we submit them to the Ministry of Defence. I've yet to submit them though, as I've told my bosses I need another week to look through them all – and thought that you might want to see them yourself, to see if your contacts in the Saudi Defence businesses you represent could use them."

"I see." Sergei nodded. "Very wise of you. So, at present, the only one who knows of these reports are yourself and the authors of the reports, these five civil servants? Correct?"

"That's correct."

"And each author does not know how many other reports have been written, nor what they contain or the identity of the other authors, is that also correct?" Sergei cocked his head slightly as he asked.

He nodded in reply as he took another sip of his tea, savouring the taste.

"Good!" Sergei beamed again as he leant back in the seat. "That is very good news. Now the reports that we have seen, these first four are very good, we liked those, and we thank you for showing them to us – they'll be very helpful to us in the future, but it's the fifth report that we really want to discuss with you. We like that a lot, but we don't wish for anyone else to see it. You see, we feel that our businesses would really benefit if your government did not know of this report. Therefore, we would like you to bury it."

"But my boss would know there were five reports, he would question why it had disappeared."

"No, he would not, because when I say bury... I'm sorry, my English is not as good as I thought. I meant to say that if after reviewing the report, you were to say it was not viable, it would not get submitted. It would get lost. After all, that's your job, is it not? To *review* and then submit these reports. Simply say that it was not realistic, not feasible and that you have destroyed it, all copies that is, except, of course, for the copy we have now." His smile became a grimace as he added, "Of course, to help you decide I have been authorised to tell you that all your previous debts will be considered repaid and that we will also offer you more. Much more."

"More?" His eyes lit up. "More what?"

"What does every person want? Money, power, control, respect, which would *you* want? Take your pick."

He watched as Sergei leant back, smiling back at him, his cold eyes calculating what he would do. When he had first found himself in this position, it had been to merely repay the debt, a debt he knew he had already paid at least five times over. In the past, the files and information he had handed over had no doubt helped the companies Sergei worked for win contracts, valued in the millions, if not billions. He had wanted rid of this greedy little man for months and in getting the folders to him had seen this as a way out, not a way further in. He needed rid of them once and for all. He thought about the risks he had already taken and the punishments if he

317

were caught, and seeing Sergei sitting opposite, with that greedy look in his eyes and the thin smile on his puffy face, he saw for the first time something he hadn't before, something evil and calculating. Without knowing why, he felt the need to get out and get out quickly.

Calmly and forcefully, he replied, "Sergei, I think I've done enough for both you and your friends. You've seen those files, you've seen what's in them and that's enough for me. I'm not going to be helping you any further. Clearly, they're worth something to you, so I'll consider the debt repaid in full and our business concluded. Please don't call me again or I'll report it to the Parliamentary Standards Committee, and I don't think your friends in Saudi Arabia would want that kind of publicity."

He stood to leave, suddenly noticing that the chef had silently approached the table and was blocking his way out, his white chef's clothes and apron, bloodied, giving him a menacing, threatening appearance. The chef's hands were folded across his body in defiance and in each hand, he held a large, wicked-looking knife, still covered in blood and scraps of meat. The chef's stare sent a chill down his spine, almost daring him to try to push past. Without realising he had done it, he found himself sat back down, and pushed himself further into the booth, trying to create distance between them. He looked over to Sergei, who sat still, the smile gone, a cold face that looked impassively back at him. *What the hell is going on?* he wondered. He looked over to the waitress who was staring back, unconcerned with the events that were unfolding. He looked over to see the trucker walk over to the restaurant door, locking it and turning the sign over to say, '*closed.*'

"Who the fuck are you, Sergei?" he said, the panic in his voice rising, "what the hell is this? What do you want?"

"Calm down, please calm down. Now we only want to be friends. These people here are all friends of mine and they want to be friends with you, but they don't like rudeness. So, if you insist on being rude, if you insist on wanting to leave before we've finished our business here, then..."

The looks on both the chef and the trucker filled him with dread and left him in no doubt that they would hurt him badly. *Fuck!* What had he got himself into, he thought angrily. Why was no one else in the restaurant?

Sergei now said something to the waitress in that language again. Was it Polish? he wondered, having his doubts. She walked over, carrying a laptop and placed it in front of him. He looked at the images on the screen; good quality and clearly at close range. In the picture he saw himself handing over a flash drive to Sergei whose own face had been digitally faded out. He remembered the exchange; it was last year, when he had been shown information on the details for a new lightly armoured vehicle for Afghanistan, to replace the Viking vehicles currently out there. The details of the vehicle he had seen had belonged to another defence contractor in Singapore and he had felt that Sergei could use the competitor's information to help swing the contract his way. There had been several bids to build the replacement and he had assumed the winning bid belonged to one of Sergei's companies.

"You see the way that the light hits your features? Very good at identifying you I think. Of course, my profile requires work." Sergei wore a mock expression as he nodded towards the chef. "Lieutenant Laratov deserves the praise for this image, it was his camera work that set you in such a good light."

Quickly composing himself and thinking quickly, he said, "So what, Sergei? So what? I sold a few bits of information to you, gave you an inside track on the competitors – who cares? It happens all the time. I'll get a slap on the wrist and moved out of the offices for a while. What will happen to your companies you represent if it comes out that I helped you to get those contracts? All that bad publicity and all those defence contracts now cancelled. They'll lose billions, have their shares plummet on the markets and it won't be me they're after, it'll be you and your thugs here. So go ahead, sell those photos, that's still not going to make me do what you want. It's still a no. Those reports – all *five* of those reports – are going in. And if anything does happen to me then another person, one you don't control, will simply get the job and do it anyway. So, there you go, you can't blackmail me!"

Sergei still sat there, unmoving, his face showing no recognition, no anger to his outburst. *Damn*, he thought. He really hadn't known about Sergei at all.

A look of mischief crossed Sergei's face as he began, his tone condescending. "Ah, but that's where I'm afraid you're mistaken, my friend. You see, on that flash drive that you so kindly gave me, were the plans for the *winning* bids' vehicle details. Vehicle size, engine and more importantly, its *protection* aspects. My own company was unsuccessful in its endeavours, the UK military deciding instead to go with *this* vehicle design and the Singapore company. I believe it should start arriving in Afghanistan at the start of next year, just in time for the information you have provided to help the insurgents in their battle against the corrupt and fascist government that *your* government helps keep in power. The information you kindly gave to us will now help them to fight and defeat this new threat."

As Sergei continued, the laptop scrolled through other photos, all of him and all from the other meetings they'd had in the past. Clearly, they had been planning for this for a long time.

"I never agreed to any of this," was all he could stammer.

Sergei continued, unperturbed. "These companies that you say I work for, can you name one? Can you prove which one it is? No, you cannot, because they don't exist. It is all, how you say, smoke and mirrors. I instead used the information you gave me in the other, more darker aspects of my work. For the past two years you have been providing us with detailed knowledge of your country's latest defence vehicles and capabilities. For that you have my extreme gratitude. Now, of course, if you no longer wish to help us then I'm afraid that we can no longer help you – already, copies of these pictures and videos of our other meetings have been leaked out to people, people who, shall we say, do not share the same views that I do, as to what constitutes business and what constitutes treason or espionage." He pointed to himself. "I am a businessman; I have a business brain and see the value in our little agreement. Others, though, perhaps in your own intelligence community, may say that what you have done is espionage, sabotage and dare I say it even treasonous."

A feeling of dread and confusion came over him. With his voice rising he replied, "No! That's a fucking lie, I never agreed to that. I NEVER AGREED TO THAT! You lying bastard! You fucking—"

He was quickly stunned into silence as with a loud thud the chef buried one of the knives into the table in front of him, spilling his half-empty cup of tea. Fear took hold then, and he kept his mouth shut, watching Sergei who, enjoying his discomfort, merely put his finger to his lips.

"Ssshhh. I already told you; my friends hate rudeness. Their concept of the English language is limited, yes, but they understand enough words to know when you are beginning to insult me."

Tutting, Sergei watched as the tea ran down the table, pointing to the waitress. She hurried over with a dishcloth and cleaned up the mess, before producing another cup of tea and placing it in front of him. Sergei smiled in thanks before pointing to the chef.

"Lieutenant Laratov here really is a qualified chef, did you know that? He trained for four years at a top London hotel. Of course, that's not his real job though – he works for me. But sometimes his training as a chef does come in useful, especially when I need to send out a message. One of his favourite dishes, or as he modestly calls it, one of his 'specials', is a dish called *truth stew*, have you heard of it? No? It involves the removal of a person's testicles, then they're fried up in a lovely red wine sauce with onions and then fed to the same person, all whilst keeping them alive. Imagine that. It's good to see those four years were not wasted. According to Lieutenant Laratov, it's a dish to die for and it doesn't matter if the lucky recipient is male or female, because if the person enjoying the dish is female, you get the same result by removal of the breasts."

He felt like he was going to gag, the way Sergei jovially described the man's talents. He stared up at the Lieutenant with growing fear, finally realising the danger he was in. *You stupid fucking fool*, he thought.

"Now, who I work for is irrelevant, but what we want is. You now have two choices. Option one is to go to prison, have your reputation destroyed, your family despise you and your own country loathe you. Of course, the trouble is that the information you have submitted will be used by your country's enemies for many, many years to come, so there will never really be an end to the shame or suffering. As each year passes, as you finally think it is ending, another life will be lost, aided by the information you have given us, then the blame will resurface and all that hate and loathing will begin again. I'd even go so far as to say a man of your calibre would most likely kill himself from the shame after no more than a year inside, leaving your poor family to carry your burden and debt. I would, of course, be there to help your family in their time of grief at your loss."

"Please, Sergei, leave my family out of this. They've done nothing wrong."

Sergei left him to dwell on the thought of what being in prison could be like for a few moments and the impact on his family, before offering a lifeline.

"Of course, there's option two..."

He looked up, hope in his eyes.

Sergei carried on, counting on his fingers. "You do as we ask, and you submit only the four reports and help us to get rid of the fifth, and you get a promotion. You have our backing and support, you have access to our help, and you begin to rise up the ranks of political power that you so long to climb, and... your family will love you, and your beautiful, precious son will grow up without ever getting to know me or my associates."

He watched as Sergei now stood up, buttoning his coat, and about to leave.

"But I haven't given you my answer yet?" he said, confused.

Sergei leaned towards him, a menacing look on his face as his hand pinched his cheek roughly. "I already *know* what your answer is. You're a smart man, you'll work it out."

Releasing him with a look of disgust and wiping his hand on his coat, he now stood back and began to chat animatedly to the trucker, who up to now had been stood behind them. After a few brief exchanges the trucker stepped forwards, a brand-new phone in his hand. He placed it down on the table in front of him before disappearing out of the diner door and into the rain.

"What's this?"

"This is a new phone that you will always keep on you, it is not to be shown to anyone else, and you are to never use it. No texts, no emails, nothing. When we want to chat, we will call you, so make sure the battery is always fully charged and it's switched on. If you go into a meeting and they tell you to remove your devices, you keep this with you. *Never* leave it behind anywhere. Do you understand?"

"I do." He nodded meekly. "Keep it on me, and fully charged."

"And tell *no one* about it or about our agreement." His tone was low and menacing. "Remember, we are watching you *all* the time. If we find out that you break these simple rules, then the footage and images you just saw will be released to the press and I may even send my chef to go round and cook for your family – perhaps they would like to sample one of his specials?"

"Okay, okay," he replied dejectedly. "I get it, I fucking get it, just keep away from my family."

"Good, now before you go, you're going to give Lieutenant Laratov the name and address of the author of report number five. And you're never to mention this man again. Give him the details and then forget all about the man."

"Why do you need to know that? Does that matter?"

"Why do you need to know what we need to know?" he countered, his tone dripping with malevolence. "It is insignificant what you know about us. In fact, it's probably best if you don't know why we want to know, but let's just simply say that there's already too many people who know of this report. Tell the Lieutenant quick enough and then perhaps you can still make it back in time for your 17:30 appointment with that lovely young aide of yours... Samantha, is it? Aren't you married?" Sergei's eyes lit up again when hinting at the affair.

Fuck, how does he know so much? he thought, as Sergei walked towards the door.

As if suddenly remembering something, he stopped and turned to face him one final time. "Oh, and I almost forgot, when the phone does ring, every time you answer you are to say you are Acorn – not your name, nor any another name – just Acorn."

"Acorn?" he said, confused. "Why the hell, Acorn? Why would I answer as that?"

Sergei gave a dazzling smile as he said, "Simple. It will confirm that we are speaking to you, because that is now your agent name, Acorn. Because starting from today, with our help, we will grow you into the mightiest of English oaks."

Laughing at the last part he turned and exited the diner, the bell ringing in his wake.

And just like that, he was alone in the booth with just the cold-faced chef and the saggy-faced waitress for company. Not wanting to spend any more time there and wanting desperately to see Samantha, he took a deep breath and then proceeded to tell the Lieutenant what he wanted to hear.

28th Sept 2022

The traffic was light at this time of evening, as the convoy of armoured black Mercedes G-Wagon cars drove through the streets of Moscow, helped by the Russian police, who, on their motorbikes, stopped the traffic at every junction, their hands outstretched, warning the traffic to ignore the green lights and to wait. As soon as the four-vehicle convoy shot past, the police would then kick the bikes into gear, leaving the bemused motorists in their wake, the diesel fumes belching from their own older Soviet-era cars.

In the back of the second armoured G-Wagon, watching the lights of Moscow flash by was Dimitry Smolov, one of three senior directors of the FSB. He shared his power equally with the two other directors, both of the same rank and standing, all unable to use leverage on the other. Purposely done, so as to prevent any one person from becoming too powerful, preventing them from wielding their power or pursuing their own agenda or ambition. Only one man had managed to do that before, the current Russian President, and now that he had that power, he fought all the harder to keep it, which was one of the main reasons why Dimitry was forced to share power with the other two directors. He watched out of the four-by-four's bullet proof window as the shopping centres sailed by. Some of the more high-end stores already being boarded up, as the embargo and sanctions the west had put on Russia were beginning to bite. How long would this last? he had thought. How long can the President remain in power for?

Dimitry's own ambition had been to become sole director of the FSB, the Russian secret service police. Already partway there, he just needed to remove the other two and then assume overall control. He'd learnt long ago that in order to be the king, you first had to have the ear of the king, and it was for this reason that he had risen through the ranks of power to become the President's most trusted of advisors and allies. At his age of fifty-six years old, he was still young enough and hungry enough to want to lead his country, but he also knew that with the current conflict in Ukraine going badly and the world uniting against them, to do so now would be the final nail in the coffin for his country. Already, there were small voices in the Russian states who were crying out for the country to break apart. And he knew those small, quiet voices could quickly grow in volume and strength to help break apart his beloved country and that was something he could not bear to see. So, he had decided to put his own ambition aside, and help his President, and more importantly help his country. In doing so, his next move would come at considerable risk to himself and all he worked for, but he had to do something, always believing that fortune favoured the brave.

On the seat next to him was the folder he had kept hidden in his safe for nearly ten years, waiting for a time when he thought its contents could be used. And he thought that finally that time was now.

The four-vehicle convoy crossed through the main gates and into the famous parliament buildings of Moscow's Red Square, the sun glinting off the tiles on the large domes and illuminating the vivid colour of the red bricks of the building. Ushered through a side gate and then down into a vast underground car park with a squeal of tyres, three of the vehicles peeled away, leaving Dimitry's vehicle to continue alone, being driven up to a large set of double lift doors, ornately carved with a gold gilded eagle sat atop the centre. A Russian flag hung off the wall on either side. The lift doors opened, and two large men in oversized suits stepped out, wearing earpieces and stern looks as they appraised the car parked in front of them. Quickly recognising the occupant, they opened the rear door, stepping aside as Dimitry confidently strode into the lift, purposely ignoring the guards as the doors closed behind him.

Within a few seconds the lift doors reopened, revealing a vast hall, with twelve marble columns extending floor to ceiling, each on its own weighing over twenty tonnes, and capped with gold-leaf banding at head height on the columns. The hall was one of six within the building and rivalled any palace or capital building seen around the world. At the far end of the room hung a vast Russian flag over two large bronze doors and, stood to attention beside every column was a member of the elite Presidential Guard, the red-and-green uniforms and black gloss knee-high boots standing out amongst the white of the marble. As he walked into the hall, he saw the guards turn their heads as one to look at him, watching him closely as he passed them, following his progress as his footsteps echoed off the high walls and ceiling. He'd seen them do this hundreds of times and the effect was now lost on him, but he knew the guards practised for hours to perfect this technique, a form of intimidation to unsettle visiting dignitaries to the palace. As he walked, he made a point to look every guard in the eye, to show them he was not afraid and that they should fear him. Soldiers respected strength and in him they needed to see that he was strong. He took satisfaction in the fact that some of the guards looked to the floor, whilst others nervously swallowed, showing him that he had unsettled them. *Good, that is good,* he thought proudly.

In between every column on the wall stood huge gold-framed pictures, each depicting a Russian military victory from the past – a far cry from where the country was now, he thought, as he passed. Finally coming to the end of the long hall, the two guards flanking the doors slammed to attention, their boots making a loud crash on the floor to rival any gunshot. The two doors opened inwards and he walked through into the vast presidential briefing room, seen before on the world's media, with white marble and gold leaf adding a level of grandeur more befitting a ballroom than a briefing room. Behind the double doors and stood ramrod straight were yet another pair of presidential guards. With military precision they slowly and gracefully closed the doors behind him. At the other end of the room stood another two guards, guarding the white-and-gold leaf doors that led into the President's personal office, which was closed for the moment.

In the middle of the room stood a forty-foot-long table, able to seat twenty comfortably, and at its head sat the President's chair, larger than the others with its arms encased in gold leaf and green padding. It had once belonged to the Tsar and was where he had sat to open his royal correspondence from his cousins the King of England and the Kaiser of Germany. Now it sat alone, a relic of the past. Seeing he was not alone, he walked up to the table, recognising the two men sitting there as Mikhail Gelenekov and Arkady Kirov, both the other directors of the FSB; younger, inexperienced men. He'd played this game long enough to know the people smiling at you and calling you friend were the ones you watched the most. He enjoyed seeing the confused looks on their faces as they saw him in the room with them, confirming his suspicions. He'd already been briefed from his informants working in the highest levels of both men's departments that they were already putting plans together to move against him. A plan he already knew that would begin with him being alienated from the President and then removed from office. No doubt, he thought, they would try some fake operation, some fabricated evidence to achieve this, which was why he had beaten them to it. He smiled as he saw they had both been made to sit at the end of the table, furthest from the head. With a small degree of satisfaction, he pulled out the chair next to the President's, watching their faces aghast as he sat himself down comfortably, placing his folder on the table. The effect was not lost on them – he had a seat near the President whilst they were sat furthest away – a political snub.

"Dimitry, I am at a loss, may I ask how you knew about this meeting or how you came to be invited?"

Ah, Dimitry thought, *so the fool Mikhail speaks first; he must be the one in charge.*

"It is simple enough, Mikhail, I *knew* about this meeting, because I *called* this meeting."

"You called it?" Now it was the turn of Arkady to speak. "What the hell gives you the power to call that? Where is the President? We came here to speak to him alone, not you, you old bastard!"

Ah the wit and charm of Arkady. Always the one to rush to temper, so easily barbed. Always a weakness that will eventually lead to his downfall, he thought.

"You will not get to speak to the President, not tonight or any other night. Tonight, your empires come crashing down. You have failed comrades."

"Failed, Comrade Dimitry, failed in what? We are all on the same side here, are we not?" said Mikhail.

Dimitry looked at Mikhail as he spoke, slowly and loudly clapping his hands. "Well done, Mikhail, Well done. An Oscar-winning performance no doubt." The confusion on both men's faces was almost comical to see.

"Tonight you came here to inform the President of a plot to assassinate him, a plot that was to be led by me, no doubt, with fabricated evidence and fake witnesses. A plot that was to see me removed and my department dismantled. Leaving power to be shared equally between you both. Where once there were three, there would now be two."

As he spoke, he watched both men intently, watching their reactions. Mikhail remained impassive, but he saw the rage inside Arkady build, his face flashing red and his teeth showing. *Ah, good old Arkady*, he thought, *I can read you like a book.*

"Dimitry, I think you're seeing enemies where there are none, perhaps you've been in this line of work too long and need a break? I mean, come on, why would we do that? I couldn't manage your department without you?" said Mikhail.

"You can save your time and breath by trying to deny this. I have good people already deep within your departments ready to replace you. It was these people that you trusted with your plans and now these plans are on my desk. I have all the evidence I need to know what you've both been planning."

"So what?" It was now Arkady who, tired of listening, began to speak back, his voice dripping with hate. "Yes, we were going to replace you. So what, Dimitry, what of it? You're old news. We're the future, not you. You died with Glasnost, an old relic of a bygone age. Look at where our country is heading thanks to the likes of you. Go fuck yourself. When the President gets here, I'll happily tell him what we were up to, He needs to know, he respects strength and action. We need to be strong as a country, not weak. Weak is your world, old man."

"Arkady!" It was the voice of Mikhail who cut through to him, his hand resting on his arm to emphasise the fact that he had already said to much.

Dimitry smiled, genuinely pleased with the outburst as he replied, "Thank you, Arkady, for that colourful confession. As much as it pains me to say it though, you're probably right, our country is weaker, and we need to strengthen it. Which is why we find ourselves here tonight."

He sat there amusedly watching the men's faces as they look confused. He was about to speak when he was interrupted.

Behind them the double doors of the President's office opened sharply. Upon instinct all three stood up. Arkady and Mikhail wore looks of genuine shock, but only Dimitry looked relaxed and calm as the Russian President stood in the doorway surveying the room. He stared hard at the men at the far end of the table, who looked nervously about, their eyes darting between the President and Dimitry. The President said nothing, assessing the two men with his gaze, the silence terrifying. With deliberate intent he smiled and walked over to Dimitry and clasped his hand, a brief gesture that showed the other two that whatever had been said, they were the ones out of favour. Dimitry picked up the folder and without saying a word handed it to the President, who nodded his thanks, turning once more look at the two men, a cold hard look that told them they were in serious trouble. Without another word he took the folder and walked back to his office as the guards closed the doors behind him.

After he had left the room Dimitry sat back down. The others went to sit, but were held in place as he shouted, "remain standing!"

Both men were about to ignore the order, when out of instinct they looked over to the guards by the doors. Instead of standing to attention, both guards had now unslung their polished AK-74 rifles and had them aimed directly at the two. With cold precision and fingers resting lightly on the triggers the guards walked slowly up to the two men, taking up perfect firing positions beside them. With a mere order Dimitry could have them executed on the spot.

Mikhail looked across at him, a look of congratulations on his face. "Dimitry. Okay. Well played, comrade, well played. You're older and wiser than the two of us. It was a fool's game to play and we should never have underestimated you. Now you have our attention, our loyalty, we won't do it again. We work for *you* now. Imagine the power that we could bring—"

"Silence!" he yelled. "Traitors do not speak here!"

"Traitors? For trying to replace you?" Arkady countered, confused. He was about to speak again when the guard next to him slammed the butt of his rifle into his stomach, winding him and causing him to double up in pain. He struggled to his feet, his breath coming in gasps as he tried to compose himself.

"Traitors, because that's what you are. You see, you both always looked at the small game, the short game, that was always your weakness. My guess is you you always want everything now, never willing to wait for it. I spoke to the President last month. I told him of your plot to overthrow him, I told him that I myself was part of it, that I had agreed to help, to be part of it, until things began to get bad for our country – the sanctions, the threats of the country tearing itself apart – but then I realised, we were helping to destroy it ourselves, weakened by our own small ambitions."

Both men looked on, confused.

"I informed the President of your plan, and that I had changed my mind and would try to prevent you from implementing it. I told him that realising I was now a threat to you both, you would work together to get rid of me, to paint me as the threat so you could get closer to him, so that you could *get* to him."

"That's a lie, there was no such plan!" Arkady shouted.

This time the guard decided to hit him in the face and Dimitry smiled in satisfaction as he heard his nose break and saw his blood run freely. Arkady staggered forward, his hands resting on the table as blood dripped onto the marble floor. As he stood there struggling, Dimitry continued, his voice rising. "You see, I do have a plan to get our country back to its former glory, to make it strong again, but that plan calls for sacrifice and it calls for strength. Strength that I see you both lack. You're both weak men, weak with greed and weak with ambition. Perhaps thirty years in the Siberian salt mines will strengthen you both into men more fitting to lead." He stood up, his face filled with anger as both men were led out of the room by the guards. Once the far doors were closed, the doors to the President's office were opened again and he entered the room.

"Mr President, thank you for letting me do that, I found it most... satisfying."

"I never tire of it, Dimitry; true power. And sometimes not even a word needs saying."

Pointing to the table he said, "My apologies but there was some blood spilt on the floor over there. It will need cleaning up."

"Ach," the President replied, "there's been blood spilt there before. One of the guards will take care of it."

He gestured for Dimitry to come into the office, to sit at the couch by the window overlooking Red Square.

Sitting comfortably, he watched the President walk over to his desk, ring a bell and a hidden door behind a bookcase then slid open. A pretty blonde woman, impeccably dressed in a pencil skirt and suit jacket entered.

"Yes, sir?"

Looking over to Dimitry he said, "Anything for you?"

He nodded. "Thank you, Mr President, I think a black tea with lemon will do."

The lady nodded in reply, and the President added, "And a green tea for me, thank you, Natasha."

Both men waited patiently as the young secretary reappeared moments later carrying two beautiful silver-and-glass tea jugs. She expertly poured both drinks into ornately decorated silver-handled glass cups and left the drinks in front of them, before leaving the room, the door sliding silently behind her. Dimitry looked at the cup as he picked it up, noting the decoration and design. Clearly the President liked to be surrounded by beautiful things, he mused, as he also remembered the woman's pert bottom as she walked away.

He was interrupted in his thoughts as the President, now seated on the couch opposite, began. "Firstly, my congratulations on your promotion, Director Smolov now, sole head of the FSB."

"Thank you, Mr President. I believe I will be kept very busy over these next few days."

The President countered, "Arkady and Mikhail. Are you certain there can be no fall out from this? The country cannot, will not, allow another grab for power. I need you to confirm to me, Dimitry, that this will all end tonight."

Stirring his tea, he looked up as he replied, "Mr President, as we speak, both traitors' homes and offices are being raided by my men. We will find out from the files we obtain just how deep this rot goes. Those we arrest will talk – as you know our people can be very persuasive in their methods. Both traitors' families will be arrested and sent east. We cannot have their sons and daughters free to flee to the west as some kind of beacon for them to be used against you as propaganda. Already

I have a list of trusted men and women ready to replace those who disappear and I'm confident that within a month we can rid ourselves of the rot that the west has spent decades growing here."

The President drank his tea, watching Dimitry, assessing him no doubt. Dimitry had to remind himself that this was not some easily led or deceived politician before him. This man had been like him, a trained agent and was more than capable of reading people's reactions. He had to be very careful when sat this close to him, he thought.

"Good. Then this report you've shown me, your idea?"

"It is," he lied, keeping himself composed. *Calm, Dimitry, keep calm...* still those calculating eyes watched him.

"And when did you write it?"

"I had the idea and the plan put together when I planted Acorn in 2012. I suppose you could say the two became linked. I sat down and thought of ways I could bring down the UK and its monarchy at the same time."

Smiling, the Russian President replied, "I like the thought of two kings of the same family becoming unseated by Russia and replaced by a government of our choosing."

Drinking his tea, Dimitry also smiled at the thought, as the President asked, "And this Acorn, is it bearing fruit? Would the agent be ready in time for this plan if we were to go ahead?"

"If you gave the go-ahead for the plan, then Acorn will be ready."

The President looked at his cup, swilling the tea inside as he asked thoughtfully, "Why, Dimitry? Explain to me why you think we should go ahead with this plan?"

Finishing his tea, Dimitry set the cup aside on the table and settled himself in the armchair.

"Mr President, I always vowed to be honest with you and that sometimes I would say things that you would not *like* to hear, but that you would *need* to hear."

Draining his tea in one go, the President placed the empty cup on the side as he settled himself in, his arms resting across his lap.

"I understand, Dimitry. Feel free to tell me, I need to know. I promise I won't warm up the firing squad just yet..."

Grimacing at the joke, he continued, "At the moment, Mr President, our country is economically, politically and militarily weak. Our ambassadors overseas are becoming the laughing stock of the world stage and our military hardware, once feared and respected, is now, along with the reputation of our forces, being eroded. Our economy is shrinking, and every day I see the value of the rouble fall further against foreign currencies. Our defence industry once boasted of supplying over a third of the world with their arms and ammunition, but now it's a shell of its former self, as our friends and allies overseas now turn to purchase the western equipment being advertised and performing well in Ukraine."

"But we ourselves have advanced weaponry, Dimitry, we just can't get at the finer items, like microchips and semi-conductors to be able to build them. If we could, then we'd build such weapons too," he countered.

"Mr President, I recommended, if you remember, that we held off the invasion of Ukraine until our own defence industry could replicate the complex electronics that western and Chinese equipment enjoy. Until that time, we were always going to be reliant on either one. As it is now, the west will no longer supply us and the east no doubt will begin to renegotiate harsher terms to us. Am I correct?"

The President nodded slowly in agreement as he replied, "Yes, that fucking crook Xi Ping has slowly been ratcheting up the pressure, demanding more supplies of gas and oil, whilst demanding we lower prices. He's recently even asked for military access to some of our naval yards to help secure a new deal on some more shipments of microchips. We need these items though, Dimitry – without them, we can't rebuild our forces."

"But, Mr President, this is exactly why I feel the time is right for this plan to be put into play. If we do nothing, we will slowly fade away and become a vassal of the Chinese or another western-backed politician will attempt to take you down. I think we have no choice *but* to go ahead with the plan. It will propel you and our country back to a position of strength, it will prove to our people that we can and will fight back, it will prove to our armed forces that they are good enough and their equipment is as powerful as we tell them. It will undermine NATO and bring down one of NATO's most powerful partners and it will provide us with a springboard into Europe. It will also allow you to tell the Chinese that they would be helping us to take down NATO, helping them in their own long-term goal to reclaim Taiwan. There would be no reason for them *not* to send us every available microchip and processor they have. We can rebuild our military, restore its faith in our equipment and soldiers and finally we can rid ourselves of the reliance on the industries of the east and the west. Imagine in ten years how our country will look if this plan works!"

Without realising it, the Russian President had allowed himself to be swept along in a tide of patriotic fever as he thought of the power and prestige they could regain if such a plan were to work. He smiled as he thought of the look on the Chinese President's face as he told him NATO was collapsing.

"And how much time would you need to prepare for such a plan?"

Without needing to think he quickly replied, "Two to three years."

"Why so long? That's not going to help us now, is it?"

"Mr President, nothing we do now will be able to help our country in the short term, we're in this for the long game and for that we'll need the time to prepare the logistics, not to mention prepare the groundwork for what's to come. Training our soldiers will take time as will preparing the ships and all of this must be done under a tightly squeezed veil of secrecy. Think of it this way – we were always going to be on borrowed time once the Chinese began to squeeze us, this way instead of going out with a whimper we will instead strike back with a bang!" He slammed his fist into the palm of his other hand.

The Russian President could see the fire and determination in his security director's eyes. There was ambition there, but to what purpose? he thought suspiciously.

"Okay, Dimitry, time to negotiate. I know how much you love our country and understand why you want this to happen, but what do you want? What would be in this for you? Would you use this against me, I wonder? Would you want all of this to happen only to usurp me in our moment of triumph? Or could you want this to fail, to be the architect of my downfall?"

Slowly shaking his head, Dimitry replied, "Mr President, I have forgone my own aspirations of power, my own ambition died in that room tonight when those two traitors were dragged away. I saw the empty Presidential chair at the head of the table and did not picture either you or myself sitting there. Instead, I saw another man."

Blinking in surprise at his candid honesty, the President replied in surprise, "Really? Then who did you see in the chair?"

"Mr President, you asked me what I wanted, why I have sacrificed my own ambition. It's simple. I want you to name my son as your successor, to be the President in fifteen years' time. You have no sons yourself and we both know your two daughters are too clean and innocent for the dirty tricks of power. With your endorsement and your help, my son will assume the leadership of our great country. If you agree to this, then I will guarantee you, promise you another fifteen years of my loyalty, with no risk to yourself or to your family. That is what I want, that is my price."

With a cold hard face, the President stood up and walked over to the folder, opening the pages and glancing at the contents. Dimitry said nothing. He had already said enough. Now it was up to the Russian leader.

"Dimitry, I can work with that agreement," he said, his face serious. He picked up the telephone, as Dimitry sat immobile, trying to look composed, but inside was a maelstrom of thoughts and emotions. *Keep calm Dimitry, keep it together now*, he kept thinking to himself. He waited with his heart in his mouth. Who would the President call? Would his security detail now come in to bundle him away, to disappear with the others? Had he played the last card too early or too late? He held his breath as the President finally talked into the receiver.

"Natasha, get me a direct line through to Beijing. Yes, that's correct, the Presidential Palace... Yes I want to speak to him now... I don't care about the time, get him on the phone now... Yes, I'll wait..."

The President looked back at Dimitry again as he said, "Okay, you help me set this up, get this Acorn of yours ready in time and we have a deal. Fifteen years, though, Dimitry, give me those fifteen years, agreed?"

Dimitry stood up, his heart pounding in relief as he looked him directly in the eyes, his voice full of pride. "Agreed, Mr President. We will be ready, my Operation Fools Mate will be ready."

20

All Going To Plan

Eagle-Four

"Sir, report's now incoming, all primary targets neutralised. All Kestrels are now proceeding to secondary objectives."

Colonel Bresavik punched the air, elated; all targets had been hit. He turned to his air Captain. "I want all our radar systems turned on now, tell all aircraft *we* are now providing eyes over the UK. Have all our air superiority fighters converge on us. I want maximum defences on us for the next thirty minutes. I don't care about their fuel states, they can run out of fuel if they have to."

He tuned his radio to the command net. "Sea Hawk, this is Crowsnest, Lightning, Lightning, Lightning. Out."

MV Leyberg

On board the MV *Leyberg*, the crews had completed their checks on all the missiles and were now down from the launch containers and safely shielded within the ship's superstructure. On the bridge, the crew had pulled the blast shields down across the windows to protect their eyes from the rocket flashes and were now monitoring the launch through a camera system; with everyone poised waiting for the launch signal. The Captain stood, finger hovering over the button to release, the safety now flicked open, his face sweating, more from the thought of what he was about to do, rather than from the heat of the day. All eyes were on the radio operator who was facing them all. His expression was blank, waiting patiently for their moment to come. Suddenly, with eyebrows raised, he looked at the Captain, his face confirming what he was about to say. "Sir! Lightning! Lightning! Lightning! WE HAVE LAUNCH AUTHORITY!"

"Good God!" muttered the Captain as he pressed the button to launch. Inside the bridge they all heard the thud followed by the shriek as the rocket motor ignited, as the first missile began to fire away, a noise that repeated every two seconds as the one hundred and sixty Kaliber missiles began to launch. A huge pall of smoke slowly rolled over the ship, covering it from view, flashes emanating from inside the cloud, as the missiles launched, then streaked out of the maelstrom, screaming to an altitude of two thousand feet before levelling off and heading for their targets.

On board the MV *Majestic* and *Trojan*, the scenes were repeated, as both ships were quickly smothered in clouds of thick smoke as their deadly cargo began to launch, streaking across the east coast of England to their designated targets.

After three hundred and twenty seconds the final missiles left the launchers, screaming into the evening sky and leaving the ships to slowly emerge from the smoke, the only sound now the deep throb of their engines. Cautiously the missile crews emerged onto the deck wearing respirators to protect them from the lingering smoke. Quickly, they climbed onto the launchers, checking that all the tubes were empty and confirming with the bridge over the radios before climbing down, the smoke making progress slower than before. With a flick of a switch the containers slowly closed, hiding their true nature, and once again the ships were all back to being one of many container vessels sailing the seas. The only telltale sign was the blackened scorched marks on the containers from the rockets' hot exhausts. The crews on all three ships had already practised for this, though, and as the ships all turned to their new headings, the paint crews were already climbing, ready to hide any evidence of what they had just unleashed.

Jackal-Five

Flying at forty thousand feet, Flight Lieutenant 'Jacko' Jackson was scanning his threat radars, checking for any aircraft in the vicinity that might be emitting any form of EW signatures. He'd already been given Zulu Zero-Zero-One's last-known position and was about a hundred miles north of it, ten miles off the northern coast of Scotland, looking to see what was there when his wingman's voice suddenly burst through on the radio.

"Five, this is Six. Look below us, heading southeast. What do you make of that?" Quickly peering down and to his right, he saw the distinct contrails of an object, flying fast and low and passing beneath them. The speed he estimated to be about Mach .08. He recognised its flight profile.

"It's a cruise missile. Why the hell is that out here?"

"Shit. Look right, there's more of them! What the hell?"

He looked right and his eyes widened in alarm. Even in the dim light he could see perhaps another forty or fifty coming in. Without thinking he sent out over the radio, "Blackdog Control, Blackdog Control, this is Jackal-Five, I have eyes on multiple cruise missiles inbound. I count approximately sixty at this time, I say again six-zero, course one-six-zero and altitude around three thousand feet. All inbound. Over."

"Roger Jackal flight, wait one..."

Jacko looked over to his wingman, already making the decision. "Merv, we're going to engage them, we'll never get a better time than now. Cannons only. Save the missiles. We've got the altitude and speed. Let's turn left to intercept new course one-six-zero; turn now. Now. Now."

Both Typhoons banked left at the same time, bringing themselves onto a course directly above and behind the first missile. With his wingman closely remaining behind him and to the right, Jacko began to descend from forty-thousand feet, activating his gun station and trying to keep his mind focused.

Blackdog came back over the radio, the voice of the controller more urgent this time. "Jackal-Five, Blackdog Control. New mission – intercept and destroy missiles as they bear. Keep us updated, we're scrambling fighters to assist. We believe missiles are on course to strike Lossiemouth, I say again they are inbound to Lossiemouth. Over."

"Blackdog, Jackal-Five, understood, engaging with cannons now. Out."

Jacko had never fired the Typhoon's Mauser twenty-seven millimetre cannon in anger before and realised the missile he was to engage would no doubt be on course to kill or injure people he knew. Shaking off any thought of failure, he settled himself into the task at hand. *Come on Jacko*, he thought, *you've got this, just like killing the target drones when practising, now you and the weapon are one...* He checked his airspeed, throttling right back, the engines almost at idle, not wishing to overshoot as the airspeed increased and the altitude began to fall away. Quickly he thought about the other missiles as he keyed his radio. "Merv, let's not waste time here, I want you to line up on the next missile, we'll take the bastards two at a time. Watch out for the inbounds, we don't want a mid-air collision with one of these."

"Roger, Five, I'm breaking right now. Good hunting, out."

Slowing his breathing, he watched the numbers counting down on his computer display in his helmet's visor; his altitude was now down to eight thousand feet, the white missile now visible flying low over the coast. Although the targeting computer had locked on, all it could do was give Jacko the range to target. In his heads-up display a simple dot was shown – the gunsight – showing Jacko where to aim. If any corrections or aim-offs were required, then that was down to Jacko alone to correct by adjusting the nose of the fighter. Basic, good old-fashioned dog fighting, except instead of taking avoiding action, the missile remained on course, low and dumb. He waited until he was close enough to be confirmed of a hit then sent over the radio, "Jackal-Five engaging," and pulled the trigger, feeling the aircraft shudder as the one thousand seven hundred rounds per minute cannon began firing. He watched the tracer rounds tear out, hitting the body of the missile as it continued to fly, but with its aerodynamics compromised it began to wobble in flight, as more rounds hit it in a shower of sparks. He was tempted to fire another burst when suddenly it exploded in a huge fireball, far bigger than he imagined and he had to quickly increase power and pull away for risk of flying through the debris. Banking up and to the right he reported excitedly, "Jackal-Five, splash one," as he heard his wingman begin his own engagement on another missile. He brought his aircraft round, quickly spotting another missile inbound and began to line up with it, ready to begin the engagement sequence again. His excitement and euphoria of the destruction of the first missile was short lived when he saw on radar just how many missiles were incoming. "Blackdog Control, this is Jackal-Five, we will *not* be able to stop all the inbounds, there's just too bloody many. Get whatever you can off the ground now. Over!"

He began his gun run on the second missile as Blackdog replied, "Roger, understood, Jackal-Five. Do what you can for now, out."

His face pinched in concentration, he watched the second missile explode as he gave another two-second burst, this time from further out, giving himself more of a safety margin from the explosion. As he banked up to search for other targets, he could already see two of the missiles were out his gun range, having made it through, and more were heading his way. Frustrated, he turned to line up on another missile, his thoughts darkening. *Come on, keep it together and let's stop what we can, buy them time.* Once again he began to dive onto the next target.

RAF Lossiemouth – Scotland

The controller stood in the control tower, a look of shock on her face as she heard the words blasting out of the radio telephone. "I repeat, we are tracking thirty-plus bandits inbound to you. Time to target is two minutes. Scramble everything you can, get aircraft in the air and get personnel into shelters and prepare for attack. Acknowledge. Over." She looked out of the windows as aircrews scrambled to get fighters fuelled, armed and ready to fly. Some planes were fuelled and not armed, some were armed and not fuelled, and she looked on apprehensively as she realised they would soon be out of time. Some pilots were already running out to the aircraft, getting themselves into the cockpits and pre-start checks completed ready to go, even though the aircraft were far from ready. One pilot in desperation was attempting to attach a fuel hose himself, such was his eagerness to get airborne. The controller looked at the growing chaos below her and knew she had to make a tough decision.

Looking to her two Flight Sergeants, she activated the base's attack alarm, the air-raid warning beginning to blare as she picked up the handset for the tannoy system to talk through the base.

"Attention all personnel, air-raid warning, air-raid warning, launch all aircraft *now*, regardless of states, get them off the ground. All non-essential personnel make their way to the shelters. This is not a drill, we are counting thirty bandits inbound, time to target is two minutes! NOW MOVE IT!"

She nodded to her two Flight Sergeants. "That includes you two. Get yourselves away to the shelters. I'll stay here to launch the aircraft, I'll follow along shortly."

"But, ma'am, you'll need help, we're not leaving you here. We'll all get the aircraft away and get to the shelters together. Come on, let's get it done."

Deciding not to waste time arguing further, she nodded, "Thankyou."

Realising the incoming danger, some of the aircraft that had been fuelled and armed were already taxiing to the runways, the pilots checking in with the controllers before preparing to take off. With a roar of engines four of the aircraft powered down the runway in close formation and lifted off into the sky, getting the vectors from her to join the others now attempting to shoot down the incoming missiles. Another four began to line up, these were fully fuelled but low on ammunition. She quickly gave them the course to fly to RAF Kinloss a few miles to the west, hoping they could get away to be rearmed. She watched them take off, engines screaming as they all became airborne.

Another three aircraft began to taxi to the runway, these low on fuel, but fully armed. "Tell Blackdog we'll need a tanker up here, I'll have birds in the air that are thirsty," she said to one of the Flight Sergeants. Nodding, he began to relay the message when suddenly they all heard an explosion at the far end of the airfield. They were out of time, she realised, had two minutes really passed already? Without waiting for permission from the tower she heard the three aircraft's engines spool up, the pilots deciding to get airborne rather than stay as sitting ducks on the ground.

Looking around her, she realised with horror that most of the aircrews had ignored the order to seek cover and were all working hard to get the remaining aircraft in the air. Four Typhoons with pilots already inside the cockpits were sat by the bowsers waiting for fuel, the ground crews swarming over them, trying to get the work completed. A missile struck one of the hangars, exploding deep inside and sending shrapnel high into the air over the airfield. Another missile struck, then another, and she turned to watch the flight of three aircraft still accelerating away. A missile struck the runway behind them, obscuring them from her view. *Come on, get up*, she thought, *get up, get airborne*! She watched fearlessly, ignoring the danger as another missile slammed alongside the tower, the windows imploding from the blast and covering everyone inside in glass as she was thrown to the floor.

Outside, another explosion, louder than before, shook the building as one of the waiting Typhoons took a direct hit, its own missiles and fuel adding to the explosion as the ground crews, fuel bowsers and three other aircraft exploded into a huge fireball, vaporising the Typhoon and incinerating anyone within a two hundred metre radius. Her ears ringing, she tried to stand, feeling something heavy on her legs preventing her from getting up. She looked down to see the body of one of the Flight Sergeants strewn across her legs, his eyes lifelessly staring back at her, multiple cuts across his face and body and his uniform shredded from lacerations. Her arms ached and she struggled to breathe. Feeling a tugging on her arms, she looked up and with blurred vision saw the figure of the other Flight Sergeant now pulling at her, trying to drag her along the floor to the stairs. Was he shouting? she thought. She could see his lips moving but could hear nothing with the ringing in her ears. She opened her mouth to say something, when another explosion went off, closer this time. She could feel the tremor through the floor as the roof came in and she felt the ground beneath her give way as the tower began to collapse around her. *Tell my parents I wasn't scared.* Her last conscious thought as she closed her eyes and descended into the darkness.

The last three Typhoons to get airborne quickly climbed to altitude to the relief of the pilots, but relief quickly turned to rage as they banked overhead, watching their home and colleagues become overwhelmed by the attack on their base. All three had seen the destruction and they could only watch helplessly as the missiles streaked in one after the other, cratering the runways and destroying the base's infrastructure. After the attack, not one building had been left standing and all the hangars were destroyed. At the far end of the field one of the Typhoons had been caught in the open, attempting to taxi. It was rolling slowly down the taxiway, burning, the ignited jet fuel pouring out along the runway leaving a fire trail in its wake. Its cockpit canopy was still raised, the pilot sat lifelessly at the controls. They watched as the plane rolled onto the grass, before one of the onboard missiles detonated, collapsing the landing gear and leaving the plane and pilot to burn in the inferno. After two minutes of circling overhead the Flight leader decided he'd seen enough.

"Okay, flight let's try for Kinloss, we need fuel and a place to call home."

"We can't just leave them, they need help" the voice of one of the younger pilots chimed back.

"And just what the hell are you going to do?" he shot back angrily. "The runways are cratered, and the base is gone. Those poor sods down there don't need your pity. They died helping to get us airborne, now let's make it mean something. Now, if you don't want to be walking home, I suggest we go find some motion lotion."

Already he'd seen his fuel warning light come on, indicating that he had no more than forty minutes of flight time remaining. Taking one last look at the base he said quietly, "Come on, let's head for Kinloss."

The three aircraft began to turn towards Kinloss, as the other four aircraft already ahead of them and flying over the base reported back, "Jackal One-Two this is Jackal Eight. Forget Kinloss – it's also gone. Looks like they took some missiles too."

Cursing softly the flight leader reported back,

"Blackdog this is Jackal One-Two, Lossiemouth and Kinloss are now out of action, runways are cratered, and towers are gone. I have seven aircraft in my flight, three are bingo fuel, and four are Winchester. I've got about thirty minutes of flight time, what do you want us to do? Over"

"Roger, Jackal One-Two, standby..."

ASACS - RAF Boulmer - Northumberland

The controller, callsign 'Blackdog', was looking at the map on the display, a growing number of red crosses being displayed on the locations in the north of England and Scotland. He turned to his team. "Right, so we've now lost Lossiemouth and Kinloss, along with most of our northern radar stations. I'd say someone wants us out of the north completely. Try to get us some eyes in the sky from RAF Waddington will you. The sooner we get eyes on, the sooner we can get a plan together. Also, try to get a tanker into the air, make sure it has an escort. I want Jackal flight to be refuelled as best we can. Now I'd better check in with command on this." He picked up the phone to talk directly to the WOC, when suddenly the base's attack alarm sounded. Looking up, confused, he saw one of the Corporals look up, phone in hand, shouting over the noise of the alarm.

"SIR! ENEMY MISSILES REPORTED INBOUND OUR LOCATION!"

"What?" he just managed to exclaim as outside he could already hear the shriek of the first missile followed by the thud of the explosion, followed quickly by another, then another, the explosions sending shockwaves echoing through the bunker, dust and plasterboard falling in great chunks over the computers and desks.

"TAKE COVER!" he managed to shout, as with a loud crash a missile exploded directly overhead, causing a huge crack to appear in the concrete ceiling. He dived under one of the desks, falling beside one of the Corporals, both crouching together as the operations room descended into chaos and everyone dived to take cover. They could hear the thuds of the impacts outside, the shockwaves reverberating through the bunker, which thankfully was situated two floors below ground. He could only imagine the havoc being wreaked onto the base above as they remained where they were, in relative safety. Within minutes, the attack was over, but everyone remained where they were, waiting to hear the sirens announcing the 'all clear' for the base.

After another two minutes of waiting, and hearing no alarm, the controllers finally grew impatient, picking themselves up off the floor, dusting themselves down and clearing away the mess across their stations. All the computer screens were off and Blackdog looked over to the Flight Sergeant who shook his head dejectedly.

"Power's off, sir, looks like the backup generators are offline as well."

He crawled over to one of the phone lines, picking it up and hearing the line was cut before slamming it back down in frustration.

"Dammit, Flight, we need power! Go topside and get the backup online immediately."

He waited as the Sergeant took two airmen with him and ran back upstairs to the surface, hoping to fix the generator. After a few minutes they came back down, the shock clear to read on their faces as the Sergeant stood covered in dust with blood all down the front of his blue uniform.

"What is it?" he demanded, his eyes drawn to the blood, already fearing the worst.

All three looked at each other in disbelief as finally the Sergeant reported, "Sir... The base, it's... It's gone, destroyed!"

Tidworth Garrison Guard Room

Corporal Jennings, with his feet up on the guard desk, was watching the DVD playing on the telly, with the six members of his guard force all lolling around in their chairs, laughing and talking animatedly at the comedian onscreen. He smirked at the jokes, finding the comedian no longer as funny as when he'd first watched the same DVD five years ago. But with the TV stations now all offline, and no internet, it was all they could do to while away the time before they were called to stand their two-hour shift on the gate.

He looked out again at the camp gates, seeing the other four members of his guard detail talking together next to the barriers. He was tempted to shout out of the window, to tell them to get back to their own posts, but then thought better of it. Besides, he'd reasoned to himself, it's not like anyone's around to see. There were only ever a small number of visitors to the camp over the stand-down period. Most of those were contractors to help maintain the many buildings, whilst others were soldiers still living in the accommodation blocks with nowhere to go, either waiting to be sent back out to their units overseas or waiting to do their own stint of guard duties. Nobody liked to be left behind on 'rear party', the name given to the group chosen to stay and guard the camp whilst the main unit was away. But he hadn't grumbled – from what he heard of his mates in Estonia, he was the lucky one. The tales of half-finished camps and no hot water hadn't exactly been the posting they had been promised before deploying. Still, he missed his mates and looked around disappointedly at the bunch of new recruits all laughing again at the old jokes.

"Oi! Jones!" he barked out, the Trooper looking over immediately.

"Yes, Corporal?"

"What comes after the letter S in the alphabet?"

The young Trooper frowned before replying, confused, "T, Corporal?"

Smiling, Jennings leaned over, handing him his empty mug, adding, "Why thank you, don't mind if I do. Milk, two sugars."

The Trooper's eyes darted to the mug, then to the Corporal before he finally realised the trick that had been played on him. Looking glum, he stood up, sighing in resignation.

"Okay, Corporal."

Jennings watched on, smiling as the Trooper disappeared into the kitchen area, thinking to himself, *There's one born every minute.*

He looked back over at the TV, smiling at another joke when suddenly he heard what sounded like a low-flying jet aircraft screech overhead. He looked out of the window, seeing the gate guards were all looking upwards and pointing, as another jet seemed to shoot across the sky. In the distance he heard the thud and boom of something hitting the ground.

He sat forwards, looking up at the clock, noting the time.

Bit late to be conducting live firing, he thought, as yet another low-flying jet flew over the guardroom. He could hear shouting outside and quickly he jumped up, startling the other soldiers into action. They jumped out of their chairs and looked at him for direction.

The explosions sounded closer this time, as he pointed at them, shouting,

"Get your fucking helmets and body armour on! Come on! Stand to! Stand to!"

Dashing outside, he was met by one of the guards sprinting towards him from the gate, the look of disbelief clear to see on the soldier's face as he pointed skywards.

"Corporal, we've got fucking missiles flying overhead, they look like Tomahawks!"

344

Looking upwards, he watched open-mouthed as another screamed in low over-head, then another, then two more. It was as if suddenly the sky was full of them. He ran towards the sentry box, quickly climbing up onto its window ledge to get a better viewpoint, seeing towards the far end of the camp the smoke already rising from the direction of the vehicle hangars and tank parks. More missiles roared over-head, this time striking closer, now smashing into the accommodation blocks, the ground trembling beneath their feet as shockwaves reverberated towards them. A large piece of one of the building's roofs came raining down, landing just metres from them, shaking them all from their stupor. He looked down at them, shouting, already knowing they were too late.

"FUCK! SOUND THE ATTACK ALARM!"

The soldiers looked back at him in shock, not knowing what to do, so he jumped down and pushed past them towards, his hand smashing into the red attack button. Within seconds the alarms began to sound all over the camp, echoing off into the distance as more missiles came screaming in. Jennings watched as one came lower than the rest towards them, pulling up rapidly into a vertical climb directly over the guardroom, to around a thousand feet before its rocket motor cut out and it seemed to slow down and hang in mid-air above them. He looked up at it, just having the time to see it tip over as gravity now took hold and finally the realisation hit him as to what the missile was targeting.

He looked back over to the guardroom, seeing through the windows the soldiers still inside getting their equipment on as he heard the rocket's motor firing again – the missile was accelerating back down towards them, executing the perfect top-down attack.

"GUYS! GET OUT! GET OUT OF THERE!" he shouted, about to run towards them, as two of the other soldiers, already sensing the incoming danger, grabbed him and threw him and themselves to the ground.

He closed his eyes and covered his head with his hands, hearing the deadly shriek as the missile screamed earthwards, coming closer. He knew he was powerless to stop it, and a feeling of helpless rage enveloped him, as with an earth-shattering explosion the missile exploded less than fifty metres from him...

Eagle-Four

Onboard Eagle-Four, Colonel Bresavik smiled as he watched the air picture now begin to take shape – the British fighters were split into three groups off to the north of the UK, with no clear plan, flying aimlessly around trying to chase their own tails. The missile attacks had achieved a good rate of success. Ninety per cent of the missiles had hit their targets, more than enough to achieve their objective, he thought. Now, with the British blind and most of their bases destroyed, he could begin the next phase of the mission.

"Air Captain, how long until Eagle-Two has secured its objective?"

"Comrade Colonel, Eagle-Two is now five minutes to objective. They should be landing shortly."

Good, he thought, *it was all going too well*, he mused.

Bournemouth Airport

In the control tower Steve shook the desktop fan again. "Piece of shit! Come on, work!" *This really is turning into a crappy shift*, he thought, as for the tenth time in as many hours the fan refused to work, simply stuttering to a halt. *Why do they always buy the cheapest piece of crap?* he thought angrily. He looked around for someone to moan to, but he was alone in the control tower. Usually there would be two controllers working the tower, but Andy had called in sick, leaving just him alone to manage the shift. He walked over to the flights board, checking when the next incoming flight had been scheduled for. It looked to be 20:30, one of the cheap regional carriers flying in from Spain. At least he'd have something to look at, he thought, as he picked up the telephone to talk to the ground controller stationed one floor below.

"Hello, Ground Controller," she answered.

"It's me again, I'm bored, what's happening in your neck of the woods?"

"Steve, you shouldn't be calling me, I'm busy." Her voice dripped with sarcasm. "Look, it's the same as before. It's all quiet here, NATS is off the air and currently the RAF are contacting everyone. So far, all the planes I can see on our screens are being diverted to Bristol, Heathrow and Gatwick. Don't ask me why, but that's all I know. I don't think our 20:30 from Palma will be coming in either. From what I'm hearing, the UK airspace is being closed to all new arrivals."

"Shit, that must be big. What do you think it is? Terrorism? Hijacking?"

"Look, I don't know; all I know is that Swanwick are not picking up any of the phones or answering the radios. Perhaps it's all linked to this cyberattack earlier?"

He was about to answer when, with a burst of static, the radio loudspeaker next to him squawked to life.

"Attention, Bournemouth tower. Attention, Bournemouth tower, this is Canadian cargo one-eight-two, we are declaring an emergency and requesting permission to land, we have an onboard fire and require permission to land immediately. Over."

Keeping the phone in one hand he reached over to the headset. "Roger, Canadian cargo one-eight-two, you're declaring an emergency. Can I ask for fuel state and souls on board? Over."

"Fuel state is two-two thousand pounds and number of souls on board are four. Over."

"Did you hear all that?" he said into the receiver to the ground controller.

"Got it. I'll get the fire trucks stood by and try to pass it up the chain. We've nothing scheduled for another twenty minutes, so runways will be clear."

"Thanks," he replied as he threw down the receiver. At least it was something to do, he thought, a break from the monotony. He picked up the radio and walked over to the localised radar screen, his voice remaining calm. "Canadian cargo one-eight-two, this is Bournemouth tower, runways will be clear and fire crews standing by. Do you need a vector to the airport? Over."

"No, we are already ten miles out and coming in on your runway eight, we just need you to turn the lights on and confirm it's clear. Over."

How did you manage to get there so quickly? he thought. *That's cheeky. Normally you wait to be told which runway to approach. Perhaps another controller has vectored them in.* He was about to ring downstairs when the radio again burst to life. "Bournemouth tower, this is Canadian cargo one-eight-two, please, we must hurry. The fire is beginning to spread, we need to get down now!"

Hearing the urgency in the pilot's voice he was pushed into action. "Canadian cargo one-eight-two, clear to land on any runway, I'm turning on the lights now." He raced over to the control panel flicking on the three banks of switches and watching the powerful runway lights flicker on in the distance. He could just make out the aircraft in the distance turning on its landing lights, now about eight miles away. He picked up a set of binoculars to try to see the aircraft but with the light being poor and the distance too great he decided to wait. After a minute he picked up the aircraft through the binoculars, expecting to see smoke pouring from it or some signs of fire, but he couldn't see much. What he could see, though, was that the plane was big, very big. He'd seen 747s land at Bournemouth before and even from this distance he could see that this plane was larger than that. Doubt began to creep into him as he picked up the phone to speak to ground control. "Okay, I've got him, visual, about seven miles out, coming in on runway eight. I think we should put the fire equipment out there. I can't see any signs of fire yet. Something's not right. The plane is big, I mean *really big*. It looks military."

"Well, military or not, Steve, if they've a fire onboard, we need to let them land," she said, matter of factly.

"Yep, of course, I'll let you know when they're on the ground." Hanging up, he went back and took another look through the binoculars. This time it was five miles out, landing gear down and flaps lowered. *What a monster*, he thought. He watched as the fire engines, lights flashing, took up their positions alongside the runway and noticed their movements had attracted the attention of passing motorists, some of whom had stopped to park up and watch the action unfolding. There were always rubberneckers, he thought moodily. At the far end of the field, he saw the collection of plane spotters, binoculars and radios in hand, no doubt listening in and realising an emergency had been called. Watching the windsock, he went over to the radio again. "Canadian cargo one-eight-two, wind is one-eight-zero and speed one-five, cleared to land. Over."

He waited to hear the acknowledgement, but nothing came. He was about to resend the information when he realised the plane was no more than twenty seconds from touchdown and he didn't want to add to the pilot's already busy workload. He watched in shocked silence as the huge plane floated gracefully over the perimeter fence, its fuselage no more than fifteen metres above the road as its huge bulk settled onto the runway, no more than twenty-five metres from its edge, the large banks of tyres smoking as they made contact with the asphalt. The pilot had called the move perfectly, he thought admiringly, as he heard the huge engines begin to roar as the pilot requested full reverse power and applied the brakes. Steve looked on, impressed at how quickly a plane of that size could decelerate as it slowed halfway down the runway, far earlier than he had expected. He watched as the plane continued to taxi off the runway and onto the apron, heading for the tower, its huge wingspan dwarfing the planes around it. The plane was moving faster than usual and Steve wondered if perhaps the fire had damaged the brakes. Two fire engines followed at the same high speed behind the plane, their foam nozzles moving, ready to douse any sign of fire.

"Canadian cargo one-eight-two, can you please hold there, our fire crews would like to check for signs of fire before you taxi in. Over."

Again, no answer. *What is it with these guys?* he thought. *One minute they're screaming about a fire, the next they're happy to roll into the taxiway.*

The radio chirped to life, an annoyed voice sounding, "Control, this is Fire Chief, what's going on? Are we checking for fire or not?"

"Roger, Fire Chief. I'm just trying to raise the pilots now, plan for brake failure with the speed they're going. Continue as instructed and remain behind. Over."

The plane continued past the tower and finally it came to an abrupt halt outside the passenger terminal taxiway. Where it was now parked, it blocked all access to and from the terminal buildings for any other aircraft.

"No, not there!" Steve said to himself, annoyed. "Canadian cargo one-eight-two, you cannot park there, sir, you're blocking the taxiway. Please continue forward to the charlie-seven ramp. Over."

He stood gobsmacked as instead of the plane moving, he now heard the four huge engines begin to whine down and shut off. The huge ramp behind began to slowly open as did the side door and in absolute disbelief he saw armed men dressed in military gear begin to run down the ramp and outside of the aircraft, in groups of four.

What the hell was going on here? he thought, as he watched them begin to yank open doors to the passenger terminal and enter. Suddenly two large, tracked vehicles raced out and began to speed along the runway, setting up menacing positions at each end of it. Soldiers began to pour out into the taxiway and ran up to the fire engines. He heard shots being fired and the doors to the fire trucks were yanked open, the crews being bundled out and thrown to the ground spreadeagled.

He quickly picked the phone up, panicking. "Listen, something's wrong! The plane, it's full of soldiers, they're driving along the runway and shooting."

"Steve? What? What's going on out there? You're not making any sense."

Suddenly he heard a loud bang and screams and muffled shouts from the phone, and then the line went dead. *God, they're already inside the building*! He tried to gather his thoughts, his fears consuming him. He picked his phone up and began to dial 999, but the dial tone indicated that the call had not connected. Quickly he tried again and again. "COME ON!" he shouted, "answer the fucking phone!" He could hear gunshots and screams coming from the terminal buildings. *What is going on in there*? Suddenly he could hear the shouts getting louder. They were coming up the stairs. Dropping the phone in shock, he ran over to the control-tower door, it was armoured to prevent unauthorised access, but it was never locked, and with the heat of the day and the fan not working he had foolishly left it jammed open. He charged across to it, hearing the heavy footsteps on the metal stairs clanging up to the door. He could hear shouts in an unknown language. *Who are these people*? he thought, as he grabbed the door to close it.

He'd almost made it, when suddenly, like an apparition, a soldier appeared. A menacing-looking man, with a face all blackened with camouflage cream and dressed in military gear, feet planted firmly and the barrel of his rifle pointing straight at him. Not wanting to be a hero, Steve put his hands up and slowly backed away. The soldier roughly grabbed him and led him back into the centre of the room, indicating one of the console seats, directing him to sit. Doing meekly as he was told, he watched as more soldiers now came in. Risking a look outside he witnessed more men and vehicles coming off the aircraft and being deployed around the airfield, setting up some kind of perimeter. He heard shots at the far end of the field, and saw the plane spotters were being forcibly moved on. The road at the side of the airport was now closed. A sinister-looking armoured vehicle sat astride it, the turret a warning for people to stay away. Two soldiers stood over him, both shouting at him, their voices rising. Not understanding the language, he stared blankly at the soldiers as they became more and more animated until eventually, he said, "Look, I'm sorry, I don't understand you. I don't understand you! Who are you? What do you want? What are you doing here?"

One of the soldiers slapped him across the face and spat at him before walking off. The other laughed coldly at him, as Steve began to wish that things could go back to being boring again...

Eagle-Four

Onboard Eagle-Four, Colonel Bresavik joyfully slapped his air Captain on the back as he heard the words transmit over the radio: "Crowsnest, this is Eagle-Two, the Eagle has landed and we now have the nest. No casualties and we are in complete control. Over."

Smiling, he looked to one of the controllers furthest away. "Send to all aircraft, begin recovery now, nest is ready and waiting." Then turning to the air Captain he said, "Okay, Captain, let's send the final code, now finally it's time for rain."

He sat back with satisfaction. Taking Bournemouth Airport had been a major part of the plan. Now at least they had an airport with which to base themselves and refuel their fighters and planes. Within a matter of hours Bournemouth would become their airbase, fit for operations, and integral to them in the future. Now, with the RAF out of the skies, the next part of the mission could begin.

21

Here Comes The Rain

Mike watched the crews outside, feeling a slight chill as the wind blew through the hangar. All the doors were open and all ten of the ATDU tanks and the CRARRV stood outside with turrets facing forward and crews running between the vehicles and the cages, grabbing last-minute items and checking the tanks' systems were working. Thankfully the ATDU had the armouries located at the back of the hangar, so all the vehicles had their mounted weapons fitted and ready to go. However, with no ammunition available to fire they would be of little use. The personal weapons had proved to be more of a problem. Usually soldiers would each have a weapon assigned to them when back at their home camp, but Bovington, being a training regiment, meant there were only thirty-eight of the short-barrelled L22 carbines, twenty of the SA80 assault rifles and only ten Glock 17 pistols to be shared amongst all the assembled officers and soldiers.

The Colonel had done well though – with the GSM and the rest of his team corralling anyone in camp still around, they had managed to assemble one hundred and twenty soldiers of various ranks, cap badges and skills and immediately sent them off to get the vehicles ready. Not including the ATDU gun tanks, they had a further four Challenger 3 gun tanks at Lulworth, six Challenger 2 Driver Training Tanks, (DTTs), ten Warrior armoured fighting vehicles, able to carry six infantry soldiers in each, and eight armoured engineer vehicles. In essence Mike had joked that the Colonel had a mini battlegroup of sorts. The real problem now, though, was the lack of ammunition for any of the vehicles, and only a meagre amount for the personal weapons. In total they had just four hundred rounds of 5.56 millimetre for the carbines and rifles and fifty rounds of nine millimetre for the pistols. Anyone lucky enough to get their hands on a pistol had only four rounds each and anyone with a carbine or rifle had to make do with just one magazine containing eight rounds. All any of them could do for the time being was withdraw.

Twenty of the soldiers had since been tasked to dash away to the married quarters, as the families living in the military homes still needed to be evacuated. Mike had seen them from a distance, rushing out of their houses carrying hastily packed bags as they were told to leave immediately. Some were lucky enough to have family in the nearby area, others not so, and with no idea where to go next, they jumped into their cars ready for a journey with no destination. Still, it was better than staying here, Mike had thought as he'd watched them go. If things went bad, then staying put could be a nasty place to be. He watched two of the soldiers carrying fill guns, jumping from tank to tank, filling the radios with a secret code that would allow them to talk securely. That at least was one blessing – when the helicopter had landed and Major T-P had jumped out, it had also been carrying two signallers fresh from headquarters, who went to work immediately on all the armoured vehicles' radios. At least they would all have working comms, he thought.

He watched as a Land Rover raced into the compound, its brakes squealing as it came to an abrupt stop beside him. He watched Chris get out, struggling with his arms full of maps and head inside the hangar, his face strained and showing the pressure he was under. Mike decided to wisely keep quiet as he followed his friend in.

Putting the maps atop one of the large yellow concrete bollards, Chris turned to face his friend. His face was pinched in thought.

"Mate, thanks for helping me out, I appreciate this. I know it's not what you came here for."

Mike looked seriously at his friend. "Are you kidding me? Right now, you need all the help you can get."

Chris had stayed behind with the command group as the Colonel had formulated his plan. Mike, however, knowing that he would not be going with them – he was, after all, a civilian – had instead volunteered to go to the ATDU to help the crews get their vehicles ready.

Chris looked behind Mike to the crews working and he asked, "So all set? You think we'll be ready to go shortly?"

Looking at his watch, conscious of the time constraints, Mike replied, "Yeah, you should be good to go. I've got the radios being filled now, then the final thing will be to get the tanks over to the fuel point, top up with fuel and then you're off. Who did they send over to Lulworth?"

"Major Noakes, the training squadron OC, with fifteen soldiers. At least they've got access to the tank ammo over there. If they do manage to get the four tanks out of there, we'll all try to link up north of Dorchester."

"North of Dorchester? So that's where you're all going to be heading then?"

They were distracted by one of the soldiers, a Lance Corporal, walking over with two large mugs of tea. Mike could hear his London accent as he said, "Here you go, sirs,, two cups of Rosie Lee."

Chris looked at the man, smiling. "Baz, thanks mate, always a welcome distraction. Do me a favour, get me all the vehicle commanders over here in five, will you."

"Sure thing, boss," he replied as he handed the second cup to Mike.

Nodding in thanks he took the cup, sipping immediately, the hot sweet tea a welcome distraction to the aches and pains he felt in his arms and legs. The cuts and scratches were already beginning to heal and the blood had mostly been wiped away. Even so, he still looked like he'd been in a fight with a Tasmanian devil. Mike could only hope the other guy was feeling as bad or hopefully worse. His mood began to darken as he thought of the dead gate guard and he quickly distracted himself by looking down at the mapping. He asked, "So you were saying, Dorchester?"

Chris slurped his tea, wincing as the heat burned his tongue, and he replied, "Yeah, there's some plan in play regarding Dorchester. Apparently, we're to rendezvous there to get an ammo resupply and then go on the defensive. Look, I'll be honest, mate, it's all pretty vague. I don't even have enough maps for all our commanders. The Colonel's hoping to get everyone out together, but we both know it's going to be a fucking 'Ging Gang Goolie', and I've got three pistols and four carbines amongst my unit. I think the official term for all of this is a grade-A clusterfuck."

Seeing his friend's mood darken, Mike quickly changed tact, his voice mischievous as he leant forward, offering his arms out for a cuddle. "Aw, poppet, remember it's warfare not welfare. Want to hug it out? Because it sounds to me like someone's whinging and needs to get it off his big hairy chest!"

Looking up sharply to respond, Chris saw the playful look in Mike's eyes. Realising why he had mocked him he shook his head and laughed. "Okay wanker, you win, I *was* whinging then, I'll give you that. I'm not going to lie though, Mike. I'm glad I've got you here with us. One of the few people who I still lovingly let kick me up the arse occasionally."

"Yeah, but Chris," he quickly countered, his face serious, "you know I'm not going with you, don't you?"

"Oh," Chris's face suddenly showed surprise, "I thought that after everything you did earlier and all the effort to help me that you were in this for the long haul? We could use your help, you know. In case you haven't realised we're lacking manpower, more importantly lacking commanders, and I need all the help I can get. I'm asking for your help mate; I *really* need your help."

Mike could see the desperation in Chris's eyes, the feelings of past loyalties and his friendship tugging at him. But then the thoughts of Kate and her family came into focus. He promised her he'd always be there for her; he'd had his time in the military, he'd been a soldier once, but now he was a husband. His commitments had changed. He wasn't going to leave her and her family alone with what was coming. His loyalties lay with his family now. He swallowed hard, putting his feelings aside.

"Chris, come on. Be realistic. I'm a civilian. I'm not even legally allowed to carry a gun let alone ride in one of those tanks. What the hell can I do? I'm not in the army anymore, plus I've got my own things to look out for. I intend to see you all away, quick kiss on the cheek and loving wave and then I'm heading home, mate. To *my* home – that needs protecting as much as anything else. What will Kate think if she comes home to find the house abandoned? I'm sorry, mate, but I'm not chancing that. I've already done my time in uniform and now it's time for someone else to do theirs. I've got my family to think of and that's who I'm thinking about now."

Seeing the disappointment on his friend's face hit Mike like a hammer in the gut. He knew he'd have to explain this at some point and had been planning to quietly slip away once the tanks had left to refuel, but seeing his friend expecting him to be with him all the way, he knew he had to say something now.

His friend looked up, his face a mixture of feelings, not saying anything for a few moments. Then, slowly nodding he began to reply, "Okay, mate, okay, I get it, I get it. But just think on this and I'll leave it for you to mull over. You've seen what we're working with here, you've seen how green some of these guys are. In about an hour the world as we know it will change, and you'll go home. But to what? This could be your chance to help us, to help stop what's coming. I get the fact you say it's not your fight, but it *is* your fight. Your home and your family are living in the combat area. Do you think the enemy are going to leave you alone, Mike? Do you think they're going to leave you sitting in that lovely house of yours driving your fancy cars while they fight us?"

"Chris..." Mike began to say, as ignoring him, his friend continued, raising his hand to silence him, his face growing red in anger.

"No, let me fucking finish. You've said your piece, now hear mine."

Mike took a deep breath, knowing better than to try to reason with his friend when his blood was up.

"Okay, so what if we do lose, what then? Do you really want to live in that kind of country? The same tin-pot dictator-led shitholes that we spent most of our youth fighting in? I'm not trying to beat the patriotic drum here, mate, but if this war is coming tonight, then there's no such thing as our war and your war. You're either someone who helped to stop it or someone who helped to make it happen. You need to pick a fucking side, mate, because from where I'm standing, you're one of the pricks now helping to make this happen."

Mike decided it was best not to argue as he watched Chris throw the tea away angrily and pick up the maps, walking away to the hangar, the anger clear in his voice as it echoed off the hangar walls.

"ALL COMMANDERS IN TO ME NOW! DON'T MAKE ME FUCKING TELL YOU AGAIN!"

Mike looked about him: everyone was busy and for the first time all day he suddenly felt redundant, a spare wheel. Not wanting to part ways with his friend in a foul mood, he stepped outside to finish his tea. *I'll wait for him to finish the briefing and make amends*, he thought. He stood there, enjoying the cool summer breeze and watching the first of the stars appear in the evening sky as overhead he heard the roar of an aircraft. It sounded low, large and very close. *Strange*, he thought, *we're nowhere near any flight paths, what the hell could that be?* Craning his neck, he looked up, seeing nothing but clear evening sky and the tops of trees. He realised that he'd have to get a higher vantage point. Climbing onto one of the tanks, he stepped up onto the turret roof and saw the dark-grey shape of an aircraft coming in from the north. It looked like it was preparing to land with both its landing gear and flaps fully down. *What the hell?* he thought. *Where the hell is this guy going?* The plane was about a mile to their north, overflying the glider club. Mike remembered that he'd been there in the past, having been given a voucher as a present to fly in one of the gliders. Still confused, he watched on, open-mouthed, as the first parachute began to deploy out of the back.

Eagle-One

Onboard, Golgolvin was watching the Dorset countryside flash beneath him at three hundred feet, the excitement and adrenaline now building. He closed his eyes and felt the fresh air whip around him as the heavy ramp was opened and lowered into position. His eyes were focused on the red and green lights above the cargo door. He knew they were only minutes away now. He saw the red light blink on and heard the loadmasters screaming through the plane, "RED ON, CLEAR THE SLEDS!" Out of habit, he and his men shouted the order back, acknowledging that they had heard and to ensure the message was passed up the plane. Stepping closer to the fuselage, he looked up to see all three hundred of his men do the same, ensuring they were nowhere near the huge sleds and giving them plenty of clearance for what was about to happen.

Already the sleds were moving rearwards closer to the ramp and he thought at first, that they were going to deploy too early, his excitement building as he found himself staring at the green light, waiting for it to illuminate. *This is it,* he thought, *no stopping us now.* The green light flashed on and almost immediately he saw the first of the sleds' parachutes deploy, the fabric fluttering in the turbulent air as it whipped out, the cable uncoiling quickly. It became taut and suddenly the sled with its fourteen tonnes of cargo was ripped out, sliding smoothly along the ramp, the armoured vehicle disappearing quickly. The speed of its deployment made him flinch and as the second vehicle came shooting backwards, he found himself involuntarily squeezing further against the fuselage, a human instinct that he tried to fight. Suddenly the third vehicle was sliding past, the last of the Sprut -SD tanks, then the sled carrying the two Kamaz Typhoons whipped past him. *Damn, that was fast*, he thought, as the final sled disappeared into the evening sky.

He heard the engines powering up and felt the plane bank over to the left, as he made his way to the centre of the aircraft, clipping his parachute harness to the guideline above him. The loadmasters were quickly sorting the cables and harnesses left behind and were clearing the jump area for the men. He looked back at the first hundred men lined up behind him, faces focused and intent, etched with concentration. Some of the more senior men smiled at him, giving the thumbs up sign and showing their lack of fear. So far so good, he thought. The loadmaster came up to him, quickly running his trained eye over his parachute and gear. Checking that he was securely fastened to the jump line and happy with the rig, he gave him a thumbs up and shouted over the maelstrom of wind, "Good luck, Colonel and give them hell!"

Nodding and grimacing, he turned to face the ramp, his eyes focused on the lights. Feeling the plane turn again he knew they were heading back for the drop zone. He heard the loadmasters behind quickly checking the men, and double-checking the rigs. No one wanted to fail the mission early from falling out of a plane. The loadmaster stood beside him with his arm across his chest, a visual prompt to wait. Not that he needed it, he thought, but people did silly things when the adrenaline was pumping and it wouldn't be the first time someone had jumped early, eager to get to the fight.

His thoughts were interrupted as the red light now flicked on. "Red on!" he shouted, then further shouts echoed down the plane as the first one hundred men repeated the order. *Come on, Yuri, this is it*, he thought. *Here we go. Keep a clear head, your men are depending on you.* Before the light come on, he saw the loadmaster's arm move away and heard, "Green on, GO! GO! GO!" His legs were already moving as the light then flicked green and he jumped with his arms tucked into his chest. There was an explosion of noise and heat. The back blast from the engines was thunderous and there was a strange sensation of being weightless as he fell forward out of the aircraft. He heard a noise like tearing fabric and for a split-second panic took hold. *Has my chute ripped?*

A violent jolt ripped his arms out to his sides and yanked him so hard, he felt his eyes almost tear from his head. Feeling himself decelerating he looked up to see his canopy was fully open and then realising he was out and his chute deployed, he began to look around and take in the new environment he was about to land in. He only had a few seconds to look though, as already the ground was rushing up to meet him. He saw the area was a large and open expanse, surrounded on three sides by heavy woodland. A road ran parallel to the drop zone and he saw no sign of any hostile forces ready to meet him. Already the vehicles were on the ground, the parachutes covering them up as they had deflated on landing. Seeing the grass clearly he knew he had seconds to go, so braced his legs together at the knees, ready to transfer the shock of the landing through his body. With a crash he hit the ground hard, rolling over to his side, whilst keeping his legs straight and together, a textbook paratrooper landing, he thought proudly. Within a second he was on his feet, rolling his parachute up quickly and expertly, preventing it from blowing around the drop zone, and releasing his harness. Already his men were landing around him, mirroring his movements, getting themselves ready for battle as the noise of the aircraft faded off into the distance, ready to conduct drop number two.

At the side of the drop zone he saw two men. He had been told to expect a meeting party and out of instinct he unfolded the stock of his AK-12 rifle and walked towards them, his weapon at the ready. Seeing him approach, the two men stood with outstretched arms, faces impassive, showing no signs of aggression or threat. As Golgolvin stood before them, he asked, "Captain Lunyou?"

"Yes, Colonel," one of them answered, "welcome to England."

Golgolvin lowered his weapon, noting the other man's face was heavily bruised and seeing his nose broken he asked, "What happened to you?"

The man remained quiet as the Captain answered for him, "Ah, Sergeant Feodor was careless with the locals, he won't make the same mistake again."

Pointing to the body on the ground behind them with his rifle barrel, Golgolvin enquired, "Is that the local?"

"No, Colonel, that was someone who decided to stick his nose where it didn't belong."

Nodding, satisfied, he turned to watch his men as they all began to form up into their units. Already, senior commanders were issuing orders, with some of the men now running up to the vehicles, unclasping the huge chutes and opening the hatches, getting the vehicles ready. Others were sent off to defensive positions, providing an outer perimeter to protect the drop zone in case of an attack. Not that there would be. All seemed quiet from what the Colonel could see, and the surprise looked to have been complete. Hearing the huge plane in the distance turning in for another drop he said, "Okay, Captain, while I'm waiting, give me an update on what's been going on today..."

ATDU Hangar Bovington Camp

Mike watched dumbfounded as vehicles began to appear from the plane, parachutes deploying above, the vehicles slowly rocking beneath their canopies as they floated to the ground. They were only visible for a few moments before disappearing behind the treetops. Quickly realising what he was witnessing, he jumped down off the tank and ran into the hangar. Chris was briefing the assembled soldiers, and looked up as he saw his friend sprinting in.

"What do you want? I thought you were going home?" he said testily.

"Chris, there's paratroopers landing right now at the glider club! I've seen vehicles being deployed on parachutes, they're here and you guys need to move NOW!"

Seeing the look on Mike's face, he knew better than to question him, but the anger was still there as he raced outside to look, replying with, "We're not going anywhere until the CO says so; besides they told us the threat wouldn't be here until 21:00."

"I know what they said, but for fuck's sake look for yourself!" Mike exclaimed as he pointed to the aircraft flying overhead. "That's an Antonov An-124, it's a heavy-lift cargo plane, able to carry one hundred and fifty tonnes of equipment. Think about what they could have on board right now!"

Both men climbed onboard the tank turret as Mike pointed to the plane again coming in low and slow. This time the distinct shape of parachutes was clear to see as they floated down. Mike wasn't sure on the numbers, but he felt sure it was over sixty parachutes dropping from the sky.

Seeing it with his own eyes Chris shook his head in disbelief, his anger gone, replaced with a growing dread that they were already out of time. He looked back over to the assembled tank crews all watching with interest and some pointing up curiously to the parachutes.

Shaking them into action he yelled, "MOUNT UP! BE READY TO MOVE IN ONE MINUTE!"

He jumped off the tank, running over to the signallers. "Hey, you two! Forget all about that now, get over to the tank park, tell them we've got enemy incoming now! Paratroopers with vehicles landing at the glider club. Well, don't just stand there, move your fucking asses!"

The two female signallers were about to race away when another Land Rover came screaming in, driven by the GSM. Quickly jumping out, Chris looked at him. "GSM we've got—"

"Yeah, we fucking know!" the GSM interrupted, "paras coming in on the glider club, we can see it better than you from up the hill. Looks like one hundred plus. No doubt they're coming here to capture the base. The CO's ordering all vehicles to bug out now – including you, you have your orders and know where you're going?"

"We do."

"Good, then this is goodbye. I won't see you for a while."

"You're not going?" Mike asked. "Why not?"

"We've got three tanks unable to move, my orders are to stay with a handful of men, fire what we can in the base and then get the fuck out. Sooner I get away to do that the better."

The GSM looked over to the two signallers, indicating with his thumb for them to climb aboard the Land Rover.

"Okay you two, times up, I've got you a ride out of here!"

As they climbed aboard, the GSM said with genuine emotion sounding in his voice. "Mike, I just want to say thank you. If it wasn't for you, I'd be the dick on the golf course now watching this lot coming in to land."

Not wanting to get too emotional Mike countered back with, "I don't know if that's a compliment or an insult. I thought you liked golf?"

Smiling, the GSM replied, "I *love* golf, but I love my country and my freedom more. Good luck to you both."

Without allowing them time to reply, he turned and raced back to the four-by-four, climbing into the driver's seat, before accelerating away in a cloud of exhaust smoke.

Mike watched him go, startled suddenly as behind him he heard the heavy diesels of the tanks begin to cough and roar into life. He turned to see the crews mounting up, getting their headgear adjusted and ready, the smells and sounds bringing back memories. He watched Chris jog up to his tank, about to climb up onto the mudguard, when he stopped himself and ran back towards Mike, his headgear and helmet in hand.

Mike was about to speak when Chris cut him off.

"Look, I'm sorry. I'm just angry with everything and I just wished that you could be with us. I had no right to ask that of you, you've already done enough, more than enough. You just take good fucking care of yourself and that wife of yours, okay?"

Christ, thought Mike, *if this continues, I'll need a tissue*, and he felt the lump in his throat. The throb of the tank's diesel engines made both men have to shout above the noise.

"Chris, you take good care yourself, best of luck to you and your troops, and I'll see you when I see you next."

Grimacing, Chris touched his forehead to Mike's, recognising the saying they'd used in the past when about to go out on a tough mission. It was never goodbye.

"I'll see you when I see you next," Chris repeated softly.

Both stayed there for a second, until eventually it was Mike who, understanding time was against them, pushed him away lightly, retorting with, "Now fucking move your ass, you crazy sod, before we both end up in a POW camp. God, I can't imagine sharing a cell with you."

"I can," Chris called back, "but I'd have to insist you shave that arse of yours, it looks like a fucking sasquatch!"

Both laughed, happier that they were leaving on better terms, and Mike watched his friend run up to the tank and climb aboard, settling quickly into the cupola and plugging his headset in. He could see his lips moving as he spoke to the crew. With a final wave to his friend he heard the engine roar as the heavy monster began to move forward in a cloud of fumes and smoke, the noise deafening as the tank turned and headed for the gate, quickly followed by the second then the third. He turned and began jogging back to his car, leaving the tanks to it, the engines revving away. He still had to get home, and he didn't want to be here when the paratroopers arrived. With luck they'd find nothing but an empty camp and big sign saying, *Fuck You*. He smiled as he fumbled in his pocket for his car keys.

Eagle-One

Watching the second drop coming down, Golgolvin nodded in satisfaction as another one hundred of his men began to descend, checking that all the chutes had opened. Satisfied with the count he turned back to the FSB Captain, his face angry.

"So, Captain, you were explaining to me why you left your position at the camp and why it's been four hours since you've had eyes on it?"

"Colonel, we couldn't stay any longer, after the shootout we had with the British, they would have seen us if we stayed."

"So, you decided to just leave and come here?" His voice rising in anger, "Your primary task was to keep us informed on what was going on at the camp. And for the past four hours you haven't done that, instead you waited for me to land here, killing civilians and dogs before telling me this. Did you not have a radio?"

The Captain was about to answer when Golgolvin held up a hand to silence him, cocking his head to hear. "What is that in the distance?" His eyes opened wide in recognition, as snapping his head round to his officers he shouted, "Engine noises, that's heavy tanks moving! Prepare to defend against armour!" The British must be onto them, he thought angrily. He rounded on the Captain. "It would appear that things *are* happening at the camp."

"But Comrade Colonel, the camp is quiet, its men are all away, we were only there four hours ago. Two men with automatic weapons had them on the run, there's no way they can attack us here." His face showed confusion as he, too, heard the distinct rumble of the heavy engines in the distance, followed up by smaller engine noises. Whatever was happening the British were certainly on the move.

"Captain, you and your dog of a Sergeant may be in the habit of underestimating our enemy, but I am not." Turning to another Captain he shouted, "Get those vehicles ready to move now!" He watched as the engines of the Spruts came to life, belching thick black diesel fumes as the crews cleared away the last of the rigging and began to move them forward. The Typhoon wheeled vehicles were already clear and lined up by the roadside ready to move. Golgolvin quickly keyed his radio, relaying orders to the vehicle crews. "Get me eyes on that road, I want to see if we have the enemy coming at us or not." Watching them drive off to carry out his orders, he began to look around at his men. *Damn it, I still have one more drop to come in, where is that bloody plane?* he thought, as he looked skywards. All around him his soldiers began to organise themselves into teams and then ran to the perimeter, ready to conduct a hasty defence, pulling anti-tank weapons out of cases and setting up machine guns, ready to pour fire on anyone stupid enough to come close. *Okay*, he thought grimacing, *let them come, we'll be ready.*

ATDU Hangar, Bovington Camp

Mike climbed into his car, about to start the engine when he looked back over to the hangar, surprised to see one of the tanks was still there, gun forward and lights on but not moving. He could hear the engine idling but couldn't see anyone in the turret. Surely it would be moving now, he thought. He watched as the last vehicle of the convoy, the REME CRARRV, reached the road junction and turned left, the engine screaming as the driver fought to catch up with the rapidly disappearing convoy. The commander was so intent on chasing the convoy that he hadn't looked back to confirm the vehicle behind was following too. Confused, Mike got back out of the car and ran up to the tank. It was Megatron, the tank that he'd seen before with the add-on armour fitted. Given that the driver's hatch was open and empty, he banged on the hull to see if anyone would appear out of the turret, fully expecting someone to be there. *Where the hell are the crew?* he wondered.

"Hello? Anyone onboard?"

He quickly climbed onto the turret and peered inside, seeing the headgear all assembled and in position. The turret systems were on, too, but strangely no one was home. He looked skywards, hearing the noise of the plane over the tank's engine, watching as yet another parachute drop was being conducted. *How many was that, was it three or four?* he wondered. Seeing movement in the hangar behind him, he quickly jumped off and ran in. At the back of the hangar, carrying five empty mugs, was a Trooper. Mike recognised from his black beret and badges that he belonged to the 24th Tank Regiment – Mike's former regiment. He looked young and nervous and Mike identified him as one of the recruits from the camp.

Mike couldn't help but sound surprised as he exclaimed, "Trooper, what the fuck are you still doing here?"

The young soldier blinked in surprise at Mike's outburst, replying, "I was told to clean up the hangar, sir, while the tanks go to the fuel point."

"They're not going to the fuel point!" he said. "Where's your crew? Where's your commander?"

Looking around at the empty hangar the Trooper stammered, "Er, I'm not sure, sir, I was told they'd give me someone when I got down here. I've just been told to get the tank ready to go. It's outside, now, for when you're ready," he added.

The army never changes, thought Mike. Even with the threat of an attack some asshole made this lad remain behind to clean the bloody hangar. He shook his head in disbelief, walking outside to the tank, as the Trooper followed him out, asking, "Sir, if the tanks aren't coming back then when are we going?"

Oh shit, thought Mike, *this lad thinks I'm part of his crew*!

Mike stood looking over to his parked car, thinking all he had to do now was simply jump in and drive away, leaving the camp and all that was coming to it to be someone else's problem. Then he looked at the deserted ATDU hangar, and then at the young soldier, knowing there was no one left to help the lad. Already he could hear the engines of the vehicles over the road firing up, preparing to leave. In two minutes, there'd be no one left at all.

"How old are you, Trooper?"

"I'm eighteen, sir," he said proudly.

"And where you from, I'm detecting an accent there?" Mike asked, already knowing the answer.

"Plymouth, sir, born and bred."

"And what do I call you, Trooper? What's your name, I can't see a name tape."

Seeing Mike's eyes flicking to the empty space on his combat shirt he quickly answered, "Sorry, sir, I'll get a name tape on there soon, the tailoress just had trouble getting my name tapes made up. I'm Trooper Hickok, sir, the lads call me—"

"Bill?" Mike interrupted with raised eyebrows.

"That's correct, sir, how did you know?"

"Call it a hunch. Okay, Bill, we don't have long, so are you a recruit here, are you a trained driver, can you drive that tank?"

"Yes, sir, I passed my training two weeks ago. I've been kept here while everyone went on summer leave. I'm off to join my regiment in two weeks. Are *you* my commander, sir?"

Mike saw the young lad's eyes look him up and down, no doubt wondering about his attire and why he wasn't in uniform. It would do him no good if he told the lad the truth. He could imagine the young soldier's reaction as he said, "No son, I'm not an officer, I'm not even a commander. Your own troops left you behind. Oh, and by the way, there's soldiers coming to kill you. Good luck on your tank though, with only six weeks of training."

Mike knew he wouldn't last the night. *Damn it, Chris, how could you be so fucking careless!*

Making the decision on the spot, Mike decided to lie instead.

"Okay, Bill, all right, I'm your commander. I want you to jump in and get yourself ready to go. We're leaving in one minute, do you have everything you need on board?"

"Yes, sir, I've got my body armour and helmet already in the cab, but I don't have a weapon. Where's the gunner and loader though?"

"I don't have a weapon either, Bill, so I guess we'll just have to manage without one. For now it looks like it's just you and me, so no loader or gunner. Now come on, we've wasted enough time, let's get the hell out of here and catch the others up."

He ran back to his car, pulling out his jacket from behind the driver's seat, then closed and locked the door, removing the car keys from his pocket and placing them on the rear tyre, hidden from view. He didn't know when he was coming back, but he knew he didn't want his keys with him in case anything happened on the tank. As he ran back to the tank, he saw the silhouettes of the other armoured vehicles now begin to race away up the road. It looked like the vehicles were moving in smaller convoys of threes and fours. With a sudden fear of being left behind, he quickly climbed up into the turret, the familiar sensation of adrenaline returning.

He sat in the commander's station and quickly checked over the switches; the gun kit was on, the sights were on, all the radio switches were on. He flicked over the interior lights from white to red, checking they were all set to low, bathing the turret interior into a soft fiery red, so as not to disturb his night vision. He quickly looked over the radios – they were on, but he had no idea if it was the right frequency or not, but right now he didn't care. He looked to the operator's side, giving it a visual once-over. Seeing the headgear and cable were lying across the turret and not wanting it to get caught in the traverse, he climbed over the huge breech of the gun and tucked it safely away, quickly scanning the loader's side to check everything was in order. Seeing the loader's hatch was still open he jumped back out to close it, before darting back inside the commander's cupola. Once happy that everything was ready and secure he put his headset on, adjusting the straps for comfort as the 'bone dome' helmet now sat on his head.

He blew into the microphone to check he had feedback and could hear himself as he spoke. "Okay, Bill can you hear me?"

"I can hear you, sir, loud and clear."

"Okay, firstly, don't call me 'sir', call me 'boss' when on the wagon okay?"

"Okay, sir... Sorry, boss."

Closing his eyes Mike thought back to all those years ago, trying to remember the drills and procedures that once upon a time were second nature to him.

"Right, Bill, have you tensioned the tracks yet?"

"Not yet, sir – sorry, boss – you want me to do that now?"

"Yes, let's get that done please." Mike stood up, checking out of habit that the tank was clear on both sides. He listened as the engines revved and the tank pirouetted slightly on the spot to the right, dragging all the slack of the right track to the front. He heard the high-pitched whine of the hydraulics as the motor now pushed against the forward tension wheel, making the right track tighten, to stop it from slipping off the wheels when they moved off. He wanted nothing more than to get going, but he knew from past experience that if the track were too slack it could fall off the sprockets, and if that happened, they were going nowhere, especially with only a crew of two. "Okay, boss, right track done, doing the left."

Again, the engine revved and the tank pirouetted to the left, with Bill repeating the procedure, reporting back with, "Okay, boss, tracks are done."

"Right, Bill are you closed down? Is your hatch shut?"

"Er, do I have to? I'm not really all that good with driving with the periscope."

"Yes, you have to – last time I checked, heads were not good at stopping bullets. Besides, if you're not good now, then by the end of the night you'll be a pro. Close your hatch please."

"Yes, boss."

Mike heard the dejected tone in his driver's voice, followed by the grunts of effort over the headset as the young driver struggled and heaved the seat back and down and the heavy hatch was closed. On a tank the driver could drive two ways, heads up, with his head out of the hatch and seeing the world with his own eyes or closed down, meaning the seat was collapsed backwards, allowing the driver to be almost lying down and viewing the world through a periscope. Usually in peacetime, drivers preferred driving heads up, but seeing how things were unravelling, Mike knew the driver would have to drive closed down from now on. But the benefit he had was that this was the upgraded tank and Mike knew the periscope was a visual display unit, so the driver would see outside via two cameras mounted forward and rearward. This would allow Bill to reverse the tank if he had to without Mike's guidance, something that the other tanks couldn't do.

"Bill, this is different to what you've driven before, you'll notice your periscope is actually a camera feed. Can you see out of it?"

"It's all backwards, I'm looking at the hangars," he exclaimed.

"Okay. that's your reversing camera. When I tell you to reverse that's what I want you to look at. See the lines on the display? That shows you where the tracks will be, it's similar to reversing a modern car, okay?"

"Understood, boss, but won't you be telling me where to go?"

"I might be a little busy up here. Now, on the side of the periscope are four switches, one is on/off, to power up the sight, one is to switch the camera between daylight and thermal, allowing you to drive at night, one is to select white hot and black hot when on the thermal camera and the fourth one switches between the front and rear camera. Have a feel, make sure you're happy where they are. I want you to be able to switch them without having to look. When you're happy let me know."

He could hear the clicks of the switches being pressed, and the subtle breathing of the driver as he finally said, "Right, boss, I've got it facing forwards, I think we're ready to go."

What next? thought Mike, resting his eyes on the brow pad of the commander's sight. *Have I forgotten anything?* Gripping the turret controls he pulled in on the grip switch, the dead man's clutch that powered the gun kit, designed to prevent someone accidently moving the fifteen-tonne turret when in the hangar. Usually it would click, indicating it had been engaged, but as he pressed it there was silence. Something wasn't working. Quickly thinking, he looked down to the gunner's station, checking the controls. Each station on the tank had a large GCE (Gun Control Equipment) safety switch, designed in case of emergency to allow the crew to cut the turret power. Usually it was needed in case someone, or something became trapped in the turret. With the turret weighing fifteen tonnes it could mangle body parts and would crush most things, so the switch was there to prevent that from happening. He checked the gunner's station; the switch was set to live. He looked over to the loader's station, again live.

"Bill, is your safety switch set to live?"

"Er, no. Sorry, do you want it to live?"

"Yes please, without it I can't move the turret. Remember every time you get in or out of your cab, put it to safe, but then check it's back to live. Understand?"

"Yes, boss. Sorry, I'm not used to a gun tank, all of my training was done on a DTT."

The driver also had a safety switch – when exiting or entering the driver's hatch they would, out of instinct, put it to safe, to prevent them being crushed by the turret. The DTT training tanks were turretless, so Bill had yet to get used to flicking the switch back. Mike remembered it had taken him a few attempts to get it right when he was a new driver.

He heard the clutch engage this time as he pulled in on the grip switch. Using the thumb controller, he checked the turret would traverse left and right and then the gun would elevate and depress. It was a little bit shaky. The thumb controller was designed to be relative to its input; the harder you pressed, the quicker the turret would turn. Mike was a little rusty, he felt, but not bad considering. Finally happy with the turret controls he said, "Right, Bill, let's get out of here. When you're ready, let's go."

"Okay, boss."

Mike heard the engine rev, but the tank remained stuck, refusing to move. He heard the engine rev again then again and the driver exclaim, "Something's wrong. We're not moving."

"Bill, let the revs die down, take your foot off the accelerator," Mike said calmly.

He heard the revs die down and the engine idle again as his driver exclaimed, "What is it? Are we broken down? Have I broken something?"

Shaking his head and laughing at the situation they found themselves in, Mike just calmly replied, "No, we haven't broken down, just do me a favour and take *off* the handbrake."

With a clunk he felt the handbrake release, and the tank jolted forward into gear. Now they were ready to go.

"Sorry, boss, er... I'm—"

"It's okay, Bill, it's been a while for me too. Now let's get going, shall we?"

Finally with a roar, the tank moved forwards as Mike looked back to his car, realising he had been moments from leaving. Something Chris had said had now rung true – he couldn't just sit by and watch everything he knew and love fall apart. Kate would understand, he thought. He'd get the tank and the young lad away to safety and back with his unit, get a crew for him and then he could come back, and hopefully the car would be there waiting for him. Turning to face his front he watched the road junction appear. It was going to be a long night, he thought, a very long night...

22

Tigers Without Teeth

As the tank approached the road junction out of the ATDU complex, Mike looked both ways to check the road was clear. There were still civilian cars to be aware of on the roads and he didn't want his first time back on a tank to involve a collision. *Besides*, he thought, *who the hell would insure me?* Seeing the road was clear he said, "Okay, Bill, you're clear on the left, clear on the right, out we go."

He felt the tank jolt as the driver went down a gear and with revs increasing and the turbos whining the tank began its turn, the tracks squealing on the road surface. All armoured vehicles had track pads fitted to stop them from chewing up the roads in peace time, but this also meant the rubber would squeak on the asphalt at low speeds. No doubt anyone within a mile would hear the tank moving, as stealth on a road was not a tank's strong point, Mike thought.

The road ran straight for two miles, parallel to the driver training area, a forested space measuring four square miles, where the military's new drivers would learn how to control an armoured vehicle. An all-weather tarmac ring road ran around its perimeter to simulate road driving, complete with road signs and junctions. The centre of the training area was made up of broken, undulating ground with ditches, forestry blocks, railway tracks, steep inclines and banks and berms, all designed to test new drivers on every type of terrain that could be thrown at them when driving an armoured vehicle on operations. Mike knew that the glider club's airfield sat on the opposite side of the training area and that any threat would come from either the road to their front or the training area to his right. He didn't feel comfortable being exposed driving down the road, but he could see through the thermal sights the tell-tale track marks left on the tarmac from some of the armoured vehicles that had already left. He knew he was heading in the right direction and just hoped he could catch up to someone soon. He sat himself lower in the cupola as the wind increased around his head and the tank gained momentum, accelerating up to thirty-five miles per hour.

Feeling a little uneasy at the speed and just to reassure himself, Mike confirmed with his driver, "Bill, on your driver's sight, the two lines marked on the display are showing you where your tracks are. So long as you make sure they are lined up on the road, we won't hit anything coming towards us and won't go off the road. You understand?"

"Okay, boss, I got it. I'll keep us in the road, promise."

Checking again the tank's road position, and mildly confident that Bill had understood him, he lowered himself into the commander's chair and used his commanders controls to check the radio frequencies. *Let's see if anyone's chatting on here*, he thought. There were two radios fitted on the tank, the A and the B set; each was set to a different frequency, allowing him to hear in his left and right ear the two different radios individually. Whatever radio he heard in his left ear would be the one he would be transmitting on. Usually he would hear someone chatting, but all he could hear at the moment was static. Lowering the volumes slightly he peered over the cupola, looking towards the treeline, expecting any second to see armed men rushing to stop them, or the flash of gunfire. But all was quiet. *Where are they?* he thought.

Eagle-One

"What do you mean, leaving? Stop them now! Yes, of course, OPEN FIRE!"

Golgolvin raged into the radio before turning to the Major who now ran to him. "Third drop completed and everyone ready to move, sir."

"Good," he fired back, "we need to move now; it appears the British are *not* attacking us but instead are running away. I want those vehicles stopped. Get as many men mounted on our vehicles as you can, the rest will have to run there. We'll go through the training area, it'll be quicker. Now let's move, Major!"

Golgolvin turned to the FSB Captain. "Your four-by-four, I'm taking it with my command group."

"But, sir! I need that vehicle to get back!" Captain Lunyou protested.

"You can both *run* to the base with the rest of my men, I'll expect you there shortly."

Snatching the keys from the open-mouthed Captain, Colonel Golgolvin and six of his men raced over to the four-by-four, unceremoniously dumping the equipment inside onto the grass to make room for themselves.

Captain Lunyou and Sergeant Feodor stood in mute rage as the heavily loaded four-by-four shot off with all its wheels spinning and flicking mud in all directions, as it chased after the light tanks. The Spruts had already raced away down the road and were cutting through to the muddy tracks that cris-crossed the driver training area. Shaking their heads in anger, they began to pick their equipment up off the ground, before falling in behind the paratroopers who were already jogging out of the area. Sergeant Feodor fumed to himself as with sweaty hands he heaved a backpack onto his shoulders. To top it all off, he still hadn't had a decent cigarette. *Fucking paratroopers*, he thought, as he ran after the men who were already leaving the other two struggling in their wake. In the distance they could hear gunfire. *Finally*, he thought, *time to make someone pay.*

Tango One-One

The tank had travelled about a mile down the road, the vast open area to their right had now closed in, giving way to heavy woodland, at least shielding them from where the enemy were coming from. Mike relaxed slightly, feeling a little bit more confident. *Whatever the enemy are doing, it isn't here*, he thought.

His left earpiece squawked and made an uncomfortable high-pitched sound, as wincing he turned down the volume. Suddenly it burst to life.

"Any callsign, any callsign this is Golf Two-Zero, we need urgent assistance, contact enemy vehicles... they're tearing us apart!"

Mike quickly looked around the cupola for any signs of a fight going on near them. It wasn't until he looked behind that he saw them. Back in the direction of the camp he saw the distinct flashes of green tracer fire shooting over the road. Something was already on fire down there; he could see the smoke rising into the darkening sky but he couldn't make out what.

"Bill, stop the tank!" he ordered, bracing himself in the cupola as the tank slewed to a halt. He quickly spun the commander's sight to the rear, using the high-powered optics to see back up the road. He could see a vehicle lying half off the road in a ditch. It was one of the Warrior AFVs, an infantry vehicle that they referred to as a 'battle taxi'. It looked like smoke was pouring from its engine deck and the turret was turned over to the right. Mike could see the turret moving; whoever was inside was using the vehicle optics, he guessed. Knowing that they had no ammunition and that they were a sitting duck, it would only be a matter of time before the vehicle burned itself out. Behind the stricken vehicle he could see another three Warriors, lined up one behind the other. They were using one of the camp's buildings as cover, but whatever was firing at them had them trapped there. They couldn't proceed any further. Having a mile of open road to cover, they would be picked off easily.

"What is it, boss? What's going on?" Bill asked.

"Behind us, some of our vehicles, they're under fire and pinned down. They're asking for help on the radio."

"Okay, so what can we do?"

"Give me a second, Bill, I'm thinking."

After a few seconds of silence the radio again screamed out, "I repeat, any callsign, any callsign, this is Golf Two-Zero. For Christ's sake, is anyone there, we need help!"

Mike sat there thinking quickly, trying to formulate a plan. He didn't want to answer up on the radio offering help, only to have to drive away. He had no weapons and no ammo. What he did have, though, was a tank, a big, beautiful fully armoured tank. Making his mind up he said,

"Bill, up ahead. One hundred metres off to the right, there's a track that leads off the road and back onto the training area, do you see it?"

"Yeah, I got it, boss. You want me to cross over onto the training area?"

"Yep, that's it, get us onto the training area and head back down the track, the trees will keep us covered from view. We're off to make some new friends."

With a jolt, the tank began to accelerate down the road. Mike was impressed at the way Bill managed to keep the revs high enough to make the turn. Usually new drivers would bog the vehicle down, the revs dying away, resulting in the tank turning slower than usual, sometimes even stalling and being forced to make a half-hearted three-point turn. Bill, however, did none of this and the tank whipped around with speed onto the dusty track, the hydro-gas suspension easily able to overcome the bumps. Now they were driving back the way they came. This time though, they were hidden from the view of the enemy by the trees. About four hundred metres ahead of them, the forestry block opened onto a large muddy plain and Mike had Bill slow down as they approached, not wanting to just burst out into the open like some panto dame on stage.

Mike keyed the pressel to talk on the radio. "Golf Two-Zero, Golf Two-Zero, this is..." *Ah, bugger,* thought Mike mid-sentence, *I don't have a callsign. Sod it, I'll use Tango One-One, my old callsign.*

"Unknown callsign, unknown callsign, this is Golf Two-Zero. You were cut off, say again. Over."

Mike could hear the desperation now on the voice over the radio; things were getting serious over there.

"Golf Two-Zero, this is Tango One-One. I'm on my way to assist you now, hang in there. Out!"

The tank crept along, Mike peering through his sight, checking the ground in front of him. He could see only two vehicles firing on the Warrior, both were wheeled types, and he didn't recognise them from anything he'd seen before. Mounted on the turrets were rapid-firing canons, he guessed them to be either twenty or thirty millimetre, and though not dangerous to the tank, to the Warrior they would eventually start to punch through its lighter armour if they kept hitting in the same area for long enough. *Where are the other enemy?* Mike thought. *Surely there will be infantry in support.* One of the Russian vehicles, the closest one to him, sat three hundred metres away, behind a berm, a small rise in the ground, providing it with cover from incoming fire – not that there would be any with the Warriors having no ammunition onboard. Its gun was hammering at the stricken vehicle, sparks firing off it, as so far, the armour held up against the onslaught.

The farthest enemy vehicle was back on top of a hill in the middle of the training area, its gun trained down onto the road, firing into the buildings on the camp, the green tracer sparking through and setting fires. *They must think there are still troops on camp*, Mike decided.

Both vehicles were facing away from him, not expecting any threats to come from where Mike was approaching from.

Seeing how close the nearest vehicle was to the berm Mike knew what to do.

"Okay, Bill, check your instrument panel and check you know where the smoke generator switch is. Have you found it?"

"Boss, we were told never to use this, it's bad for the environment."

"Bill, there's a lot of things they would have told you not to do, and I'm afraid that tonight I'm going to get you to do most of them. Now look for the switch, tell me when you've found it."

He waited a few seconds as he heard Bill fumbling with the switch panel.

"Okay, yep, I got it. Smoke left and smoke right."

"That's the one. Now I want you to smoke the side I tell you to smoke, you got that? If I say 'smoke left', you press the switch over to the left."

"OKay boss, I got it, but what are we doing?"

"You ever played dodgems?"

"What?"

"Trust me, we need to get going, times a-wasting. For now, I want you to drive down this track. Not too fast though; I don't want to kick up a dust cloud. Right, let's go!"

The tank began to move down the track. All the while Mike kept looking over his left side, expecting to see enemy troops, but still none appeared. It was as if the two vehicles were on their own. Perhaps they were the lead elements, he thought, and the rest were yet to appear. He didn't care as long as the two vehicles to his front kept looking away from him. To add to the deception, he now asked over the radio, "Golf Two-Zero, Tango One-One, I'm just north of you. I need you to keep these two distracted, keep them looking your way. Over."

"Roger, Tango One-One, what are you going to do?" The voice was sceptical.

With no time to explain further Mike simply replied, "Golf Two-Zero, just keep them looking your way. Be ready to move in sixty seconds. Out."

The tank was now one hundred and fifty metres away from the lead vehicle, the enemy's turret still trained away from their tank and firing at the others. *Whoever the commander is, he isn't watching his arcs correctly*, thought Mike.

Mike watched as one of the Warriors hiding behind the building accelerated forwards, jamming on the brakes and then quickly reversing back into cover, the enemy fire hammering into the empty ground where the Warrior had stood. *Good, it's working, the plan is working. All the enemy's focus is on the Warriors.*

Now with less than one hundred metres to go Mike said, "Okay, Bill, our target's off to your left, I'm going to guide you in on him, now turn left stick."

He felt the tank turn to the left. Once Mike had him lined up, he shouted, "On!" The tank continued forward, now leaving the track and going cross country, the gun remaining straight and level as the gyroscopes and computers kept it on target. *If only we had some ammo*, thought Mike, *this would be so much easier.*

Now less than ten metres separated the vehicles. Mike had kept the speed low, trying not to give away their location until the last second. Not wanting to damage the barrel of the tank, he spun the turret to the left, putting the turret and gun over to the side of the tank and out of harm's way, having to now peer cautiously out of his side periscopes. He'd lined the tank up to come in over the top of the berm that the enemy were using for cover; the height difference meant the tank would now pass up the higher ground and come down over the top of the enemy vehicle.

He was so close now he saw the gunner, who was hiding behind the armoured cupola, aiming the weapon and firing. Sensing something wasn't right he saw the gunner look sideways and up, his face a mask of shock at seeing the tank bearing down on him.

"Okay, Bill, right stick a bit, right stick a bit, on! Okay, FLOOR IT!"

Mike ducked and winced as he heard the engine race and the tracks scrabble for grip as the shrill shriek of metal on metal filled the air. He felt the tank judder slightly as the seventy-four-tonne Goliath rode over the enemy cupola as if it were tissue paper. He didn't see what happened to the gunner, he didn't need to, he felt the tank rise up before crashing down on top of the vehicle, his head smashing into the side of the turret. Without the helmet on he would have knocked himself out no doubt. He peered over the cupola, seeing the tank had stopped. Whether he had meant to or not, Bill had stopped the tank on the roof of the armoured vehicle. Weighing only fourteen-tonnes, the lighter vehicle had never been designed to carry the seventy-four-tonne tank in a piggyback. The enemy driver panicked and tried to move the vehicle, the tyres scrabbling uselessly in the mud. As all four of the huge tyres blew out, Mike and Bill could only sit as passengers and watch as the vehicle exploded under their weight. Slowly the armoured sides began to splay out and the chassis howled as their tank crushed the vehicle below. Mike felt explosions beneath his feet, quickly followed by the smell of smoke.

"Bill, quickly get us off this thing before we catch fire."

With a shriek of tearing metal, he felt the tank move forward and drop back down onto the ground behind the berm. Looking behind him, Mike saw the shattered remains of the vehicle begin to spark up and catch fire as the ammunition began to ignite, setting fire to the dry grass around it.

"Okay, one down. Let's get over to the Warriors, quick as you can, Bill."

The tank roared away, leaving the dead vehicle in its wake as it raced across the open ground towards the stranded Warrior.

Mike was about to transmit on the radio when he was interrupted by a flash of sparks on the side of the cupola. He ducked down as thirty millimetre rounds began to hammer the sides of the tank.

"Okay, Bill, can you see the Warriors?"

"Yep, I got them, boss."

"Good, make your way to them, I want you to stop on this side of the broken vehicle, we're going to provide armoured cover for it, okay?"

"Okay!"

Leaving his driver to it, Mike quickly brought the turret back to the front. The enemy vehicle was still where he had left it, on top of the hill and now firing down at them. Mike lined his sight onto the vehicle, the dot sat squarely in the centre of the observed mass. *If only we had just one round*, he thought angrily, as the enemy fire kept thudding into the vehicle's side. He pressed the align button and the gun swung round and elevated to match what his sight was seeing, aimed directly at the enemy vehicle. Suddenly the firing stopped, and he watched the enemy vehicle quickly reverse off, hiding itself from view. Perhaps they thought the tank had been about to fire. He didn't care why. All he cared was that for now the firing had stopped. He transmitted over the radio, trying to keep his voice as calm as possible, but the urgency still there.

"Golf Two-Zero, Tango One-One, now's the time. Move your arse, get your stranded vehicle hooked up, we'll provide cover."

The tank took up a blocking position next to the Warrior – the military term was called 'sandbagging' – the bigger vehicle now able to shield it from fire, as Mike saw the hatches open and the crew begin to get out. They manhandled the driver out of the front of the vehicle. Mike watched them carefully place his limp body down alongside the tank. Keeping the tank's turret pointed at the area where he last saw the enemy, he leaned over the cupola to shout down to the crew, lifting his headset away from his ear to listen to the response.

"How bad?"

One of the soldiers, a Corporal who seemed to be the commander answered up.

"Driver's been knocked about a bit, apart from that we're okay."

"Right, and the vehicle can it drive?"

"Engine's gone, so has the gearbox, it's fucked. We'll need a tow."

"How long do you need to rig up?"

Mike was interrupted as more thirty millimetre rounds began to ricochet off the vehicle's side. *Fuck, this guy isn't giving up easily!* Careful to keep himself low in the cupola and looking back down to the Corporal, Mike shouted, "Forget the tow, there's no time! I'll get your other vehicles to pick you up!"

The Corporal replied with a thumbs up, before taking cover around the other side of the Warrior as Mike ducked back down and transmitted on the radio.

"Golf Two-Zero, this is Tango One-One. Forget the tow, leave the vehicle. Pick your guys up and get out of here, we'll cover you as best we can."

Another voice, one he didn't recognise, answered up.

"Tango One-One, this is Golf Two-Two. Golf Two-Zero is on the ground near you. Acknowledge your last message and are on our way. Out."

Mike waited until all the Warrior's crew were safely hidden around the other side of their vehicle before ordering,

"Okay, Bill, go forward now, nice and slow and smoke left please."

The tank began to move slowly over the ground, thick white smoke belching out of one of the two exhausts. The pièce de résistance of the Challenger 2 was its ability to inject diesel fuel directly onto the hot exhausts, allowing the tank to create its own smoke screen. The gunner in the enemy Kamaz could only look on in frustration as the tank and the Warrior quickly disappeared like pantomime villains into a cloud of smoke.

The smoke wouldn't last forever, though, and Mike could only watch with concern as the Warriors now raced out from cover to pick up the stranded crew. Thankfully the wind wasn't blowing too hard, and the smoke lingered longer than usual. As his eyes burnt from the diesel smoke, he watched the shadows of the vehicles drive up along the road, stopping beside the stranded vehicle. One crewman lingered. *What is he doing?* Mike thought. As if in answer, a jet of flame shot out of the engine deck. They'd set the vehicle alight to stop it being used by the enemy. The military term for it was to 'deny'. *Smart*, thought Mike, and then Bill reported, "Boss, the smoke's clearing."

He was just about to speak when a crash hit the front of the turret, the shockwave sending a vibration through his bones. *Fuck, that wasn't a thirty millimetre*, he thought, as another round smashed into the hull, the flash whizzing past into the trees behind the road.

Whatever was hitting them was big. Mike suddenly remembered the tanks he'd seen under the parachutes. *Finally*, he thought, *they've arrived.*

The air around them seemed to come alive with whizzing, buzzing metal as hundreds of bullets began to strike the tank, flashes bouncing off and sparks flying in all directions. Weapons of every type and calibre were aimed at them as through the bushes and undergrowth of the training area burst men and vehicles of the enemy paratroopers. Mike saw them through the periscopes, no more than five hundred metres away.

"Bill, reverse! Get us moving, smoke left, NOW!"

The tank juddered forwards slowly, as in his haste the driver forgot to engage reverse.

Mike sent over the radio, the urgency in his voice plain to hear, "Golf Two-Two, we're out of time. Go, go, go, head up the road, we'll cover with smoke."

Seeing they were going the wrong way, Mike shouted, "Bill! Fucking wake up! REVERSE!"

"Shit! Sorry, boss, sorry!"

"Don't be sorry, just get us going backwards!"

The tank again shuddered as another round hit, the vibration passing through the tank, causing Mike's head to ring.

He tried to focus through the periscopes to find where the enemy vehicles were, his eyes still stinging from the diesel smoke that was now drifting into the turret. He felt the tank finally begin to move backwards, through its own smokescreen and pick up speed. Unfortunately, as well as hiding them from view, the smoke was now hindering them, as they found themselves reversing through their own thick bank of fog. With a huge clang from behind, the tank shuddered to a halt, throwing Mike backwards and over the gun breech, his back and shoulder roaring in protest. Had he been wearing body armour he wouldn't have felt it, but unfortunately as he was quickly finding out, he was lacking all the tools necessary to do the job.

"I think we've been hit from behind. I think we're hit!" Bill shouted over the intercom.

Watching in a daze as green tracer buzzed through the smoke above his cupola, Mike slowly raised himself up off the heavy gun breech, his teeth clenched against the stabbing pain from his back.

Confused, and with his back screaming in agony, Mike peered over the cupola looking out into the diesel fog at the back of the tank, seeing flames and smoke coming from that direction. Thankfully it wasn't from their own tank – in his excitement Bill had driven them into the abandoned Warrior vehicle.

"Bill, have you got your reverse camera on?"

"No, should I?"

"What do you think?" Mike exploded, his back aching in response. "You're going backwards, so where should you be looking? You've just driven us into another bloody vehicle!"

"I'm sorry, I'm so sorry!"

Realising now was not the time and the place, and not wanting to waste any more time, Mike replied through gritted teeth against the pain, "Don't be sorry, just do what you're fucking told, now GO FORWARD!"

Trying to ignore the pain, Mike quickly manoeuvred the tank around the dead vehicle, the smoke generator belching out more and more, helping to cover them from view. Still, bullets tore through the smokescreen – no doubt the enemy were firing blindly into the moving cloud, anticipating hitting something. Thinking that the Warriors had more than enough time to move, he reversed the tank onto the main road, the turret still facing towards the threat, the toughest armour on the tank being at the front.

"Right, Bill, get your *reverse thermal* camera on and go backwards down this road, on your own, no input from me. Keep the lines in the sight—"

"On the road," Bill interrupted, quickly wanting to prove he'd been listening.

"Good, now let's get going in reverse, keep the smoke on for now, alternate using both left and right smoke and let me know if you see the Warrior vehicles behind us. I don't want us hitting another one!"

"Okay, boss, okay!"

The tank began to move slowly backwards, the thick white smoke still belching out of both exhausts as Mike concentrated on what was in front, using the tank's thermal sight and scanning left to right with the turret, trying to locate what had fired at them. The smoke was still doing its job and Mike held his breath, as four hundred metres in front of them, two of the enemy tanks burst onto the road, the turrets scanning for them, their own basic sights unable to pierce the smoke. Out of desperation one of them began firing dumbly up the road, the one hundred and twenty-five millimetre round whizzing past and into the trees. Mike watched open-mouthed as the distance increased – thankfully they were not following. As if finding easier prey both tanks turned and headed off back towards the camp area. Mike hoped there was no one still there, remembering the GSM's last job had been to torch anything of value left behind. His thoughts were interrupted as finally his driver reported back.

"Boss, the vehicles have stopped at the junction behind us."

"Okay, keep us going backwards, let me know when you're near them."

Quickly keying in the radio, Mike asked, "Golf Two-Two this is Tango One-One, do you have a problem? I can think of better places to stop."

"Tango One-One, this is Golf Two-Zero, I'm back on these means, can we have a face to face?"

Mike recognised the codewords – 'back on these means' meant the commander had commandeered another of the vehicles after losing his own, and 'face-to-face' meant the commander wanted to chat off air. But seeing that they were less than two miles from where the enemy were still attacking, Mike wanted to put more distance between them.

"Roger, we can do, but not here." Mike knew the area well. He'd lived here for ten years, so thinking quickly he said, "We're too close to the enemy, let me take the lead and follow me in. I'll take us somewhere safe to stop."

"Golf Two-Zero, roger, understood. We'll move over and let you past. Out."

Looking through the tank's sights back up the road, and double-checking it was clear, Mike finally said, "Okay, Bill, stop using the smoke, let's save the fuel."

Lifting himself up, he looked back as the smoke began to dissipate. He hadn't realised how dark it had become since he'd first stepped on board and he could just make out the darkened silhouettes of the Warriors now parked over to the left-hand side of the road. Carefully, he guided Bill past the vehicles, the dull green glow emitting from the Warriors' turrets as the crews now had their night-vision optics turned on. As the tank reached the junction he backed it onto the opposite side of the road so that the tank ended up facing the way he wanted it to go. Mike saw the red glow from behind the tank, as its brake lights illuminated the road. "Bill, check your convoy light is on please and blackout your lights, I don't want anyone to see where we are going," he said.

After a slight pause he heard, "Okay, boss. Blackout is on and convoy light is on."

All the armoured vehicles had a small convoy light that shone from the back visible at night and only when close. It would allow the driver behind to make sure they were following the correct vehicle. It would be no good if Mike stopped later to find the convoy had disappeared up the road, following a taxi. The blackout switch was designed to kill all of the vehicle lights that made the vehicle road legal, such as the brake lights. Now that people were shooting at them, it wouldn't do to advertise their presence.

Checking with the other vehicles Mike said over the radio, "All Golf Two-Zero callsigns, Tango One-One, confirm blackout and convoy are on."

"Golf Two-Zero."

"Golf Two-One."

"Golf Two-One-Alpha."

Good, everyone was ready to move. Mike acknowledged with, "Roger, moving now. Out."

The tank moved off down the road, now the lead vehicle in its own little convoy. Mike looked back and checked the other three vehicles' dark shadows followed onto the road. Satisfied they were all there, he settled himself into the seat, turning down the brightness of the screens around him as his eyes began to adjust to the dark. He knew of a large wooded area four miles from the road they were on where they would get some distance between them and the enemy and then he could chat to the commander of Golf Two-Zero. He hoped they may even run into the other tanks; he could already see the mud and debris on the sides of the road, indicating they had at least come this way. His back still ached and he tried to roll his shoulder to flex some movement there, to get some relief from the pain. As if to add to his discomfort his stomach now began to grumble. *When was the last time I ate?* he wondered, *was it lunchtime?* Knowing that thinking about food wouldn't help him, he tried his best to ignore his stomach and zipped up his jacket against the chill of the darkness, settling in for the long ride to come.

Bovington Camp, Driver Training Area

On top of the hill, overlooking the road, Colonel Golgolvin fumed as he watched the smoke cloud dissipate to reveal an empty road. He had been certain that his Sprut tanks would come in to finish the enemy tank off. He could only watch in disbelief as four of their one hundred and twenty-five millimetre rounds had hit and bounced off – the armour was indeed as good as the British had bragged about. And then the way the tank had slowly backed away into the smoke, like some medieval beast, daring them to follow. No, he wouldn't take the bait. He had called his tanks off the hunt, he could see the road for what it was, a perfect ambush point. Instead, he would get his men to sweep the woods on both sides of the road before venturing down it.

His second in command, Major Lenosky, tapped his shoulder and pointed to the fiery wreck below them. One of their Typhoon vehicles was crushed and burning, the explosion looked like it had almost flattened the vehicle. *The enemy tank must have knocked it out*, he thought, as he watched the flames spread across the surrounding grass. Turning to the Major he nodded, "Yes, I see Sasha it looks like the British tanks were armed after all, not quite the tigers without teeth that we were led to believe. Pass that up to command, they need to know to be careful in future. Now come on, let's get inside this camp and see what the enemy have left for us."

By the time his four-by-four had bounced down the rutted track, his men had already torn open the back gate and begun to search the huge camp. Carefully they made their way up through the tank park, seeing the disarray that had followed as the British had left in a hurry. Scorched papers blew through the air and pillars of smoke rose from some of the buildings, monuments to the hasty fires that had been started. Gunfire could still be heard at the far end of the camp, as his soldiers still fought through. It had not been the simple walk-in he had been told to expect. They stopped outside one of the rows of tank hangars, its doors open and a thick pall of smoke rolling out and upwards into the night sky, the orange and yellow flames visible deep within the hangar. Off to the side, four men in camouflage knelt, their hands on the backs of their heads, looking down at the floor. Alongside them lay the two bodies of their comrades, their jackets pulled up, covering their faces, pools of crimson spreading out beneath them. Four paratroopers stood behind them, guns at the ready, watching for any signs of defiance.

A Captain stood ready to greet them, quickly saluting the Colonel as he stepped out from the vehicle.

Colonel Golgovin looked past the Captain at the inferno raging inside the hangars as he listened to the officer's report. "Sir, most of the hangars are empty, but we have found some lighter vehicles – some wheeled and some tracked – that are still in working order. We'll try to see if we can utilise them."

"And what about the tanks?" he asked suspiciously, his eyes narrowing.

"We've found seven tanks in total, five with the turrets removed. We think that the British use them to train their drivers and we've found three gun tanks. It looks like they have all been stripped for spares, all had the tracks and most of their wheels removed, probably the reason why they were left behind..."

"And where are they?" Golgolvin demanded, already fearing the answer.

"They're in the hangar you're looking at now, sir."

Golgolvin clenched his fists in rage. The heat and intensity of the fire told him that anything of value in the vehicles would be destroyed soon enough.

The Captain, as if sensing his Commanding Officer's anger, continued, "I'm afraid the British were able to set the fires before we could get in to stop them." Pointing to the four prisoners sat nearby he added, "We caught these men leaving the hangars as they set the fires. All the vehicles have had their fuel tanks opened and some kind of flammable jelly poured in that reacts to water – the more water you put on the flames the more intense the fire. I've pulled our men back in case they exploded, but—"

"Okay Captain, I've heard enough." Sensing that the man stood to attention before him had more to say, he then enquired, "Is that all?"

"Well, not quite sir, it looks like the British knew we were coming. The camp is mostly empty, we captured a few prisoners but nothing near the amount that we were led to believe, and..."

"And *what*, Captain? We don't have all night."

The Captain swallowed before replying, "Some of the prisoners have mentioned that most of the vehicles including some tanks left about ten minutes before we arrived. They said that they were expecting us."

"Okay, leave that to me. Leave these men here to guard our prisoners and go rejoin your men. Let me know when the rest of the camp is secured."

Watching the man run off to carry out his orders, he turned to his second in command stood nearby. "Major Lenosky, round up all the prisoners and find out exactly how many tanks left and in what direction. Also, I want to know what the British know – how did they expect us?"

The Major nodded, heading towards the guards and shouting out orders, leaving Golgolvin watching the hangars burning fiercely, the heat now becoming uncomfortable for him. *Shit*, he thought, as he stepped away into the cooler air, his mission had been to destroy the tanks or capture them. He was supposed to have rolled up into the camp and met light resistance, finding them all securely tucked away in the hangars. Hearing now that they were scattered throughout the countryside had complicated things. Now it would be a hunt to try to track them down. With only three hundred men and light armour he didn't have enough resources to hold the camp and go hunting through the woods. All he could do for now was wait for the rest of his battalion to arrive with the ground troops landing at Weymouth. Sighing to himself, he watched the prisoners being roughly pulled to their feet and frog-marched away. *Okay*, he thought, *let's go find out what they know*. At least he could have the answers for when the General arrived.

23

Breaking The Ice

B3390, somewhere near Affpuddle, Dorset.

Mike looked around him, surprised at the lack of cars on the road. Usually in the summer months these roads were packed, but he'd only seen one car coming the other way. The driver had flashed angrily at the armoured vehicles, as if trying to provoke them to turn on their lights. Mike had ignored the threat – so long as people were shooting at them, he would keep the lights off. Besides, he had no idea where the enemy were. For all he knew the location he was taking them to could already contain a company of enemy infantry. He shrugged off the dark thoughts that threatened to engulf him and focused on the road. It wasn't much further.

Seeing the forestry block and track on his right, he got Bill to slow down, ready to make the turn. Checking behind and happy that the other vehicles were still following, they turned the tank right, leaving the main road, and drove along the muddy wooded track in between the trees. Mike made sure that the gun barrel overhanging the front was low enough not to hit any of the overhanging branches. He knew the track they were on would continue for another mile before rejoining another main road, so once he felt sure that they were far enough away from the road he ordered Bill to stop, watching the shadows of the other vehicles as they closed behind the tank. Not ideal tactically, he thought – usually the vehicles would keep a safe distance in case one was hit. However, given what had just happened, he knew everyone would probably feel safer at the moment if they were grouped together.

"Bill, I've raised the gun so you can get out of your cab easily. I want you to do a quick running check. Check all the tracks and road gear. The tracks must have taken some damage with what just happened. Also, check there's nothing leaking out the back. And remember your driver's safety switch, safe to leave, it's back to live once you're out."

"Okay, boss, will do; do you have a torch?"

Ah, thought Mike, *of course*. No one had been prepared for this, and it was dark now.

"No, I don't, but do you have a mobile phone, can you use the torch on it?"

"Okay boss. Yep, will do. It's probably the only use I've got for it now."

"Bill, one more thing, what's our fuel state? How much fuel do we have left?"

"Er, just checking now... Yep, half a tank on both sides."

"Okay, thanks, now let's get those checks done. I'm off the tank to go and chat to the other commanders. Off comms."

Mike took off the headset and helmet and laying it on top of the cupola, stepped out and onto the turret roof before jumping down to the ground swiftly, both feet landing together. Rubbing his eyes, which were still red from the diesel smoke, he looked up to see the dark shapes of three soldiers approaching him, all wearing helmets and body armour. Behind them he could see other shadows of figures milling about the vehicles, some out stretching their legs and, thankfully, he could hear laughing – no doubt some were already talking about their recent near miss.

Walking towards them, he stopped by the lead Warrior, its engine softly throbbing away, the heat from the decks giving Mike a welcome blast of warm air as the three commanders walked up to him, one offering an outstretched hand.

"I just want to say a big fucking thank you, you saved our asses back there."

Taking his hand in reply, Mike shook it as he countered, "Not a problem, we should be safe here off the road for a few moments, but before we get too cosy, we need to chat about what we're going to do. Now firstly let's find out who's who. Who's in charge here, who's Golf Two-Zero?"

The man who had shaken his hand and Mike recognised as the commander from the destroyed Warrior stepped closer and introduced the men around him. "That's me, sir, I'm Corporal Webb, lads call me Spider, this here is the commander of Two-One, Corporal Patterson, lads call him Patty, and this ugly fucker here is the commander of Two-One-Alpha, Lance Corporal Jones, lads call him Jonah."

Mike nodded to all three as they were introduced, before asking, "Okay, Spider, what's the plan, where are we heading?"

Mike saw the confusion on the man's face as he looked to the others and then replied, "I was hoping you could tell us, sir? That's why I wanted to have the face-to-face with you, find out what the plan is."

Mike looked at them all as he replied calmly, "Right, guys, firstly I'm not an officer, I'm not even a serving soldier anymore. I'm ex-military, been out eleven years."

"Fucking hell!" exclaimed the one called Jonah, "I knew this was too good to be true. He's not even in the fucking army, a fucking weekend warrior."

Mike saw the demeanour on all three soldiers change in an instant. Jonah looked angry but the other two, Patty and Spider, looked more despondent, as if they'd hoped that Mike had been the answer they were looking for. He saw the shoulders drop on one and the other look to the ground shaking his head.

Jonah, the loud one, now stepped forward aggressively, his voice rising. "What the fuck, what the FUCK! Who the fuck are you, man? Playing the hero!"

Patty held up his hand. "Okay, Jonah, calm down, mate. Let's just find out what's going on here." Looking to Mike, he said, "Okay fella, mind telling us what you're doing driving one of our tanks? Is Jonah right, did you just fancy playing at being a soldier?" His tone was condescending.

Mike quickly countered, not rising to the barb. "No, I was visiting a friend who works at the camp. I used to be a tank commander and in the confusion this tank and its driver got left behind. I thought I'd take the tank, rather than leave it there to be captured along with the driver and try to get them both back to their units. Now here we all are, one big happy family. If you're not happy with me being in that turret then fine, I'll leave it to you guys, the *real* soldiers to carry on without me. I can probably walk home from here."

Mike saw them all look at each other as his words hit home, and he continued, "If, however, you do need my help, which looking at the state of you I'm guessing is a yes, then I've got years of experience, *combat* experience, plus I'm local and can help you to get where you're going."

Jonah was the first to reply, his tone sarcastic. "We don't need your fucking help, fella, but thank you all the same. Why don't you just fuck off back home and get your slippers on, get yourself a nice hot cup of cocoa and tell everyone else who'll listen all about your fucking combat experience. Leave the real fighting to us, the professionals to sort out, eh?"

Mike said nothing, leaving the soldier to rant. Instead, he looked over at Corporal Webb, the one called Spider. He could see he was thinking it over. Jonah was about to say something again when, tired of his whinging, Spider interrupted, turning to face him. "For fuck's sake Jonah, give it a rest will you, you weren't so bloody picky when this guy turned up and saved all our asses a minute ago. Don't forget that the next time you start gobbing off at him."

He turned back to Mike, asking, "What rank were you when you left?"

"Staff Sergeant, eighteen years in tanks, two tours of Afghan, two tours of Iraq, two tours of Kosovo and one tour of Bosnia. Name's Mike by the way." Mike wanted to show these lads he was no amateur.

Nodding in response and thinking quickly, Spider replied, "Okay Mike, that's good enough for me. For now he stays."

Patty smiled and nodded in agreement. Only Jonah remained the odd one out, the expression on his face letting everyone know how he felt.

"Good," said Mike. "Now that we're all acquainted, Spider, what were your last orders? Where were you told to go to?"

He shrugged his shoulders as he replied, "We didn't get time for any orders. I was ordered to get to the fuel point and get these vehicles filled up. We only managed to fill one up before the fuel point ran out of diesel. We were supposed to get an officer to lead us out, but he never turned up. We were the last out of the gates when those two vehicles showed and started brassing us up. The rest you already know."

"So fuel-wise, how much have you all got?"

Spider looked to the others before replying, "The vehicle I'm on now has a quarter of a tank."

Patty replied next. "We've got half a tank."

And finally, Jonah spat on the ground before replying, "Yeah, we've got enough fuel, mate, don't you worry about us."

Mike looked at him intently. "How much is enough? I need to know."

Jonah scowled before remarking, "Oh, you need to know do you? Are you in fucking charge now?"

Patty had decided he'd heard enough and intervened. "Jonah, stop fucking about and answer the man. How much fuel have you got onboard?"

Looking at Mike and then at the others, Jonah responded, "We've got less than a quarter of a tank."

"That's not enough fuel, Jonah!" Spider responded angrily. "Next time just tell us and stop with all the fucking about. This guy's trying to help."

Mike watched as Jonah turned and stomped off towards the other vehicles, his rage clearly getting the better of him, leaving the two Corporals alone with Mike.

"I'm guessing that the vehicle you managed to fill up with fuel was the one you had to leave behind?" Mike said.

Patty nodded in reply as Spider shook his head, frustrated. "Yeah, my old vehicle. Bloody typical ain't it?"

Mike grimaced before asking, "So, are you all from the same unit? How do you know each other?"

Patty looked back along the line of vehicles before replying, "We're all from the Regiment of Fusiliers, half our platoon was sent down here to do a refresher course on the Warrior before being sent out to Poland to train the Ukrainians on how to use it."

"How come you're not away with everyone else on summer leave?" Mike asked.

This time Spider answered. "Time frames – they wanted us out there ready to go for the end of August, we were told we'd get our leave after we'd completed the tour."

"Well, I'd say that's lucky for you both, at least you're with your own troops, they'll be used to following your orders."

The two Corporals looked at each other, as if sharing a thought, something unsaid. Mike watched them, clearly sensing that something was troubling both men. Looking around and seeing people were still stood within earshot, he motioned for them both to follow him. Walking to the front of the tank and checking no one was there to hear him he then turned to them.

"Okay, Patty, Spider, what's going on? What was that look between you back there all about?"

Both men checked behind them again to confirm that they were alone, before finally with a sigh Spider spoke first. "Look, you've got to understand both of us, we're not... Fuck! I mean we were only both promoted to Corporal to do our courses here, we're not meant be in charge. Our platoon Sergeant was sent back home yesterday, his wife's in labour, and suddenly we're in amongst all this shit. We're the ones having to decide where to go, what to do. The guys, they listen to us, but fuck we don't want to be in charge of them like this. We should have a fucking Rupert or at least a Sergeant with us."

Mike smiled at hearing the nickname he'd heard long ago still being used to describe an officer.

He understood the turmoil they were going through; he'd been there before. When you're in the lower ranks, you're one of the many. Life is simple; you get told what to do, you do it, you even have the luxury of bemoaning those at the top, criticising the decisions and getting to say you could do it better, safe in the knowledge you would never have to. But then one day, you're promoted; now you're at the top, you look around and you're not surrounded by friends anymore – you're on your own. No one tells you what to do, instead *you're* the one giving out the orders. And all those people below you, the looks, the stares, the comments. Suddenly *you're* the one being talked about in the bars. When you do well, no one notices, it's just put down as you just doing your job, but when you make a mistake; everyone knows about it, now it's your decisions being criticised. Suddenly people you used to call mates won't drink with you. There's a reason they show the rank structure in the army as a pyramid – the higher up you go, the less space there is at the top. Someone must be at the top though; it's a lonely place and some people just can't hack it. Now, due to the extreme circumstances, these two young inexperienced Corporals found themselves suddenly in charge, with no one else to help them. They weren't being weak, Mike thought, they were just being honest.

Patty now continued from Spider. "Look, we just thought – we hoped – that you were an officer. The way you spoke on the radio, it sounded calm, cool, in charge. Now we find out you're not even in the fucking army. I'm sorry, I'm not ungrateful, you helped us all out back there, but the lads, they'll... oh, fuck it, I don't know what I'm going to say to them now that Jonah's probably back there causing a mutiny."

Mike watched them both look at the ground, the weight of responsibility bearing down on them as they took in what lay ahead. Mike knew what both men needed, but would they want to hear it? he wondered. It was time for some tough love.

"Guys, listen up," Mike began. "Firstly, I'm not going to pretend to be something I'm not, so let's get that out of the way." Pointing to himself and then to the other two men he continued, "I'm not an officer and you two don't want to be in charge. Boo fucking hoo, isn't life unfair."

Mike saw them both stiffen as he spoke, his words lashing out like whips. "Well, now we've all had a little whinge about how unfair it all is, how about we dry our eyes and play a game. Let's pretend that we're all in this together and that the soldiers back there are counting on all of us to know what we're doing." He watched both men stand a little straighter at the barb. Mike was never known to be tactful and would always say it as it was. Sometimes it worked, and sometimes it didn't. Keeping a close eye on them both he continued. "Spider, Patty, I know you don't want to hear this, but tough, you've got to. You're the men in charge now, but you're not alone, you've got each other to help carry the load. Forget all the other guys because now they're no longer your mates. They don't need your friendship, they need leaders, *good* leaders, leaders they can trust and *will trust* with their lives. Now I'm not going to say it's easy, because I can tell you from experience it won't be. You'll both have to make decisions that you will think seem tough, unfair, even cruel sometimes, but you're going to make those decisions anyway because if you do nothing, if you just give up now and walk away, then you may as well go back there now and put a bullet into all those soldiers' heads. Save them the pain, the time, the hurt and suffering that's going to come. Because that's the price of being a leader – you either lead, you follow, or you get the fuck out of the way. So, what's it to be with you two?"

Mike could see they were both nodding in understanding and standing a little taller; it looked like his words had the desired effect. He broke into a smile, his voice softer, as he added, "Now, you're both lucky in the fact that I'm here. I know I'm modest, my wife always tells me so, but I'm also fucking good at my job. I used to be *very* good at my job and that's where I come in tonight with you guys. Now officially you're in charge, you're both the senior ranking men here in uniform; unofficially, I'm going to tell you both what to do. You wanted an officer, how about instead I'll be your advisor, a civilian advisor? Now Spider, Patty, would you be happy with that arrangement?"

Both men looked at each other in thought, before nodding in agreement, Spider replying, "In that case what do we call you? you don't have any rank, but we can't just call you Mike in front of the others, that just sounds far too casual."

"Right, on that front, when it's just us three, it's Mike, Patty and Spider, but in front of the others it's Mr Faulkes, Corporal Webb and Corporal Patterson, understand?"

Both men nodded and Mike said, "But remember, if anyone asks, I am *not* an officer. I don't want anyone thinking I'm posing as something I'm not." Wanting to concentrate on the task at hand he quickly added, "So getting back to our situation, fuel-wise, it could be better, what about weapons? Do you have all the vehicle weapons onboard, the thirty millimetre Rarden and the chain guns?"

Patty answered quickly this time, his tone admiring. "Ooh, so you know all about our vehicles then?"

Mike smiled as the mood lightened. "Yes, I've worked on them before, a long time ago but I can still remember. Anyway, so are they fitted?"

"Yes," Spider replied, "all vehicle weapons are fitted and operational. However, personal weapons are not looking so good, we're looking at two pistols with no rounds and three SA80s with about seven rounds each. We won't be going on the offensive just yet."

"Right, and how many people do we have with us? How many were you all carrying?"

"Shit, I didn't count," replied Patty. "Fuck, what if we've left someone behind?"

"Okay, okay," Mike replied, "forget the people left behind, there's nothing you can do about that now. Let's all go and see who we have on the vehicles and from now on, when we move off, I want you to check, physically check that those people are back on board. The responsibility lies with the vehicle commanders now. I think it best if you guys tell Jonah what we've just discussed, I don't think that right now he's in the mood to listen to me."

Spider answered up with, "Yeah, he won't take to kindly too being told what to do by a civvy."

Mike nodded. "Well, I'll leave that for you two to manage, you've got the rank to pull him in line. Remember what I said, your soldiers will want leaders, it's not a popularity contest. If Jonah becomes a problem, deal with him immediately."

Both men nodded as Mike walked with them back down the line of vehicles. They stopped by the first Warrior, its back door open, the sound of voices coming from inside. Jonah was standing by the door, illuminated by the red light shining out, chatting to the guys inside. As soon as he saw Mike, he stopped and walked away to the second vehicle. Clearly there was no love lost there. Inside the back of the vehicle Mike saw three people all staring back. One, a huge mountain of a man, was a big Fijian with a bandage on his head. The other two were smoking, silently staring back at Mike, their eyes full of curious amusement. What had Jonah told them, he wondered? The Fijian looked at Mike in surprise, before his eyes settled on Corporal Webb.

"Sir, this big lump of Fijian rock here is called Fusilier Changayaty. It's a bit of a mouthful so we just call him Changa."

Mike nodded to him as Spider added, "Changa's my driver, he got knocked about a bit when our vehicle was taken out."

One of the soldiers chuckled, playfully mocking the big man. "You bloody wet blanket, eh, Changa? Bloody fainted didn't you, you big bloody wet fart!"

Ignoring the banter, Spider pointed to the first soldier, who was inhaling deeply on a cigarette. "This is Lance Corporal Martin. We call him Doc. Former commander of this vehicle, till I took it from him. And yes, he also happens to be our team medic."

Mike nodded in greeting, the Doc merely staring back silently and blowing smoke into his direction. Spider waved it away, irritated, coughing at the smoke as he continued.

"And the other soldier you see, taking the piss out of Changa and happily killing himself slowly on those fucking cancer sticks is Fusilier Pong, lads call him Ping, he's the driver of the vehicle."

Mike again nodded in greeting, but the Fusilier was silent and merely gazed back, aware that both soldiers were scrutinising him.

Sensing the awkwardness of the moment Spider spoke out again.

"Lads, this here is Mr Faulkes, he was the one on the tank who saved our asses back there."

Spider's words seemed to have the desired effect, breaking down the barrier as both now nodded in thanks. Meanwhile, the Fijian, as if finally understanding what had been said earlier in jest, leant forwards to cuff the one called Ping around the ear. The soldier laughed and ducked backwards, easily moving away from the blow as Changa shouted back in his broad Fijian accent, "Ping, you cheeky bastard! Fuck off! Bloody fainted? I was headbutting those bloody rounds!"

Seeing Mike looking on, confused, Spider quickly explained, "Changa here is one lucky boy, his driver's hatch wasn't closed properly, so when those rounds came our way, his hatch was torn open. He ended up sat there, trying to hold his hatch in place with nothing to protect him except his good Fijian humour. And those legs you see through the turret belong to my gunner, Fusilier Jenkins, Jenks to his mates."

"Okay, so including you Spider that's now five onboard Golf Two-Zero," Mike replied, looking around for something to write with. Quickly, Doc leaned forward with a permanent marker in hand. Mike nodded his thanks as he wrote the number on his arm.

"Mind if I borrow this?" he asked Doc, who simply nodded whilst drawing deeply again on his cigarette. "Keep it, I've got more," he replied uninterestedly as he began making circles with the exhaled smoke.

Mike turned to walk away, when the Fijian with speed belying his size shot out a hand, grabbing his. Without realising it, Mike quickly countered, his reflexes and training coming on instinct, even being as tired as he was. The Fijian yelled in surprise as Mike got him into a wrist lock and dropped low to the ground, the movement almost pulling him out of the armoured vehicle's door. Quickly realising there was no threat Mike had to stop himself, trying now to help keep the soldier from tumbling out onto the ground.

Changa sat back, a surprised look on his face as Mike replied, "Shit, I'm sorry, Changa, I thought you were trying to hit me. It's a—"

The Fijian's face broke into a huge grin as he began to laugh, interrupting Mike and pulling him closer into the vehicle into a friendly bear hug, Mike feeling the power in the man. He was glad he'd seen the funny side, as the thought of having a fight with this man-mountain filled him with dread.

Releasing him, Changa said loudly, "I was only going to thank you, Mr Faulkes, thank you for coming back for us. But that was quick – you're quick!"

Chuckling more out of relief than humour, Mike replied, "You're welcome, Changa. Now if you'll excuse me." He turned and followed the two Corporals as they walked to the second vehicle, hearing the laughter and animated chatter fade away as they left the three men no doubt talking about him again, hopefully now in a more positive light, he thought. Approaching the rear door of the second vehicle was a repeat of the first. Jonah was chatting to the occupants, and with Mike's arrival, he simply turned and walked away to the third. He was obviously chatting to the soldiers within, warning them about Mike. *Every unit has one*, he thought, *a troublemaker who loves the gossip, painting people in the worst possible light and making a hard task even worse.* Looking into the back of the vehicle he saw two people. Both stepped out into the darkness as Corporal Patterson introduced them. "Mr Faulkes, this is my vehicle Golf Two-One and these are my crew; this is my gunner Fusilier Siddal – we all call him Sid – and this is my driver, Fusilier Whipp – lads call him Whippet."

Both soldiers assessed Mike, looking him up and down. Sid spoke first, a strong Liverpool accent bursting through, "Eh, mate, were you the one driving that tank? Did you really ram and crush that vehicle like Whippet here says?"

Mike was about to answer when Patty quickly cut in, his tone forceful. "Now, Sid, there's to be none of this 'mate' shit, you're to call Mr Faulkes either sir, or Mr Faulkes, but never mate, okay?"

The young soldier's face creased in confusion and he replied, "Fuck that, la. Jonah says he's a civvy like, I ain't calling no fucking officer wannabe *sir*!"

Spider was about to say something when Patty stepped forward, his forehead almost touching the young soldier's, his eyes boring into him, anger rising in his voice. "Now you fucking listen here. I don't give a fuck what Jonah says, we're in charge. If I told you to call him your fucking highness, then that's what you call him, do you understand me? You're fucking embarrassing yourself *and* you're embarrassing me. Is this how we say thanks to people who help us?"

The young soldier looked to the ground, realising that Mike now had the backing and support of the two Corporals as Spider stepped closer to stand by Patty, confirming who was really in charge.

"I'm sorry Patty, I didn't—"

"Corporal Patterson!" Spider interrupted him. "Right now, it's fucking Corporal Patterson, do you understand, *Fusilier*?"

The young Fusilier looked up, stiffening immediately, knowing he'd crossed the line. "Yes Corporal, my apologies."

Mike looked further into the back of the vehicle, seeing the other empty seats. Looking over to Patty he asked, "Just these two, Corporal Patterson? You've no one else in the back?"

"Just these two, Mr Faulkes," Patty replied as Mike wrote on his arm saying, "Golf Two-One, with three onboard."

Nodding goodbye to the two young soldiers, Mike turned and continued further down towards the last Warrior, with the two Corporals in tow. Like the others, its back door was sat open, and two other soldiers were stood by it, chatting to each other.

The conversation stopped as the three men approached, the two soldiers nodding towards the two Corporals in recognition.

It was Spider who spoke first. "Lads, this is Mr Faulkes, he's the one whose been helping us tonight."

Both soldiers nodded and said hello out of forced courtesy. Clearly, they'd heard and seen the earlier encounter between Patty and Fusilier Siddal.

"Mr Faulkes, I'd like to introduce you to the crew of Two-One-Alpha. The commander, Lance Corporal Jones, you've already had the pleasure of meeting. This here is Fusilier Grimm, the vehicle gunner, we all call him Reaper, I think you can understand why, and this is the driver, Fusilier Kerr – the guys call him Jo."

Mike nodded to them both before turning to look into the back of the vehicle, expecting to see the angry face of Jonah staring back, but he could only see the legs of the soldier as he stood in the turret. Clearly, he wanted to be left alone. He saw another person, sat on the furthest seat away from the door, almost hiding in the shadows. He stepped into the vehicle to get a closer look, seeing a face he recognised straight away.

"Trooper Smith! What the hell are you doing in the back of here?"

"Mr Faulkes! Sir, how did you get here? I thought you were left back at the camp?"

Seeing them chatting, and not recognising the soldier, Spider looked to the vehicle gunner, asking, "Reaper, who the fuck's this, and how did you end up with him in the back?"

"I had no idea he was in there!" the Fusilier replied, confused, and then he demanded, "What about it, mate, mind explaining how the hell you got into the back of my vehicle without me knowing?"

The young Trooper leant forward, his eyes darting nervously between the faces of the men staring back at him as he spoke. "I was at the fuel point when it all kicked off. The GSM had grabbed a few of us from the guard detail to help him sabotage the camp. We'd been to the cookhouse to grab bags of sugar, the GSM was using it to start fires, some kind of sticky napalm he knew how to make. We'd made our way to the fuel point waiting for you all to leave, so we could sabotage it – he was going to pour the sugar into the fuel tanks after you left, but before we could do that, the enemy arrived and everyone just started to leave. Then the firing started, and everything went to shit. The GSM grabbed us and pushed us into the back of this vehicle, told us to get away out of it and that he'd do it all himself. We told him we'd stay, that we shouldn't leave him behind, but he wouldn't have it. As he pushed us in, and the door began to close, I saw him smiling. He was actually laughing about it, Why? What was so funny? We should have stayed with him."

Seeing his eyes welling up and hearing the sadness in his voice, Mike quickly reached in, putting a hand on his arm, hoping to distract him from his dark thoughts. "Listen, I never found out, but what course were you here on, was it driving or gunnery?"

He swallowed, his Adam's apple bobbing up and down as he looked up, more focused now. "Gunnery, I'm trained to be a gunner. I haven't live-fired yet on the ranges, that's the only thing left to do before I'm qualified. I was supposed to be doing that next week when everyone came back from leave..."

Smiling sympathetically, Mike replied, "Okay, well that's good enough for me. Let's get you out of the back of here, I want you to grab your gear and go to the front of the line of vehicles. You'll see the Chally 2; get onboard and settled in, driver's called Bill. Introduce yourself and tell him I'll be along shortly."

They watched as the Trooper picked up his helmet and carbine and jumped down out of the back of the vehicle, wiping his eyes. As he was about to walk away Spider stopped him, a confused look on his face as he enquired, "Hang on. 'Us' ? You said, 'us' a moment ago – does that mean there's more of you?"

Nodding, he wiped his nose with the back of his hand and replied, "Yes, Corporal, there's me, Private Nock and Private Jackson. I think they're AGC, they're from the admin office."

"Clerks?" Mike said, surprised. "There's two clerks with you?"

"Yes, sir, they're just out in the woods over there, they needed to... well, they needed the bathroom."

"Why not just go here, by the side of the road?" Patty asked, confused.

The Trooper's face creased incredulously as if to highlight the obviousness of the question as he replied, "Well, because they're women, Corporal, they wanted privacy."

"How long they been gone?" Mike shot back, looking over at the treeline.

"About five minutes. I watched them go that way," he replied, pointing in the rough area.

Watching the Trooper walk away, Mike quietly walked off the track and into the woods, the sounds of the heavy diesel engines fading into the distance as he looked for signs of the two other soldiers. Carefully he crept forward, his footsteps slow, checking his footing – the last thing he wanted was to fall over now. His eyes had adjusted to the dark and he could make out the distinct shadows of the trees, but out of habit, to protect his eyes he walked forward with one hand raised in front of him, to ward off the thinner branches and bushes that came his way. He couldn't see any torches flashing in the woods and couldn't hear any branches breaking, so he knew they were not in any trouble. Usually when people walked away from vehicles and into woods in the dark, the danger would be from not seeing the ground ahead and falling over and becoming disorientated. Then getting lost could become a real possibility. He stopped to check how far he'd come, when he was aware of Patty and Spider following him. As they drew near he said in a hushed voice, "We'd best find them, with these woods and the darkness, if they get lost, they'll wander off in any direction, and we may never see them again."

Patty whispered back, "Yeah, happened to me a few times when I was a young lad, walked off for a shit in the dark, lost sight of the vehicles and suddenly every tree looks the same. I walked for miles before I found the guys again. And you know what the biggest kicker was?"

"No?" Mike whispered, expecting something serious to have happened.

Patty nudged Mike as he smirked and said, "I lost the toilet roll for the crew and for the next two weeks I was wiping my arse on my socks!"

Spider quickly fired back, "I bet for those two weeks your socks were the cleanest part of your body."

Smiling, and happy to break the tension, all three men spaced out a few metres and continued to walk forward, stopping every ten paces to try to hear any noises. Mike would open his mouth, his jaw hanging slack to hear better. He'd never understood the science behind it, but just knew that for whatever reason it worked and he'd always been able to hear better at night, so now, he stood there, his jaw slightly open, with his head cocked to one side, listening for anything that sounded human. Suddenly, he could hear something on the wind, a faint noise from the bushes over to his right. He waved his hand over to the other two soldiers, who in the dim light could see him signal over to the noise. Patty could hear it too and nodded confidently, confirming Mike's suspicions. Mike walked forward, the noise becoming louder and more pronounced – someone was crying.

Mike began to walk confidently forward now, forgetting himself, as underfoot a large twig cracked, the noise as loud as a thunder cracker.

Shit, thought Mike, as all three men froze mid-step.

Immediately the crying stopped, replaced by a female voice, loud and scared. "Who's there? Who is that?"

Mike closed his eyes, desperately trying to remember the last names of the two soldiers. Without wanting to alarm the crying soldier anymore he quickly replied, "Listen, we're here to help, we're with the—"

He got no further, as with a flash of blinding light, he heard gunfire, the sound making him jump. Bullets ripped through the trees around him. He threw himself forwards, seeing the two others do the same, as shouts of alarm began to sound from the direction of the vehicles.

After a few rounds had passed overhead, he heard the voice shout back, "Fucking stay back, stay back. I'll fucking shoot you. I'm armed and I'll shoot you!"

Great, he thought, *she's afraid, and armed with one of the few weapons we've got, and now she's wasting ammo trying to shoot her own side. This night gets better and better.*

He heard Patty trying to get his attention. Looking over, he saw the Corporal had removed his rifle and was pointing it towards the direction of the clerk. Quickly shaking his head in reply, Mike realised he'd have to talk the clerk down.

He shouted back, "Listen, Private, we're here to help. I know you were with the GSM back at the camp, Trooper Smith has told us. We're with the vehicles you were just on. We were just coming over to see if you're all right, that's all. We don't mean you any harm, okay?"

"Trooper Smith? I don't believe you. You're here to get me. I saw the bodies, I saw people being shot back there. No, fuck off, you're lying. Stay away, STAY AWAY!"

Sensing she would fire again he quickly countered, "Bags of sugar! Bags of sugar, you were told to get bags of sugar and go to the POL point. He's already told us. The GSM was there, he pushed you all into the back of the vehicle. There were three of you and you didn't want to leave the GSM behind, but you had to. He was laughing, the GSM, he looked like he was laughing."

Mike could hear the sobbing again, this time louder. He could hear the others coming loudly through the undergrowth from the vehicles, getting closer. He was about to say something when Spider shouted in warning, "Everyone stay back, stay well back. We've got this sorted. We're all okay, just stay where you all are."

He recognised the voice of Doc shouting back, "You okay? No one hurt? We heard gunfire."

"Yeah," Spider shouted back, "it's all good. We've got a scared lady and she seems to have more ammo than we have. Just wait there, Doc, we'll call you forward if we need you."

Slowly standing up, Mike began talking again, keeping his voice low and calm as he walked towards the sound of the sobbing. "Listen, Private, I'm walking towards you slowly. I'm not armed and I don't mean you any harm. I just want to check that you're okay. Can you talk to me? Can you let me know you're okay?"

Mike slowly walked closer, the sound of crying getting louder. He kept talking, not wanting to startle the girl. He suddenly stopped as he realised he had almost stood on her, his feet making contact with her feet, she had been that close. He stopped and looked down, now able to make out the shape of her in the darkness. Were there two of them down there? Mike wondered, as his eyes adjusted further to the dark, and he could take in the scene fully. The Private was sat on the floor, her back against a tree stump and her legs splayed out in front of her, the rifle lying by her side. Across her lap was the body of another female soldier, wearing body armour, but with her helmet removed and her head being held in the arms of the sobbing soldier. She looked to be asleep, almost peaceful, with her eyes closed. Mike could see the dark stain running down her legs, the blood being the only telltale sign that anything was wrong. Seeing the rifle on the floor, Mike slowly sat down beside the soldier, gently moving the rifle away out of reach. The bolt was forwards, and it felt heavy, so there were still rounds left in it, he thought.

"Hey, what's your name?" he asked softly, as the girl continued to gently stroke the hair of her friend.

In between sobs she said, "Rachel, my name's Rachel."

"Okay, Rachel, and what's your friend called? What's her name?"

"Sharon."

"Okay, Rachel, listen to me, look at me, I've got some friends over there who can help us. They can come and help Sharon, but I need them to come in now. Would you be okay if we do that, if they come closer to help Sharon?"

"She told me she was fine, that everything was fine," she carried on, oblivious to what Mike had asked. She was in shock; he'd seen it before and he knew he had to be very careful with how he treated her. She carried on explaining. "She only said she wanted to go to the toilet when we stopped, asked me to come with her, said she needed the company. We came here, she sat down, and then asked me to hold her. That's when I saw the blood, lots of blood..."

Mike heard the others slowly walking forwards so as not to startle the soldier. Patty came into view, his weapon held at the ready, shining a torch onto the scene before exclaiming, "Oh shit. Doc! Man down! Man down! Get over here!"

Ignoring the others, she carried on softly, playing the events over again. "She asked me to sit here with her. I told her we should get the others, to go get help, but she didn't want to, she said it was too late. It was peaceful, tranquil. She said this was her place, that she wanted to die here, that she was going to see her mum again..." Her voice trailed off as she began sob again.

The undergrowth burst into life around them as Doc ran over, quickly followed by Ping carrying the medical Bergen, setting it down beside them. Doc quickly began opening the pouches and pulling out bandages and equipment as he looked over the body. "I need some light here," he said urgently, as Patty tried his best with the torch. Mike took the shoulders of the Private, gently lifting her up and taking her to one side as Doc moved the body onto the floor and began cutting off her body armour and checking her wounds. Others now burst through the bushes to join them, standing in mute shock with the sight of the body on the ground.

"What happened? Was she just shot?" Doc asked, looking up to those around him as he worked.

"I think she was shot earlier," Mike replied, looking back. "I think it happened before we left the camp."

"What's her name?" Doc asked as he began to cut carefully away at her smock.

"Sharon," the girl replied, looking up, the tears streaming down her face. "Her name's Sharon."

Seeing the big Fijian, Mike quickly walked the girl away from the scene over to him. "Changa, she's had a bit of a shock, can you take her back to your wagon, see if you can get her anything sweet to eat or drink, but don't leave her alone, and don't let her near any weapons."

"Sure thing. Come on, love, let's get you somewhere warm."

Mike watched the big hulk of a man disappear into the darkness back to the wagons with the clerk, his arm gently comforting her. Mike turned to check on Doc; four of the men were trying to light the scene with torches or mobile phones as best they could. Doc was kneeling next to Sharon, and Mike could see clearly now with the light just how much blood there was soaking into the mud and the leaves. Doc began to work and was talking loudly to the girl. "Sharon, can you hear me? I need you to talk to me, love. Come on, wake up, tell me where it hurts, where are you hurting?" The girl's face was deathly white. Doc said, "Fucking hell," as he cut away her combat shirt, revealing a large mass of blood that had been hidden. A single bullet wound was now visible to her lower abdomen, the blood dark, almost black in colour. Sighing and shaking his head angrily, Doc leaned forward to check her pulse. After a few seconds he looked up, his face strained. "She's gone. Even if she hadn't lost so much blood, it looks like she took a round to the liver. She'd be dead now even if I'd managed to treat her up at the camp." Annoyed, he threw one of the bandages covered in blood into the bush next to him, shouting, "Fuck!"

He sat shaking his head, his anger quickly replaced by confusion when he looked up to the others around him, asking, "Where did she come from? How did she get here?"

"We think she was in the back of Jonah's wagon," Spider said dejectedly before sighing.

"Why didn't he tell us? Fucking Jonah! He's the vehicle commander," Sid exploded.

Spider rounded on him. "It doesn't fucking matter now does it? She was always going to die, even if we knew she was in there. Doc's already said so, now let's save it for the enemy."

The Fusilier looked away, his face full of anger as Mike knelt to remove her dog tags, quickly realising she didn't have any on. Looking at her blood-stained name tag on her shirt, he read the name 'Jackson', so this was Private Jackson, he thought. He looked closer, recognising her from the tank park. She wasn't a clerk like Trooper Smith had said, he thought, she was one of the signallers that had left with the GSM in his Land Rover. Mike guessed that after leaving the tank park the GSM had taken them to the fuel point to get them onboard one of the vehicles.

Patty knelt down, picking up the dead girl's rifle, expertly removing the magazine, checking the action, making the weapon safe.

"Girl's got a full magazine here, where the hell did she get the extra ammo?"

Looking up, Mike replied, "She flew in with the other girl and an officer earlier on the Wildcat. I'm guessing wherever they came from they were given a full bomb load of ammo."

Reaching over to confirm, Mike opened the magazine pouches of her assault vest, pulling out six blood-soaked magazines full of ammunition, handing them to the nearest soldier. "There you go, get the blood washed off and you've got more rounds for your guys, plus we've now got two more weapons. The other signaller's weapon is over there by the tree stump." Ping reached over to where Mike pointed, and removing the magazine, made the weapon safe to handle before looking inside the magazine and whistling softly to himself.

"Phew! Fuck, you were lucky, Mr Faulkes, there's still half a magazine here. The lady could have taken your head off and still had change."

Looking down at the dead body Mike replied, "Well, somehow, Ping, it doesn't feel very lucky."

Doc began to pack his kit away. Mike was snapped from his thoughts by Patty asking, "So what shall we do with her? Do we bury her here?"

Looking around at the darkened sky Mike said, "I think we're wasting time here, we need to move on quickly, who knows who heard that gunfire. There's no time to bury her. Let's get her wrapped up, put her in the back of Jonah's wagon for now and keep moving. We can bury her later when we get more time. We're still too close to the camp and from what I heard we've got more enemy landings taking place at Weymouth and Poole. We need to put some distance between us and them before daylight comes. If, of course, you agree?"

As he said that last part Mike had nodded towards the two Corporals, keen to show in front of the other assembled soldiers that he was merely offering advice.

"Okay," replied Spider, "but where do we go? We don't yet know where the others got to, and for all we know we could be heading in the wrong direction."

"Whatever the plan is, the vehicles were told to head north of Dorchester, something to do with getting to Yeovil. I wasn't in on the O group where they discussed this. All I know is that afterwards, Chris, my friend, told me that's where they were heading to and that sounds like a better bet than sitting here."

"What about fuel?" Patty asked. "There's no way we've got enough fuel to get there."

"No, we don't," Mike countered, but we've got enough fuel to get some of the way. Let's head off and see what we can find along the way. Besides, with plenty of farms around the area, we can always borrow some if we have to."

Patty and Spider looked at each other in agreement, and Spider replied, "Right, guys, we'll do it like he said. Let's get ready to move. Make sure you all do a head count before we go – no one is getting left behind or forgotten about again."

Doc looked down, pointing to the body. "Who's carrying her back to the wagon?"

Mike replied, "I'll take her, she won't be that heavy."

"I'll help you," Reaper added softly. "I was on that wagon too, I should have seen her in the back, the responsibility is mine to share."

Nodding in acknowledgement, Mike leant down, buttoning up the soldier's clothing, trying to give her some dignity back. He then grasped the body under the arms. Taking her legs, Reaper counted to three and they both lifted her together. Even with the added weight of the body armour she couldn't have weighed more than ten stone. They walked slowly as Patty lit the way for them using his torch, treading gently, careful not to drop the dead woman.

Arriving at the back of the Two-One-Alpha, they could see the door was still open. Mike looked up to see the silhouette of Jonah staring down from the turret, watching with curiosity. Stepping inside the vehicle, he carefully placed the woman's body on the floor, folding her arms across her chest, in the typical undertakers' pose, before carefully stepping out of the back. As he stepped out of the Warrior, Reaper put out a hand to stop him, looking at him, his face full of regret and guilt.

"Mr Faulkes, I didn't know she was in there. Had I known—"

"Reaper, stop fucking about and get onboard, we're leaving shortly!" Jonah shouted down from the turret.

Mike looked back at Reaper, his voice low. "I'll let you tell him. Good luck." Waving farewell, he jogged back towards the front of the vehicles, passing the crews as they all began to mount up, the rear doors closing as the turret crews put their headsets on. He jumped onboard the tank. Seeing the driver's hatch already closed, he stepped up and carefully lowered himself into the commander's seat, his feet feeling the gunner's back rest was now up. Putting on the headset and helmet, he leaned forward, checking the gunner's station was occupied. Tapping gently with his feet, he saw the face of Trooper Smith look back at him, giving a thumbs up and a smile. *Good,* thought Mike, *maybe amongst more familiar surroundings he'll forget for the moment about what he saw earlier.* He didn't want to mention the dead soldier just yet, remembering the Trooper had already witnessed another of his colleagues dying in the guardroom attack as well as the GSM. Mike decided for now to stay quiet and to give the young lad time to process it all.

Adjusting the microphone and blowing into it to check feedback in his earpiece, Mike reported, "Okay, everyone, back on comms now."

Looking down to the gunner Mike added, "Right then Trooper Smith, we need to know what to call you when on the tank. So, do you have a nickname?"

"My training Corporal called me Smudge sir, if that helps?"

"It does. So, Smudge it is from now on." Mike replied smirking, thinking to himself, *good old army nicknames. They never change.*

Going back to his driver Mike said, "Bill, did you find anything wrong with the tracks or running gear?"

"No, boss, a few links were bent slightly, and we've got some deep gouges in some of the road wheels, but we should be all right."

"Good. Now then, *Smudge*, you all settled down there? You happy with everything?

"Er, yeah, sir, umm, yeah, I'll be okay."

Mike could sense something was wrong.

Leaning forwards again to look at him Mike asked, "Smudge, what is it? That answer didn't exactly fill me with confidence just then. You are a gunner, right?"

"Oh yeah, I'm a gunner, sir. It's just, er, I've never..."

"For fuck's sake, Smudge, just spit it out. What is it?" Mike demanded.

"I've never driven around in a gun tank before, sir. I mean, I've been in the turret of a tank, just not when it's being driven about. It's a lot smaller than I thought, and it's just I'm trying to remember where to keep everything."

Mike remembered when he had first sat in the gunner's seat. It was a small, cramped position and offered the easiest way to get sick, when the tank was bouncing across country. With only the gun sight or a small periscope to look out of and all the computers, sighting systems and main gun crammed around him, heating him up, it was a great seat in the winter but hell in the summer. There was an air-conditioning system fitted to cool the computer but not the crew, and with the hatches open, it would rarely work, if ever. Now as Smudge was finding out for the first time, the reality of being in the gunner's seat was different to the light and airy spacious simulators that he had learnt in.

"Right, Smudge, fair enough. Before we get going, make sure to keep the gun-kit switch on your control panel set to 'trav' okay? This way the computer will keep the gun within its travel limits, so unless you press the grip switch the gun will stay front. Okay?"

"Okay," Smudge replied, a bit more confidently this time.

"For now, we're going to leave the gun front, but as we're going along, I want you to look around your gunner's position and get used to where everything is. It should be second nature to you already, but just use the time as we're travelling to know where all the switches are and get used to opening and closing your sight hoods. When carrying out an engagement you shouldn't have to remove your head from the sight to keep looking at the controls. Keep checking your Gun Position Indicator every two to three minutes, it'll give you an idea of where the turret is pointing – if you know that, then it will help fight the motion sickness."

"Yes, sir. Will do."

"And don't call me sir, call me boss when we're on the wagon, okay?"

"Sorry, sir, I mean boss..."

Mike grinned as he thought back to his own past experiences as a gunner. Using the red light of the turret, he pulled the permanent pen out and scribbled on the turret ring the figure sixteen. Then, with a start, remembering the dead girl, the grin disappeared as quickly he crossed it out and rewrote fifteen – the number of people still alive that he now had with him. Keying the pressel to talk over the radio, he said,

"All callsigns, Tango One-One, call back when ready."

"Golf Two-Zero, ready."

"Golf Two-One, ready."

"Golf Two-One-Alpha, ready."

He looked around at the darkness, thinking to himself long and hard. It wasn't too late, he could still jump off the tank and leave them all to it, get himself home and safely out of the way of it all. Was it his fight anymore? he questioned. Who the hell did he think he was, playing at being the leader. He wasn't in the army anymore, did he even have any right to be there? Thinking of his family and about Kate again, he looked down at the numbers he'd written on the cupola, his eyes drawn to the crossed-out figure of sixteen, thinking of the dead soldier, then thinking of the other fifteen still alive. He couldn't leave them, not now, not with what he'd just seen.

Closing his eyes for a second, he took a deep breath, clearing his mind of the distractions and fear of failure and focusing on the task at hand. Then, with renewed clarity he opened his eyes, his resolve firm again. He could do this, they could all do this.

"Okay, Bill, let's get going..."

24

Choices

Dorset Police Headquarters, Winfrith

"Ma'am, we've still no word from the armed response vehicles that were sent to Weymouth, and now we've lost contact with the two patrol cars in the Bovington area. I'm trying to send it up the chain, but no one's picking up on the radios. It's strange, because we've got communications with Poole Police Headquarters but not with anyone outside of the county. Poole are reporting the same issues. I'll keep trying the phone lines but they're still out. It's bloody strange and I've never seen anything like this before."

The Chief Superintendent looked across the control room as the Sergeant relayed the report. She walked quickly over to the regional map, the coloured markers on it denoting the locations of her patrol cars. She'd already sent three of her ARVs to Weymouth after hearing a panicked radio message from a patrol car reporting shots being fired. Then another patrol car had reported seeing explosions and flames from the area around Bovington. The recently rebuilt police headquarters was only seven miles from the camp, and from the building's windows they could see the glow from a large series of fires on the dark horizon. Perhaps the army had an accident at the camp, she'd thought. She'd dispatched another two cars along with an ambulance and the fire brigade to the camp. And now nothing. Radio silence. It was as if everyone had just disappeared into thin air. The ambulance crews and fire brigade never stayed silent for this amount of time, and she could hear the dispatchers over the radios trying to raise them on their own channels. As for her own ARV teams, they were the best she had and now they were all off the air, the usual radio traffic falling silent. What the hell was going on? she thought, quickly snapping out orders to the Sergeant.

"Get me through to Poole, I want their three ARVs here immediately and I want any available units that they have to be sent to us. Tell them all to stay clear of Bovington. Also, I want a car sent to pick up the Police Commissioner, I want him here now."

"But, ma'am, it's nearly midnight, the Police Commissioner—"

"Is paid twenty-four seven and works twenty-four-seven. He needs to be here to see this, we need the additional support and I need his input. Now go bring him in."

"Yes, ma'am." The Sergeant turned and raced away to pass on the orders. The headquarters would usually have a staff of over three hundred working there, but at this time of night, it was only the duty team with an ops room staff of twenty. The Chief Super knew that Dorset only had eight-armed response vehicles at any one time covering the whole county and now she'd just allocated six of them to Weymouth. She was taking a gamble. If they were needed elsewhere quickly, then she'd compromised that, but something was going on there, she knew it... something just didn't add up.

Quebec Charlie Five-Four

"Christ, Sandra! You nearly clipped that car!" he exclaimed as he clung onto the side pillar of the car as it weaved through the deserted streets. The ARV was screaming through the narrow roads, closely chasing the other two ARVs as they approached the outskirts of Weymouth town.

The driver simply smiled back, replying, "Nearly, but didn't, so stop bitching will you!"

He didn't argue, he wanted her concentration solely on keeping the two-tonne vehicle from crashing as they tore through at eighty miles per hour. The last message they'd received was that a patrol car in the area of Portland had reported shots being heard. Most times these call-outs turned out to be false alarms and he was fully expecting nothing more than a few drunken louts and a bag of firecrackers. Still, until they knew for sure, every shout was to be treated as a threat. The blue lights reflected a hue off the darkened shop windows as he looked down to change his radio frequency to the chat net.

"Five-Seven, this is Five-Four, do you have any more details on this shout?"

He heard the calm voice of their team Sergeant reply over his earpiece. "One of our patrols reported shots fired west of the bridge. We'll deploy from there and check it out on foot. I'm struggling with comms back to Control. Five-Four, can you give them a shout, tell them to wake the fuck up will you."

He smiled, replying, "Roger, Five-Seven, I'll try them now." Flicking back to the main frequency he asked, "Control, this is Quebec Charlie Five-Four, are you receiving me. Over?"

He released the radio pressel to hang on again, as the three cars negotiated a roundabout far faster than they were supposed to, the tyres squealing in protest as they passed through the town centre. He looked over to see his driver still smiling, thankful that she was top of the class of her advanced driving course. Looking ahead, he could see the other two cars were still wildly weaving, no doubt thanks to the erratic inputs of their drivers. He certainly had the better deal with Sandra behind the wheel.

He tried the radio again. "Hello, Control, this is Quebec Charlie Five-Four, radio check. Over."

"These fucking comms never work round here," Sandra shot back.

He gave her a knowing look, quickly changing back to the chatnet.

"Five-Seven, this is Five-Four, no luck on comms, looks like we're in a dead spot."

"Roger, Five-Four, thanks for trying. Out."

He looked out of the left side of the car, seeing its reflection in the shop windows as they shot past, the streets narrowing as they approached the town's quay bridge and out of impulse he felt his foot go forward to press the imaginary brake pedal. Seeing the action, his colleague replied mockingly, "For Christ's sake, will you relax and let me drive? I do know what—"

She was cut short as a blinding light lit up to their front, illuminating the bridge as if it was daylight. The three vehicles instinctively jammed on their brakes as the drivers struggled to see. The lead vehicle screeched to a halt whilst the second swerved across the bridge, blocking both lanes, with their own vehicle stopping just short of the bridge. They shielded their eyes as suddenly they heard the sharp reports of automatic gunfire. The lead ARV tried to reverse, its engine racing and tyres scrabbling for grip as it launched backwards, slamming into the side of the second ARV, disabling them both as glass and metal was torn from them. Upon impulse he shouted, "Contact front!" as Sandra slammed their ARV into reverse, the tyres and engine squealing in protest as it tried to get away. With his eyes still blinded from the light, he could feel rather than see the incoming rounds began to punch through the car's metal. He could almost feel the air parting as they whizzed close to him, the noise like angry hornets as they buzzed past. The windscreen shattered inwards, the glass coating them both as the car lurched to a halt. He looked over to see Sandra, her face now a bloody mask from the flying glass and metal as she pulled her pistol out and began firing back randomly from the driver's seat, yelling over to him, "The engine's dead, bail out! Bail out!"

He saw the rounds punching into the seat around her, seemingly in slow motion, as he pulled out his own pistol, yelling as he did so, "We're on a hill, take your foot off the brake, let it roll off the bridge! LET IT ROLL!"

The vehicle rolled slowly backwards, as she did just that, gathering momentum, each metre taking it further away from danger as the rounds continued to thunk into the bodywork and ricochet off the tarmac in a flurry of sparks. He waited until they were a further ten metres clear of the bridge before saying, "Okay, that's enough," feeling the jolt as she stopped the ARV. He jumped out, keeping his body low as he ran to the back of the vehicle. He knew what the plan was, they'd practised this thousands of times.

Opening the boot, he shook his head and rubbed his eyes to clear his vision from the bright light, before keying in the code to open the strong box, pulling out his G36 assault rifle, connecting the sling to his body armour and fitting a magazine and making ready, pulling the cocking handle rearwards to load a round. Then he grabbed Sandra's rifle. He knew then that all he had to do was come round to the front of the car, covering her whilst she got out, then together they'd storm forward to regroup with the other ARV crews and take down whoever was firing at them. They'd spent hundreds of hours practising and perfecting the technique on the ranges and now, this time it was for real. Taking a deep breath to steady himself, he stepped around the driver's side of the vehicle with the weapon held in front of him, as he scanned for targets. He could hear the gunfire still coming from the bridge, but it was now out of sight. He ran up to the driver's side, placing her G36 onto the bonnet, then, while waiting for his partner to get out and get ready, he walked slowly forward, the far end of the bridge coming back into view. He was expecting to see the other cars' officers deployed, putting down covering fire, taking control of the situation and winning the firefight, but instead what he saw left him open mouthed.

The lead ARV was fully in flames, illuminating the grisly scene as the second ARV was still under heavy fire, pieces of its body ricocheting off in all directions as the vehicle seemed to dance and jolt on its suspension as the rounds impacted into it. The body of one of the officers was lying beside the open door. At first, he thought hopefully that the officer was alive, but realised that the movement he saw from the body was the macabre jig of arms and legs twitching as the rounds being fired slammed into his colleague. No body could sustain that amount of gunfire, he thought in horror. The second ARV's blue lights were still flashing, and the glow cast a ghostly haze over the scene. Whatever was firing at them, though, was still concentrating on the second ARV. Thanks to Sandra's quick reactions they were now off the bridge and enough distance away to be out of view from the shooters. Looking over to the bridge's far end he stared in disbelief as he saw the three distinct dark shapes of the armoured vehicles, their turret cannons firing. Nothing they had in their armoury would defeat those. Who were these people? Could it be terrorists? He turned to see what was keeping his partner, she was still sat in the car. *What the fuck is she doing?* he thought angrily, was she trying to restart the car? He turned to go back, suddenly feeling a punch to the ribs, almost knocking him over. Thankfully he had the body armour on, as the incoming round had hit him squarely on the plate. Another three inches to the left and it would have hit the fleshy part of his body. Cursing his stupidity and with his back in tremendous pain, he ran back to the car.

"Sandra, what you playing at? Get out the fucking car!"

She looked back at him, ghostly white. "I'm fucked. I can't move my legs."

Looking inside, he saw in the dim light the driver's side was a mess of blood, glass and torn metal. He could see that Sandra's trousers were shredded and blood-soaked and realised he'd have to carry her out of there. Hearing shouts from the bridge's direction, he reached in, prying open the driver's door, cursing as the ripped metal caught his arm, cutting him. He picked up her rifle, slinging it over his back and slung his weapon across his chest as he reached in and grasped her around the waist, ignoring her shouts of pain as he pulled her out of the car.

"Not yet, give me a second. Wait! WAIT! FUCK!" she yelled as agonising pain shot through her.

"Yeah, yeah, yeah," he replied, ignoring her outburst. "I love you too. I'm sorry if it hurts though. Come on, girl, let's get the hell out of here." He pulled her up and hoisted her over his shoulder, relieved that she didn't weigh as much as some of the other members of the team.

She muttered through the pain, "But what about the others? We need to go help them."

Through gritted teeth he replied, "Don't you worry about them, now shut up and keep your eyes on that bridge. Let me know if you see anyone appearing, we need to move."

He began carrying her down through the darkened streets, the pain in his back getting worse. He'd prided himself on his fitness and was shocked when only fifty metres later he found himself struggling to breathe. *What the fuck?* he thought. *Come on, you can do better than this.* He looked further down the dimly lit street, noting it was another two hundred metres to the junction; he knew what he had to do. He'd find somewhere safe to hole up, call for backup and then tend to his partner's wounds. But for now, all he had to do was walk two hundred metres. With his gaze focused and ignoring the shouts of pain from his colleague, he set his head down and powered on.

Dorset Police HQ, Winfrith

In the control room, the radio loudspeaker burst to life as the controllers heard the scratchy voice of someone shouting and breathing heavily. The three controllers looked over to the Chief Super as they heard the excited voice. "Control, this is Quebec Charlie Five-Four, officer's down, officer's down... We are under fire. I repeat, we are under heavy automatic fire... we have evacuated east on foot, our vehicle has been destroyed... We were ambushed by soldiers and armoured vehicles, say again armoured vehicles... Quebec Charlie Five-Two and Five-Seven are down. Over."

The Chief Super tried to remain composed. Already the other controllers were relaying the information to the remaining patrols on the ground. Hopefully someone could get there to assist, and soon.

She hurried over to the microphone, grabbing the receiver and trying to keep her voice calm. "Quebec Charlie Five-Four, this is Control. Roger your last, we've got support on its way to you now. How many armoured vehicles and what's your location? Over."

The seconds felt like minutes as she stared at the speaker, then finally the voice came back through, this time the breathing more controlled. "Quebec Charlie

Five-Four continuing, we were ambushed on the Weymouth Bridge. I counted three armoured vehicles. They looked military. They just opened fire on us without any warning. My partner's been injured... she's got multiple gunshot wounds to the legs and we've taken cover in a shop doorway... I can hear more automatic gunfire to my south and from my position I can still see the bridge."

"Roger, understood, Five-Four, can you move yourself out of danger? Can you extract east to RV with units coming in?" She clicked her fingers to get the attention of the controller in contact with the three new ARV units racing in from Poole; looking at the map display, pointing to the area she now wanted them to go – two miles east of Weymouth. The controller nodded as she continued directing them.

"Five-Four, I've got more ARVs coming in from the east, can you move there to RV with them? Over."

Quebec *Charlie Five-Four*

Move there? he thought, disbelieving as he stared at the radio handset, *didn't you just fucking hear what I said? Our car's been destroyed and my partner's been shot multiple times in the legs.* He was tempted to send that in reply, but thought better of it – it wasn't the control room's fault and he knew they were doing all they could, but he still felt alone. He'd only managed to stagger another sixty metres from the bridge before he'd stopped and reached behind him as the pain increased with every breath. His hands came back dark, sticky and wet – fresh oxygenated blood, he thought, so he'd been hit in the lung, which explained the difficulty in breathing. Whoever had shot at them had used armour-piercing bullets, easy to defeat the body armour he wore.

Finally, exhausted, he settled for a shop doorway, raised on some stairs that afforded a small, elevated position. It wasn't ideal, but right now it was the best he could do. From their new position they could now see back up the street and onto the bridge again and at least if anyone came for them, they'd have a chance. He placed his partner carefully down, with her back against the doorway and placed her rifle into her trembling hands. She'd already dropped her pistol in the street as he'd carried her. He leaned back against the wall, sliding down to sit next to her. Together they must have looked like a couple of hobos, he thought as she looked over at him. Her face wore a mixture of pain and focus as he said, "Sandra, we can't go any further, I can't..."

She smiled weakly, her own voice soft, and the words slurred as blood pumped out of her. "It's okay, it's okay, we're here now. Let's just sit here and wait for a bit..."

He nodded, his breathing ragged as he fought to reply. "I need you... to cover the street with me, we've got... help coming but we need... to stay with it."

She said nothing but smiled back at him, her hand reaching up to weakly pat his face before falling over her chest, her usual banter and joking gone as her wounds began to take their toll.

The control room burst through his earpiece. "Five-Four, this is Control, acknowledge my last, can you move east to RV with the incoming units, over."

He rested his rifle barrel on his knee and scanned back down to the bridge, keying his radio to transmit as he did so.

Dorset Police HQ, Winfrith

There was a long delay until finally the voice replied, this time sounding weaker, "Negative, Control, I'm also hit and won't be going any further... One GSW to the back, looks like they used armour-piercing bullets... We've made it this far, but we won't be going any further. Keep the other ARVs away from here... They'll need something that can penetrate armour... We're going to stay here; I'm still watching the bridge for now... Five-Two is burning... looks to be twenty men on the bridge now... All armed, approaching Five-Seven... They're pulling the officers out of the car – one of them is alive! It looks like Quebec Charlie Two-One-Six is still alive!"

She could hear the relief in his voice over the radio as she listened in, and the armed officer continued to relay what he was seeing.

"They've got Two-One-Six out of the car... They're talking to him, looks like they're asking him questions. I can hear more armoured vehicles in the distance... Coming towards us. I think it's the port area, I think that's where they've all come from."

"Roger, Five-Four, I'll try to get that information passed up." She looked over to the controller, urgently asking, "ETA on Poole ARVs?"

"Twenty-five minutes, ma'am," was the reply, the Chief Super looking on aghast at the answer. *That's going to be twenty-four minutes too late,* she thought.

"Five-Four, this is Control. Stay with it, we've got help on the way, it will be with you shortly, hang in there, over."

"Control, they're picking him up, they're walking him to the... Oh fuck! They've just thrown him off the bridge! The bastards just threw him off the bridge... Police Sergeant Jones... Sam... They've just fucking killed him in front of us."

With the combined weight of his body armour and weapons, and even without any injuries, throwing the policeman off the bridge and into the water was a guaranteed death sentence, as he would sink like a stone to the depths of the harbour.

Her mouth hung open as she fought to regain her composure. She still had injured officers to help. They could still be saved.

"Five-Four, we've logged that, no need for you to dwell on it. You need to think about yourselves now. Can you and your partner crawl to safety? Can you break open the shop doorway and get inside?"

"Negative, Control, the door's locked with a shutter... I don't have the strength... to break through. My partner's unconscious now... I'm struggling to breathe... lung wound... I'll try to stay with it... doorway is a charity shop... raised stairwell."

"Five-Four, hang in there! Stay awake!" she yelled, the feeling of helplessness making her angry.

"I can see torches... they're coming for us now... About twenty men... In military uniforms... Another three vehicles are... by the bridge... look like tanks... they're nearly on us now... not much longer..."

No one in the control room could speak. All eyes were on the loudspeaker, the tension in the air palpable as they heard the officer's final moments play out. Over the radio they could hear the voices in the background getting louder as the officer began to speak.

"Can someone... get a message... to... my—"

The Chief Super held her hand over her mouth in shock as the gunshot echoed through the speaker and into the ops room. She'd had colleagues die in the force before, but never like this, never a cold-blooded execution played over the air. She fought back the urge to throw up, closing her eyes for a second, calming her thoughts.

One of the other controllers began to cry. She quickly rounded on her. "And who is that going to help now? If you want to cry, do it on your own time, but for now, keep it together."

The controller quickly wiped her tears away, nodding as she fought her emotions. The Sergeant returned to the control room, sensing the mood had changed when he saw the looks on the faces of those around him.

"Ma'am, what did I miss?" he asked apprehensively.

"We've just lost the three ARVs that were sent to Weymouth. They were ambushed on the bridge by men wearing military uniforms, armed with automatic weapons and armoured vehicles and tanks."

"*Tanks?*" he asked, puzzled. "Are we sure about that?"

"We just heard it now; they killed three of our officers whilst we listened in on the radio."

The shock was evident to see on the Sergeant's face. He stammered, "But tanks, we need to get the army, surely. This can't be happening, can it?"

She walked him over to the window, the glow of the fire on the horizon clear to see. "I'm betting *that* has something to do with what's going on in Weymouth."

As she looked out the window, she saw a series of quick flashes in the distance, over by Bovington camp. Was that lightning? she thought. How long before daylight? she wondered. She longed for daybreak to come quickly; with it the day shift would appear and she desperately needed the extra manpower and resources. She looked back over to her Sergeant.

"The car for the Police Commissioner?"

"Has been sent, Ma'am."

She tapped her fingers on the console in front of her as she thought through what to do next. Fifteen years of policing and she had never had a night like this. *Damn these communications blackouts*, she thought. She needed answers and she needed backup. She was interrupted from her thoughts as another controller called over.

"Ma'am, Poole are requesting the ARVs back, they're getting reports of gunfire in Poole harbour and reports of armoured vehicles and tanks with people in military uniform there!"

"What?"

She looked over at the map, first Bovington, then Weymouth and now Poole. *What the hell is this?* she thought, *is this all connected? Where the hell was the army?* Studying the map she quickly came to a horrifying conclusion.

She looked over to the controller, her voice urgent. "Rescind that request, tell Poole, on my orders that their request is denied. I want every patrol car and every ARV to pull out of the areas of Weymouth, Bovington and Poole. Those areas are now too dangerous for our officers."

The controller nodded and began relaying the orders over the radio as the Sergeant looked on confused, responding with, "Ma'am?"

She quickly pointed out the areas on the map she had just checked. "Look, reports of armed personnel and armoured vehicles, here, here and here. That's the whole area from Weymouth to Poole. What does that look like to you?"

Recounting back to his own military service the Sergeant replied, "It looks like a military invasion, ma'am, but that's not what it is. It can't be," he replied.

"Why not?" she countered. "How else can you explain it?"

He shook his head in disbelief as the controller now said, "Ma'am, the ARVs and patrols have asked where you want them to go for now?"

She looked back at the map, quickly thinking to herself before replying, "Tell all units to get to Dorchester until we have further orders for them, from there we can deploy them as we see fit."

She watched as the map symbols on the screen began to change direction as the units followed her orders. She'd already sacrificed six of her officers needlessly, she wasn't going to be responsible for the deaths of others. Until she knew what was going on, this was the safest play she had.

***

They came for them at 02:00. She remembered she had been stood by the map, briefing the Police Commissioner on the events so far, telling him about the ARVs being lost, the missing police patrols, the communications failures, the vague reports, her own thoughts on what was happening. She'd remembered seeing the disbelief on his face, the way he'd almost dismissed her out of hand. And then they burst through the door. There was no warning, there were no shouts, suddenly they were just there. Twelve heavily armed men, in camouflage with automatic weapons at the ready.

Her police officers had looked to her for instructions, they were as confused as she was. Thinking about it now, it had always been stupid to stay, caught in between Poole and Weymouth they were always on borrowed time, but even so, to see them standing there, in the middle of *her* control room, had rankled her. She had defiantly tried to tell them they had no right to be there, that this was illegal and they would pay for their actions, but they had merely laughed at her, and she winced in pain at the broken nose she had received in response. That should have been the end of it. She knew she shouldn't barb the aggressors. She'd attended plenty of police negotiations, she'd been told that you always played along with the kidnappers or the aggressors, you never angered them. But even after she picked herself up off the floor, even as the blood poured from her nose and down her white blouse, she couldn't help herself. She looked the soldier in the eyes, a fire now ignited and raging inside her and told him again to get out. She'd called him a fool and a coward – only cowards would attack unarmed people. This time there'd been no smile and she blacked out as his fist connected with her head. When she came round, she was lying on the floor of the conference room, her Sergeant kneeling next to her. This was where she found herself now, her hazy foggy memory trying to piece together the past few hours.

She slowly raised herself off the floor as white spots danced before her eyes. Her head throbbed, her nose ached, and she was forced to breathe from her mouth thanks to the congealed blood blocking her nostrils. Her cheeks felt like they had daggers being stabbed into them, but at least she was alive, she thought. Others had not been so fortunate. She could see the daylight through the windows and confused, she looked across to her Sergeant. "How long was I out for?" Her voice was croaky.

"About six hours, ma'am, we've been locked in here ever since they..." His voice trailed off, almost as if the shame of it was too hard to talk about.

"Six hours?" she exclaimed. "There was a time, you know, when I could at least take a punch in the face."

The Sergeant cocked his head, confused, replying, "One punch? Ma'am, after you hit the floor, that bastard started laying into you with his rifle butt. You're lucky to be awake at all. Five of us jumped in and pulled him off you. Davies managed to give him a black eye before we were pulled off."

She winced in pain as her chest ached and suddenly all the cuts and bruises came to life – perhaps her defiance hadn't been such a good idea after all.

She looked around the room to see everyone from her night shift was accounted for, all except the Police Commissioner. Five of her officers sported cuts and bruises, no doubt from when they had jumped the soldier, but like her they were alive, for now. She counted another thirty-five officers who she didn't recognise. Perhaps they were from Poole, she thought, or the surrounding areas. Everyone was sitting and all had the same dejected unbelieving look on their faces and no one was talking.

"Who are all these other officers?"

The Sergeant shrugged his shoulders. "I've no idea, ma'am, they've been bringing them in all morning. I'm guessing they're stragglers from other areas and they're bringing them all here."

"And where's the Police Commissioner? What happened to him?" she asked.

"They took him away after we were placed in here," the Sergeant replied angrily, "I can't believe this is fucking happening."

She slowly stood up, leaving him to his anger, not trusting her shaky legs as she reached out to the table for support. Tentatively she walked over to the window, as one of the PC's said quietly, "Ma'am, they warned us not to look out the window, if they catch you looking, then they'll shoot you." She gave the PC a look of defiance as she saw the fear in the young face looking back. To prove a point, she walked slowly over to the window and looked out at the car park. She saw five armoured vehicles out there, big green-wheeled things with wicked-looking cannons in turrets. She had no idea what they were, only that they were here. There were lots of soldiers out there, the uniform was the same black-green disruptive pattern that she'd seen their own army wearing, but the weapons were different. Whoever they were, they were not friendly.

She wondered if these soldiers had been the ones who had killed her officers early this morning. She watched them chatting and smoking; some were laughing, their body language told her they were animatedly discussing last night's events. Her anger began to rise again as she thought of the events of that morning. Where were the military? Had they really expected the police to deal with these people? She heard the door to the conference room unlock and keeping her hand out on the desk to steady herself she turned to see who had entered.

The Police Commissioner entered first, looking at the floor, not meeting her gaze. What had been said? she wondered, what could make him look so dejected?

Refusing to submit, she looked up defiantly as two soldiers pushed into the room, barging the commissioner aside and making way for a fourth man. He was stocky, with a round face and she saw the jet-black hair protruding from under his peaked cap. His physique was like a wrestler with a slim waist and huge shoulders filling the doorway as he entered. She guessed his height to be five feet eight and he wore the drab green uniform of the Soviet military. The silver braids on his shoulders shone in the sunlight and the ribbons on his chest made it clear he was a man of rank. His eyes scanned the room, revelling in the sight of the defeated officers, until they settled on her, narrowing slightly. She refused to be intimidated and made sure he knew it. She saw his mouth twitch; was it irritation or enjoyment?

He removed his cap, placing it on the desk in front of him as he looked around and announced confidently, "I am Colonel General Terekhov." They all looked up, surprised at the General's perfect English. "For those of you who may not know it yet, your army has now been defeated in this area. They will not be coming back. No-one will be coming to save you." He paused to let his words sink in before continuing, "Now I have just been speaking to your Police Commissioner, who I believe is your superior and until recently was in command of the police force in this county. He has given me his guarantee and assurance that I can count on your support and assistance. We are, after all, here at the request of your own government."

She looked over in total disbelief to the Commissioner who kept his head low, looking at the floor, ashamed of what was being revealed, as the General continued.

"Now, even though the Commissioner has assured me of your co-operation, I know how strong the urge can be to resist change. Especially so soon after... well, after last night's events." She watched as he stared directly at her as he added, "To some of you, the urge to resist will be strong. Therefore, I am going to give you all two choices. One, you can swear today, in this room, to assist me and my men. If you choose this option then there will be no change to your daily lives, you will still be the police and you will be free to go home and be with your families. You will continue to do your jobs alongside my men."

She looked at the General with disgust. He made it sound so appealing, so easy, she thought to herself. What about all those people you murdered last night? She was tempted to shout out, but her eyes met with one of the armed guards. The savage grin he gave her was almost daring her to try, and as if to hammer home the point he shifted the assault rifle slightly, his finger loosely resting on the trigger, making it very clear he intended to use it if provoked. She knew this was not the time to be brave or foolish, and wisely decided to stay silent.

The General walked slowly around the room as he spoke, looking down at the police officers sitting on the floor. Some looked up, listening to what was said, others simply looked at the floor, too ashamed, or too proud to look at him.

"However, if you reject this offer, if you feel perhaps that you cannot do as we ask, and will not be comfortable working alongside us, then I give you option two. You will be free to leave us, no more will be asked of you and nothing more will be expected of you; however, you will no longer be working police officers."

She watched her fellow officers as the words sunk in; some exchanged glances. She could see what they were thinking; free to leave, to just walk away? Could it be true? Was this a lie?

One of her junior police Constables looked up. He was one of those sporting a black eye. Clearly, he'd helped her last night. His voice was almost condescending as he glared up at the General.

"Just like that, you'd let us go? simply walk out that door and away from all this?"

The General walked over to him. His own eyes bored into the young man, his voice firm and controlled. "Yes, young man, it's as simple as that, you are *not* our prisoners, and we are *not* your captors. We are here to help you, even if you do not see that yet."

Unperturbed, the brave young officer countered, smiling through bloody gums. "Here to help? Not your prisoners? Yet here we sit with your guns pointed at us. And what about last night, all the people you've killed in cold blood, are we to just forget all about that and go back to our day jobs because you're here to help?"

The General looked over to one of his guards as the young officer's voice grew louder and his anger grew. "You're not here to help us, you're here to help yourselves! Fucking murderer! Fuck you, and your offer. Kiss my ass, and then kiss it again! Go on, pucker up, you—"

Taking the prompt from the General, the guard stepped forward, slamming his rifle butt into the back of the officer's head, who, groaning, crumpled to the floor. The General shook his head slowly, displeased with the outburst. Ignoring the young officer's moans, he addressed the room again.

"Last night was unfortunate, but my soldiers were merely defending themselves. After all, it was *your* soldiers and armed police who fired on us first. Sometimes the price of freedom comes at a cost, does it not? Wasn't it your own country who bravely fought alongside my own to help us defeat the Nazis and rid the world of them? Didn't that come at a cost as well? Well, now your own government, your *own people*, have asked for our help to rid itself of another tyrant, another Nazi." The General walked over to the table. Picking up one of the police helmets, he pointed to the crown on the badge. "This tyrant, however, wears a crown. *This* crown."

She'd heard enough. Deciding to risk another beating she shot back at him, "You haven't answered the Constable's question, General. Will you let those who choose to, walk away from here?"

He turned to look at her, smiling, dropping the helmet to the floor. He walked over with mock concern on his face. "Ah, the voice of defiance. My soldiers tell me you were very courageous last night, and where did that courage get you?" His eyes scanned over her injuries to prove his point. He waved his arm with a flourish around the room and said, "Tell me, Chief Superintendent, where are your soldiers? Where is the brave British Army now that you need them? My soldiers tell me that they all ran away and that they abandoned you to your fate. Even now, after such a betrayal by your own military, you still see *us* as the aggressor?"

She said nothing as he turned to address the room again. "I am wasting time here, as I have already said, the choice is simple: either you work with us, or you're against us. I shall give you all five minutes alone to decide."

She watched as the General walked out of the room, stopping by the doorway to look back at the Police Commissioner who stared mutely at the floor. What the hell had they done to him? she thought.

"Police Commissioner, we still have much to discuss," the General hinted, the request sounding more like an order. The Commissioner looked up, and then for only a brief second, she got eye contact. She could see him imperceivably shake his head at her. Was that a warning? she thought. What was he trying to tell her? Without further ado he left the room, following behind the General and his men, the lock of the door snicking into place behind them.

Everyone looked at each other. Some began to mutter amongst themselves, discussing what to do next.

Realising she was the senior person there, she decided to take charge. She walked slowly into the middle of the room, the conversations and chatter dying as they saw her standing there.

"Is everyone okay? Is anyone injured? Apart from, that is, the bruising?" She looked over, relieved to see the fiery young Constable was now sat back up and looking back at her, rubbing his head.

"We're okay, ma'am. It looks like you've taken the brunt of it yourself."

She smiled as she replied, "And to think, I thought the days of me getting a beating on the street were long behind me."

She was glad, as a ripple of nervous laughter, more out of relief than anything, sounded around the room.

She looked at the faces of those before her. Sensing the defiance there, she could see they were expecting her to have a plan. Part of her wanted to join with them, to defiantly tell the General to go fuck himself, and refuse to co-operate with them. But then as quickly as the anger surfaced it was quashed, as she remembered the voice of the dying armed response officer last night. Hearing her officers die like that had really hit her hard, and she had been powerless to stop it. Now in this room, there were close to forty officers, all looking to her for leadership and answers. She had the answers, but she felt sure they wouldn't like them.

"Look, I know some of you are considering not co-operating, or maybe even thinking of walking out of here, hoping to take the fight back to them another day."

The nodding heads told her she was right. She winced in pain, holding her chest before continuing.

"I'm going to tell you all now that I think that's a mistake, these people will *not* let you walk out of here alive if you refuse to help."

Some of the officers looked back shaking their heads, their scowls clear to see on their faces. The young Constable that had spoken against the General stood up, rubbing the side of his head and wincing with the pain, but his voice was full of fire.

"But, ma'am, what would you have us do? This is *our* country. Are you telling us to simply roll over and spit in the eye of every person we vowed to protect? Just give up on all our oaths, on everything we believe in about law and order? My older brother's in the army, he was based at Bovington. For all I know, he was probably killed last night and you want me to shake hands with the people who killed him, smile sweetly and then help them? No. NO!"

She held up her hands to quieten down the chatter that broke out amongst the group. "Please, everyone, hear me out first, just listen, please," she reasoned, as the chatter died down. "I can't, and won't order you to do this. Everyone here is free to make their own decision, but last night I had to listen to them execute some of our officers over the radio. There was no chance for them to surrender, and they won't think twice about killing anyone who defies them. I couldn't help those officers last night, but I can help you all now, today, in this room. Please, all I'm asking is that you put your anger and shame aside and think of your families, think of your loved ones. If you're gone, who will protect them? Who will look after them?"

Her Sergeant looked across to her, his face puzzled. "So, do you want us to give up and go along with them?"

"No," she reasoned, "I'm not asking you to give up anything, all I'm asking is that for now, you put yourselves before your emotions, swallow your pride, roll with the punches and dust yourselves off. Today we lost, there's no shame in admitting that. We can live to fight another day, but to do that, first we must *live*." She looked around the room as she continued, "As well as your families, think of the public – they'll need us now more than ever. If you're gone then who is left to do your jobs? Them?" She scowled, pointing to the door. "Those murdering bastards out there? At least by agreeing to work with them – as much as it makes me shake with contempt and anger – we may be able to protect our public from the worst of it. Because that's our job now – we protect our communities, we keep everything safe as best we can, and we hold on. Because despite what the General said, our country won't just forget about us."

Some of those looking back began to nod, finally she was breaking through the barriers. The young Constable still looked defiant. He slowly shook his head.

"I'm sorry, ma'am, but I still won't do it, I'd never be able to look my mum in the eye again."

She stepped closer, her voice softer, "Please, I can't bear to think of any more of us dying today. Let's survive the day and then plan for tomorrow. Besides, what if your brother is still alive, there's still hope isn't there?" She gave him a little smile, hoping the gesture wasn't lost on him as he sat back down deep in thought.

A few moments later and the doors were flung open, the soldiers' boots thumping heavily on the floor. The General strode into the middle of the room, his eyes darting around, an arrogant sneer plain to see. His eyes settled on one of the newcomers, a young Constable sat alone in the corner.

"Well, what did they say?" he asked loudly in English.

To everyone's surprise the demeanour of the Constable changed in a second. Gone was the timid, scared look; instead, one of confidence and pride replaced it. He stood up confidently and walked towards the General, slamming to attention and pointing to the Chief Superintendent.

"Sir, she has told them all to accept your generous offer for the time being, but has plans to betray you in the future. She is not to be trusted."

"Really?" The General stared over at her. "A pity. I was hoping she'd see things more clearly. Never mind. Anything else?"

The Constable pointed to the officer whose brother was in the army and had been vocal before. "This man will refuse your offer and will be nothing but trouble for us in the future."

She stood open-mouthed at the Constable who had betrayed them. Her Sergeant was quicker to respond as he shot out, "What the hell are you doing, man? You fucking traitor!"

The General laughed at the outburst, remarking, "Traitor? No, just one of my men wearing one of your uniforms. You didn't really think that I'd leave you all alone in here to talk amongst yourselves, did you?" His laughter vanished as he turned and quickly shouted to his soldiers. She couldn't understand what was said, it was an alien language to her, but four guards quickly came in; two grabbed her roughly under the arms, pulling them back and tying her wrists with zip ties, the other two guards doing the same to the young Constable. She almost cried out and had to bite her lip against the pain in her chest as she was manhandled to the door, trying to take the weight on her feet as her shoes scuffed along the carpet. She heard the shouts of her officers fading into the distance.

"Where are you taking them?"

"She agreed to help you, bring her back."

The last thing she saw was the familiar corridor leading to the double doors of the entrance to the Police HQ as a black hood was roughly pulled over her head and then the world as she knew it went black.

B3413 North of Dorchester

After they had left their stopover point, Mike had led them down the back roads, with his local knowledge helping them to stay away from busier roads, trying to keep themselves hidden. They had driven the eight miles to Dorchester in silence, seeing the flash of explosions on the horizon to the south of them. Mike thought it could be Weymouth or Lulworth and he had remembered they still had four tanks there. He'd hoped whoever had been sent there to get them had managed to escape. They made good time, managing to get north of Dorchester quickly, before being stopped by a police car blocking the road, its blue lights flashing and coating the area of countryside around it in a blue hue.

The armed response officers had been happy to see them, thinking they were part of some defending force sent to help, and had listened glumly as Mike told them that they were unarmed and low on fuel. "Not much of a bloody defence," he remembered the policemen remarking. The officers had warned them not to go further south, they were getting reports of large amounts of armoured vehicles coming up from the Weymouth area, shooting at anyone they saw, clearly hostile. Mike had asked them if they'd seen any other tanks or friendly military vehicles in the area, to which he was told they were the only military vehicles they'd seen all night. Where the hell was everyone else? he'd wondered. Wishing the police officers the best of luck, he had continued driving further north, away from Dorchester and the distant sounds of battle and into the safety of the farmlands and countryside.

Mike led the convoy down some of the older backwater roads, going across country where needed, trying to find somewhere suitable to stop; already the cold grey light of dawn was starting to appear over the horizon and he knew everyone was tired. He was fighting to keep himself awake too, his head nodding forward, hitting the cupola, waking him back up. He'd had to shout at Bill a few times to wake up as he felt the tank veering off the road, before snapping back to the centre, his driver replying, "I wasn't asleep. Honest." It didn't help that they could hear the snores from Smudge the gunner over the headset, who had fallen asleep with his head resting on the sight.

For the first two hours of the journey Smudge had been happy to check and test the gunner's controls, and Mike had him carry out some practice engagements, tracking targets using the gunner's thermal sight as they drove along. Mike was careful not to let the turret traverse too much though; the last thing he had wanted was to play baseball with a car coming the other way, using the barrel as the bat. Now, though, his gunner was asleep and for the tenth time he'd gently nudged him with his foot, waiting until he was awake before saying, "Smudge, if you're going to sleep, at least take your mic away from your mouth."

They'd made good progress, but before long it was the voice of Jonah, who had dictated when they would stop, as he now came over the radio. "Tango One-One, this is Golf Two-One-Alpha. Fuel level now critical, we're going to need to stop soon or run out of fuel."

Mike acknowledged him on the radio, then after another two minutes of driving, he finally decided they would stop on a wooded hill overlooking a farm, the plan being to see if they could stay hidden from view during the day and borrow fuel from the farm to continue the following night. Leading the vehicles through the fields and up to the woodland, he was about to dismount when he saw the flash of a torch off to his right from the farmyard. Someone was walking towards them.

Seeing how steep the slope was that the vehicle was on, Mike said, "Bill, make sure your handbrake's on nice and tight, I don't want you rolling away without me."

"Okay, boss," the tired voice replied, as Mike removed his headgear and stepped off the tank, satisfied at hearing the handbrake ratchet on.

The farmer approached him and jovially said, "Morning army, bit lost are we? This is private land after all." The Dorset accent was clear to hear in the farmer's voice.

Mike was taken aback by the farmers jolly tone, fully expecting him to be angry at having the vehicles trashing his field. He also noted that the farmer had kept the torch beam low, and not shone it angrily in his face.

With a little bit of hope Mike replied, "Look, I'm sorry for the bother, sir, but we really need to use the woodland here. I need somewhere safe for us to hide out for the day. I've got vehicles low on fuel, and tired people on board and no time to mess about. We won't be any bother to you or your family, and any damage we do to your fields will be compensated by His Majesty's Government."

The farmer shone his torch along the side of the tank. Mike could see for himself the scratches and dents from the bullets and two large deep furrows in the armour on the turret, caused by the earlier battle. The tank would certainly need more than just a paint job, he thought.

The farmer, as if in agreement, whistled softly. "Phew! Well, army, it looks like you've been in the wars, that's for sure." Explosions could still be heard in the far distance, faint, but still a reminder of the ever-present danger. The farmer turned to the sounds, his eyes scanning the horizon, before stating, "It seems that someone somewhere has a bit of a beef with us."

The farmer's torch shone along the line of vehicles, then onto the deep ridges across the ground that the vehicles had made when they'd churned up the grass, the telltale marks leading up to their current position.

"Well," the farmer continued, "you can't stay in that there woodland."

Mike had been about to argue when the farmer quickly added, "That woodland isn't as dense as you think, army, your vehicles will be clearly visible from the air. Even if you use your cam nets and thermal sheets, you'll all stick out like the dog's bollocks."

Mike listened, wondering how the farmer knew so much about camouflage and concealment.

"And those bloody great tracks leading up to the woodland, well, even Stevie Wonder could follow them. No, you can't stay there, and seeing as it'll be daylight in about forty minutes, I can't exactly turf you away now, can I?"

"What are you saying?" Mike asked curiously.

"What I'm saying, army, is that you can all go down into that there feed barn on my farm. It's empty now and plenty big enough to hide all your vehicles in. You'll have cover from the air, and no track marks to give you away. Come on, let's get you all in there, you look like you could all do with some shut-eye."

Stepping forward, relieved, Mike shook hands with the farmer, his voice almost emotional with fatigue. "Thank you! Thank you. I'm Mike by the way."

"Sam, Sam Collins," the farmer replied breaking into a big beaming grin before continuing. "Pleased to meet you, army. Now let's get you in there, I've got to get this field ploughed, best to hide those tracks again..."

To be continued...

Here ends the first instalment in a series of books that make up 'Operation Fools Mate' The second book in the series titled '48' is available for purchase now.

Acknowledgments and Authors notes

They say that inside every person is a good book, and that we all have a story to tell. Well, if that's the case, then this story is mine, and I do hope you've enjoyed reading it as much as I have writing it. So, this page is dedicated to all of those in my life who helped me along the way. Firstly, to Paddy and Victoria, with whom whose guidance, advice and keen eyes helped with the editing of the book, you'd be surprised how quickly those typos add up! Then to all my friends and family who took the time to read the book, such as Natalie and Tim who took the time to give their honest reviews and opinions, on how the story progressed. Finally, I'd like to reserve the biggest thank you for my unofficial editor in chief and wife Emily, who not only helped me edit the book, but had to put up with my constant chatter about the story!

I'd like to also thank you, the reader, for taking a chance on me and purchasing this book, hopefully you've enjoyed the story so far, and will afford me a little bit of creative license when it comes to the story, as I must confess, I've never been anywhere near a Cabinet Briefing Room. What I can say whole heartedly though is that I have been in the Military, which is probably where the idea of doing the book came from. During my 19 years in the Army, I was lucky enough to meet and work with some truly extraordinary people, and some of the characters and scenarios you have just read about in this book, although with a fictional enemy, are based on some of those people, and their experiences, albeit with a different enemy at that time. The military minded amongst you will see that I've changed the names of the Russian and British units to fictional ones, there is no 24th Royal Tank Regiment, or at least not anymore, neither is there a Regiment of Fusiliers nor a Kings Company Royal Hussars as I felt it necessary not to be too close to the truth, with the world as it is when writing a story like this. Likewise, the same applies to the creation of the country of Tumat, totally imaginative but necessary in order to make the story work. But hey, why let a few facts get in the way of a good story. But speaking of facts, some of the things you've read about in the book, from the Kinzhal missiles used to attack London through to the 3m Kalibr Cruise missiles are very real. In fact currently the Russians are exporting those very cruise missiles already pre-loaded into shipping containers re-appropriated for that exact use as demonstrated in the book. I'm not trying to scare anyone, just making you aware that the threat is out there. Sometimes the truth can be scarier than fiction!

Anyway back to the fiction, and if you have enjoyed this book could I ask that you let me know by posting a review on either amazon.co.uk or goodreads.com It'll only take you two minutes, and would mean so much to me. Also, if you want to know how the story continues for Mike, Peter, Spider, Patty and the rest of the characters then please could I recommend you strap yourself in and read the next exciting book in the 'Operation Fools Mate' series titled '48'. I can promise nothing except more action, twists and plots as the newly formed group try their best to stay alive for as long as possible. For more information about the new book, myself, or the book you've just read, then please visit www.mlbaldwin.co.uk

So, I guess there's not much more to say now except, thank you, I wish all my readers the best of luck in whatever life throws at you and,

"I'll see you when I see you next..."

Glossary

5.56mm – Standard NATO round – What all NATO assault rifles fire, standardised in size to make logistics easy

7.62mm – Standard Russian Round – Larger than the NATO calibre, able to cause more damage

ADJ – Adjutant – usually a Captain and in charge of a units administration

AGC – Adjutants Generals Corp

AK-12 – Russian Assault Rifle

AN124 – Antonov 124 Russian heavy lift cargo plane

ANPR – Automatic Number Plate Recognition

APU – Auxiliary Power unit

ASACS – Air Surveillance and Control System

ASRAAM – Advanced Short-Range Air to Air Missile

ATC – Air Traffic Control

ATGM – Anti Tank Guided Missile

ATDU – Armoured Trials and Development Unit

Bingo – Codeword used by pilots to describe an aircraft low on fuel

BMP-3 – Russian Armoured Infantry Vehicle – Used to transport troops into combat zones under fire

BV – Boiling Vessel – Square shaped large kettle used on armoured vehicles to heat water and rations

BVRAAM – Beyond Visual Range Air to Air Missile

CAS – Chief of Air Staff – Head of the Royal Air Force

CDI – Chief of Defence Intelligence – Head of UK intelligence agencies

CDS – Chief of the Defence Staff – Head of all Military forces

CGS – Chief of the General Staff – Head of the Army

CNS/1SL – Chief of the Naval Staff/ First Sea Lord - Head of the Royal Navy

Chally 2 – Nickname that crews use to describe the Challenger 2 Tank

CO – Commanding Officer

COBR(A) – Cabinet Office Briefing Room (A) – Emergency response meeting usually chaired by the PM and other senior figures of government

CPO – Close Protection Officer

CPS – Commanders Primary Sight – What the Commander uses to sight and fire the tanks weapons. Also has its own laser to acquire the range to target for the Fire Control Computer

CRARRV – Challenger Armoured Repair and Recovery Vehicle – Used by the REME to assist broken and bogged vehicles

DASS – Defensive Aids Sub System – also called **Praetorian**- provides threat assessments, aircraft protection and support measures to the Typhoon

DTT – Driver Training Tank – Turretless Tank used to train new drivers

DZ – Drop Zone

ETA – Estimated Time of Arrival

EW – Electronic Warfare

EWO – Electronic Warfare Officer

F-35 Lightning – RAF's next generation multirole fighter plane

FCC – Fire Control Computer – Calculates the computations required to help the crew to aim the gun

FSB – Russian Federal Security Services

GCE – Gun Control Equipment

GCHQ – Government Communication Headquarters

Glock-17 – Standard British forces 9mm semi-automatic pistol

Gold Commander – Police designation for the overall commander of a situation or emergency at the scene

GPS – Gunners Primary Sight – What the Gunner on a Chally 2 uses to sight and fire the tanks weapons. Also has a laser to acquire the range to target for the Fire Control Computer

GSM – Garrison Sergeant Major

HF – High Frequency

IFR – Instrument Flight Rules

IL-80 – Iiyushin II-80 'Maxdome' – Russian Airborne Command Centre, similar to the USAF 'Airforce-One'

Javelin – Portable Anti-Tank Guided Missile System, used by most NATO countries

JNCO – Junior Non-Commissioned Officer

3m54 Kaliber – Russian cruise missile – can be launched by sea air and land

Kamaz K-4386 Typhoon – Russian oversized armoured 4x4, air portable with a rapid firing 30mm cannon

Kinzhal – (KH-47M2 Khinzal) Russian hypersonic air launched ballistic missile. Nato designation is 'Killjoy'

L-7 GPMG – General Purpose Machine Gun – Belt fed, rapid firing machine gun

L-22 Carbine – Short barrelled variant of the SA-80-A2 assault rifle issued to armoured crews

L-94 Coax – Coaxially mounted Machine Gun, located next to the Main gun

MBT – Main Battle Tank

MiG-31 – Russian Fighter Bomber

MoD – Ministry of Defence

MP443 Grach – Standard Russian forces 9mm semi-automatic pistol

NATO – North Atlantic Treaty Organisation

NATS – National Air Traffic Services

OC – Officer Commanding

PIRATE – Passive Infra-Red Airborne Track Equipment – allows long range visual identification of a target using cameras, sensors and computer

PSTN – Public Switched Telephone Network – Copper telephone landlines

PM – Prime Minister

QM – Quartermasters Department – Where kit and equipment for vehicles and troops are stored and distributed

QRF – Quick Reaction Force

QRA – Quick Reaction Alert

R-37 Vympel – Russian long range hypersonic air-to-air missile

RAC – Royal Armoured Corp

RAF – Royal Air Force

REME – Royal Electrical and Mechanical Engineers

RMP – Royal Military Police

RSM – Regimental Sergeant Major

RUPERT – Nickname given to officers by junior ranks

RWS – Remote Weapons Station – fitted to tanks that are classed as TES

SA80-A2 – Standard British Army Assault Rifle

SBS – Special Boat Service

SNCO – Senior Non-Commissioned Officer

2S25 Sprut – SD – Russian air portable light tank, able to field a 125mm gun

SSM – Squadron Sergeant Major

SU-57 – Russian next gen multirole fighter plane

T-80 – Russian Main Battle Tank

TES – Theatre Entry Specific – designation given to the Challenger 2 'Megatron' that has been heavily modified with add on armour, RWS and forward/rearwards facing cameras and other upgrades

TU-54 Bear – Russian Cold War era turboprop bomber

Typhoon – RAF multi role fighter jet – also known as Eurofighter

UHF – Ultra High Frequency

UN – United Nations

VDV – Vozdushno-Desantnye Voyska – Russian Airborne Forces

VHF – Very High Frequency

VID – Visual Identification

VOIP – Voice Over Internet Protocol – A phone line that is digital and relies on the internet instead of a landline

Wildcat – Upgraded version of the Lynx, fast, lightly armed, multirole helicopter used by the British Army and Royal Navy

Winchester – Codeword used by pilots to describe an aircraft out of ammunition

WO2 – Warrant Officer Class 2 – Sergeant Major rank or equivalent

WO1 – Warrant officer Class 1 – RSM or GSM rank or equivalent

WOC – Wonderland Operations Centre

Rank Structures of the UK Armed Forces

Rank structure of the British Army

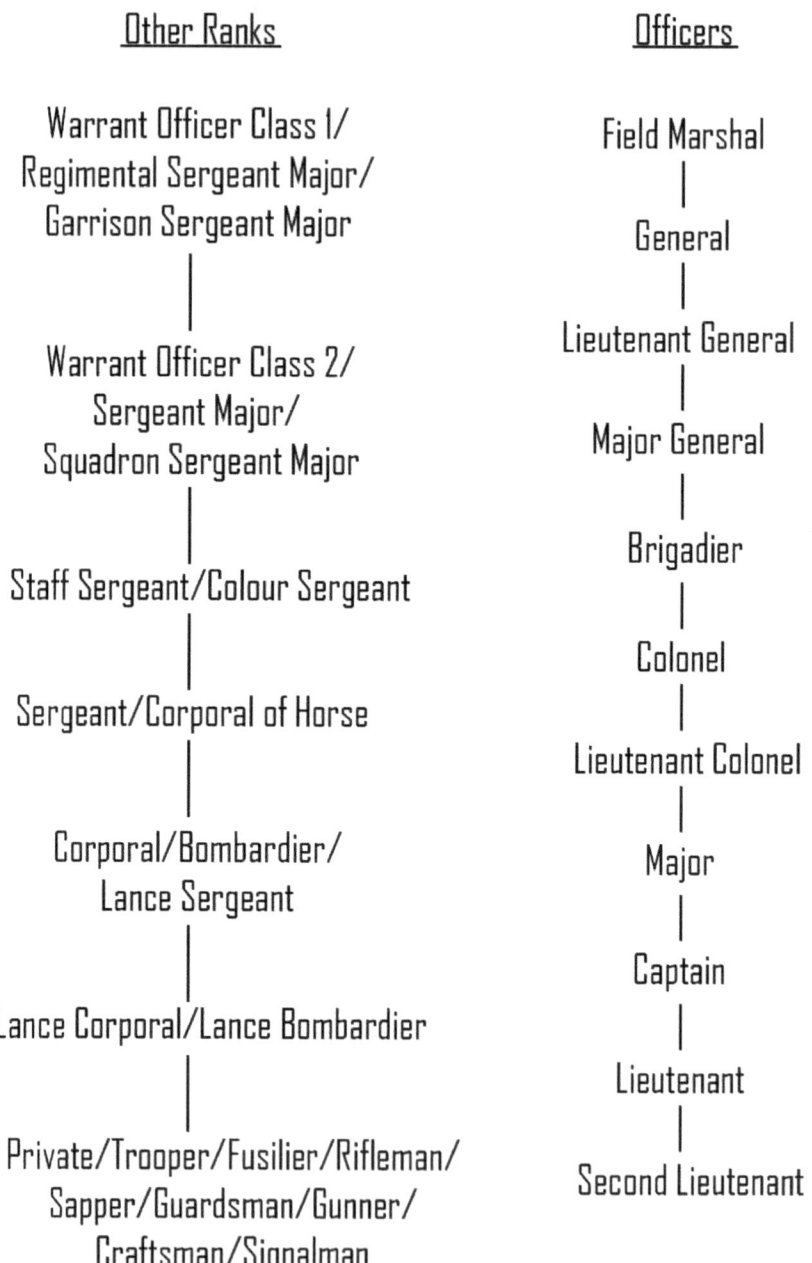

Other Ranks

Warrant Officer Class 1/
Regimental Sergeant Major/
Garrison Sergeant Major

Warrant Officer Class 2/
Sergeant Major/
Squadron Sergeant Major

Staff Sergeant/Colour Sergeant

Sergeant/Corporal of Horse

Corporal/Bombardier/
Lance Sergeant

Lance Corporal/Lance Bombardier

Private/Trooper/Fusilier/Rifleman/
Sapper/Guardsman/Gunner/
Craftsman/Signalman

Officers

Field Marshal

General

Lieutenant General

Major General

Brigadier

Colonel

Lieutenant Colonel

Major

Captain

Lieutenant

Second Lieutenant

Rank structure of the Royal Air Force

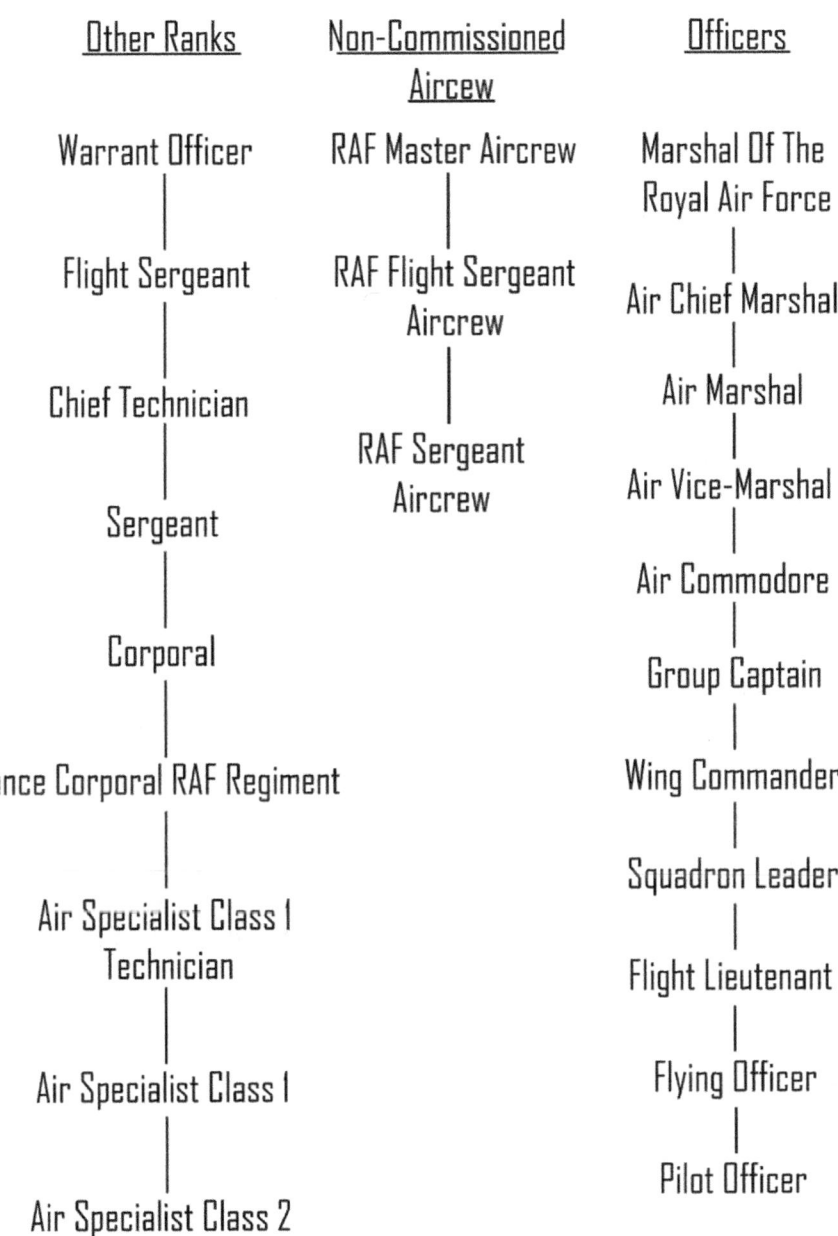

Other Ranks	Non-Commissioned Aircew	Officers
Warrant Officer	RAF Master Aircrew	Marshal Of The Royal Air Force
Flight Sergeant	RAF Flight Sergeant Aircrew	Air Chief Marshal
Chief Technician		Air Marshal
Sergeant	RAF Sergeant Aircrew	Air Vice-Marshal
Corporal		Air Commodore
Lance Corporal RAF Regiment		Group Captain
Air Specialist Class 1 Technician		Wing Commander
Air Specialist Class 1		Squadron Leader
Air Specialist Class 2		Flight Lieutenant
		Flying Officer
		Pilot Officer

Rank structure of the Royal Navy

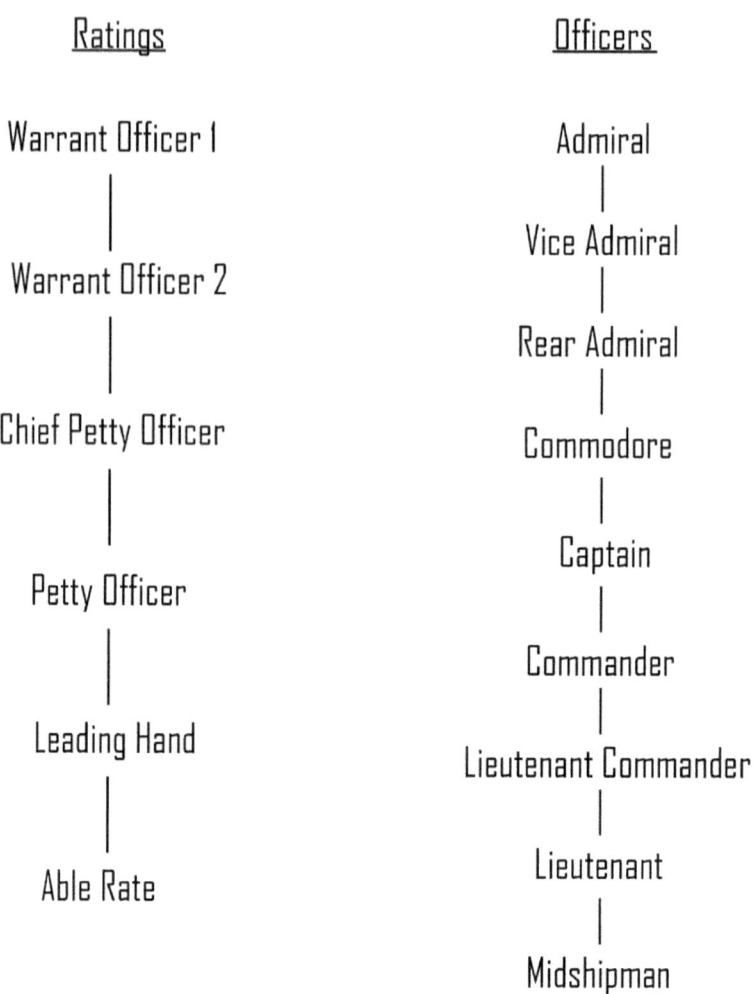

Ratings	Officers
Warrant Officer 1	Admiral
Warrant Officer 2	Vice Admiral
Chief Petty Officer	Rear Admiral
Petty Officer	Commodore
Leading Hand	Captain
Able Rate	Commander
	Lieutenant Commander
	Lieutenant
	Midshipman

www.ingramcontent.com/pod-product-compliance
Lightning Source LLC
Chambersburg PA
CBHW072000110726
47910CB00005B/1603